I0673913

Mr. Knightley

...in his own words

_____

SHANNON WINSLOW

A Heather Ridge Arts Publication
Copyright © 2023 by Shannon Winslow
www.shannonwinslow.com

All Rights Reserved.
No part of this book may be reproduced or distributed in
any manner whatsoever without the written permission
of the author.

The characters and events in this book are fictitious or
used fictitiously. Any similarity to real persons, living
or dead, is coincidental and not intended by the author.

Cover art by Shannon Winslow
Cover design by Micah D. Hansen

Soli Deo Gloria

~~*~~

Mr. Knightley, a sensible man about seven or eight and-thirty, was not only a very old and intimate friend of the family, but particularly connected with it... He lived about a mile from Highbury, was a frequent visitor and always welcome.

~~*~~

"Mr. Knightley's air is so remarkably good, that it is not fair to compare Mr. Martin with him. You might not see one in a hundred, with gentleman so plainly written as in Mr. Knightley." – Emma Woodhouse

~~*~~

Emma, by Jane Austen

Prologue

M r. Woodhouse is my hero and always shall be. This assertion will no doubt come as a great surprise to some, especially to his more recent acquaintances, for he may not appear heroic in any way.

Mr. Woodhouse is now a somewhat elderly man with what I will call habits of gentle selfishness. He is not autocratic or demanding. On the contrary, he is mild mannered and the soul of charity itself. It is simply that he wishes to keep those he cares about near to him and cannot reconcile himself to change of any kind. These predilections seem so obvious and natural to him that he can never suppose there to be any good reason for other people to feel differently. *Why should anybody wish to marry? It is so disrupting to the family circle. What reason could there be for one choosing to leave Highbury, when it is not to be supposed that there is a more comfortable place in the whole world?* I have heard him say as much.

His scope of interest has contracted over the last twenty years to where his view now rarely reaches beyond his own village and the nearest concerns of himself, his two daughters, and a few intimate friends. Moreover, his valetudinarian propensities have in this same period taken a firmer grasp on him. Mr. Woodhouse is afraid, if not of his own shadow, then certainly of the threats posed by an unwholesome piece of cake and a chill draft.

But it was not always so. No, I have known him all my life, and I remember him as the man he once was, the mentor and champion of my youth. Do not mistake me; he was never by nature brave-hearted or bold. There was at least one time, however, when he faced up to a formidable foe to see that right was done. This is true heroism, not that one has no fear but that one is willing to go into battle anyway. Mr. Woodhouse did that, and he did it for me. I can never forget the priceless service he rendered those many years ago. It is for that I honor him still.

I owe him everything, perhaps even my life. So, as long as I have breath, I will be his grateful servant and faithful friend. I will do my best to see no harm comes to him or to anybody he cares for. I will put his needs and wishes above my own in every case – even when it is most painful, as it is now. For the sake of that longstanding debt I can never repay, and respecting certain promises I made, I will deny myself as long as… Well, as long as it is necessary.

It would be tempting to say, "Oh, but things are different now. Circumstances have changed. One must not feel bound by promises made two decades ago."

Yes, many things have changed in that time – it would be easier if they had not – but Mr. Woodhouse's wishes remain the same. Therefore it is my clear duty to keep my promise to him, even now. If there is one thing a man can and always must do, it is his duty.

Part One

~~~

The Early Years

−1−

Inconvenient Cataclysm

I have come away to think.

Ostensibly, I am come into London to visit John and Isabella, but I am a very poor guest, for I neglect my relations to a shocking degree. No doubt the whole family is quite put out with me, especially the children, who are used to claiming their Uncle George as their personal property, to climb upon and make the center of their sport. Their parents are more perceptive, I believe. They merely shake their heads over me and look worried.

I have no heart for socializing, and perhaps I have made a mistake in coming here at all. But I had to do something. The situation at home had become intolerable. The unfortunate case is this; I have recently had to admit to myself that I am in love... in love with Emma Woodhouse.

Such a revolutionary circumstance *must* change everything! And yet it can be allowed to change nothing at all. Such a brilliant revelation should be shouted from the rooftops, and yet I cannot speak of it to a single creature. Such a glorious cataclysm of the heart and mind demands to be celebrated, and yet I cannot. Alas, it brings only misery.

Oh, that Frank Churchill had never come to Highbury! I abused the blasted young man for not coming sooner, but now I could wish it all undone. Except on his father's behalf, I could wish him to the other side of the moon for all the mischief he has made! Had he never come, we might then have all gone on comfortably as we were before. No revolutions or revelations. No inconvenient cataclysms of any kind.

But now! Now the situation is irrevocably altered, at least for me. For the genie, once out of the bottle, cannot be put back again.

I thought the risk of falling in love was well behind me. I was not immune in my younger years, I admit, twice succumbing to that temptation then, but never since. No, truly only once. I do not count dear Isabella. Not anymore, for to admit to remembering my brother's wife with any passion would be inexcusable. To imagine it, offensive. Besides, despite how sincerely fond I was of her – and still am – I am now quite convinced that there never was any serious attraction between us. Not on her side, presumably, considering her later actions. As for myself, I can only judge by comparison, and what I felt then for Isabella does not begin to equal what I cannot help feeling now for her sister, God help me.

Everybody expected *me* to be the one to marry Isabella, of course, especially after...

However, I am run ahead of myself.

As I said, I came away to think. I had the idea that, by putting a little distance between myself and my 'problem,' I might recover my perspective. By allowing my head to clear, I might talk myself into being sensible again – in short, to talk myself out of being in love with Emma Woodhouse.

Oh, but so sweet was our manner of parting that it has made the task even more difficult. Perhaps it would have been wiser to leave without seeing her, but how could I? How could I let the last words between us on the old footing be ones of acrimony? Next time I meet her, everything may have changed. She may no longer be my free and easy friend but Mr. Churchill's future bride: a disaster on so many levels.

And so I waited with her father, and then also Harriet Smith, at Hartfield until Emma returned from calling on Mrs. and Miss Bates.

I rose immediately when Emma entered. My, but how well she looked! – although perhaps a little embarrassed at seeing me. No doubt she was remembering, as I was, the unfortunate manner of our leave-taking the day before at Box Hill. Her eyes begged my approval and that we should be friends again. All I could think was that I had best get away at once. As appealing as she looked at that moment, I did not trust myself to do and say what was wise, what I knew I must. Indeed, were it not for the safeguard of others present, who can say what might have happened? For I longed to take her into my arms and tell her all was forgiven. I longed to tell her the truth about everything. But instead, I was obliged to hold myself in check, to appear calm and indifferent when I felt anything but.

"I would not go away without seeing you, Emma," I told her in as neutral a tone as I could affect, "but I have no time to spare, and therefore must now be gone directly. I am off to London, to spend a few days with John and Isabella. Have you anything to send or say, besides the 'love,' which nobody can carry?"

She looked confused, perhaps even a little distressed. "No, nothing at all. But wait, is not this a sudden scheme?"

"It is… rather," I said. "Although I have been thinking of it for some little time."

I told myself to go without further delay, to stop staring at Emma and leave at once. Somehow, though, my feet refused to move, and then Mr. Woodhouse was talking, praising his daughter's kindness to the Bateses, which served to heighten Emma's color even more. By the way she looked at me then, with a wan smile and slight shake of her head, she clearly told me she knew this praise was unjust – unjust and undeserved.

If only I could have stayed angry with her, as I had been the day before! How much easier it would then have been to go. But remaining angry with Emma Woodhouse is something I have never been able to do, not from when she was a small, mischievous child until this day. No, I was in fact very proud of her at that moment – for apparently acknowledging her mistake, repenting of it, and humbling herself in order to attempt some reparation to Miss Bates. What an excellent creature she is – flawed but excellent nonetheless!

I am afraid the grave look I had been determined to maintain melted away. No further words were spoken between us, but, just as I had understood her silent communication moments before, I am certain she could not have failed to read the warm glow of regard I felt burning in my heart for her then.

I cannot exactly say what happened next. Did I reach for her hand or did she offer it? It seemed the work of simultaneous thought. In any case, however it came about, I took her hand, pressed it, and held it for a moment, even going so far as to lift those lovely white fingers partway to my lips before stopping myself. I had kissed Emma's hand, casually, many times before. This would have been different, however. This time would not have been a casual, meaningless gesture. There existed far more consciousness now, at least on my side, and far more significance than I had any business communicating to her.

I released her hand instead, leaving the room and the house at once.

~~*~~

Coming away to town has not made my mind any easier, though. I have the strong sense that we are at a critical juncture, and no one but myself seems to be aware of the danger. Little does poor Mr. Woodhouse suspect that Frank Churchill is about to cut up his happiness and destroy his peace of mind forever. As for Emma, I fear she is about to make the biggest mistake of her life. My own painful situation aside, I must think and do what is best for them; this I have resolved. And yet, what *can* I do? I have been over it time and again and see no useful measures to be taken. Emma will not heed my warnings. Neither will her father. And so my comprehending the imminent danger avails nothing at all.

Having concluded that there is no relieving action I can take myself, I have no choice but to await the outcome of events that are in other hands. Meanwhile, here in Brunswick Square, I intend to distract myself as well as possible.

John and Isabella's children will serve as an excellent diversion, if I will allow them to be. And to the extent I can give them pleasure, my time here will not be wasted. My other strategy is to set down a record of the past. Perhaps these ramblings of mine will be fit only for the fire in the end, but while I confine my thoughts to the past, I may at least forget my current trouble for a little.

I suppose I should start this narration at the beginning; that would make the most sense. I must go back to the events that established the rule for all the rest: why it is that I owe Mr. Woodhouse my complete loyalty, and why our two families are forever bound together – not only now by John and Isabella's marriage, but many years prior to that. I must start in 1791, the year before Emma was born.

Until that time, nothing extraordinary had occurred to me. Life was quiet, pleasant, and good. Both my parents lived, and my brothers and I went on well together, making all Highbury – Hartfield and Donwell Abbey in particular – our personal grounds for play and exploration. I say "my brothers," because there were three of us then, you see. I was in the middle at the age of fifteen, with John four and a half years my junior and poor Miles less than two years my senior.

But then my uncle Spencer Knightley came to stay.

I must have intuitively understood the event's significance even at the time, for I remember with preternatural clarity the conversation between my parents that heralded my uncle's arrival. It was a quiet evening at Michaelmas, and we were all gathered in the drawing room. John sat on the floor playing with his collection of toy soldiers, and the rest of us divided our time between conversation and reading – Miles and I with books, my father with his paper, and my mother reading the letters that had arrived earlier.

Mama's little gasp of surprise suddenly drew my attention. "Your brother is coming!" she told her husband with a certain tone of wariness that seemed to always be employed when speaking of my uncle.

"Spencer?" asked Papa, looking up from his paper with a scowl. "I wonder what he can possibly want here at this time of year."

"Heaven only knows. He just says that we are to expect him tomorrow. Gracious!"

"Steady, Margaret. Now then, let me have a look," he said, reaching across to receive the letter from my mother's extended hand.

Mama said no more; she quietly waited for my father's opinion, as she always did. She had a very good mind of her own, but a natural timidity of spirit and diffidence as to her rightful claims had given her the habit of always deferring to others, especially her husband, on serious matters. His good judgement and benevolence made this practice no bad thing, while he lived.

She sat poised on the edge of her chair, the perfect picture of the refined lady. She was a bit taller than average with a figure only mildly the worse off for the three sons she had borne. Her hair was still a fine shade of auburn, I remember, although laced with a little silver filigree by that time. She seemed to me somewhat advanced in years, although I suppose she was no more than five years older than I am now, and still a very handsome woman.

After briefly scanning the single-paged letter for himself, my father said, "Spencer can mean nothing serious by this – only a short visit. After all, he must be back in town for the beginning of next term, you know."

"Yes, of course. Well, I suppose we can put up with him for a few days, can't we?" Although she sounded none too sure.

"We can and we must. He is my own twin, after all, and this is his home too, in one sense of the word. I can hardly turn him away at the door."

"No. No, of course not."

My father, who was ten years older than my mother and fully gray by this time, tossed the letter aside, tended his pipe, and returned to his paper. Mama kept silent for a few minutes, as if she agreed the matter was settled and meant to say no more about it. And yet, from the corner of my eye I observed her restless fidgets. Finally she seemed not to be able to stifle her disquietude any longer.

"It is just that..."

"Yes, my dear?" said my father, looking over the top of his spectacles at her.

"It is just that with Spencer's history... Your history with him, that is... His implacable resentment. Well, I do not like his coming unexpectedly like this. Uninvited too. I cannot help thinking it does not bode well. No, it does not bode well at all, and I shall be uneasy until he has been and gone again."

My father frowned and gave his wife a significant look accompanied by a slight tilt of his head in my direction, which put an end to the discussion of Uncle Spencer, at least within my hearing, and left me to wonder what it all meant. To what "history" did my mother refer? And why was she so uneasy about my uncle's coming?

Later that night, I decided to talk it over with my brother Miles in private. We were quite close – in age and even more so in temperament – and we had always shared a bedchamber by choice. Oh, how I miss him, even now! He was my best friend as well as an excellent brother, always there by my side to defend and guide me. So naturally I wanted to hear his opinion on the business with our uncle. He had nearly two years more life experience, if nothing else, but I also thought it possible my father had confided more to him, since he was the heir.

"Say, Miles, what do you know about this business with Uncle Spencer?" I asked after we had retired for the night. I had lain awake in the dark, thinking, and was quite sure by the sound of his breathing that he was still awake as well.

His instant answer confirmed it. "What do you mean?"

"The mysterious 'history' with our father that Mama spoke of, and why is she so nervous about his coming?"

"Oh, that. Well I know very little – probably no more than you do – but I have always supposed there to be some bad blood between them because of Father's inheriting and Spencer's not."

I considered this. "But why should Uncle resent Father for that? It is not *his* fault. I do not resent *you* because I was born second."

"That is because you have a nobler spirit, George. You always have had. Honestly, though, it does not seem fair, does it? – that I should get it all, and you and John practically nothing, just because of an accident of birth?"

"Not when you put it like that. But then, I have never considered it an accident. It is all part of God's plan somehow. Is not that right? I am sure I have heard the vicar preach on that subject before."

"Yes, and I do *hope* so – that it is God's plan, and that I will prove worthy of the responsibility when it comes my time. Still, think of Uncle Spencer. If younger sons resent not inheriting, as I believe they often do, think what Uncle must feel as the younger twin. He missed his chance by only a few minutes, not years. It must make the bitter pill even more difficult to swallow. Do not you think so? Like a cruel trick of fate."

"Miles?" I said after a little silence.

"Yes, George?"

"You do not suppose Uncle means to make any trouble over it, do you?"

"No. I cannot imagine how he could, even if he wished to. Donwell belongs to Father, all legal, right, and tight. Nothing can change that."

"And after father, it will be yours, not Uncle's. Is that not so?"

"Exactly so. And I will always look after Mother and you and John. You can rest easy on that head."

I lay awake a while longer considering all this. Miles had explained the probable source of the conflict so well that I thought I could understand. He was correct, too, as I would later learn, although there was more to it than that.

Uncle Spencer came the following day, and so began a very dark period of our lives.

-2-

The Trouble with Uncle

I happened to be nearby when my uncle arrived and so was the first of my family to greet him, right there on the front steps when he swung down from his horse and retrieved his bulging saddlebags.

"Good day, Uncle," I said with a slight bow.

He responded in kind and said, "Miles, isn't it?"

"No, sir. I am George."

"Of course you are. Well, George, I trust my letter arrived and I am expected."

"Yes, sir."

"Good, good. Now, while I would like nothing better than to stand here talking with you, I have had a miserable journey. So I hope to Heaven my room is ready for me. I must change before seeing anybody."

"It is ready. The same bedchamber as usual, Uncle."

"Very well, then. You may tell your parents that I will be down shortly. There's a good lad." He tousled my hair and went on inside.

I should have been glad to shake his hand but, at fifteen and well grown, I thought I was much too old to have my hair tousled anymore. I raked it down again with my fingers as I watched him go, delaying to obey his order as a small protest against him.

Although Spencer was my father's twin and they were nearly identical, there were some discernable differences between them, which a sharp eye could detect, especially when one saw them side by side. Uncle Spencer was slightly taller and broader in the shoulders. His nose was also longer, ending in a bit of a hook, which Father's lacked.

But the minor discrepancies in their persons were nothing compared to the noticeable disparity of their manners. Whereas my father seemed to have matured into a rather stodgy, straightforward gentleman who did not suffer fools gladly, perhaps Uncle Spencer had failed to mature at all. He had never borne the responsibility of a family – an entire community, really – depending on him, as my father had. And even now, in his middle years, he was reputed to still play fast and loose with the truth on occasion, for the sake of a joke or to gain his own end.

Father had said that he and Spencer often passed for each other as children but could do so no longer. I imagined that their differences had grown more marked over the years until now anybody who knew them at all would never be fooled.

After a moment's delay, I did run inside to find my parents, even though I knew Jenkins, the butler, would have already alerted them. I thought to improve my chances of being on hand when their inauspicious reunion with Uncle Spencer took place. For it seemed likely that answers to some of my questions might be gained by observing that scene.

I witnessed only the initial civilities, however, which were stiff and formal. They told me almost nothing I did not already know. Then the two somewhat estranged brothers retreated to the library for a private discussion of some kind.

My mother and I stood shoulder to shoulder (for we were then of similar height), both of us still looking at the closed door the men had disappeared behind. I asked her, "What do you suppose they are talking about in there?"

"Heaven only knows, George," she said, threading her arm through mine and giving it a squeeze. "Your uncle must have something particular on his mind to have come to see us at this time. I hope it will all be well, though."

I looked at her. "Why should it not be?"

She shook her head. "It is something from the past. Something I may not speak of." Then she approximated a smile. "Your father will sort it out, I trust. He is so wise and always looks after us so well. Do not worry."

Of course that is precisely what I *did* do: worry.

Later at dinner with the whole family, including Uncle Spencer, gathered round the table, my father made an announcement, which seemed directed at his three sons, my mother having been previously informed, I supposed.

"Your Uncle Spencer will be staying on at Donwell indefinitely, to help with the estate," he stated matter-of-factly. "I am not as young as I once was, and I could use a hand managing things, especially while you older boys are away. Spencer has offered to work alongside me, and I have accepted. So that is that."

By his tone, we knew that no further information would be forthcoming and no impertinent inquiries entertained. We knew our place and what was expected of us; we were expected to look pleased and raise no difficulties. "Yes, Father," we all three answered nearly simultaneously.

For myself, I did not much mind Uncle Spencer staying. It could make little difference to me, since Miles and I would be returning to Eton shortly in any case. For my mother, though... Judging from what she had said before and her subdued mood now, I knew she could not be well pleased at this turn of events. It was more difficult to develop what my father might be thinking. Was he really glad for Uncle Spencer's help, or was he only putting the best face on a disagreeable development?

Uncle Spencer himself seemed the only one at table in the mood to celebrate. "This is an excellent scheme; do not you think so?" he asked of no one in particular. "And it comes at such an opportune moment. I have grown weary of the noise and dirt of London. And the practice of the law is, I assure you, very dull indeed. Nothing could be better than to be returned to the country, I find – to the family estate, to feel myself made useful doing real work again. It is high time I get to know my nephews better, too. You have all grown so since I saw you last. It is no wonder I could not tell one from the other when I arrived. But I shall soon master your names and faces." Nodding at each of us in turn and meeting our eyes, he went on. "Miles, who is seventeen; George, who is fifteen; and little John, soon to be eleven. There, you see, I have it already!"

Uncle's cheerfulness and the effort he made to be obliging in the days that followed went a long way towards setting my mind at rest. After all, what was so remarkable about a man wishing to return to his origins, to his native soil? I understood that young men often felt the need to strike out on their own and have adventures. But perhaps as one grew older, one was drawn back to home and hearth with a deeper appreciation. To my fifteen-year-old mind, that seemed perfectly reasonable.

In any case, I had no choice but to hope for the best. Father's attitude was all reassurance and goodwill towards us when Miles and I made ready to take our leave and return to school. We would be gone scarcely more than two months before returning for the Christmas holidays. How could we have known that everything would have changed by then?

~~*~~

Miles's and my departing for school always occasioned some distress – both for those leaving and for those left behind.

Father never let on that he would miss us, of course. He would lay his left hand on my shoulder while shaking my hand with his right, solemnly look me in the eye, and give some sage piece of advice. "Remember you are a Knightley," or "Mind your studies," or "Make me proud of you, son." Then the same for Miles.

Mama was more demonstrative. She made free to embrace each of us at least twice in the leave-taking ceremony – something that, once we were past the age of twelve, she rarely imposed on us at any other time. We would pretend to object, naturally, but I never truly minded. Then Mama's lace-trimmed handkerchief was sure to come out as we climbed into the carriage, the article to be employed both for waving and for the blotting of her tears.

It may have been the worst for John, however, being left behind. I remember when Miles first went away to school without me, how much I regretted his going. At least I still had John with me, though. When I went too, John was left all alone. He carried on his day lessons with Mr. Bates, the vicar of Highbury, just as his brothers had done before him. But there were few suitable playfellows in the neighborhood who could fill the place of his absent brothers.

I always returned to Eton with mixed feelings: sorry to leave my home, eager for my friends and the academic world, and yet a little apprehensive as well. Would I be able to keep up with my studies? Would I comport myself as I ought? Or would I run afoul of an unforgiving instructor or a vindictive older student?

School is an odd environment, impossible to fully explain to anybody who has not experienced it – a strange mix of regimented time and unregimented behavior. In fact, one might justifiably call it rather wild. Like dogs thrown together in a pack, boys sort themselves out every year, not just by class but by establishing dominance. The lucky ones rise to the top and enjoy their privileges: extra food extorted from their fellows, menial tasks done for them by their subservients. But for the boys who come out at the bottom, it can be a cruel existence, being forever pecked and picked on, even brutalized. It is a fight for survival, with little or no help to be found from the adults. On the contrary, some of the masters are very quick to resort to the cruelty of corporal punishment in the name of discipline. I daresay there are few boys who have passed through the ranks without at least one caning.

After receiving my first at age thirteen, for quite a minor infraction, I complained to my father when I was next at home.

"I trust you did not cry!" was his first concern.

"No, Father," I said.

"George?"

"Well perhaps a little. Only a very little. It was extremely painful. And mortifying."

"Very well, then. Next time you will know what to expect, and you will do better."

"Next time?" I shuddered. "But why should it be allowed at all? I did not do anything so very bad."

"Perhaps not, my boy, but trust me; it will make you stronger in the end. It happened to me, too, you see. Oh, yes! More times than I care to count. And I am sure it helped to make a man of me. Enduring hardships and suffering, even when unjustly applied, builds character and fortitude. There is something in the Bible about that. In Romans, I believe, or perhaps it is Galatians. No, Romans. I remember now. So we can be confident it is true."

"Yes, sir."

"There, now. And experiencing discipline helps you to understand the chain of command as well. I should imagine you will be very careful not to disobey orders of a superior again."

Remembering the searing pain, I agreed.

"One day, George, you may be in charge of other men – in the Army, for example; second sons often choose a military life – and you will know something about what it is to command and what it is to follow orders."

I gave my father's words careful thought, but I cannot say I was completely convinced of the benefit of a caning, especially when it happened to me a second time a year later.

In any case, I did my very best to avoid displeasing my masters; that is certain. As for dealing with the potential abuse of the other boys, I was among the more fortunate. Although I was not especially high ranking or large for my age, my saving grace was that I had a brother there who had gone before me and already established for himself an acceptable place in school hierarchy. Because of Miles, I did not have to fight so hard for respect when I arrived at Eton; I instantly acquired a measure by proxy. Plus, Miles was a prefect by then, and he used his position to watch over me.

Oh, Miles, dear Miles! I do not know where I should have been without you!

I never had the chance to repay him; I could only try to deserve his kindness and to follow his example later with John.

Latin and Greek always comprised the greater share of our studies, but some attempt was made for a competence in history, mathematics, and the sciences too, the bookwork broken up by instruction in the physical arts: dancing, fencing, and so forth. I generally excelled, and I resented none of it except for Greek and dancing lessons. Greek was always a struggle for me, and I could have cheerfully foregone that discipline altogether. As for dancing, I did not appreciate having learnt until much later. Still, one took the good and the bad in stride; one had no choice.

Such things occupied my thoughts and expectations as Miles and I returned to Eton that autumn after Uncle Spencer arrived, and life at school soon settled again into its usual pattern. A week before the end of term, however, a letter arrived by express from my uncle, summoning us home early. My father was ill.

-3-
Transfer of Power

I suppose I should have been alerted to the seriousness of the situation by the summons itself and by the fact that my uncle, not my father or mother, had written it. Thinking back, I believe it was so inconceivable to me that my father could be dying that I did not even consider that possibility. On the contrary, I expected to be reassured by my mother the moment we arrived that all would soon be well. Perhaps Father would even be fully recovered by that time, and it only meant an early beginning to our Christmas holidays.

Full of anticipation, I remember stupidly saying to Miles at one point during our drive home, "I wonder if the pond is frozen over yet. We simply must skate every single day, Miles… once Father is better, of course."

He only smiled wanly and remained subdued, apparently having a much better idea of the potential graveness of the case. What a terrible son I later felt myself to be – thinking of my own pleasures while my father had lain, as it turned out, on his death bed.

Uncle Spencer met us at the door and took us aside into my father's study. "You boys must be brave now," was his opening remark, said sternly but not unkindly.

I looked from him, to Miles, and back again. "What do you mean, Uncle?" I asked.

"Your father had a riding accident a few days ago," he explained. "He struck his head and has never come to his senses since. The doctor says there is no hope, and it cannot be long now. So it is well that you have come promptly. You must prepare yourselves and then go up to your father's bedchamber to say your farewells before it is too late."

I felt my face crumbling and my eyes stinging, which could only mean one thing.

"No tears, George," admonished Uncle Spencer, gripping my upper arms and giving me a bracing little shake. "You know your father would not like it. He would expect you both to behave like brave soldiers. After all, you are nearly grown. Is not that so?"

"Yes, Uncle," said Miles with shoulders back and chin up, although I saw how it trembled.

"May we not see Mama first?" I asked instead of agreeing.

"She sits with your father, so you will see her when you go upstairs. You must not upset her with questions and wailing, though. Is that understood? This thing is difficult enough for her as it is. You must be strong – to do your father proud but also for your mother's sake. She will depend on you now more than ever."

I only nodded. I could not bring myself to speak.

Uncle looked me sternly in the eye and nodded in return. Then he did the same for Miles. "Very well, then. Off you go," he said, giving us each a little push to get our heavy feet started.

Slowly, we advanced to the stairs. But when we were only about halfway up, a loud, pitiful wail from above cut through the stale air of the house and sent a shiver up my spine. It also sent us running the rest of the way. It was my mother's cry, of course, and it emanated from the direction of my father's bedchamber.

When we burst through the door, Mama threw herself at us, crying out, "He is gone! Oh, Miles, George, your father is gone!" As she continued to sob, she clung to us as tightly as a drowning man would a lifesaving rope, and between her stranglehold and my own choking emotions, I could barely breathe.

I had meant to control my tears, as Uncle Spencer had commanded me to do, but the sight of my mother in such anguish brought me to the brink. And then my eyes were inexorably drawn to the bed beyond. I did not want to look. I told myself not to look, for as long as I did not see him lying there, a portion of my mind could deny that my father was dead. But I could not seem to help it. I looked, and the irrefutable evidence was before me: the body lying still as stone, the eyes closed, the jaw hanging slack, and the face unnaturally ashen. I knew it was my father, of course, and yet it did not quite look like him somehow. My mother was right; the man I knew as my father had gone, and there was only this lifeless form left in his place.

It was like a hand reached out and pushed me over the edge of a precipice. I was falling into an abyss with no one to catch me. My father, who had always been the rock at the center of my world, was dead, and nothing would ever be the same again. Tears flooded down my cheeks, and I no longer cared who saw it.

~~*~~

The next two weeks reside in my memory as little more than a painful blur. People came and went, making the necessary arrangements, I assume. But none of that involved me. I remained in my rooms upstairs as much as possible, not wanting to see anybody beyond my mother and brothers.

Then came the funeral itself. Nearly the whole countryside was there to see one of its leading citizens laid to rest. No doubt the vicar performed the rites admirably, too, saying all that was good and right on such an occasion. But I could not attend to anything much beyond my own pain and bewilderment. *How could this be happening?* That is what I kept asking myself. Fathers were supposed to be there at least until their children were grown. The fact that I knew it did not always happen that way could not stop me asking.

One thing I *do* remember, though, is that after the service Mr. Woodhouse made a point of speaking to me, personally and privately. I saw him glance in Miles's direction too, perhaps to include him in the conversation, but Miles was engaged with listening to something my uncle was saying to him and to my mother, who was being supported by them both. In any case, Mr. Woodhouse laid a hand on my shoulder and drew me a few more steps away from the others.

"I am sorrier than you can imagine, George," he told me. "Your father was a good man and one of my dearest friends. He will be sadly missed; that goes without saying."

Here, one must picture my friend Mr. Woodhouse prosperous and in the prime of life. He had a beautiful young wife, to whom he was devoted, and two small offspring – a girl and a boy – upon whom he doted, and the hope of more children yet to come. He was active in the management of his estate and gratefully sensible of the blessings God had supplied to him. True, he was sometimes over fastidious in his tastes and habits even then, but otherwise he was as sociable and even tempered as anybody could wish him to be. And this is what he said to me that day:

"What I want to tell you, though, is this. I wish you and your brothers to know that you can come to me at any time – if you should need help or just wish to talk. You still have your mother, of course, who is an excellent woman. And your uncle... Well, he is no doubt a very good sort of fellow too. But if I can ever be of any service, I hope you will not hesitate to ask. You boys are like sons to me, you know. And so for your own sakes as well as out of respect for the memory of your dear father, I will always do whatever I can – to stand in his place, as you might say. Remember that, and tell your brothers. Will you, George?"

I thanked him and promised that I would.

It was a kind invitation, and I thank God that Mr. Woodhouse meant what he said, for we sincerely needed his help and friendship in the months to come.

~~*~~

My uncle seemed to rise to the occasion, now that the mantle of responsibility had naturally passed to him. Far from acting the immature fellow we had believed him to be, he instantly undertook to manage whatever wanted immediate attention as if no interruption had occurred. He was a tower of strength. I could not imagine how we should have got through without him.

Uncle Spencer's manners were pleasing as well during those early weeks. He was very civil to each of us boys, and more importantly, very patient and solicitous of my mother. He regularly leant her his strong, steadying arm and his shoulder to cry on when needed, which it often was. He would invariably sit beside her in the evenings as well, engaging her in quiet conversation. I remember appreciating his being there to condole with Mama, for I was certain he knew how to comfort her much better than I or my brothers ever could have.

And so we went on together as well as a family can be supposed to do in such gloomy circumstances.

The first troubling sign I noticed came a month or so after my father was gone and buried. Mama and Uncle Spencer were walking arm in arm together in the garden as I emerged from the house that day. Then I saw Mama suddenly try to draw away. Uncle Spencer would not allow it; he kept hold of her wrist, looking down at her and saying something, which by all appearances was quite severe. I was on the point of interfering when he released her and they walked on together.

I quietly withdrew unseen, for some reason feeling more embarrassed than worried at having witnessed this exchange. So I said nothing about it to anybody.

A few days later, though, Uncle Spencer summoned us all together into the drawing room and shut the door. My mother sat limply on one of the sofas with my younger brother John leaning against her. Miles and I shared the other sofa, and my uncle stood before us with his hands clasped behind him, rocking from heels to toes and back again.

"I have called you here because there are important things we need to discuss: things required by the difficult circumstances that have been thrust upon us."

I noticed at once a subtle yet unmistakable shift in his manner. The kind and solicitous uncle we had begun to expect and trust had receded slightly, while a man of business, brooking no nonsense, had advanced to the forefront.

"I know it is early days yet, and we are still adjusting, but this really cannot wait any longer." He then turned to address my mother. "Margaret, I am sure you will not mind the boys being here. These things will involve them as well."

"Whatever you think best, Spencer," she said without even looking up.

"Good," Uncle continued. "The first thing you all should know is that I will not desert you in your hour of need; I will stay on here at Donwell as long as I am wanted. How fortuitous it was that I came when I did, for I am now well able to take the wheel and pilot the ship. I make no doubt that was my brother's intention when he appointed me guardian for the boys and for the estate."

My mother did look up then. "But I thought... Oh, dear. What I mean is that we are all very grateful for your help in this sudden crisis, Spencer, but I thought it was to be Mr. Woodhouse who would see us through the long course. That is what my husband told me. If anything ever happened to him, Mr. Woodhouse would look after things until Miles was of age."

"Ah, yes," Spencer replied. "What you say is true, or at least it used to be. But that was before I arrived and became so familiar with the workings of the estate myself. I am sure you would agree that it makes much more sense now that I should step into my brother's shoes since I understand the situation so well. And besides, I am family. No need to burden your good neighbor with the business."

Mother was silent a minute and then only nodded. Spencer apparently felt empowered to proceed.

"I am sorry if you were not made aware of the change, Margaret. Perhaps your husband also failed to acquaint you with the precarious state of his business affairs?"

Mama gave a start. "Precarious? I knew of no such trouble!"

"I thought not," he said with a sigh, shaking his head sadly. "No doubt he wished to spare you, my dear. Well, then, it is my unhappy duty to inform you that the situation at Donwell is precarious indeed. Some changes will need to be made immediately to bring the ship about, to return it to its proper course again."

"But it can be done?" Mama asked, her voice trembling. "Surely all is not lost?" She looked at Miles, and I knew she was thinking how dreadful it would be if there was nothing for him to inherit when the time came.

"Do not fear, my dear sister," Spencer answered with a coldness that belied his words. "That is exactly what I have been working on since I arrived: a plan of retrenchment. In two or three years, with careful management and good harvests, I daresay we will be on secure footing again. That will be my goal – to return Donwell to a prosperous state before Miles takes the reins."

Miles spoke up. "Well, I thank you for that, sir, but just what does this 'retrenchment' you speak of entail?"

"This is the part that will most involve yourself, Miles, and George as well. I am afraid there is no more money for Eton. Your father meant to tell you that when you came home but did not live to do it. You boys will therefore all have to remain here and make do with taking your lessons from Mr. Bates, as least for now. It is a sacrifice, I know, but we must all be prepared to forgo extravagances of every kind for the time being. Hopefully, when you are ready for university, the situation will have vastly improved."

"Of course," replied Miles, evenly. "I am ready to do my part. So will we all." Miles glanced at the rest of us to receive our assurances. Mama nodded perfunctorily. John and I said nothing, but Uncle Spencer went on as if we had.

"Good, good," he said. "I knew that once things had been explained, I could depend on you. I think that is enough to take in for now, though. I will keep you all informed if and when other changes are needed."

"Thank you, Spencer," said Mama, wearily rising. "It is very good of you, I am sure."

He bowed. "It is my honor as well as my clear duty, Margaret, to look after my dear departed brother's affairs and his family."

I had remained silent throughout the meeting, trying to absorb this latest blow. Afterwards, though, I wanted to talk to somebody about my questions and doubts. But who? John was obviously too young, and I did not wish to upset Mama or Miles, both of whom seemed to be reconciled to all that Uncle Spencer had told us. They would probably think me strange and ungrateful to question it. Then I remembered Mr. Woodhouse's invitation.

Suspicious Minds

The next morning, I stole from the house, ran the mile to Hartfield, and asked to speak to Mr. Woodhouse. Mrs. Woodhouse came to meet me instead.

"Why, George! What do you do here?" she asked. "And all out of breath too!"

Mrs. Woodhouse was the most beautiful lady of my acquaintance. Beauty was not her only virtue, though. She was also esteemed for her open nature, kindness, and sense well applied. In my youthful folly, all these caused me to hold her in some considerable awe, as a kind of ideal female. When in her presence, I was always torn between wanting to bask there and fearing I would embarrass myself by letting on how I felt about her. I judged Mr. Woodhouse a very lucky man.

"I ran all the way," I said, feeling my warm cheeks begin to burn.

"Oh, dear! Is anything the matter?"

I hesitated. "No, Ma'am. I just need to speak to Mr. Woodhouse. He told me I might come anytime."

"Well of course you might, but he is not in the house at the moment. Come in and sit down. Rest yourself, and I will send to have Mr. Woodhouse fetched in from the stables. I am sure he will be with you shortly."

"Begging your pardon, Ma'am, but I would not want anybody put to trouble on my account. I can go to the stables just as easily myself."

"Very well, if you really had rather. It would be no trouble at all, though," she added as I slipped back out of the door.

The stables at Hartfield were not large, but they were well built and neatly kept. Mr. Woodhouse himself took a great deal of interest in them and their occupants, stopping by frequently to pass a few words with the groom and a few more with the horses. So I should not have been surprised to find him there.

When he saw me at the open doorway, he came to meet me, saying cheerfully, "Well, George, what can I do for you today, my boy?"

"I need to talk to you, Mr. Woodhouse. Remember, you said I could anytime."

"Yes, and I meant it. But let us leave the stable yard and find a comfortable place to sit down, somewhere we will not be disturbed." I walked at his side whilst he led the way to the part of the garden furthest from the house, which was made up mostly of lawn and hedges in geometric designs. When we had settled on a bench there, he asked, "Now, what is this about, George?"

And so I told him everything Uncle Spencer had said the day before: that my father had named him guardian, that we were to retrench because Donwell's finances had nearly collapsed, and that Miles and I would not be attending Eton anymore. Mr. Woodhouse calmly listened as I unburdened myself, finishing with, "Mama and Miles seem to accept everything my uncle has said without question, but I... I cannot."

"You *have* questions, then?"

"Yes, like did my father really change from you to Uncle Spencer as our guardian? And if Donwell was in difficulty, why did he never tell us? I am sure even Mama did not know anything about it."

I paused, and he asked, "Is that all of your questions?"

"Yes. No! Why did Uncle Spencer come to Donwell in the first place? I do not dislike him, except that he sometimes makes my mother nervous. I suppose he is very kind to help us now, so I am probably very wicked to doubt him, but…" I trailed off, not knowing how to finish.

Mr. Woodhouse picked up from there. "You, George, wicked? No, I would not say so. Although it is good to think the best of people whenever possible, sometimes we need to choose being wise instead. Being wise, especially in business, means asking questions, as you are. It means staying apprised of the facts instead of blindly trusting. Unfortunately, that advice sometimes needs apply even to a family member, particularly one who has proven untrustworthy before."

"Uncle Spencer?"

He nodded and then took a moment to think before continuing. "I… I do not know the whole of the story, you understand, but I know there was some conniving on his part years ago, disputing your father's right to sole ownership of Donwell and so forth, I believe even going to so far as to claim that he himself was the older twin. I'm afraid it left bad blood between them. It was a long time ago, though, and people change. Your father must have been convinced that your uncle's motives in coming to Donwell this time were honorable, convinced he deserved another chance, or he surely would not have taken him into his confidence as he did these past months.

"Your father was very closed-lipped with me since your uncle's arrival, so I cannot confirm or disprove much of what you have told me. He never confided to me that the estate was in trouble, for example. One thing is certainly true, however; your father did, only a few weeks before his accident, change his will. I saw his solicitor soon after his death, because I wished to be clear on my responsibilities as guardian. That is when I learnt that it was to be your uncle's honor and not mine. Rather irregular for a man to appoint his younger brother, though." He stopped, but he looked as if he had more on his mind.

"Why would it be, Mr. Woodhouse?" I prompted.

"Oh… Well, it is to do with the law, but you need not concern yourself with all that now. The important thing for you to remember is that your father must have thought your uncle the very best person to take charge or he would not have appointed him guardian. Does that help to set your mind at rest?"

"I suppose so." Even if I did not entirely trust my uncle, I did entirely trust my father to have known what was best for us.

"At this point, there is nothing to be done but to give your uncle the benefit of the doubt, to hope that he is just what he appears: an honest soul with your family's interests at heart."

"And if he should not be?"

"Then we will know it, by... and... by," Mr. Woodhouse said, patting my arm to emphasize the last three words. "You must not be so impatient, George." Then his countenance grew serious. "But do take care. I feel it my duty to caution you against poking your nose into your uncle's affairs – you or Miles either. Even an honest man would not take kindly to that. A dishonest one... Well, just promise you will not confront him or hurl any accusations at his head. Come straight to me instead, if you notice anything truly worrisome. Agreed?"

"Yes, sir, Mr. Woodhouse, sir."

"Ah, there's a good lad. Shall we solemnly shake hands on the bargain?"

We did so, I feeling very mature. Then I took my leave. On my walk home, I considered all Mr. Woodhouse had said. At least I knew that Uncle was not deceiving us about being Father's choice for our guardian. That did give me more confidence. I also felt mightily relieved to have unburdened myself to Mr. Woodhouse, to know that he would be on the watch for anything irregular as well.

His manner had been reassuring. And there certainly was no proof, or even any clear evidence, of wrongdoing at this time. My suspicions were probably exactly that and no more – the products of an unnaturally suspicious mind. I was glad my uncle could not know of it and neither could my mother. I preferred both of them would think better of me than I probably deserved.

I could not keep any secrets from Miles, though, not for long. It all came out that night in our shared rooms.

"...I just wanted you to know, Miles," I concluded after confiding to him the whole of the conversation, my worries and Mr. Woodhouse's advice. "But I suppose you will say that I am only imagining things."

"I would never say that, George, although I am of a similar mind to Mr. Woodhouse. In the absence of any clear evidence of wrongdoing, we should trust Uncle Spencer because he was Father's choice. How good of Mr. Woodhouse to watch over us, though! His motives are completely disinterested, since he cannot possibly gain from helping us."

...unlike our uncle, as I later came to understand. A named guardian is normally a person who, like Mr. Woodhouse, can have no personal interest in the estate – generally a close friend or a relative on the wife's side – not somebody who stands a chance to inherit something from the estate. This is the 'irregu-larity' Mr. Woodhouse spoke of, and on these grounds he had already filed a complaint with the Court of Chancery on our behalf, questioning Uncle Spencer's suitability to be guardian of his nephews and Donwell Abbey. However, months would pass and many things would happen before I knew about this.

-5-

A More Immediate Threat

My concerns about Uncle Spencer's guardianship soon disappeared from view, swallowed up by a larger, more immediate threat: influenza. Although it was known that London was awash with a particularly bad version of the stuff, we all felt reasonably secure in Highbury, where the air is so superior. But then a change in the prevailing winds was blamed for the city's miasma finding its way to our neighborhood.

Sickness was everywhere, it seemed, with barely a household left untouched. The apothecary was kept extremely busy, Buchan's book was consulted front to back for assistance, and the contents of still rooms were nearly exhausted in search of an efficacious remedy. Yet the illness raged on. Most eventually recovered, of course, but there were sad exceptions.

Mr. and Mrs. Woodhouse's little boy, Henry, who had never been of stout constitution, was one of the first to be buried that terrible winter. Other children and infants, especially among the poor it seemed, also succumbed, as did a few of the elderly. Those well enough to leave their homes attended many funerals.

At Donwell, we had our share of disease – amongst the servants and tenant farmers, but also in my own family. John contracted the illness first, then Mama, then Miles, and finally I myself was afflicted. We were each miserable in our turns but then, at long last, began to improve. Still, it was a slow process and full recovery was not to be expected immediately.

Only Uncle Spencer escaped unscathed, crediting his being spared to hard work and a strong constitution. The rest of us dragged through the sick days, one after another, with no interest in much of anything beyond our own health.

When the time came that we boys should have been beginning lessons again, Mama read aloud Mr. Bates's note, advising us of a postponement of uncertain length. She sighed and then tossed the missive away, forgotten.

John was the only one who would have been in any condition to resume the routine of daily lessons. Having become ill first, he also recovered first and then became impatient for activity. "Come along, George," he cajoled me one day. "Let us go out for a grand explore, as we used to do. I cannot sit about the house one minute longer."

It was impossible for me to do as he asked, but I roused myself enough to give him a half-hearted answer. "Another time, John. It is such a cold, gray day that I cannot face it." I pointed to the window. "See how the rain and sleet are coming down heavy. It is not safe, and I am still quite unwell."

After John had given up on me, and having had the same result with Miles, he went out on his own.

Mama spoke languidly, as much to herself, it seemed, as to me or Miles. "I hope he will not catch a chill. At least little John has some energy. I have none myself. Thank goodness Spencer is able to carry on and look after us all. He has proved himself a real godsend these past weeks."

I made no reply to this. Mama had a point in that we probably should be glad Uncle had been able to, once again, carry on the important business of Donwell without interruption. But still, somehow I could not think of him as a true godsend. After all, everything had been well with us until he arrived.

It was glorious, though, when the day finally came that we were all well enough to resume our daily lives after being confined for weeks. Miles and I waited no longer than necessary to take the air, reacquainting ourselves with all the environs of Donwell.

Our pleasure at the outing did not last, however. When we visited the stables, I sensed at once that something was amiss. It was too quiet. I glanced about for the head groom but only saw the stable boy. "Where is Webster, Jimmy?" I asked him.

"Gone, Master George."

"Gone?" my brother repeated. "You do not mean... You do not mean he has been taken by the influenza."

"Oh, no, sir, Mr. Miles. Sent packin', so he was."

"Discharged! It cannot be," continued Miles. "I knew nothing of this. Why was he dismissed? For what cause?"

Jimmy shrugged. "Don't know. Mr. Spencer Knightley jus' told 'im he weren't needed no more, 'n that was that."

An inkling of dread crept up my spine, and I ran off down the aisle between the stalls, looking left and right. It was as I feared.

"Over half the horses are gone!" I reported a little out of breath when I immediately returned to Miles. I looked at Jimmy. "Sold?"

He nodded.

"Not Sheba!" Miles, without waiting for an answer, dashed towards his favorite mount's stall. He came dragging back a minute later.

"Cinder too," I choked out. Cinder was the charcoal grey gelding everybody knew as mine. "It seems Uncle Spencer has been very busy indeed."

Miles thanked Jimmy then took my arm to lead me away. In a hushed voice, he said, "This is quite shocking, George. I wonder what else has gone missing while we were laid up. We had better have a look around."

So we did. Miles and I made a tour, discreetly speaking with tenants and servants, looking into barns and outbuildings, taking an informal inventory of equipment and stock. Everywhere it was the same: things unaccounted for, workers gone without explanation, jobs left undone, tenants' concerns unaddressed.

"It must be the economies Uncle spoke of," I told Miles at last, "his 'retrenchment' plan. He said sacrifices would have to be made."

"He also told us he would keep us informed, which obviously he has not. No, I cannot believe that completely accounts for all this. It goes too far. We are depending on good harvests to recover our footing; Uncle has said so himself. But there will be no harvest brought in if the workers are dismissed and the equipment left to rust and ruin. Something is wrong; I am sure of it. I will speak to Uncle at once and demand an explanation."

"No, Miles, you mustn't! Remember Mr. Woodhouse's warning. He made me promise I would not confront Uncle Spencer but come to him instead, should I see anything amiss."

"*I* made no such promise. Besides, George, I would not trouble Mr. Woodhouse for the world, would you? Not when he has just lost his son. The man must be eaten up inside with grief. The last thing he needs right now is more worries heaped on his shoulders. I must manage this myself."

I could not fault my brother's logic or his consideration for Mr. Woodhouse's feelings. I had seen him at Henry's funeral, and he was a changed man. He seemed barely to recognize me when I spoke to him. God willing, he would recover in time, but Miles was right; Mr. Woodhouse was in no condition to help us now.

Miles moved off towards the house, obviously intent on finding Uncle Spencer.

"Wait, Miles," I said, trailing after him. "What can you hope to accomplish by this? Even if your suspicions are correct, Uncle Spencer will be under no obligation to do what you say. He is the legal guardian and the estate is in his control. You will only make him angry."

"He may not be obliged to do as I say, but I think I am well within my rights, as heir, to expect an explanation. You need not become involved, though, George. I am prepared to face him alone. As oldest, it is my responsibility."

What could I do? I wished to keep my promise to Mr. Woodhouse, but I also wanted to stand with my brother. I could not do both. So, in much trepidation, I went with Miles, intending to at least be nearby when he confronted Uncle Spencer. We found him in my father's study, which he had commandeered for his own use, and he gave permission for us to enter.

Miles had promised to be calm and respectful – as if seeking information rather than come to make accusations. And he began well enough, but as he ran through his list of grievances, he became more and more agitated. I hovered in the doorway, watching and listening in fear and trembling for what would happen next. Would Uncle throw us out? Would he yell and shout? Would he devise some cruel punishment for having questioned his authority and methods?

Nothing as dramatic as that happened… at least not at first. Uncle Spencer merely leant back in his chair behind the desk, appearing aloof and impassive as my brother delivered himself of his complaints. When Miles came to a sputtering finish, Uncle planted his fists on the desk and drew himself up to his full height to face his accuser.

"I have let you have your say, Miles, and now it is my turn. Agreed?" Spencer said in a milder tone than I had expected.

Miles gave a curt nod and remained silently at attention.

"Very well then. First," he continued in a business-like tone, "in consideration of my dear brother's memory, I have allowed you some latitude. You are still young and have much to learn. But do not mistake my indulging you this once for weakness. Going forward, this is how you will behave. You will not attempt to dictate to me or challenge my decisions. You will treat me with the respect my age and position in this family demand. You will obey me as you would have your father. That is what he decreed when he named me guardian.

There is no room for discussion on this matter; I merely state the facts.

"Secondly, as to the changes you see that I have made, why should you be surprised? I did warn you to expect more measures of economy to come. In fact, I remember how boldly you promised at the time to do your part. But now you come crying because I sold your horse?" he asked in apparent perplexity. "That is the act of a child and unworthy of you, Miles."

I saw my brother flinch at this.

"Difficult decisions had to be made," Uncle continued, "and I have made them. I did not bother you with the details when you were all so ill. As for the harvest, when the time comes, we will manage perfectly well with temporary workers. There is no reason to pay men all the year round when we only need them for a brief season. Besides, you boys can help.

"Now listen carefully," he said in the manner of one whose infinite patience has been tested to the limit. "*Both* of you," he added, a keen glance in my direction letting me know my presence had not been overlooked. "Until you are twenty-one, Miles, I am in charge, and this estate will be managed as *I* see fit. Is that understood?"

"Yes, sir," said Miles. "I understand you perfectly."

"Very well. See that you remember it in future. I may not be as generous should you create such a scene again. Now please go. I have work to do."

To Uncle Spencer, Miles may have sounded compliant in the end, but I knew better. Nor was I fooled by my uncle's calm demeanor. I was sure there were stronger emotions on both sides being carefully kept in check.

"Come along, George," Miles mumbled as he led the way out of the room and then the house, moving so rapidly that I struggled to keep up. Neither of us said another word until we were well away and Miles had expended some of his pent up energy stalking across a fallow field. There, he finally stopped and stooped over, hands on his knees.

"Are you well, Miles?" I asked timidly.

There was a long pause. "I will be," he said at last, "as soon as I am able to control my temper."

"You did not like what Uncle said." It was a statement, not a question.

"Of course not."

"He was not very kind, but at least he forbore to yell. And he made what he said sound very reasonable. I suppose he must be firm."

"Do not be taken in, George. Skilled liars can make the most outrageous falsehoods sound convincing. Uncle Spencer is up to something. I just do not know exactly what it is... yet."

"Oh, Miles, do be careful!"

"I will be, but I must discover what he is about before it is too late. You remember that deer carcass we found in the field last summer?"

"Yes, of course," I said, puzzled by the abrupt change in subject. "But what is that to do with anything?"

"It came to mind when I thought of how our *dear* guardian seems to be dismantling, piece by piece, all Father built up in his lifetime. I cannot stand by, doing nothing, while Donwell is picked apart until there is nothing left but dry bones."

Is that what Uncle Spencer was really doing, I wondered? – devouring the estate, bit by bit? I was concerned too, but somehow I could not quite believe possible such a desperate prospect of the future.

Rumors Abound

Once the fearsome specter of influenza had passed, life in Highbury began slowly to return to normal, at least for those who had survived with their families and faculties intact. Townspeople emerged from their cottages; Ford's and other shops were open again; and market day recaptured its vitality and bustle.

Mr. Bates also resumed giving lessons at the rectory. He had two or three boys who boarded, and now, with the addition of me and Miles, several day pupils as well. And so we three brothers walked together to the rectory every day.

"I am glad you did not go back to Eton, Miles," John said, smiling up at us, that first day along the road to Highbury. "I am glad you did not, George, but do you mind?"

"No," I answered, "not so very much." That was true. Of all the changes and misfortunes that had occurred in recent months, the loss of Eton was far down my list. I only minded the reason I could not go back, not the actual fact of it.

"Uncle Spencer says I must begin working on the farm, though," continued John in an abrupt change of subject. "I do not think I shall like that."

Miles gave me a speaking look over John's head. "Perhaps not, John," he said, "but it will be necessary for us all to help out, now that there are fewer workers on the estate. George and I have farm duties too, you know, much more than you will, since we are older. I daresay it will be good for us, so that we understand and better appreciate how Donwell operates."

"But *I* am not going to have a farm or an estate when I grow up," my younger brother declared. "I am going to live in a fine house in London and be a solicitor, or maybe even a barrister. So I do not need to know about crops and harvests and dairies and tenants."

"Is that so?" I asked him. "Where did you get that idea from?"

"From Uncle Spencer. He is a solicitor, you know."

"I *do* know that, John, but he told us when he came here that he found the law a very dull pursuit. Has he told you something different?"

"He just said that to know the law gives one power over other men, or something like that. Besides, it is a respectable occupation for the younger sons of gentlemen. Uncle told me that too."

"As are the army and the church," said Miles. "Do neither of those professions interest you?"

John thought a minute. "George will probably go into the church. Is not that so?" he asked looking up at me.

"Probably," I confirmed.

"...but I should not mind being a soldier and wearing regimentals."

"There is a good deal more to soldiering than wearing regimentals," Miles informed him. "Perhaps your first idea was best after all: the law. It would be a pity to have you away in London, though. Could not you content yourself with being a country attorney?"

"Oh no, that will never do! Uncle says country attorneys are low and commentable."

I thought for a moment. "Did he perhaps say they were 'contemptable' instead?" I asked.

"Yes! That was the word. At least I think it was. Anyway, it is something bad, which I do not want. Uncle says I should have more pride than that."

Another look passed between Miles and myself. I did not like the idea of my younger brother patterning himself on Spencer, using him as his source of information and counsel. But with our father gone, I supposed it was only natural for a boy of ten to look to the one who stood in his father's place. For the time being, at least, that was Uncle Spencer.

~~*~~

One day, Mr. Bates asked us to stay after our lesson. "You run along with the other boys," he told John. "Your brothers will be with you presently. When John and the others had gone, he continued, "Sit down a minute; I would have a word with you."

Miles and I looked at each other, and it was clear that we both had the same questions and no answers. *Why did the rector wish to speak to us? Were we in some kind of trouble?*

"Is there a problem with our work, Mr. Bates?" Miles asked as we three took seats close together.

"No, not at all," answered the rector. "You boys are doing very well in that line. I have no complaints against you. No, this is something else altogether."

He paused, fidgeted, and frowned, and for a minute I thought he would not continue. There was nothing to do except wait, however.

Presently, Mr. Bates resumed. "You observe my discomfort, do not you? It is all too true. I am reluctant even to mention this subject, you see, since it amounts to passing along gossip, and the last thing I wish to do is add to your troubles. I know things cannot have been easy since your excellent father passed on. But on the other hand, I cannot help being concerned. There is talk, I'm afraid, throughout the village and the parish." Here he hesitated again.

"Talk?" Miles prompted.

"Very well," the rector said with a sigh. "I will leave off my shillyshallying and just have out with it. There is talk of strange doings at Donwell – servants and workers turned off, much stock sold, and so forth. Suggestions from bankruptcy to highhanded interference on your uncle's part. It may be nothing, and of course I sincerely hope that is the case. But if there *is* trouble, I should like to do anything I can to help."

Miles and I exchanged another look. He lifted his brows in a question. I understood, shrugged, and nodded. What could it hurt to have a good man like Mr. Bates knowing the truth, especially when all our neighbors were apparently talking about it anyway?

"It is true, Mr. Bates," said Miles. "Our uncle, Mr. Spencer Knightley, who Father appointed our legal guardian, says it is all a necessary part of his retrenchment plan to return Donwell to a solid financial footing again. That is as much as I know or can tell you."

Mr. Bates looked surprised. "Indeed? I am sorry to hear it. I had no idea there were difficulties of that kind at Donwell!"

"Neither did we until Uncle said…" I abruptly stopped, seeing the dark expression on my brother's face.

The rector resumed, filling the awkward silence. "No doubt your father was trying to spare you. He was a proud and private man. He would not have wished everybody to know his troubles. Now, however… Well, now it is still nobody's business but your own, I suppose, and you can be sure I will do what I can to curb gossiping tongues."

Mr. Bates let us go then, with the promise of his support and to call on our mother soon.

"Why did you stop me saying more back there?" I asked Miles when we had achieved the street.

"As Mr. Bates said, what goes on at Donwell is nobody's business but our own."

"But perhaps he could have helped us. And besides, you cannot be concerned about preserving Uncle Spencer's reputation, not with how ill you think of him."

"Perhaps not, but still, he *is* family, father's brother, and we therefore owe some loyalty to him, at least until we are sure he is a no-good scoundrel. That is why I keep such a close eye on him. Until we are sure of the truth, nothing can be done about it."

So we lived in an uneasy truce at Donwell. Spencer carried on as he saw fit, while the rest of us danced, however unwillingly, to the tune he played. We boys did our lessons and the work our uncle assigned to us, Miles and I also keeping watch for some proof of his perfidy, if indeed such proof existed.

None of us was happy, as once we had been, but we carried on as best we could. I think what grieved me most was seeing what recent events had done to Mama. Six months had passed since my Father's death, and she had, naturally, come nowhere near to the end of her mourning for him, if she ever would. In the absence of her husband, she had fallen into the habit of taking her lead from Spencer instead. Whatever misgivings she had at first harbored about him, seemed to have been forgot in the process, perhaps drowned out by her greater need to have a leader to follow – any leader. She even accepted without complaint his measures of economy, degrading though they must have been to her.

We entertained no company, and the quality of fare at our own table had suffered sadly under the reduced budget Uncle Spencer had imposed. Although she had less to work with, at least the cook kept her position. Caruthers, Mama's personal lady's maid, was not so fortunate. Her services were deemed an unnecessary extravagance. Now Mama had to make do with only whatever time Amy, the chamber maid, could spare from her other duties.

"A lady with no lady's maid has entirely lost her self-respect." I had heard Mama say it of others, and now, sadly, others were probably saying it of her.

She rarely left the house anymore, even to go to church. Perhaps she was sensible of the gossip, as I was. Ever since that conversation with Mr. Bates, it seemed I could not meet a neighbor or enter the village without becoming painfully aware of the furtive looks and whispered comments. Most, I believe, were regarding our family's situation with kind concern rather than scorn, but it was still distressing.

In the midst of all of this, however, a small beacon of hope emerged. Little did I guess at the time what meaning that event would have in my own life.

-7-

A Beacon of Hope

It transpired that Mrs. Woodhouse had been with child when her little boy was carried off by the influenza, and apparently there was some fear at the time that the shock would cause her to lose the unborn infant as well. But instead, a healthy baby girl was born to the Woodhouses in July. They christened her Emma.

This occasion was sufficiently momentous as to rouse Mama from her lethargy and tempt her out of her self-imposed seclusion. Despite everything, she knew what was due to her friend Mrs. Woodhouse. Her pride would not allow her to ignore the fact that a call to Hartfield was definitely in order.

Our finest carriage had been sold, along with the horses that used to draw it, and there was no dedicated coachman anymore. So I drove Mama myself in the gig. I liked driving and often fancied I had a talent for it. I did not object to the destination or the company to be found there either. Although a new baby did not interest me, I *was* partial to Mrs. Woodhouse and thought to have opportunity to gaze upon her unobserved while she conversed with my mother. I also expected to enjoy entertaining seven-year-old Isabella. As for Mr. Woodhouse, I hoped to find him returned to more his old self.

I had seen little of them since before the influenza struck, and no continuation of my earlier conversation with Mr.

Woodhouse had occurred. Nor did I plan to renew the topic on this occasion.

Miles, who was feeling poorly or otherwise might have come along, had charged me before I left, "Remember, George, do not burden Mr. Woodhouse with our troubles. He is still grieving one child and adjusting to the presence of this newcomer. Besides, there is no need; I can manage things myself."

So he said, but I wondered... Wondered and worried. Though he had promised to be careful, Miles had sometimes pushed his luck a little too far. The worst had occurred when he attempted to gain a view of Uncle Spencer's ledgers one day, considering that it would be the likeliest place to find the proof of misconduct he was looking for. But Uncle had discovered him in the act and berated him severely, apparently not believing the excuse Miles had invented for being in the study. Since then, even more tension filled the air, and the door to the study was now locked at all times.

I was, therefore, glad for an excuse to temporarily escape my home for one which was, although not free from sorrow, at least free from intrigue and suspicion.

Arrived at Hartfield, Mama and I were shown into the drawing room and soon joined by both Mr. and Mrs. Woodhouse.

After greetings, Mrs. Woodhouse exclaimed cheerfully, "Why, Margaret! I see you are arranging your hair in a new way. It is most becoming. Caruthers is so very clever."

I waited to see if Mama would tell her friend of Caruthers having gone, but she did not. She only mumbled her thanks at the compliment, and Mrs. Woodhouse moved on.

"And so I suppose it is little Emma you are really come to see," she said. "I shall not begrudge you that! I shall have her brought down from the nursery at once. Isabella too," she added, with a nod to me and a sunny smile. "She will be happy to see you, George."

I was glad she turned away before my face could flush.

"Do you think you should?" Mr. Woodhouse said before his wife could act. "Infants are so susceptible to changes in their surroundings and their routines."

"I would very much like to see the child," Mama admitted, "but I would be perfectly happy to go to the nursery myself, if that would be more advisable. Or wait until a later date."

"Thank you, Margaret," said Mrs. Woodhouse. "That is very good of you but entirely unnecessary. The child is not made of glass. In fact, I do not know when I have ever seen such a strong, healthy infant. Nothing seems to bother her! Mr. Woodhouse has just become a bit overly fastidious recently, since..." A shadow crossed her face and then was gone, no doubt summoned by the memory of her sickly son's sad outcome. "In any case, there is no need for you to go up to the children; the children will come down to you."

She sent a footman off to the nursery with the message.

When little Isabella came in, she curtsied properly to my mother and then hurried over to me. Taking my hand, she pulled me away from the adults to a sofa at the far end of the room. "I have a new book, George," she said, showing it to me. "Would you like to look at it?"

"I would!" I answered with exaggerated enthusiasm. "I see there are some very fine drawings of animals in it," I continued, turning over a few pages. "Can you read it yourself, Bella, or would you like me to?"

"I can read. I am seven now, you know."

"I know. Your birthday was in March. Isn't that so?"

"Yes. But some of the words in my new book are too difficult. I am still learning."

"Of course you are. Then we shall read your book together. You read until you come to one of those difficult words, point to it, and I will tell you what it is. Agreed?"

She nodded and we began.

While the adults talked together at the other end of the room, Isabella and I went on very well together – our reading interspersed with teasing and laughter. Then we were interrupted by Mrs. Woodhouse coming over to us with the baby in her arms.

"Now, George," she said, "it is your turn to hold little Emma."

I was taken quite off my guard at the very idea! I had never held an infant in my life, at least not that I could remember, and I had no particular desire to do so. To add to my discomfort, all eyes, including Mrs. Woodhouse's, were turned on me.

Mr. Woodhouse provided me a chance to escape the awkward situation by calling across the room. "You do not have to, George, if you had rather not. In any case, do be careful."

Before I could think of what to say, Mrs. Woodhouse placed the child in my arms. "Just give support underneath and allow her head to rest in the crook of your arm. There! That's perfect. Nothing to it at all, you see."

I was too embarrassed to say anything. I could only comply and hope it would be over soon.

The baby was so tiny; she hardly weighed anything at all, and I felt at first as if she might crumble to pieces, like a fragile little bird, if I held her too tightly. When I looked down at her, I discovered there was really not much to see, for swaddling covered all but the round face, a few wisps of pale hair, and a pair of blue-gray eyes staring back at me, unblinking. I remember thinking how impossible it seemed that I – and everybody else I knew – had once started the same way.

I held the infant for only a minute or two. When her face grew red and she began to cry, I was very glad to return her to her mother.

"She is probably hungry again," explained Mrs. Woodhouse. "What an appetite she seems to have for such a little mite! Nurse?" She said, passing the now-squalling child off to that worthy woman, who swiftly removed the noisy article from the room.

This was my first impression of Emma Woodhouse, the distant precursor to the fully grown woman I am now in love with. It seems inconceivable that the two are one and the same person, but logic tells me it must be so.

In any case, after the infant was removed, and after Isabella had been taken back to the nursery as well, Mr. Woodhouse motioned that I should come to him. I went, of course, and sat down beside him. The ladies were busy talking amongst themselves, and Mr. Woodhouse kept his voice low. It lacked much of its former strength in any case.

"And so, George, how do things go on at Donwell? Is your uncle behaving himself as he ought? I am sorry that I have not been as attentive to you and your family as I should have. The influenza and… and everything. You must forgive me."

"There is nothing to forgive, Mr. Woodhouse. I was to let you know if your help was needed, remember."

"That is true enough, and I am glad you recall it. Still, I should have done more. Tell me what has transpired since last we spoke on this subject."

"Miles says you are not to worry. We are undergoing some uncomfortable economies, which Uncle Spencer has instituted, but… but that is all. Nothing we cannot bear."

"What sort of economies? I have heard some rumors, but I will not give credence to mere gossip."

I did not wish to say more because of Miles's injunction, but it was impossible to refuse to answer Mr. Woodhouse's questions altogether. So I made as light of the true circumstances as possible. "A few servants let go. Some of the excess stock and farm implements sold. That sort of thing. As I said, it is nothing we cannot bear, and you are not to worry."

"Hmm. 'Uncomfortable economies' indeed," said my companion, "and I am not to worry. So says Miles, eh? Yes, I see. Well, then, I can only remind you of what I told you before. Be careful to stay out of your uncle's way, and do not hesitate to come to me if anything alarming should occur. I have been knocked down a peg or two; that I freely admit. But I hope I shall still have the fortitude to do what is my duty. You will remind Miles too, will you not?"

"Yes, sir."

"Very well, then, my boy," he said, briefly resting a hand on one of my own. "You know you are like sons to me, George, you and your brothers. I told you that once before, but it is even truer now... Now that..." He choked to a halt, and I knew he was thinking of his little Henry. "No harm must come to you!" he continued presently, sounding gruff. "That is what I am trying to say, and so do take care."

I promised him we would, feeling all the while that I was lying. I wanted to tell him that we most certainly *did* need his help. I wanted to tell him that Miles had been too bold in spying on my uncle's dealings, and that he had been found out. I wanted to tell Mr. Woodhouse that I was worried for what Uncle Spencer might do next. Were it not for Miles having forbid all of this, I might even have gone so far as to admit to Mr. Woodhouse that I was afraid. Of what, exactly, I could not have articulated at the time. There was just a nagging dread that had taken residence in my mind since Uncle Spencer discovered Miles nosing about in his study.

But this I had not even admitted to my dearest brother. Miles had always been my example, and I was sure *he* was never afraid. In hindsight, though, I may have been mistaken.

New Worries

Mr. Woodhouse's most recent warning was entirely unnecessary, for Miles and I soon had no choice but to set aside any thoughts of discovering what Uncle Spencer was up to. Miles had become seriously unwell again.

Mama initially supposed that it must be a relapse of the influenza, for some of the symptoms were similar to what we had all experienced so recently – headaches, digestive disorders, and so forth. At first, the illness was not so severe as to worry her overly or confine my brother to his bed. Still, the apothecary was called as a precaution. Although he could not tell us precisely what ailed Miles, he was persuaded it was not the influenza. He left some draughts, which seemed to take the proper effect, and soon my brother was all but recovered. He returned to his studies and even to some of his lighter tasks, while I made up for the rest.

"I am glad to be done with that unpleasant business and back to my old self," he remarked to me as we were working alongside each other in the orchard. "I do so despise the helpless feeling a crippling illness gives one. I wonder what Uncle Spencer has been up to this time while I have not been looking."

"Leave it be, Miles. Please do!" I pleaded. "He is already angry with you. With us." I added the last under my breath.

"Nonsense, George. Let him be angry if he chooses. He would not dare try to beat me, for I am as big as he is! Furthermore, I do not mind that he knows I am watching him. That has more chance of keeping him honest than if he believes he can do as he pleases with nobody to answer to. No, I intend to get to the truth of the matter, now that I am well again."

Mile's boasts came to nothing, though. Just when we were feeling quite relieved about his recovered health, he was struck with another bout of the strange sickness. The headaches and digestive complaints were worse this time, but some changes to the skin and derangements of the mind were added to them. Miles was abnormally drowsy and, more worrisome still, occasionally quite confused. One day while I sat at his bedside, he began raving wildly and did not know me.

Again the apothecary was called; again he failed to account for the cause of Miles's symptoms or name the illness with any certainty. Still hopeful of a cure, however, his new prescriptions were given and faithfully applied.

We went on like this for weeks. Miles would seem to nearly recover only to suffer another relapse. Unlike with the influenza, though, no one else was effected... that is until I began to experience some of the very same uncomfortable symptoms myself.

The first headache, I quickly discounted. One could experience the headache for any number of reasons. It was a very warm August, and I had spent too much time working in the hot sun the day before. That was surely the cause. Or perhaps it was because I had not slept well, so worried was I for my brother. When the digestive disturbances began as well, though, it became more difficult to deny there was a problem. But still I kept my worries to myself.

Miles was by then entirely wrapped up in his own misery, his symptoms having become more persistent and severe. Mama was so distracted by his worsening illness that she noticed nothing amiss with me. Uncle Spencer seemed the only one whose suspicions had been aroused. He stopped me when we encountered each other in the passageway one day. Looking at me with a furrowed brow and head cocked to one side, he asked, "Are you feeling quite well, George?"

"Perfectly well," I disclaimed, anxious to get away from his sharp-eyed scrutiny. I had in fact been making my way to the privy with some determination, and I judged that I could not afford much delay.

"Really? I am glad to hear it," he said, "but I am bound to say that you do not look it. You look a bit green about the gills." He reached forward but stopped before touching me. "You *will* tell me if anything is amiss, will you not? You know you can depend on me to help you in any way I can."

"Of course," I said, adding a thank-you over my shoulder as I hurried on my way.

All the while, however – all the weeks I was denying and concealing my symptoms – a rising tide of panic was building within me until I simply had to do something about it. I could put it off no longer. It seemed my world was falling apart before my eyes. My father was dead already; my brother was failing fast; my mother and Donwell itself seemed mere shadows of their former selves; and now my own health was in jeopardy as well. It could not be allowed to go on.

But what was the proper course of action? I could not see a solution. I was loath to worry Miles or Mama with my woes, and despite my lip service to the contrary, I would never turn to my uncle for help. Consulting the apothecary in secret would be impossible. Besides he had so far failed utterly to do any good for Miles. All I could think of was to turn to Mr. Woodhouse again, and this time Miles was in no position to stop me.

~~*~~

"Good God!" exclaimed Mr. Woodhouse, shooting to his feet, when I had told him everything. "You should have come to me sooner, George. You promised you would!"

"I wanted to, sir, believe me, but Miles forbade it. He said he could manage the situation on his own, and I should not bother you with our troubles. But now..."

Mr. Woodhouse began pacing the width of his drawing room, worrying his chin with his hand and muttering – sometimes to me and sometimes mostly to himself. I watched him back and forth, waiting for what he would tell me to do and hoping his greater wisdom and experience would produce the answers I and my family needed so desperately.

"But now, what is to be done?" he began unpromisingly. "I never did trust that man, but with no evidence of wrongdoing, I was prepared to wait and see – to wait until he would be required to make his report to the courts. Then, I told myself, we should have known the truth." He stopped and turned to me. "All testamentary guardians must by law produce a yearly report, you understand. That is where I expected to discover if your uncle was conducting Donwell's business as he should. In the meantime, I had filed a brief with the Court of Chancery to challenge his guardianship, but I am still awaiting the results." He returned to pacing as he continued, "But clearly, waiting is no longer an option. Never should have been. Dreadful mistake! And now Margaret and the children are paying the price. No, something must be done at once. So much is at stake. Dear God, give me wisdom, and let it not be too late."

He carried on his ruminations, mostly in silence, for several more minutes before returning to me.

"George, he said, fixing me with a serious gaze. "You must return home and say nothing of this conversation to anybody, especially not your uncle. I have some urgent inquiries to make before I can act, but it will be no more than two or three days at most. As soon as I have my legal questions answered, I will come to Donwell myself and intervene. No doubt there will be quite an unpleasant scene. I suppose that cannot be avoided. But one way or the other, George, you and your mother and brothers will soon be removed from your uncle's control. That

I promise you. If that cannot be achieved at Donwell, then you must all come to stay at Hartfield!"

At least a part of me had secretly hoped that Mr. Woodhouse would be able to explain away all my concerns, proving that none of us was in any danger and that all would be well. But that was not the case. In fact, Mr. Woodhouse's alarm had only added to my own. He obviously believed the situation demanded immediate action and prayed it would not come 'too late.' I could only pray the same.

And so I returned to Donwell with some hope that help was near, but nervous as a cat. The house was silent when I crept inside, and so I started violently when an accusing voice came from behind me.

"Where have *you* been?"

It was Uncle Spencer, of course, the last person I wished to encounter. I turned slowly to answer him with the excuse for my absence I had prepared in advance. "Uncle Spencer, you startled me," I said, trying not to look or sound as deceitful as I was required to be.

"No doubt, but you have not answered my question. Where have you been, George? Certainly not about your work, I collect."

"Do forgive me, Uncle, but I was obliged to go into Highbury on an errand for Mama – to the apothecary for more of Miles's physic." In evidence, I pulled from my pocket a small, brown, medicine bottle I had taken with me as a precaution. It was filled only with the water I had added myself, but Uncle was not to know that. "I will get to my assigned tasks – and Miles's too – presently, just as soon as I deliver this to Mama. May I go?"

He looked dubious but begrudgingly said, "I suppose, but see that you attend to your work without further delay."

I nodded and hurried to find Mama sitting in the sick room. "How is he?" I asked her.

"Much the same," she said in a defeated tone.

I looked at Miles, feeling again that stab of grief and long-ing I always did when I saw him of late. He was sleeping or otherwise unconscious, but I took his hand, squeezed it, and leant down to whisper in his ear. "Hold on, Miles, for just a little while longer. Help is on the way!" Then I dashed out to the farmyard to turn my pent-up energy to good account.

-9-

Heroic Intervention

Why on earth I should have supposed Mr. Woodhouse's promised assistance could go so far as to rescue Miles from his perilous decline, I can only explain in this way. Mr. Woodhouse had promised we would be released from Uncle Spencer's control, and in my mind, that was the key. Illogical though it may seem upon closer inspection, I intuitively blamed my uncle for all the misfortunes we had suffered since he first came to Donwell – everything from my father's death to our financial woes and finally Miles's illness, as well as my own.

A bud of hope was now forming, and it seemed anything was possible. So of course Miles would recover, if only he could hold on a few days more.

As Mr. Woodhouse had instructed, I told nobody else that help was on the way. Indeed, how could I? I did not know myself exactly what to expect or when. Would Mr. Woodhouse ride in on a white steed, saber drawn, to somehow rescue us himself, or would he send a company of soldiers? And how would Uncle Spencer react? Would he confess his sins at once and go meekly away? No, I could not imagine him doing any such thing. An 'unpleasant scene' Mr. Woodhouse had told me to expect. Too vague to conjure up a clear picture in my own mind, though that did not keep me from trying nearly every waking minute of the succeeding days.

I could think of little else, and yet I was constrained to carry on as if nothing extraordinary was in the wind. It would not do for Uncle Spencer to become suspicious.

Finally, on the third day after my meeting with Mr. Woodhouse, John came running to me where I was working in the stable yard, grooming one of the few remaining horses.

"George, George!" he said, half out of breath. "There is a carriage coming up the drive... and two mounted soldiers in red coats besides! ...What can it mean, do you think?"

I dropped my brushes and set my feet into motion at once, dusting off my clothes as I ran, John at my side. "My guess is that it is Mr. Woodhouse, but we shall have to wait and see," I said, my own excitement now matching his. "Come along!"

Mr. Woodhouse was alighting from the carriage as I approached. "Good morning, George," he said soberly. "Where can I find your uncle?"

"He is in his study, I believe."

"Very well. I would speak to him at once. You may wish to accompany me." I nodded in answer. "But John, is your mother sitting with Miles?"

"Yes, sir, Mr. Woodhouse, sir. At least I think so."

"Excellent. Go and wait with them with the door closed and locked. Do you understand? It is very important. Close the door and lock it. Quickly now, run ahead of us, and I will come to you both presently."

John whined a little but did as he was told.

"The stables are that way," Mr. Woodhouse told one of the soldiers. "Return to us as soon as you can."

The other joined Mr. Woodhouse and myself as we entered the house.

No doubt alerted to unusual activity by the noise, Uncle Spencer was just coming out into the hall. He stood there with hands on hips as we approached. "What is the meaning of this?" he demanded. "Mr. Woodhouse, how dare you come into my home uninvited, and bringing a soldier too!"

"Ah, see there," Mr. Woodhouse answered more affably. "I had hoped we might get through this without unpleasantness, but you have made it impossible, Mr. Knightley, for I must disagree with you at the very outset. This is not *your* house, though you seem to be treating it as if it were."

"Stop speaking in riddles, sir, and state your business plainly!"

"Glad to. Now do listen carefully so that I need not repeat myself. Firstly, I do not know what kind of hold you had over my friend, your brother, that he was persuaded to be so imprudent as to name you guardian of the boys and of all Donwell, but that will shortly be rectified. My suit with the Court of Chancery will see to that. Furthermore, as I am sure you have known all along but I have only recently discovered, Miles is old enough to appoint the guardian of his choice, the stipulation of his father's will notwithstanding. And I daresay, from what I have gathered of the situation here, *you* will not be his choice."

Spencer gave a derisive laugh. "The boy is not in his right mind. He can make no decision of the kind for himself."

"If anything should happen to Miles, which you had better pray it does not, George is also over fourteen and will have the power to act in his own interest. What I am telling you, Mr. Spencer Knightley, is that you are not wanted here. You are to collect your things and clear out at once. If you are not wise enough to do as I say, I have brought reinforcements with me, as you see. I am told they can be very persuasive."

"Ha! You cannot throw me out just like that! At least for the moment, I have the law on *my* side."

"I humbly beg to differ with you, sir." Mr. Woodhouse said, slowly pulling a piece of official-looking paper from his inside pocket.

Uncle Spencer made a lunge for it, but Mr. Woodhouse quickly drew it back out of reach. "Uh, uh, Mr. Knightley. As a solicitor, I am quite confident you are able to recognize a Court Order when you see one, even from where you stand. It says that you are obliged to give up your claim as guardian of Donwell, to vacate the premises immediately, and to never set foot on Donwell land again unless expressly invited by its owner to do so."

The other soldier came unobtrusively in to join us.

"Ah, good," said Mr. Woodhouse. Then he turned back to Uncle Spencer. "These fine fellows will now accompany you to your private apartment, where you may collect your personal effects. They will also watch to ensure you take nothing that does not belong to you. You will find your horse saddled and waiting outside when you return."

Spencer looked undecided for a moment. Then jerking his waistcoat down into sharper order, he said haughtily, "Very well! I refuse to stay where I am so obviously not wanted. So *this* is the thanks I get for all my efforts on this family's behalf. A wretched, ungrateful lot, all of them!"

He turned on his heel and made for the study.

"Not so fast," said Mr. Woodhouse.

Spencer hesitated.

"What do you think you are doing?"

"Collecting my things, as you advised me."

"Your *personal* belongings, Mr. Knightley. That does not include any estate ledgers or financial records. Now," Mr. Woodhouse said, consulting his pocket watch, "you have precisely twenty minutes to pack your bags and leave this house for good. No more false moves either. These gentlemen," indicating the soldiers, "are armed and highly trained in the handling of recalcitrant criminals."

Spencer exploded with an unintelligible sound of fury, then turned to mount the stairs with the soldiers escorting him, one on his left and one on his right.

Mr. Woodhouse and I stood looking up to where the others had disappeared, listening and awaiting their return. I tried once to speak, but Mr. Woodhouse held up his hand to stop me. "Hush. Not a word until he is gone," he said. And so we waited in silence for those fifteen or twenty minutes until the three men returned.

Uncle Spencer came down the stairs with his heavily loaded saddlebags and his great coat slung over his arm. He looked quite harried and seemed intent on being gone as quickly as possible. But as he was about to pass within a few feet of me on his way to the door, he stopped short to aim an accusing glare and a pointed finger at me. "I am ashamed of you, George, for whatever part you played in this farce. When you flounder here on your own, then you will repent of the mistake you have made this day. But don't come crying to me; it will be much too late!"

"Leave the boy alone!" commanded Mr. Woodhouse. "Have you not caused enough misery already?"

In one swift movement, Uncle Spencer dropped everything and threw himself at Mr. Woodhouse, taking him by the throat and raging, "You interfering bastard, I swear I'll wring your scrawny neck!"

Just as swiftly, though, the soldiers were on him, pulling Spencer back and leading him forcibly away.

"Are you hurt, sir?" I asked my friend, steadying him by the arm.

"Surprisingly enough, not in the least," he said with a little chuckle. "Now let us watch the villain off the property and out of sight."

We went out onto the porch in time to see Uncle Spencer finish loading his horse and mount up. He turned one last look over his shoulder, his countenance betraying little of what he must be feeling, and then he jerked the reins to turn his horse's head down the drive. With a savage kick and cry of "Ha!" he was off.

"The soldiers will conduct him at least as far as the London road," Mr. Woodhouse explained, "and my guess is that you have seen the last of your uncle. It is too soon, of course, to know all he may be guilty of, but I expect that in the days to come we will discover more than enough to warrant his arrest and imprisonment – perhaps worse – should he show his face in this neighborhood again. Now, let us go to your mother and brothers."

"You were tremendous, Mr. Woodhouse!" I exclaimed then, my amazement and gratitude bursting forth. "So brave and commanding! I daresay my uncle barely knew what had overtaken him. How can we ever repay you for what you have done?"

"Let me take your strong and steady arm for a start, young man," he said, which he did without waiting for my consent. Only then did I realized that Mr. Woodhouse was trembling quite alarmingly. "Now, get me to your mother and a sturdy chair as soon as possible."

-10-
Extent of Damage

When we reached Miles's room, where Mama and John also waited, Mr. Woodhouse sat down in the nearest chair with a great sigh and allowed me to be the one to pour forth the story of all that had just transpired. The only contribution he made was to disclaim any particular heroism in the case.

My audience of three – for Miles was fortunately awake and alert – was properly amazed, and they added their own exclamations and questions along the way.

"I still do not understand how you managed it," my dear Mr. Woodhouse," said Mama at the end. "But, oh my, how brave you were!"

"Brave?" he repeated. "Not a bit of it. I confess I was shaking in my shoes the whole time. I just could not allow your brother-in-law to see it. And I had preparation on my side. After George told me of the grim state of affairs three days ago, I went to London at once to discover what could be done. But when I learnt that the Court of Chancery might not address the case for weeks yet, or even months, I knew I could not wait. I knew *you* could not wait! Fortunately, I had other resources, and my elaborate bluff paid off."

We all stared at him in amazement.

"Bluff?" I repeated. "But the Court Order, I saw it with my own eyes, and so did Uncle Spencer!"

"Quite convincing, was it not?" Mr. Woodhouse asked with a gleeful grin. "But you noticed I did not give your uncle a very close view, or surely he would have recognized it as a clever fake."

He pulled the suspect document from his pocket and let all of us have a look.

"The soldiers were another admirable touch, I thought," he continued, obviously enjoying himself now. "I called in a few favors to arrange for them. I could never have faced down such a formidable opponent without their help." Then he became more serious. "The point is that right was done. I'm sure it will prove to be so, though I did have to hasten things along a little. I believe even Spencer Knightley recognized the hand of justice at work, or he would not have responded as he did. And the business of Miles being able to name his own guardian is perfectly true.

"Now Miles, while I was in London, I also arranged for a medical man to come tomorrow to examine you. Our local apothecary is all very well, but this fellow may have more expertise of the kind required in this case. His area of specialty is... Well, what I mean to say is that I think it is possible your illness is the result of being slowly poisoned."

"Poisoned!" gasped Mama.

Mr. Woodhouse nodded solemnly. "George, too. It is only a theory at this point, you understand, but it has been known to happen where an inheritance is at stake. Although perhaps the villain only meant to keep the boys unwell enough to prevent more meddling in his affairs. In any case," he said, addressing Miles and myself, "now that he is gone, and with the help of the best medical advice available, I hope you will both begin to improve.

"One more thing," he added. "With your permission, Miles, Mrs. Knightley, I would like my own man of business to go over the estate books to see if he can discover the true situation and what Mr. Spencer Knightley was about."

It seemed Mr. Woodhouse had thought of everything.

~~*~~

The household was thrown into a great deal of confusion over the next week. Servants and workers who had become accustomed to receiving their orders from Uncle Spencer in recent months and my father before that, began of necessity to look for direction elsewhere. Miles, of course, was in no condition and my mother largely ignorant of anything beyond immediate household concerns. So much of the weight of the estate business fell to me in those early days, ill prepared for the responsibility though I was. I was now sixteen but still had little experience, and so once again I depended on Mr. Woodhouse to guide me through. I learnt quickly under his tutelage, and it felt as if we were at least moving in the right direction. There would be a long, long road ahead to set things right, however.

Mr. Woodhouse's man of business, Mr. Fancourt, came to have a look at the Donwell books and ledgers, and he quickly discovered the gloomy condition we were left in and why.

"It is true that there was a bit of a shortfall in the final quarter of last year," he explained to me and Mr. Woodhouse in a meeting called that we might learn his findings, one Miles was still too unwell to attend. "You see here," said Mr. Fancourt, extending the ledger across to us and pointing to a total at the bottom of a column of figures. "These are the last entries made while the late Mr. Knightley lived. Notice that the hand distinctly changes for the successive entries."

Mr. Woodhouse nodded, saying, "Oh, yes, quite."

No doubt he understood much better than I what we were being shown.

"It seems the harvest had been weak, and there were some ill-judged purchases made at the same time," Mr. Fancourt continued. "The situation was not serious at that point, however, and with judicious management things might soon have been set perfectly right again. But instead of making the minor adjustments to the budget necessary, the new man appears to have begun, in early February, what amounts to a wholesale selling off assets and turning away people in the estate's employ. Where the money has gone, however, is a mystery. There is nothing I have discovered yet that accounts for it among the estate's holdings. It would have been a hefty sum, too. But except for the quantity of ready money we found locked in the desk here, it seems to have completely vanished."

I exchanged a despairing look with Mr. Woodhouse, but neither of us interrupted.

"The entries become thinner and thinner, you will observe, until they stop altogether three months ago. It is as if Mr. Spencer Knightley tried to keep up the appearance of good business accounting practices for a time but then finally abandoned all pretense of such. I cannot imagine how he hoped to get away with it, Mr. Woodhouse."

"Maybe he did not," said my friend. "It looks to me as if he made the decision at some point to rob the estate blind and pocket what he could. He was too intelligent to expect to not be found out eventually, so perhaps he always meant to cut and run when the noose began to tighten. It would seem I only sped him on his way a little ahead of schedule!"

"Yes, perhaps," agreed Mr. Fancourt. "That would fit the evidence."

"I shall inform the authorities at once, of course," said Mr. Woodhouse, "but I think it unlikely we will ever see the stolen money or the scoundrel who took it again. For now, at least, we must count it as lost and go on as best we can without it. I am sorry, George. I am sorry for Miles's sake. He will inherit a much-impoverished estate, I'm afraid."

I did what I could to assure Mr. Woodhouse that none of this was his fault. On the contrary, by his intervention, he had certainly prevented a bad situation becoming far worse.

The loss to the estate was so large that indeed it seemed overwhelming. But even that paled in comparison to the concern for my brother's health.

As Mr. Woodhouse had predicted, I began to recover from my illness almost immediately upon my uncle's having gone. Mr. Finch, the doctor from London, soon confirmed the diagnosis of poisoning insofar as he was able, guided by our symptoms and his examination.

"Probably arsenic, Mrs. Knightley," he told Mama after we had left Miles's room. "Easy to come by. No doubt you even have some in this very house for killing rodents. Most people do."

"I believe so," said Mama, shaking her head and then letting it fall into her hand. "In the still room, I think."

I put my arm about her shoulders, saying, "I have seen it in the granary and other outbuildings as well,"

"There you are, then," said the doctor. "It is a white power with very little taste. A bit mixed into the food now and again, and the deed is done. Illness or death will result. Unfortunately, we still have no reliable test to prove someone has ingested arsenic, so without an eyewitness to the act, it would be difficult to prove in a court of law."

"Yes, I see," said Mama, sounding dazed. Then she came alert again. "But my boys, Mr. Finch! What can be done for them?"

"I am confident that this fine lad," he said, placing a hand on my shoulder, "will recover without any trouble. It seems he ingested a comparatively small amount of the stuff. Young Mr. Knightley, though," Mr. Finch continued in a more melancholy tone. "Well, for him the prognosis is by no means so rosy, I am sorry to say. He may do tolerably well and live out a reasonably normal lifespan. But to be honest, Mrs. Knightley, I do not expect it. He clearly received much more poison over a longer period of time. He should certainly improve, now that the dosing has stopped and with the health regimen I have prescribed. But I must tell you that I believe some permanent damage has already been done to his organs – heart, lungs, kidneys. It is likely to always limit him and also likely to shorten his life considerably. I am extremely sorry, Mrs. Knightley," he added as Mama broke down into tears.

I wrapped both my arms about her now – to steady her but also to steady myself. The doctor's report could hardly have upset her much more than it did me. Dearest Miles!

"There is a chance, though, Mr. Finch?" I hurriedly asked. "You did say that he might live a full life."

"Yes, a small chance, if he can stay clear of other assaults on his constitution in future. Medicine is far from being an exact science. Nothing should make me happier than to be proved wrong, believe me. Then there are always patients who inexplicably surpass our expectations. You must prepare yourself for the more probable alternative, however. I hope you understand. Summon me again if there is anything more I may do."

Then he was gone, and Mama and I were left to console each other as well as we might. Miles would be one of those exceptional patients who surpassed expectations, I told her. To myself I added, *May it please God, he will be. He must!*

-11-
Restoration Begins

Miles showed every sign of being the exception to Mr. Finch's rule, for he did indeed improve quite substantially. He was still somewhat weak and slept over much at first, but his mind quickly cleared, as did his digestive troubles, and soon Mama gave up trying to keep him abed any longer.

Once he had been fully informed of the situation, Miles insisted on examining the books to see for himself how things stood. Then he must be taken all over the estate, on my arm for support. As soon as we were out of doors, he drew the fresh air deep into his lungs.

"I have been given an eleventh-hour reprieve, George," he told me, "for I was certain I was a goner. And now to be free of the sickbed and the symptoms that so oppressed me... Why, it is an amazing gift!"

Although it was good to see him so cheerful, I could not help asking, "Yes, Miles, but do not you hate Uncle Spencer for what he has done? I do! You nearly died and Donwell has been robbed blind!"

"I am no saint, so of course I feel it deeply – his betrayal more than anything else. I cannot dwell on it, though. I *refuse* to dwell on it! And you must not either, George. Hate is excessively toxic. It will kill your soul just as surely as arsenic will kill the body, and we have been poisoned enough already, you and I. Do not you think so?"

I agreed, but I could by no means be so philosophical about Uncle's crimes as my brother apparently was… at least not yet.

"Besides," Miles continued, "there is too much work to be done to waste any more time thinking about our odious relation! We must save Donwell, otherwise Uncle Spencer will indeed have won. No doubt he will expect us to give up, to allow the estate to fall into bankruptcy rather than having the backbone to fight for what belongs to us. I would not give him that satisfaction, would you?"

"No, of course not. I will help you, Miles, and so will Mr. Woodhouse!"

"Dear Mr. Woodhouse! I owe him my life; I am sure of it. And you too, George, for alerting him. If he had not driven Uncle Spencer off when he did… Well, I just thank God for his prompt action, or we would not be having this conversation today. Now, let us continue on. It is a fine day for a tour."

Miles was a young man on a mission. He was anxious to get to work and determined to return Donwell to order and solvency. Naturally he was not able to take on the load of a hale and hearty man at once, but that is where I came in. The two of us worked side by side as a team, with Mr. Woodhouse (whom Miles officially named the new guardian) our mentor and advisor.

There seemed nothing much we could do immediately to restore the estate to its former glory. Unless or until the pur-loined fortune was recovered, we would have very little money at our disposal. So there was no question of rehiring servants or replenishing stock to the previous levels at once. Hence, the economies Uncle Spencer had instituted in order to line his pockets had to remain in place for the time being as a survival strategy.

Everything depended on the harvest. A good harvest and we could hope to make some progress. A bad one and… Well, that did not bear thinking of.

John continued at his lessons with Mr. Bates, but Miles and I had no time for such things anymore. We had to grow up very quickly.

"I still hope you may go to Oxford when the time comes, George," Miles told me one day as we watched John set off for the parsonage, his books under his arm, "so that you may make your way in the world – take holy orders or whatever you choose. Perhaps Donwell will have come about by then and there will be funds available."

"What about you, though, Miles? You must go as well! It would not be fair or right unless you did."

"I have thought a great deal about it, George, and I can no longer imagine that I ever shall. My health may not allow it, for one thing. As well as I am most of the time, I still feel the effects of what my body endured. Besides, my place is at Donwell, and Greek and Latin will do me no good here. The education I need is of a more practical nature: to learn how to manage this estate well, so that it may one day thrive again, and so those who depend on it can continue to do so into the future."

I could understand Miles's reasoning, but it grieved me all the same to think of his future being so diminished. A gentleman's son – especially the firstborn and heir – deserved a gentleman's education. It was his natural right to set his mind on things of a higher plane, or so I had always been taught. Let the bailiffs and estate agents deal with more practical matters; that was *their* purview. And yet Miles was being forced to let go such lofty ideals. Later it would be my turn to do the same – one more thing stolen from us by Uncle Spencer.

No, I could not be so philosophical as my brother. I must still hate my uncle for what he had done.

~~*~~

The crops were good that year – excellent, as a matter of fact, especially considering the neglect they had suffered with fewer hands working the estate and the turmoil in the household. That was a tremendous blessing.

Our difficulty came from not being able to find a sufficient number of temporary workers to bring in the harvest when we needed them. Still, despite what of necessity went to waste, we cleared enough to keep the wolves from our door for another year and some beyond.

Miles and I agreed that the first thing to be restored by the profits should be Mama's lady's maid Caruthers. Supposing that Mama would selflessly object if given the chance, we gave her none. Miles simply sent for Caruthers, who had been unable to find a satisfactory new position in the intervening months, and the happy reunion between maid and mistress soon took place. The cook's budget was also increased. We still did not entertain or eat like kings, but there was enough to see that we – Miles especially – had what was necessary for life and health. A farmhand rehired, some chickens and two dairy cows purchased: by such small steps as these, we did what we could to improve conditions at Donwell, being careful to consult with Mr. Woodhouse at every turn. Then the following year's harvest was even better.

All this time, we waited to hear news of Uncle Spencer. Mr. Woodhouse had promptly set Bow Street on the case. And, unbeknownst to us, he had hired and paid for a private investigator as well. I am sure they all did their best, and yet our larcenous uncle was never captured. It goes without saying, therefore, that the missing money was never recovered either. The best information we did receive indicated that there was every reason to believe he had boarded a boat for America, at least there was record of a Spencer Knight, esq., on a passenger manifest at a probable time. No doubt, with his stolen fortune, he was able to set himself up as a gentleman and live in some style there. I can only hope his conscience plagued him severely to where he could not enjoy it, but I am inclined to believe he had succeeded in silencing that vital organ long beforehand.

-12-

Final Rest

Only a little more, now, and I shall have done with my Uncle Spencer. He is a bad taste in my mouth that I shall be glad to put far from me. I cannot leave the story of his nefarious exploits behind quite yet, however, for there is another most unfortunate sequel that must be laid to his charge. While he may not have actually intended to murder Miles, the end result was just the same as if he had, only a little delayed. This is how it happened.

Under Mr. Woodhouse's supervision, Miles and I continued to manage Donwell together, gradually building it back to soundness, until the day finally came when my brother could go on no more. As Mr. Finch had prophesied, some of the effects of the poisoning upon Miles's constitution were lasting and limiting to his future. He never recovered completely and always suffered routine ailments that came along more severely. If he took a cold, he was in bed for a fortnight, or he might fall seriously ill for no discernable reason at all.

My mother summoned Mr. Finch for his opinion three or four times more over the course of the next two years, but the diagnosis was always the same: *His system has been permanently weakened, especially his heart, and there is really nothing that can be done for him. I am sorry.*

Then when Miles was a few months shy of his twenty-first birthday, he was overtaken by a particularly bad spell. He suffered aches and pains of every description and was too weak to rise. Indeed, with any exertion at all, he complained he was not able to catch his breath. Mr. Finch came for the last time, dispensed laudanum for Miles's pain, and told us we must prepare ourselves for the worst.

The grim news threw us into a gloom of despair, and yet we had to carry on. Miles needed us, and I was determined we would not fail him. We took turns sitting with him – Mama, myself, and John, who was thirteen by this time – so that he should never be alone. I would have stayed by his side more continuously, but as Miles reminded me, Donwell needed my attention too. Even at such a time, he did not think only of himself but of his responsibilities as the eldest. If he could not see to things personally, he would release me to do so.

Returning to the sick room one day, I asked Mama how he did. "He is a little more comfortable, I think," she quietly answered, a tear trailing down her cheek. "He was able to take a little gruel, and then I gave him some laudanum. As you see, he is sleeping now, which is no doubt the best thing for him."

We went on like this through the remainder of January and all February, while Miles gradually but steadily worsened. It was agony to watch.

I tried not to show my distress when I was with him and he awake. It was difficult to pretend all was well, however, especially in front of one who had always been privy to my open and honest thoughts. Miles must have known exactly what I was thinking and feeling, but most of the time he conspired with me to keep up a brave front. I did it for his sake, and I am convinced he did it for mine. His body deteriorated day by day, but his mind was still acute enough to understand how grieved I was on his account... and my own, for I was losing the best friend I had in the world, and not so long after losing my father too.

Despite our conspiracy to dissemble, Miles and I did have one frank discussion near the end. Uncomfortable though it was at the time, I was glad for it later.

I had been reading to him from Gulliver's Travels again – his favorite stories – when he stopped me. "George," he said in a way that immediately fastened my attention.

I looked up from the book at once.

"I want you to know something," he said.

"Yes, Miles? What is it?"

"I want you to know I am not afraid. I was at first, I admit, but not anymore. In fact I shall be glad to go."

I knew what he meant but could not bear to admit it. "Go?" I said, pretending confusion. "You cannot go anywhere just yet, Miles, not until you are well again."

He said my name again, patiently, but in that big-brother tone I knew so well, one that told me that I could not fool him. He then continued, saying, "I assure you there is no need to pretend with me. I know I am dying; nothing can stop that now. And surely you know it too. That is what I am telling you; I know, and I do not mind. May death come swiftly! That is all I pray, morning, noon, and night."

He was right; I knew. To look at my beloved brother – honestly, with eyes undeceived by wishful thinking – was to know he could not possibly survive much longer. Once so strong and vital, the standard of a fine young man upon which I had always modeled myself, he was now reduced, at only twenty years of age, to spending every hour of every day in a bed, unable to do even the most basic tasks for himself. His skin had acquired a perpetual blue hue, and he was wasting away day by day. Even speaking was a painful effort for him, I could see. He was slipping from this life to the next, and I was helpless to do anything about it.

I felt hot tears start down my cheeks, and I angrily swiped them away. "No, Miles, stop saying that!" I expostulated, wanting to shake some fight back into him. "You will get better; you must! With Father gone, it is your duty to live and look after us all. You are supposed to inherit Donwell and to have a son of your own one day. That is your destiny, what

Father trained you up to do. You know that is the truth, and nothing else can be said on the subject!"

Miles made no reply; he just gazed at me with tired eyes, full of pain, sadness, and something else. It looked like resignation or perhaps even peace.

My impassioned speech had been ineffectual. It had obviously failed to convince him that there was still a chance worth battling for. It had not even convinced me. The fight suddenly left me, and I ended in a desolate plea. "You cannot die, Miles. What on earth will I do without you?"

"You will live and go on, George. *You* will be the one to care for Mama, and John, and Donwell in my place. You will know how, for you have learnt right beside me. Mr. Woodhouse will help you. Now, promise not to grieve for me when I am gone, but be happy that my suffering is over. It cannot come soon enough for me." He closed his eyes and was silent a minute. I thought he had fallen asleep… or worse, that he was already gone, until, with eyes still closed, he added another thought. "And when you have a son one day, George, perhaps you will do something for me."

When he paused again, I desperately clutched at his hand and said, "Yes, Miles, what is it? Ask me anything."

He opened his eyes and looked into mine. "A small request. Perhaps you will consider naming your son 'Miles' after me. That would please me very much."

"I will. I swear I will, Miles. I will do just as you say," I promised, my tears flowing freely now. Then he did slip away into sleep.

That was the last proper conversation I had with my dear brother. Mama insisted he be kept as comfortable as possible; she could do nothing else for him. So the laudanum was given in larger and more frequent doses, keeping him in a persistent stupor. He persevered in a state of simulated death until, a few days later, he achieved that longed-for state in fact.

Poor Miles. How he suffered. When I could no longer bear to see it, I had, God help me, joined him in his prayer that the end would come swiftly. Then it did come, and I was lost, plunged into a deep well of despair.

I tried to remember my promise to Miles as we went through the dreadful funeral rites again. I *was* relieved at his suffering being finally over. But I could in no way be happy. I was heartbroken to a degree even more profound than when my father had died three years before.

Miles was laid to rest beside that beloved parent, and the dust of the earth reclaimed another of its own.

I dragged through the days and weeks that followed, with little interest in anything or anybody. Only my duty to Donwell kept me from floundering entirely. My mother was much the same or worse, I observed. She hardly seemed interested in getting out of bed each morning, rising later and later.

The Woodhouses, who had been attentive to us throughout Miles's illness, continued as our dear friends and benefactors after it was over. Mrs. Woodhouse served as a sympathetic companion for Mama. Her daughters, now three and nearly ten, gave cheerful diversion. And Mr. Woodhouse, standing in the place of a father to me, continued to counsel and guide me. The vicar came from time to time as well.

It was not enough. Mama, weighed down under the heavy grief of losing first her husband and then her son, seemed to lose the will to live herself. A few months later, she took an ordinary chill, and having not the strength of heart to battle it, the chill quickly enlarged into a serious putrid fever. Within a fortnight she had joined the others in the Donwell parish cemetery.

-13-

Finding Salvation

One goes on; one has no choice. At the age of nineteen, I found myself head of my household and nearly alone. Only John remained, and we comforted each other as best we could.

I would have given anything if it were not so, but I had acceded to the position of heir to the estate as well. Although the responsibility was unlooked for, there was no question of what I must do about it. I intended to carry it through to the best of my abilities. I would by no means let down my father or Miles. Donwell, which had meant so much to them both, must be kept safe and made to prosper for the sake of everybody who depended on it and for future generations.

I threw myself into the work with a vengeance, learning all the practical skills normally relegated to a bailiff, a gentleman not being supposed to soil his hands with such labors. I had no choice, though. The situation at Donwell was gradually improving, but there were still insufficient funds to hire anybody to manage the estate.

I did not so much save Donwell as Donwell saved me, though, giving me home and purpose and occupation at a time when I desperately needed them.

And so I claimed my father's chair behind my father's desk in my father's study. That is the way I still thought of these articles – as belonging to my father, not to Spencer, Miles, or myself. Although it had now been four years since he had used that desk, I still saw my father sitting there every time I walked into the room. I did not feel I had a right to take his place any more than Spencer had, but that was something I had to get beyond, for there was much work to be done.

That desk is where I studied every book I could lay my hands on concerning farm and estate management. That is where I constantly poured over the ledgers to monitor the coming and going of every pound and penny. And that is where I sat when Mr. Woodhouse came to consult with me. As my understanding and abilities grew, he gradually turned over more and more of the responsibility for the estate to me, while retaining his titular position as guardian until I reached the age of twenty-one.

One day, some six months after Mama was buried, I was again sitting behind that desk when my brother John came into the room. He knew not to disturb me whilst I was concentrating on work, but no doubt he could see I was not on this occasion. Instead, I sat leaning back and staring at a metal box in my hands, turning it over and over and absentmindedly listening to the muffled tinkling from within.

"What is that?" John asked.

I looked up in surprise, for my thoughts had been so thoroughly engaged that I had not heard him enter. "This?" I said, holding it out to him. "See for yourself."

He took and opened the box, his eyes growing large. "This is a lot of money!" he said, pawing through the contents. "What is it for?"

"To you it may seem a lot, and it has grown to a tidy sum, it is true. That is what Miles had been setting aside in the hopes that there would be enough to send me to Oxford eventually. But now…" I ground to a halt.

"What is it, George? What about now?"

"I have been remembering something Miles once told me, after Uncle Spencer left. He said he should never go to Oxford himself."

"Because of the money? Or do you think he had a premonition that... that he knew he was going to die?"

"No, well, at least I do not suppose he knew, although he may have suspected. He did mention his health as one reason. But he said it was mostly because his place was at Donwell, and that Greek and Latin would do him no good. He wanted to learn practical things that would help him here, just as I have been doing since he left us."

John waited for me to go on, which I did after some little delay to reach the conclusion of the path my thoughts had been travelling down.

"He was right, John – for himself and also for me, now that I am in the same position. I cannot leave Donwell to run off to Oxford in order to learn more Greek and Latin than what Mr. Bates has already taught us. I will not need those things, because I will never take holy orders or take a degree of any kind. Donwell will be my life's work, God willing. This is where I am needed. But you, John..."

"Yes, what about me?" he prompted after waiting in vain for me to continue.

"*You* shall be the one to take an Oxford degree." I reached out my hand, and my brother returned the box to me. "This will be *your* school fund now." I returned the box to its usual place in the bottom drawer and locked it. "You would still like to become a solicitor?"

I knew what his answer would be, for he had, over the years, consistently mentioned his plan to study the law, no longer in compliment to Uncle Spencer, but as a genteel profession that would keep him in town, since he had no great love for the country.

"Or a barrister," he added.

"Very well, then. It looks like another good harvest this year, and if it comes in as expected, you shall begin at Eton in January, then Oxford afterward. What do you say to that, John?"

His brow wrinkled. "But, George, it was *your* school money…"

"Oh, never mind about that," I said waving off his objection. "Anything I want or need to learn, I can find in books, probably right here under our own roof! Have you ever really explored our library, John? It is floor to ceiling with treasure. So you must not feel sorry for me. I shall have Donwell, after all. The least I can do in Father's place is make sure my brother – now my only brother – is well set up in life, in his chosen profession. Do you think you should like to go to Eton in January?" I could see in his eyes his building excitement, excitement which he seemed to think diplomatic to hide. And so I continued. "That is, of course, unless you should prefer to remain here and work the farm. I am quite certain a place can be found where you can make yourself useful."

This jolted a quick response from him. "Oh, no! I mean yes. Thank you, George, but I would very much like to be sent to Eton as soon as may be!"

So that was settled.

Over the course of the intervening three months, John and I talked a lot about what he could expect at Eton, the best way to stay out of trouble, and how to succeed. Although I could not be there to pave the way for him as Miles had done for me, I wanted to give him every possible advantage and the benefit of my somewhat limited experience.

The weeks ticked away, and soon it was time to say good bye to my little brother. No last-minute emergency or financial shortfall came along to give me an excuse to keep John at home with me, as I had half hoped it would. So shortly after Christmas, I shook my eager younger brother's hand, put him in a carriage, and waved him off on his adventure.

When I turned back towards the house after watching him out of sight, the full weight of it struck me; with the last member of my family now gone, I was completely alone.

–14–

Hartfield's Charms

Perhaps I did fall into a bit of a foul mood when John went away. He was going forward to new things, and I was being left behind with all the sad reminders of what we had lost. And yet, as I had told him, I had Donwell, and nobody who is the possessor of such a treasure should be allowed to feel sorry for himself for long.

Dear Mrs. Woodhouse did not allow it. Good and clever woman that she was, she must have known how I was feeling, for she summoned me to Hartfield only two days after John had gone. I wondered what it could mean – that it was she and not her husband who wished to see me.

"Well, I shall come right to the point, George," she began just as soon as I had taken a seat in her parlor as she had bidden me. "It is that I cannot bear to think of you living all alone in that great house! It has been troubling me ever since I learnt of John's being to go away to Eton. Whilst he was still with you, I would not interfere, but now I must. Your mother, God rest her soul, would have done the same for any child of mine. Do not you agree?"

I hesitated, not yet sure what she was asking. "You surely cannot mean…" I began, haltingly. "Dear Mrs. Woodhouse, kind as you are, you surely cannot mean that I should remove from Donwell in favor of Hartfield. I am well old enough to live on my own, I believe."

Her beautiful face spread into a merry smile, and she laughed that musical laugh of hers that always reminded me of bells. "Oh, dear, I see I have not been as clear as I intended. No, George, removing to Hartfield is not quite what I meant to suggest. Although I cannot think of anything that would give us all more pleasure, I only meant to insist on your coming to dinner just as frequently as possible. Every day, if you will. Mr. Woodhouse and I would enjoy it above all things, I assure you, and the girls will find it a rare treat to see you more often. You know how fond they both are of you. Now do say you will come, George. You must!"

"You are too kind," I equivocated. I was quite over-whelmed and could not think how I should answer her.

"Nonsense, George. I have talked it over with Mr. Wood-house, and he agrees. You will be doing us an immense favor if you will come very often. Old married couples like ourselves run out of things to tell over the dinner table. I have heard all his stories long ago just as he has heard mine. A third will give us someone new to laugh at our old jokes and fresh stories to hear. Isabella is a dear, but her powers of conversation are still rather limited, you know."

"As are mine. I am afraid you overrate my abilities to entertain, Mrs. Woodhouse."

"Perhaps, but honestly, George, you may sit and say not a word through the whole course of the meal, and we will still be happy to have you with us. Mr. Woodhouse and I consider you nearly a member of the family anyway, as you know. Do say you will come starting tomorrow. I would urge for today, except that I'm sure preparations are going forward in the kitchens of Donwell as we speak, and I would not put Mrs. Hodges nose out of joint for the world. You do not suppose she will mind terribly if I were to lighten her load in future though, do you?"

"She has little enough to do as it is, with only one mouth to feed in addition to a handful of servants, but I suppose my being gone on occasion would relieve her of having two separate meals to prepare."

"There! Then it is settled. You come tomorrow, and we shall see how we go on. But I warn you, I shall not be satisfied until I have you at my table at least three times every week!"

I accepted Mrs. Woodhouse's kind invitation for the following day and consented to come once a week thereafter, feeling anything in excess of that would be an imposition, despite what Mrs. Woodhouse had said. Then, as she had warned me, she lured me back more and more often – with her excellent dinners, yes, but even more so with the promise of companionship, which I so desperately needed. I could toil all day at Donwell, alone except for the staff and an occasional tenant visit, because I knew that friends and good conversation awaited me at the dinner. Besides, I was soon convinced that my host and hostess did sincerely desire my more frequent presence. And so once per week soon grew to twice and thrice, until I was travelling back and forth the mile to Hartfield nearly every day: a habit still with me.

Naturally, there would have been no point in the trouble of a carriage or even a horse for such a short distance. And in order to arrive with my person and clothing in presentable condition, I resisted the temptation to run all the way, as I had done in my youth. I almost always walked, wearing an ever more established pathway across the fields and shades between our two estates.

It is a pleasantly bucolic route, and there are always seasonal beauties or some novelty to be appreciated along the way. I am very fond of walking, whatever way I take – for the beneficial exercise but also for the simple pleasure of it. I have always found that if I have a problem to reason through or the need to clear my head, there is nothing better for it than a brisk walk in fresh country air. My life being very far from free of problems to be solved, I learnt to value the time coming and going as highly as the time actually spent at Hartfield.

The same principle applied to excursions elsewhere: to church or to the village or to visit a friend. If possible, I had much rather walk. But Mr. Woodhouse did not view my preferred mode of transportation in the same way – one of the few things on which we could not quite see eye to eye. Our frequent canvassing of the topic never concluded with our coming to agreement.

"I suppose you came on foot again, Mr. Knightley," he said one of these times. Mr. Woodhouse had taken to frequently calling me that once I had reached the age of eighteen. "For I did not hear you arrive."

"Of course I walked," I answered my friend jovially. "As I have told you before, sir, I consider there is nothing better for exercise and for ordering one's thoughts."

"Traipsing back and forth was all very well when you were younger. But you are a gentleman now, Mr. Knightley – the master of Donwell Abbey – and you should begin looking and acting more the thing if you expect to be accorded proper respect. Have I taught you nothing?"

"On the contrary, Mr. Woodhouse! You have taught me a great deal, for which I will be eternally grateful. But I have not yet learnt to put on airs and put the servants to extra trouble as well, just so that I may travel the long way round by the road instead of the short way here by the path. I prefer to come and go exactly as I please, too, rather than waiting on carriages and horses to be made ready. That is my idea of luxury. Besides, it is a beautiful evening."

"Beautiful? How can you say so? Why, it is cold enough to freeze the breath of man and beast. I hope you might not have taken a chill."

"Impossible. I never felt better. You should have seen me when I came in, sir. I was wrapped in so many warm layers that I think even you should have approved."

"I know you find me tedious, George, but I would not wish you to put yourself at risk, only to give us the pleasure of your company. If the weather is inclement, you can always send a servant to tell us you have decided to stay at home to preserve your health. Nobody would take it amiss."

"Nobody except perhaps the servant. To be sure, he might take it very much amiss to be sent out of doors on such an errand when I thought it unsafe to do the same. Now, Mr. Woodhouse, you are good to be concerned, but if I am grown, as you now credit me with being – at least most of the time – you must allow me to decide these things for myself."

At this point, our conversation was put an end to by the drawing room door's opening to admit Mrs. Woodhouse and her two daughters.

"I could not keep them away, George," she explained. "Isabella espied you from the window, and then Emma must see you as well." Isabella had come to sit beside me at once, pushing her arm under and around my own. Little Emma struggled free of her mother to follow. "That is all I hear. Every day it is, '*When is George coming?*' or, '*Is George coming tonight?*' Honestly, I am quite jealous of your popularity. I sometimes think my daughters love you more than they do their own mama!" Mrs. Woodhouse's laughter proved she was enjoying her own joke.

"Really, my dear," said Mr. Woodhouse, "you must learn to call our young friend 'Mr. Knightley,' and teach the girls to do the same. He is a gentleman now, and I have just been telling him to begin behaving as such."

"Very well, my love. I *will* try, but he has been George to me all the many years I have known him. Old habits are difficult to extinguish. Now, Emma," she continued, addressing her youngest, "tell George – I mean Mr. Knightley – good bye. It is time you were back in the nursery."

Emma, who had clambered onto my lap, cried a little as her mother led her away. At the age of four and a half, she would not be joining us at the dinner table. Isabella, now just turned twelve, would, however, and so she stayed where she was looking rather smugly superior.

"Lovely, are not they?" Mr. Woodhouse said with a sigh, his eyes following his departing wife and small child and then coming back to rest on his other daughter. "I suppose, Mr. Knightley, that I should be desperate for a son and heir – one to replace the poor little boy I lost years ago – and I shall be a very happy man whenever that should occur, believe me. But, in the meantime, I cannot help thinking myself most fortunate to be surrounded by the comfortable fellowship of such excellent examples of the female sex. What other man do you know who has such a splendid pair of daughters and a wife who... Well, there are not words sufficient to do her justice. Yes, I am a very lucky man, George."

"I could not agree with you more, Mr. Woodhouse."

~~*~~

As my brother grew older – as we *both* grew older – the gap in our ages seemed to contract until we were dealing with each other on a more even level. I keenly looked forward to the quarter breaks when he would be home from school – first from Eton and later from Oxford. He seemed to thrive in that academic world and always arrived with fresh stories of his studies, but even more of his friends, their mutual pranks and adventures.

I felt an occasional pang at what I was missing, not being able to attend these schools of renown myself. But for the most part, I simply enjoyed living the experience through John. After the grief and hardships of the former years, it did my heart good to see him happy and enthused. Not that that was always the case, for he did have his occasional contrary moods.

When he came home grumbling instead, I was not so likely to insist on keeping his company all to myself. I soon discovered the wisdom of accepting an invitation for us both to dine at Hartfield, which nearly always cured him of an ill temper, for much was made of him there. *He* was the novelty then, and a favorite with the Woodhouse females. I had to accept being consigned to second place in everybody's favor, at least temporarily.

A new female had joined the household by then too. When Isabella was twelve, it was thought time for a governess to take her in hand. And so one was sought for her and soon found in the amiable person of Miss Taylor, a young lady of about my own age or a little older.

"The daughter of an impoverished gentleman of my slight acquaintance," Mr. Woodhouse had explained to me. "She is quite a taking little thing, as you will soon see for yourself, Mr. Knightley. But with no fortune and no money to give her a season... Well, when I learnt that poor Miss Taylor was to go out as a governess, to earn her bread until she found herself a husband, I thought that she might as well come to Hartfield to take charge of Isabella's education. Then after that, you know, Emma will be in want of a governess herself. In short, I told Mr. Taylor that his daughter would most likely have a comfortable home here with us for as long as she required one."

"If she must go out as a governess," I said, "she could not have hoped to be more fortunate than to secure such a desirable position as this! The one disadvantage I see of Hartfield, though, is that there are so few eligible young men about. I cannot think much of Miss Taylor's prospects of finding a husband here."

"True, and some may say her best years are already behind her. I cannot agree, however. Look at Mrs. Woodhouse! She only grows more beautiful and charming as the years go by. If I had met her now instead of when I did, I should still have fallen head over ears in love with her."

I could not help but wonder if some part of this speech was directed at me. After all, there was at least *one* eligible gentleman in the neighborhood: myself. Perhaps Mr. Woodhouse was hinting that I should not view Miss Taylor as past her prime.

When I met Miss Taylor, I agreed with Mr. Woodhouse's assessment; she was a pretty thing with intelligent conversation and charming manners. I soon judged, however, that she and I were destined to be good friends, nothing more, and so we have been from that day.

She was a delightful addition to my slim acquaintance, though, and I could see that her talents were well suited to guiding the docile Isabella. I could not help wondering, however, if she would be able to manage Emma as well, when the time came for her to do so. For Emma, even at five and six years of age, seemed to me to have already developed a decided fondness for having her own way, as well as the clever capability for getting it most of the time.

-15-
Answering Questions

In time, Donwell rebounded. I made mistakes along the way, of course, but nothing of monumental proportions, thanks to Mr. Woodhouse's guidance. And, thanks to God, the setbacks from natural causes were few as well. I began to grow into my father's shoes, until it no longer seemed strange to be the one sleeping in the master's bedchamber, to be the one giving orders to servants or settling for myself the tasks of the day.

Much of the house remained closed up and the stables sparsely stocked, as my habits of thriftiness stayed with me long after they were strictly necessary. The entire ordeal – recovering from Uncle Spencer's plundering – left me with an abhorrence for wastefulness, and that is just what it would have been to pay extra servants to heat and clean a score of rooms that were never used. It was only I myself who lived there most of the time, and any entertaining I did was on a very modest scale. Likewise for carriage horses. No sense in throwing money away on fine stock that would be left standing idle. It seemed a better use to give what little extra I had on hand towards maintaining the parish poor.

In time, I grew accustomed to the relative solitude to where I did not mind it so much. Solitude and silence are that way. Depending on one's temperament and state of mind, they can be either bleak or peaceful, distressing or comforting. At first, they meant to me that something was wrong; they meant loneliness, that persons I cared for, who should have been there making cheerful noise, were lost and gone forever. Later, though, they only meant that all was calm; things went on in the normal, quiet way of my new life. Not what I would have chosen but what was.

Of all the people I had lost, Miles was the one I missed most. It was *his* voice I most longed to hear again echoing through the rooms of Donwell, in good times and in bad. When some problem occurred, he was the one with whom I most wanted to discuss it. If a success, I wished to share it with him. I had not yet outgrown the feeling that we had been closer than ordinary brothers, and with him gone, a part of me was missing.

I would sometimes lay awake in the dead of night, almost imagining myself back in my old bedchamber with my brother in his bed across the room. Occasionally I went so far as to speak to him aloud, reminiscent of the hundreds of conversations we had carried out that way in the dark. Though now the intercourse was sadly one-sided.

The pain of his absence lessened but never ceased to exist. Yet with the passage of time, I learnt in some measure to practice Miles's philosophy of not dwelling on the wrongs of the past, to, in his honor, let go my bitterness over Uncle Spencer, lest my own soul should be poisoned by it. But it was years after the villain had fled before I could do so, partly because I lived every day with the consequences of what he had done, and partly because there were so many unanswered questions left in his wake.

And so now, before I move on to the next momentous event in my life, I feel the need to tie up all those loose ends, to answer those questions that are answerable and lay the others to rest once and for all. Questions such as these:

Why had Uncle Spencer come to Donwell that fateful autumn, and why did my father allow him to stay on to insinuate himself into our family, going so far as to name him guardian? What was my uncle's plan when he took control, and where did he go once he had been driven off by Mr. Woodhouse?

Nobody could answer my questions at first... or at least they would not. Once I was old enough to act in my own interest, however, I had more success. This is what I was able to piece together from various sources.

It all began when Uncle Spencer had been turned out of his practice of the law upon being discovered in some dishonest dealings. Left with no means for his own support, he hatched the scheme for coming to Donwell. As to why my father allowed him to stay and named him guardian... Well, Mr. Woodhouse, years later, finally told me that it was undoubtedly blackmail. Although he did not know the details himself, my father had apparently admitted the existence of some significant indiscretion in his past, something that would have greatly pained my mother to have found out. Spencer knew of it and no doubt threatened to expose his brother's secret unless he got his way.

So Spencer stayed, began drawing a salary from my father, and in consequence of his new situation, quickly familiarized himself with every aspect of the estate. Once his brother was dead and buried, nothing stood in Spencer's way any longer. He stepped into his twin's shoes as completely as possible, setting himself up as lord of the manor and taking possession of everything that he felt had been unfairly denied him by accident of birth.

That may have been the limit of his original ambition – to live out his life in the style he had always envied. But apparently, one of the things he had long coveted was his brother's wife. Expecting to succeed to his brother's place in that respect was going a great deal too far. And so my mother told him. This I learnt from her maid, Caruthers, who had her confidence to the end.

That is when Spencer's strategy changed, as evidenced by the ledgers and our own observations. After my mother's rejection of him, and while we were all ill with the influenza, Uncle stopped managing Donwell and began plundering it instead. If he could not have it all, then he would take his revenge by ruining the estate and the family his brother had cherished. He decided to carry away as much of Donwell's wealth as he could and build a grand new life for himself elsewhere, apparently in America.

Of this much I can be fairly certain. As for the poisonings, I am strongly inclined to believe that my uncle meant only to incapacitate Miles (and later myself) to prevent our interference. For if he had really meant to kill either of us, it would have been just as easy to slip us a lot of poison as a little. There would have been no advantage to him doing so, however, since he already had complete control. Plus, there were three of us in the way of him ever inheriting Donwell himself, and three murders would be too much to hope to get away with.

However, it was another question that tortured me most of all. Although it had not occurred to me in the beginning, in light of Spencer's subsequent actions my mind could not help later asking it again and again. The question is this. Did Spencer have anything to do with my father's death?

I am far from confident of the answer. People die in accidental falls from horses every day; it is too commonplace an occurrence to excite much wonder or speculation. Yet the fact that Spencer was the only witness to the event does give cause for doubt. Short of a confession, which is highly unlikely, there really is no way of knowing for certain. Worse still, there never will be. The only two men who knew what happened that day are gone – one to the grave and the other fled halfway round the world.

That being the case, this is how I have settled the matter in my own mind. I choose to believe my father's death was a tragic accident – one that Uncle Spencer saw the opportunity to exploit only afterwards. It is entirely for my own peace that I do so. I must depend on the fact that my uncle, now being far beyond my reach and the reach of the English courts, will face his due judgement at his Maker's hands – for whatever part he may have played there and for his other crimes.

Meanwhile, I must go on. It is difficult enough to live with the knowledge that I share blood with a treacherous thief and scoundrel. If I believed him capable of murdering his own twin brother and nephews as well, how much the worse it would be for me.

Perhaps others would judge this unsatisfactory, only a convenient but ambiguous explanation. If so, then it is one I can abide, one I can and have chosen to live with. And there's an end to it.

I was far from being the only one living with personal tragedy after all. When I think of those lost by my acquaintance in Highbury alone, just since my father's death... Well, the number seems unreasonably high. There was the Woodhouses' little boy in the influenza epidemic of 1792, of course, and others I knew less well at the same time and of the same cause. Then Mr. Weston's first wife died the following year. Then Miles and my mother. The Bateses' daughter Jane, by then Mrs. Fairfax, passed away in... I believe it was in 1796.

All of them left grieving parents, siblings, spouses, and friends behind them. Some left small children. And there would be more – one more in particular.

Part Two

~~~

The Young Man

-16-
A Scheme for Happiness

When I was twenty-three years of age, Mrs. Woodhouse attacked me one day with another project she had invented for my improved happiness. I had been dining at Hartfield again, as I had never given up the habit of doing at least twice a week since it began.

She had a special gleam in her eye that day, I thought, which I attributed to the fact that, after a gap of several years, she was expecting another child. I may have been wrong about the cause of that gleam, however, for after shooing Isabella and Emma from the room, she turned those bright eyes upon me.

"George," she began coyly, "how old are you now?"

Mr. Woodhouse answered for me. "He is three and twenty, which you know full well, my dear. And do call him Mr. Knightley, if you please."

"I know I should, my love, and I do when others are present. But when it is just ourselves, behaving like family, I do not see the need. In any case, Mr. Knightley, it occurs to me that you are at a very good age to begin looking about yourself for a wife!"

I could not have been more surprised, but upon momentary reflection, her comment did not seem so out of character. I'm afraid she had made a bit of a pet of me, and likely her suggestion was nothing more than a natural outgrowth of her longstanding concern for my being alone so much at Donwell.

A wife was the obvious and permanent solution. I could see that it would seem so to her, in any case.

I was not of the same opinion, however. So I needed to dissuade her from the idea, but gently, for it was kindly meant. That did not admit a doubt. Before I could think how to respond, however, Mr. Woodhouse intervened again.

"My dear, you should not make such plans. I know you cannot help taking an interest in our dear friend, here, but Mr. Knightley is still a very young man, and therefore there is no rush whatsoever in his getting married."

"Quite so, Mr. Woodhouse," I said.

"It is a thing no person should ever do in haste," he continued, "and perhaps some had best not do it at all."

"What?" cried Mrs. Woodhouse. "I thought you were a great proponent of marriage, husband."

Looking at her with pure adoration, he reached across to take her hand. "I am, my love," he said. "But only when the right partner can be found, otherwise it had better not be attempted. Consider how long I waited for you to come along. If I had married early, only think what I would have missed out on."

Their gaze and their hands held so long, that I began to feel myself an intruder upon the tender scene. Then they suddenly seemed to remember my presence.

"And consider, my dear," Mr. Woodhouse said after releasing his wife's hand, "if Mr. Knightley were to marry, how much less we would see of him. Besides, I do not know who would be suitable hereabouts."

"Precisely!" she enthused. "That is why I mean that Mr. Knightley should go to London for a season!" Then she turned back to me. "Donwell goes on very well, does it not, George? Surely you might be gone for a few weeks without worry for anything going awry. You have William Larkins now to over-see things, and Mr. Woodhouse can look in from time to time as well."

She regarded her husband, who nodded. "Of course, if Mr. Knightley wishes it."

"Thank you, sir," I said, somewhat recovered from the initial shock. "But I am sure that it will not be necessary. I have no desire for a London season. Besides, there are plenty of other reasons why your idea would be unfeasible, Mrs. Woodhouse. Unnecessary too."

"Name your reasons, George," she said by way of a challenge, "and I will tell you why they do not apply."

That was a bold claim, but I was not afraid. I had ready answers for her. "The most obvious reason is that I have no thought of matrimony at this time. I am young, and I have plenty to manage already without a wife."

"For shame, George! A wife is not something to *manage*; she is a helpmeet. If she be of good character, she will lighten your load, not make it heavier. I trust you will choose wisely, and I cannot wait to meet the future Mrs. Knightley. I am sure she will be a delight, and we shall always be good friends. Now, have you any other objections?"

"Certainly! The biggest obstacle of a practical nature – since you have dismissed as meaningless my personal inclinations – is no doubt the very great expense! Hiring a house and servants, paying for carriages everywhere, new suits of clothes, and pin money to be thrown away every time one turns round: the sum would be staggering. Donwell is mostly recovered, it is true, but I have John's expenses to pay, which leaves little money for extravagances of any kind."

"Aha! I knew that would be your next objection, and I have the perfect remedy for it. Do not you have an aunt on your mother's side living in town, whom you visit whenever you go there?"

"Yes, Aunt Phoebe, but…" Then I was immediately interrupted.

"I think you said she was a little eccentric but harmless, and that she fairly dotes on you each time you pay her a call."

"Yes, but…"

"My guess is that she would be more than delighted to have you stop with her for a month or two…"

"A month or two! No, I could never agree to that."

"…which would eliminate at least half of the cost of the venture. No doubt she could also get you invitations into the best society and make a few appropriate introductions. I believe you said she was quite rich and very well connected, so your coming could not possibly represent the least inconvenience."

I was amazed at her presumption, but I tried to keep my countenance and to reply with a smile. "Mrs. Woodhouse, *you* may think it no great inconvenience to be always putting up with my disagreeable company, but you must not imagine everybody else as hospitable. Although my Aunt Phoebe may be glad enough to see me for an hour or two a few times every year, one must not assume the same about every day for a month or more."

"Assume? I assume nothing. That is why you must write to her at once." She paused but went on when I did not immediately agree. "Or if you prefer, I will write to her myself to plead your case. If she has any compassion whatsoever, she will take pity on your sad state."

This was going too far. I kept my temper as well as I could but very firmly told her, "Mrs. Woodhouse, I will by no means allow myself to be considered an object of pity, nor am I incapable of managing my own correspondence. If a letter is to be written, I will do it myself!"

"Forgive me, George," she said contritely. "You are quite right; the letter had much better come from you. Do write to her without delay, though. There is much to be done."

Afterward, I puzzled over exactly how it had happened. I reviewed the conversation again and again to see where it had all gone wrong. In the end, I was left with the distinct impression that I had been somehow outmaneuvered, that Mrs. Woodhouse had cleverly tricked me into agreeing to her outrageous plan.

Nevertheless, I *had* agreed, but only to writing a letter. I could do no less to satisfy Mrs. Woodhouse. I fervently hoped, however, that would be the end of it, that the business would go no farther. I did not especially care for town, and the idea of throwing myself into the marriage market frenzy nearly made my blood run cold. Not that I was opposed to being wed – eventually, at the proper time. I was simply in no rush, as Mr. Woodhouse advised. And I had always imagined, when I stopped to think of the prospect at all, that I would meet the future Mrs. Knightley in a more natural way – at church or through common acquaintances. Something along that order. Surely nothing good could come of forcing the issue.

In any case, I did write to Aunt Phoebe, proposing myself her houseguest. You may be sure that I phrased the idea in such a way as to make it sound – to my own mind, at least – an unattractive prospect, couching it in terms of "a great imposition" and "perhaps sometime more convenient, in another year or two." In short, I offered her every opportunity of gracefully declining. To my horror, however, she wrote back with alacrity and enthusiasm. I was definitely to come, she said, and as soon as possible. Not only that, but I must stay in perpetuity or until such time as she could get me well married. She even ventured to declare that she already had one or two highly eligible young ladies in mind.

Needless to say, Mrs. Woodhouse was delighted.

I was not, but I soon resigned myself. I would go to London for at least a small portion of the season. However, I would do so on my own terms. It would not be so different from my other forays into town, I told myself, only a little longer. I would visit my aunt and my other acquaintances and tend to some necessary estate business at the same time. Yes, I supposed I would have to put up with a little nonsense – engage a tailor for a new suit of clothes and so forth, attend a ball or two, dance with a few young ladies – but when I had had my fill, I would come home again. After all, I was a free agent, and nobody could keep me in London when I had made up my mind to leave.

I doubted very much that anything would come of the whole silly affair. So short a time as I envisioned actually staying would surely be inadequate to form any lasting attachment. And I was not rich enough or highly born enough to excite much interest amongst the local misses, whose mamas were doubtless dreaming of rich lords for their daughters. That in fact would be my protection. No fortune hunters need apply. I could always try again another year, when I was a bit older, more financially established, and more in the mood to fall in love. There was no rush.

What concerned me most, though, was not the discomfort of staying in town or even the prospect of being forced to consort with society types. I may have been born and bred in the country, but I was not completely green. I had spent time in town company, if only in small doses, and I knew how to behave.

No, what made me uneasy was the idea of being away from Donwell for any length of time. It had always been my home, of course, and that alone would have given me a love for it. But it had been more than that to me. For the past eight years, It had been my salvation, and in my darkest hours, my only reason for rising out of bed in the morning. For better than one third of my existence, I had lived and slaved for Donwell alone. I had poured the energy of my mind, my sweat, and my life's blood into the place. I had loved, cherished, and nurtured it back to health. And it had soothed and nurtured me in return.

Donwell was the true mistress of my heart. I felt bound to this expanse of earth and sky in so many ways, and to leave it in search of another love seemed like a faithless act, almost a betrayal. And for what? I could not imagine finding any lady as worthy of my devotion, who could mean as much to me, who could ever supplant Donwell Abbey in my affections.

But then I thought of that tender moment between the Woodhouses, along with other glimpses I'd had of their mutual love and devotion. I had thought my own parents happy e-nough, but the Woodhouses had something more. If marriage could be like that... If there might be such another woman out there for me... Well, then I would be a fool to completely close my eyes to the possibility.

-17-
London Bound

S o it was that I found myself on the road to London shortly after Easter in the year of 1799, being transported thence in Mr. Woodhouse's best carriage. I would have been perfectly content to travel by the post, but Mrs. Woodhouse looked as if she would lapse into an apoplectic fit when I suggested the idea.

"Post?" she cried in horror. "My dear Mr. Knightley, surely you know that will never do!"

"I must agree with Mrs. Woodhouse on this," her husband added. "Whatever my reservations about this scheme in general, if you are determined to go through with it, I will not see it carried out in a shoddy, haphazard fashion. A thing worth doing is always worth doing right, and a gentleman must be seen travelling as a gentleman should, especially when he enters a new neighborhood. You must be known to have arrived in a private carriage of some quality or you should be barred from all good society."

I laughed. "Why would anybody know or care how I arrived in town, pray tell?"

"If you think gossip spreads rapidly in Highbury, George," said Mrs. Woodhouse, "that is nothing to what happens in town. Were your aunt's butler to see no gentleman's carriage at the curb when he opens the door, he will look down his nose at you and then tell the story in the servant's hall. If *he* does not, then the footman surely will – how your trunks were delivered on a hired cart. All it takes is for a maid or a cook to spread the word to their counterparts in other households and the story is soon known everywhere. The lady's maids tell their mistresses, and your reputation is sunk. You will receive no invitations whatever."

"My social standing will be decided by servants, and I must spend money and exert myself to gain their approval? Is that what you are telling me?"

"Not quite," she answered. "Servants cannot *make* your reputation but they certainly can *break* it on first impression. Servants can be every bit as snobbish as their masters, you know."

I first decried the idea vociferously. Then, I proposed that if I must go by private coach, I should hire horses for my own poor excuse for a carriage – the only equipage besides a gig that remained at Donwell. I had never seen the need to procure a better, once I could have afforded it.

This notion she immediately rejected as well. "That broken-down old thing? I think not!"

I continued to argue against such a nonsensical way of carrying on, but in the end, I found it was pointless to fight these dear friends when they were united against me.

Truth be told, if I was to go to all the trouble of a season, I could understand the merit of putting my best foot forward. So I accepted the use of their carriage as gracefully as I could and rode in undeniable comfort the sixteen miles to town, arriving at my aunt's door in Berkley Square in respectable style at three o'clock in the afternoon.

In light of my earlier conversation with the Woodhouses, I felt absurdly self-conscious when the butler, who was new since my previous visit, opened the door to me.

"Ah, Mr. Knightley, I presume," he solemnly intoned.

I gave a curt nod in answer.

"Very good, sir. You are expected. Please do come in."

Although it could have been my imagination, he did seem to be sizing me up with a healthy degree of skepticism. But with a quality carriage parked at the curb, I trusted he would conclude I was a gentleman after all.

Whelan – the butler's name, as I later learnt – motioned two footmen outside for my luggage and then escorted me to the drawing room, where he left me to await my aunt.

My Aunt Phoebe, Lady Anvert, was my mother's older sister and the perpetual widow of a minor viscount, who had left her with no children but a powerful fortune to spend, so long as she remained single. Since it would all go to somebody else if she remarried, she had never found it worth her while to do so. Consequently, any liaisons she might have formed in subsequent years were carried on in an unofficial way, though not always completely in the shadows. It was generally known, for example, that she had for nearly all of the past decade conducted a less-than-perfectly-discreet affair with a certain Admiral Nugent, late of His Majesty's Navy. But since they both had money, pedigree, and were considered very amusing additions to any guest list, society had decided to turn a blind eye, pretending when the affectionate pair were seen together all over town that they were only very good friends.

It had always been less awkward for me to pretend the same, and I was prepared to do likewise again during this stay.

I stood when Aunt Phoebe entered a few minutes later.

"Oh, George, how good of you to come!" she cried. Her broad smile was natural and genuine, but little else seemed to be. Although her gown was no doubt very stylish, to my eye it looked too young for her years. Her face bore the same paint I had seen there before, but her hair looked different. Probably a wig, I decided. As she came towards me, a dense cloud of a familiar lavender perfume served as her advance guard.

Aunt Phoebe claimed both of my hands with hers, and using this advantage, turned me to one side and then the other, saying, "Yes, you shall take very well, I daresay. You are much matured since I saw you last, and a tall and handsome young man with even tolerable conversation is always considered an asset."

I disengaged myself so far as to greet her properly, make a bow over her hand, and thank her for her generous hospitality.

"None of that now, "she said motioning that we should sit down. "I can hardly wait to show you off about town. With my connections to smooth the way, you will be welcome everywhere; I have made sure of that…"

I briefly wondered what she meant by that last, but then she was off again.

"…As I wrote to you, I already have a few charming young ladies in mind, any one of which might make you an excellent match. You need only pick your favorite, like low-hanging fruit from a branch. Nothing could be easier. So you see, if I do not have you engaged by the end of the season, it shall not be my fault."

"You are too good, Aunt Phoebe, but I beg you will not put yourself to any trouble on my account. I assure you that it is a matter of perfect indifference to me if I find a bride this season or not."

"Trouble? Why, I am delighted! Having you escort me everywhere about town this season will be more fun than I have had in years! As to your indifference, I plan to do that away in very short order. You have been too much isolated in the country. When you catch sight of a society beauty or two, I daresay your eyes will be opened and your head turned. As soon as Mr. Plimpton has finished your clothes, we will begin. When do you go to him again?"

I had come into town a fortnight before to be measured and place my order with the tailor. "Tomorrow morning," I said.

"Excellent!"

With a glance towards the door to be sure it was closed, I asked in a low voice, "What happened to Kirby? I was surprised to have a new butler let me in."

"Oh, Kirby," she said with a great sigh. "I hated to lose him. He had been with me for some time, as you know, and he looked so distinguished in his livery. But, alas, it came out that he was carrying on with one of the housemaids. As you know, that sort of thing cannot be condoned, so I had to let them both go. One requires absolute discretion and decorum in one's servants. What good luck it was that I found Whelan, though, for he is just the same size and looks every bit as well in the livery. Do not you agree?"

"Oh, yes, I suppose so. I'm afraid I do not generally pay attention to such details."

"Well, you must, if you are to learn anything from me! There is much to running a household correctly, you know, the management of the servants being just one important point. Your wife, if you choose wisely, will take it all in hand. If she has been properly brought up, she will know just what to do. In the meantime, though, you must do as well as you can, so that your prospective bride will not be frightened off by a situation in disarray. I can only imagine the state of affairs at Donwell, so long without a mistress. How do you go on, poor boy?"

I knew at once that Aunt Phoebe would not approve of my practical but unorthodox style of running my household, but I could see no reason to distress her by admitting to it. "It has been difficult," I said. "Still, we manage tolerably well."

She looked dubious but said only, "Make yourself a student while you are here, Nephew, and notice how things are done. I flatter myself that you could do much worse for an example. Your own mother, God rest her soul, is not here to teach you the niceties. In any case, she had become quite provincial in her ways after residing outside of all good society for so long."

"My mother loved country life," I said rather defensively. "She preferred it."

"Perhaps she did in time, George. Perhaps she did. But you never knew her as a girl, as I did. What a gay, frolicking little thing she was when she made her debut! Pretty too. I still remember, you see – flirting with one gentleman and then another, dancing until she had to be fairly dragged from the floor!

Your father was lucky to get her, for I daresay she might have married much better – even better than I did – had she a mind to. But one cannot reason with a girl in love, and I think she was happy with her choice, for the most part."

I agreed that she was. It never occurred to me that it might have been otherwise, but it would have seemed disloyal to admit even the possibility now.

"Ah, me," my aunt said with a sigh. "I cannot think of your mother without a pang, but it is upon *you* we need focus our attention now. We need to see you looking smart and making a good impression. I trust Plimpton to turn you out in style. But dear me, you have no valet to dress you! Well, never mind, I will send Robert to you. He is first footman and does a little valeting from time to time."

"Really, Aunt Phoebe, I am perfectly capable of dressing myself. I have been doing so of necessity for years."

"I would not let that get about, George, none of it. I am sure it is very admirable how you have managed to bring your father's estate back from the brink of bankruptcy, but it is high time you were thinking and behaving very differently, lest you be fatally tainted by the scandals of the past and the loss of fortune. It was a very nasty scandal, you know."

"It was none of *my* doing, but I take your point, Aunt. I am not proud of the past either."

"I am glad we are in agreement. No talk of that reprehensible uncle of yours. No talk of self-reliance and economies that are no longer necessary. You are a gentleman of some means and need to behave as one, else no self-respecting young lady will look at you twice. They may be willing to dance and flirt with you, but they will never consent to marry you. As it is, your prospects are somewhat limited. I do not mean to be unkind, my dear nephew, but one must face facts. You have no name of particular prestige, neither have you a great fortune: two things that will weigh against you. Also, you have no house in town. Although you have a sizable estate at a location not too distant from it, it is hardly fitted out in a grand style, I surmise. That can change of course, and you should be prepared to do so to satisfy the young lady of your choice."

I responded not a word at first, so overwhelmed was I by what my aunt had been telling me. Some of it was not so different from the advice I had received from Mr. and Mrs. Woodhouse, and yet this seemed to go further than I had allowed myself to think through. I was to never speak of the Knightleys' past disgrace; I was to pretend to be richer and more sophisticated than I was; and I must be willing to change my life and my home in order to please the lady I hoped to marry.

I said what I was thinking. "That being the case, Aunt, perhaps I had much better forget the whole thing and go home. I am not currently prepared to turn my life upside down to find a bride."

"Oh, dear me! Clearly you have never been in love or you would not say such a stupid thing! But you mustn't repine too much upon what I say. In my anxiety that you should get off to a good start, no doubt I have been playing my hand a little strong again. Andrew has often cautioned me against doing exactly that."

"How is the admiral?" I asked in the hopes of an advantageous change of subject.

"How kind you are, George! He is very well and looks forward to seeing you again soon. I thought today you might be too tired from your journey, but he will join us for dinner tomorrow. Then the next day, we shall all three of us go to Lady Chamberlain's soirée. I could get you into Almacks, if you really desire it, but I thought we would start with something a little smaller, just to get your toes wet, so to speak. Then the theatre on Wednesday, or would you prefer the opera? Oh, dear, I am doing it again, are not I? I can tell by the look on your face. Enough!" she exclaimed, rising to her feet.

I rose as well.

"That is enough for now," she reiterated. "More than enough. I will have Robert show you to your room and assist with whatever you need. Have a quiet little rest and a change before dinner, my dear boy. There will be plenty of time for everything else tomorrow."

Everything else? My head was already spinning. But I calmed myself when I achieved the solitude of my own apartments.

Since I had always considered my aunt a bit eccentric, I told myself that I needn't worry; probably only half of what she said was true. I had absolutely no intention of losing my head for love, after all. No, I would behave sensibly, and if I met a lady I liked, she must be sensible as well or I should have nothing more to do with her. There would be no lies or exaggerations to impress. No strutting like a preening peacock. There certainly would be no overthrow of the way of life I held dear, just to procure the affection of the kind of lady who would require me to do so.

The knowledge that I had firmly settled this in my mind carried me right through dinner and the rest of the evening. It allowed me to listen with tolerable equanimity to my aunt speaking about this upcoming event or that person of supposed importance. I did not feel the need to take exception to things she said or proclaim my own more reasonable ideas. I simply held fast to my unspoken maxims.

The same was true of the next day. I saw the tailor without being overcome by a strong desire to admire my reflection in the glass. When I returned, I humored my aunt's fancy to see what I had purchased, which she pronounced acceptable. Admiral Andrew Nugent joined us that afternoon and stayed through the evening. As usual, I found him good company – a man with whom one could have an intelligent conversation on a variety of topics.

So it wasn't until the following evening at Lady Chamberlain's soirée that my sensible resolves were seriously challenged. There, they were put to the test… and they failed miserably.

– 18 –

Songbird

I am embarrassed to remember how quickly my good sense failed me when I first beheld Miss Julia Stibbley. Or perhaps it would be more correct to say that I failed it, for no doubt my good sense was still there somewhere, giving me faithful direction; I merely stopped listening. I was blinded by Julia's glorious person and my ears were filled with her song.

When we had arrived – Aunt Phoebe, Admiral Nugent, and myself – we went on up to a saloon on the first floor, where our hostess was holding court. Lady Chamberlain, who was an elegant looking female somewhere north of sixty, sat in a very high-backed, gilded chair at the head of the room, chatting with those gathered about her. But she looked up when we entered, spying us through her quizzing glass and motioning us forward.

"Admiral Nugent," she said, holding out her hand to him. "Charming to see you again. And Lady Anvert, this must be your nephew that you have been telling us so much about." She raked me up and down through her quizzing glass. "Yes, he is every bit as handsome as you said."

"Lady Chamberlain," Aunt Phoebe said on cue, "may I present my nephew, Mr. George Knightley?"

I bowed.

"You are very welcome, Mr. Knightley," said our hostess, further scrutinizing me. "I hope you will find everything to your liking and that you will enjoy the evening."

"I am sure I shall, Lady Chamberlain. Thank you for including me in the invitation."

Although I had said what politeness required, I was very far from sure I would enjoy myself that evening – even less so now than before we had arrived. The way Lady Chamberlain had inspected me and her allusion to my aunt having spoken of me before made me quite uncomfortable. I was aware, of course, of the "marriage market" reputation the social season had acquired, and finding a wife had indeed been the stated purpose for my coming in the first place. But still, I could not like the thought of being eyed by everybody I met as goods on offer. And what had my aunt been telling people about me?

I had little time to ponder these things for presently music carried from another part of the house to my ear – a pianoforte being played, which was momentarily joined by one of the sweetest female singing voices I had ever heard. Suddenly I could think of nothing else.

"Aaah," said Lady Chamberlain, knowingly, "I see you have noticed our principle songbird, Mr. Knightley."

"Who is she, your ladyship?" I inquired in a hushed tone, not wanting to drown out the singing. "That is, if you do not mind my asking."

"Not at all, Mr. Knightley. That is Miss Stibbley you hear singing. Miss Julia Stibbley. For now, you should go and listen, but your aunt can introduce you when the young lady has finished. Or I would be glad to perform the office myself, of course. She is a most charming young lady."

"Thank you, Lady Chamberlain," I said hastily bowing again. "Please excuse me."

I did not wait to be urged further, or even to see if my aunt and the admiral were following. The dulcet melody drew me out of the saloon and down a crowded passageway in quest of its source, which I soon found in a large drawing room filled with people, most of whom sat in rapt attention.

And then I saw her.

If her voice had shaken me like thunder, then the sight of Julia Stibbley was the accompanying flash of blinding light. She was simply the most beautiful creature I had ever beheld.

I drew as close as I could without disturbing anybody and took up a station against the wall, where I could see the fair performer reasonably well. Miss Stibbley's features seemed perfectly formed and proportioned, not greatly unlike many others of her sex. It was her coloring that made her so exceptional. Her hair, which was nearly black and arranged on top of her head in an elaborate fashion, formed an almost startling juxtaposition to her fair complexion and bright blue eyes. The dark color of her hair carried to the lashes and brows framing those remarkable eyes too. Then my attention was drawn to her lovely mouth, moving alluringly as she sang.

From my position against the wall, I could see and appreciate all this, as well as the plunging neckline of her pale pink gown, rising and falling in rhythm with her singing. Ordinarily it would have been ill-mannered to watch her so intently as I was doing, but fortunately I had the excuse of her performance. No doubt many eyes were regarding her in the same way.

I was mesmerized. That is the only term I can think to describe it. I stared at her, oblivious to everything but the sight of her and the sound of her voice. When she finished, I stood there stupidly, not moving until the noise of applause broke through to my brain, prompting me to action. I then applauded all the more loudly in compensation for my late beginning.

Miss Stibbley rose and looked about herself, nodding in one direction and then another to acknowledge the ovation. That is when our eyes met. Probably drawn by the sound of my overly enthusiastic applause, she looked directly at me, smiled a little, and then dropped her eyes. Then at the urging of her nearest companions, she addressed the instrument again and continued to entertain the company with two more songs.

Although I was already hoping to meet her, I would not have curtailed her performance for anything in the world. It was enough for the moment to watch, listen, and worship at a little distance. After three songs, however, her many admirers could not prevail upon her to continue, and soon another young lady took her place at the instrument.

My eyes followed Miss Stibbley, however, and when she moved to quit the room, so did I. Only then did I remember my aunt. I looked about myself for the first time and found her standing at the back of the room with her faithful companion. I went to her and apologized for my rudeness at once.

She only laughed. "Did I not tell you that your indifference would soon be overcome, George? Even *I* had no idea it would happen quite so immediately, though, thanks to Miss Stibbley!"

"You have excellent taste, Mr. Knightley," said the admiral. "Why, if I were only a few years younger…"

"Andrew!" came my aunt's prompt reproof. "That will be quite enough from you! I have half a mind to…"

But I could not bear to let her go off on a long tangent. "Aunt Phoebe," I interrupted, "forgive me, but what can you tell me about Miss Stibbley?"

"Well, now, young man. You do not waste any time, do you? So I will give you what intelligence I can. I am not intimately acquainted with her or her people, you understand, but I know this much. She is beautiful and talented, as you have just observed for yourself. Of good family too. The Stibbleys are established in Herefordshire, where they go back several generations, I believe. Not much money, though, if what I have heard is true, which I daresay it is. I believe her fortune will be small."

"I do not care about that, Aunt."

"Yes, so you may say now, but let me tell you, a fortune on your wife's side might come in quite handy later, especially as you have no overabundance yourself at the moment. When you have four or five daughters who need dowries, for example, there is never enough. Still, it would be an eligible match, if the money situation can be overlooked on both sides.

I suppose you would like to meet her now. Is that what you are looking so eager about, young man?"

"Yes, if you please."

"I might mention that there are some other very pretty girls in this room, but I doubt it would do any good. If you have already seen what you want, there is little point in delay. Come along, then. My guess is that Miss Stibbley has returned to Lady Chamberlain's saloon." Then she addressed her swain. "I suppose you may as well remain and listen to the music, Andrew, unless you think you will miss me too much while I am gone."

"I will miss you, my dear; that much is certain. But I will enjoy the anticipation of your return."

"Very well. I suppose that answer will do. Come along, George."

My aunt led back down the passageway, weaving between all the other guests coming and going. I saw Miss Stibbley as soon as we had achieved the saloon, but I was distressed to see she was not alone and waiting for me, as I had unconsciously pictured her. She was surrounded by men. Of course she was! Anybody as lovely as she was sure to collect admirers about her wherever she went.

"Oh, dear," said my aunt. "It looks as if we shall have to wait our turn. Or perhaps we had better try again when the crowd has thinned a little."

But then Lady Chamberlain took matters into her own hands. Although I had no idea why she should favor me with such a marked assistance, I was very grateful. From where she was still seated, she soundly rapped her cane on the floor and raised her voice. "Gentlemen, gentlemen, it is time for you to leave off admiring Miss Stibbley and move along. Give the lady some air." Addressing Miss Stibbley, she continued, "Come here, my dear child. There is somebody I would like you to meet." Then she motioned us forward. "You know Lady Anvert, I am sure. This is her nephew from Surrey, Mr. George Knightley. Mr. Knightley, meet Miss Julia Stibbley."

She turned those brilliant blue eyes on me then, and I found I could barely function. I did manage a bow, I believe, and a perfunctory "pleased to meet you, Miss Stibbley."

She gave a small girlish laugh, which seemed to only enhance her beauty. "I am very pleased to meet you too, Mr. Knightley. I believe I saw you in the other room a few minutes ago."

I exerted myself to regain my composure, venturing to say, "Yes, I enjoyed your singing very much. I hardly know when I have heard anything that gave me more pleasure, in fact." We moved away from the others a few steps as of one accord. "You are very talented, indeed."

"You are too kind, sir."

"Not at all."

She smiled and asked, "So you are from Surrey?"

"Yes, I have an estate there. Donwell Abbey it is called. You will not have heard of it, though, as I was told you and your family reside in Herefordshire."

"So we do, although we now spend the greater share of our time here in London. That is to say, Mama and I do. My father prefers the country, and my brothers are there as well."

"I see. And which do you prefer, Miss Stibbley? Town or country?"

"That would be difficult to say, Mr. Knightley. I have fond memories of a childhood in the country, but just now, town suits me better – the shops, the concerts, the music masters, the superior society. You understand."

"Of course. One cannot command so wide and varied a society in the country, nor so broad a stage to exhibit your talents."

Just then, a woman of middle years beckoned from the doorway, saying, "Julia, come with me."

"Yes, Mama," she answered before briefly returning her attention to me. "I must go. Perhaps I will see you again, though, Mr. Knightley?"

"I depend on it, Miss Stibbley," I answered. Then she glided away.

We stayed another hour and a half, during which time my aunt and Admiral Nugent introduced me to many other people, including a number of eligible young ladies. I did my best to pay each of them the attention they deserved. I did not succeed, though, or so I imagine, since afterward I could hardly remember any name or face other than Miss Stibbley's. I'm afraid I was vastly distracted by trying to catch glimpses of her through the crowd and by hoping to find another chance of speaking to her.

Glimpse I did, but I had no opportunity to speak to her again that night. She seemed always surrounded by a host of male admirers. I could see at once that I would have my work cut out for me if I were to rise to the top, to prevail over all those who would throw themselves into the competition for Miss Stibbley's favor.

-19-

Besting the Competition

I had sent Mr. Woodhouse's carriage home to him immediately after my arrival in town, and so the day after Lady
Chamberlain's soirée, it was my aunt's phaeton and horses
that I took to call on Miss Stibbley. I had had to endure some
good-natured teasing when I asked to borrow them, of course.

"And where are you in such a hurry to get to, my nephew,
as if I did not know? This would not have anything to do with
a certain young lady with a voice as sweet as her face, would
it?"

"Yes, Aunt. I was hoping to call on Miss Stibbley, perhaps to take her for a drive."

"Well, I suppose you know how to drive a pair of fine
horses like my bays."

"I flatter myself that I do, Madam. I will take the greatest
care of them, I assure you."

"Very well then, but have you any idea where to find the
young lady you seek? Or perhaps you plan to set out and depend on love to guide your way." She laughed.

"No, I hoped you might be so good as to inform me of the
lady's direction."

"Then it is fortunate for you that I had my wits about me
last night, for I thought to ask Lady Chamberlain where the
Stibbleys were lodging. It seems they have taken a house in
Hanover Square: number five. That is where you will find her,

George, and I wish you all the luck in the world. You cannot mean to make a morning call as early as this, though."

"Why, yes, of course," I said in some confusion, for it was nearly eleven.

"My dear boy, you are no longer in the country, where I suppose you must rise when the cock crows. It is very different here. Half of London is still abed at this hour!"

And so, at my aunt's insistence, I was forced to cool my heels another hour before setting out. To my dismay, however, I was not the first gentleman caller to arrive in Hanover Square. When I was admitted at the door of number five, I found Miss Stibbley, with her mother alongside, already entertaining two others, who were soon introduced to me as Lord Blankenship – a distinguished looking gentleman in his middle years – and the non-descript Mr. Crawley, who was about my own age.

It was no surprise that Miss Stibbley had multiple admirers, but I had hoped to swoop in early to steal her away before the competition arrived. Instead, I was consigned to tolerate the others and provide my share of polite conversation. To be fair, Lord Blankenship and Mr. Crawley seemed to be perfectly amiable sorts, and so the situation was not as unpleasant as it could have been.

I would have gladly put up with far worse to spend time in Miss Stibbley's presence. She looked just as lovely as when I had first seen her the night before and in my imagination ever since. *She* did not seem to mind the numbers. With considerable poise, she smiled, received compliments, and skillfully managed the conversation. She was apparently as accomplished in the social graces, I observed to myself, as she was in the realm of music. My admiration for her only grew.

Nothing of great importance was talked of, of course, only the most recent balls and parties and what was coming next. *Had we spoken to anybody interesting at Lady Chamberlain's the other night? Did we notice what so-and-so was wearing? Would we be attending the rout at the Hendrickses' on Tuesday?* That sort of thing. In such a gathering, I suppose I could have expected nothing more, but I longed for a conversation of more consequence with Miss Stibbley, that I might get to know her better without delay.

Since I had arrived last, I began to hope that the other two gentlemen would soon be gone, leaving Miss Stibbley to me at the end. But after only twenty minutes, Mrs. Stibbley rose abruptly, compelling the men to their feet as well.

"Thank you for calling, gentlemen," she said in strident tones. "I am afraid we have other pressing engagements, however."

We had obviously been dismissed, all of us.

Remaining seated, Miss Stibbley promptly held her hand out to Lord Blankenship, who was nearest to her. "So good of you to call, my lord," she said.

He bowed over her hand and mumbled some pretty parting words – to daughter first and then mother – before moving towards the exit. Mr. Crawley followed suit, and then it was my turn.

"Good day, Miss Stibbley," I said as I took her hand and bowed over it. Then impulsively, I went on. "Might I perhaps have the privilege of taking you out driving one day this week?"

She glanced at her mama before answering, receiving a solemn nod. "Very well, Mr. Knightley. Would the day after tomorrow be convenient?"

"It would."

"Then shall we say one o'clock?"

"Excellent. Thank you, Miss Stibbley. Mrs. Stibbley." One more bow, and I belatedly followed the others out though the door, where we three exchanged parting nods but no words. There was no point in pretending we could be anything more to each other than rivals for the same lady's affections.

All in all, I was satisfied as I remounted the phaeton, counting the visit a success. I had seen Miss Stibbley again, confirming my attraction to her. She had seemed pleased to see me too, although without showing any detectable preference between her three suitors. Best of all, I had obtained a definite appointment to take her driving, where I should at last have her all to myself. To celebrate, I slapped the reigns and headed for the Park to take a trial run over the route where I would drive the young lady two days later. Since it was not yet the "fashionable hour" for Hyde Park, carriages and horses were thin enough to permit a more ripping pace then I would dare to use then.

It was a fine day, and ever since I was a boy I had always enjoyed having the ribbons in my hands and the feel of speed. I was hardly a master of the art of driving – not like the infamous "whips" of the emerging London driving clubs – but I was competent enough to where I would not have to worry over that aspect of the promised outing with Miss Stibbley. I was only concerned that we should like each other and that we should be permitted to marry. There was really no question in my mind over the first; I had already lost my heart to Miss Stibbley, so of course we should like each other. The second followed the first; her parents must approve the match. The alternative had already become unthinkable.

There was a ball that night, to which my aunt had decided I must go. Accordingly, I went, but without much expectation of pleasure, since, by Miss Stibbley's own information earlier that day, I knew she would not be present. Nevertheless, I did my duty, dancing nearly every dance with this young lady or that. The exercise did at least serve to exhaust some of my pent up energy and to freshen my dancing skills, so that I should be more polished whenever I did have the chance of escorting to the floor the only girl who really interested me.

The following day was a tedious affair, as I recall, with nothing of sufficient interest to fill the long hours until it was time to go to sleep again. But at last night came, after which would dawn the day I should take Miss Stibbley driving.

I awoke far earlier than what was necessary or desirable, leaving me nothing to do but to take much more time over my dress and appearance than I ordinarily did. Once I was underway, though, I felt better. Doing something is always infinitely preferable to waiting in suspense.

And yet there was more waiting when I arrived in Hanover Square, for I was told that Miss Stibbley was not ready. So I filled my head with visions of her beauty whilst I sat, uncomplaining, for half an hour in the drawing room on my own. I was generously rewarded for my patience in the end, though, for when she came in, the reality lived up to all my expectations. Her dark, gleaming hair shone like a crown about her head, and she wore a very smart looking outfit in a shade of blue that set off her eyes amazingly.

"Mr. Knightley," she said. "So sorry to keep you waiting."

I came forward to meet her. "Not at all, Miss Stibbley," I answered. "It is very good to see you again. Shall we go?"

Mrs. Stibbley was there to see us off. "Remember what we talked about, Julia," she said in a cautioning tone.

Without further delay, we made our way out through the door and down the steps to the curb, where I helped my fair companion up to the high perch of the awaiting phaeton before climbing up myself on the other side.

"I hope you do not mind sitting so high, Miss Stibbley," I said before starting off.

"Oh, no! I have often been driven in a high flyer of this sort, and I find it vastly amusing. One can see everything that is going on about oneself."

"Very true. Then let us be off."

I cut across to Grosvenor Street, made my way through the square and the short remaining distance to Hyde Park, entering by the Grosvenor Gate. Turning north on the perimeter drive, I settled the horses into a comfortable walking pace. It was not a day for speed but for spending as much time as possible in Miss Stibbley's company.

"Do you often come to the Park?" I asked her.

"Yes, very often, and yet I never tire of it. There is always something new to see, depending on the weather or the time of year or the people one passes by."

"What is your favorite place within the park, Miss Stibbley? I believe many find the enclosure at the northwest corner particularly beautiful. We will pass by there soon, if you would care to stop."

"I know the place you mean, and it is beautiful. But we never go inside the fence anymore. Mama says it is frequented by the lower orders now, spoiling it for the rest of us. Sometimes, though, we still stop long enough to send a servant in to fill a jug or two from the spring. The water is said to be vastly good for the health."

"Indeed?"

"Oh, yes! It is the best water to be had anywhere in town!"

"Then I must try it sometime, to see if I can detect any superiority to what is drawn from my own well at home."

"Tell me more about your home, will not you, Mr. Knightley? I have never been to Surrey."

She could not have proposed a subject more to my liking. "Surrey is lovely country, Miss Stibbley. 'The Garden of England' it is often called, in fact, as I am sure you know, although I believe other counties may make the same claim. In any case, I count myself fortunate to live there. The village of Donwell – scarcely more than a hamlet, really – does not amount to much, but there is quite a large village within an easy walk of the Abbey. One can find nearly everything one needs in Highbury."

"Is Donwell Abbey a very grand estate?"

"I never know how to respond to such a question, since the answer depends on what you might have in mind for comparison. We have the usual: farmland, timber, meadows, and a fine stream. I can safely declare that the house itself is a very respectable size, and the style is pleasing to the eye. At least I think so. It is a rambling, irregular sort of structure with many comfortable rooms, as well as one or two that I believe would be regarded as truly handsome."

"And the grounds?"

"Gardens enough to satisfy anybody, I should say, although perhaps in need of more attention than they have received in recent years. My late mother was particularly fond of a garden, you see, but nobody has maintained them as well since. Are you fond of a garden, Miss Stibbley?"

"Very much so," she said and then dropped her eyes as if conscious of the possible implications of my question.

I cannot deny that I was thinking that this beautiful young lady riding beside me might be the very one to direct the restoration of the gardens to their former glory, to step into my mother's shoes as the next mistress of Donwell.

I went on before the resulting silence became too weighty. "There once was a fine prospect from the house all the way down to the meadow and stream. The trees have become too overgrown now to see much of it anymore, but I have been meaning to rectify that situation."

"It sounds delightful, Mr. Knightley. A picturesque view is by all means worth preserving."

We had by this time passed the Cumberland Gate and arrived at the point where the carriage road separated into two branches – one continuing along the northern perimeter and the other plunging south through the heart of the park. I slowed the horses and asked, "Which way shall we go, Miss Stibbley? You know the Park so well that I will trust your advice. I am completely at your service."

I hoped she would tell me to take the right branch to continue along the perimeter, since that would mean a longer drive with her. Instead, she asked me to keep to the left.

"We had much better go this way," she said as I did what she had requested, "for Mama said I should not be gone too long. We have an engagement tonight and I must rest beforehand."

"Of course," I said, trying to hide my disappointment. "Perhaps another day we will have time to see more. I do hope so."

"I will look forward to it. And I will no doubt see you at social engagements in the meantime. We have not yet danced together, you know."

"Very true."

"Are you fond of dancing, Mr. Knightley?"

"I find that my enjoyment depends entirely on my partner. I think I can guarantee that I will be very fond of dancing with you, Miss Stibbley."

As we continued on, I asked her about her home and family – she had an older brother and a younger one, she informed me – and I told her about John, my only remaining family.

By this time, we had come out to where we would need to turn left along the Serpentine to return in the direction of Hanover Square. I stopped to admire the view and to allow another carriage to pass by in front of us.

Miss Stibbley looked right and left over the broad waterway before us. "No swans today," she said with a dejected note in her voice. "You will laugh at me, but I rather regard them as my very own. I always look for them on the Serpentine and consider it good luck when they are here and bad luck when they are not. Perhaps it is a sign."

Thinking fast for a rebuttal, I said, "You must not consider them as absent just because you cannot see them from here. No doubt they are simply up at the other end of the river today. Shall we go in search of them? I can turn right instead of left, if you like."

"You would do that for me?" she asked looking hopeful.

"Certainly I would. It would please me very much to give you the sight of your swans today. As I said before, I am completely at your service."

Then she sighed. "Thank you, Mr. Knightley. You are very kind, but I think we had better not. Mama will be quite vexed with us both if I am not returned when she expects me."

"As you wish, then."

On the last portion of our drive, I turned the conversation to upcoming events – not because I cared much for a ball in general, only a ball where I might dance with the charming young lady beside me.

By the time I returned her to her mother at Hanover Square, I had memorized her social calendar for the next week and a half. Wherever Miss Stibbley went, I intended that I should follow.

-20-
Lady's Choice

I did not think I was deceiving myself that Miss Stibbley's manner to me so far had been all that I could have hoped for, and so I was sufficiently encouraged to continue my pursuit of her. Aunt Phoebe was my very valuable accomplice in this endeavor, procuring invitations for me to nearly everywhere I wanted to go – in other words, everywhere Miss Stibbley said she would be.

Julia always seemed happy to see me and would spare me as much time as she was decently able. Her other admirers – Lord Blankenship, Mr. Crawley, etc. – persisted as well, however, so I by no means had the field to myself.

It came as no surprise that Miss Stibbley danced divinely, just as she did everything else musical. And I had never enjoyed the exercise half so well before as I did any time I could stand up with her. We danced and danced during that season, always taking our two allowable together (and occasionally a third), all under the watchful eye of Mrs. Stibbley.

The daughter I counted firmly on my side, but I could not be quite as sanguine about my standing in the mother's eyes. One minute she was all goodness and encouragement, and the next she seemed to be steering her daughter towards somebody else. I suppose that was exactly the case; she wanted to be sure of me in case she could secure nobody better.

About a fortnight after my first drive in the Park with Miss Stibbley, I took her for another. This time, I ascertained at the outset that we should have no particular time constraints on us. I was glad of it, not simply because I craved as much time as possible with her, but because I wanted no extra stress pressing upon me. I had already decided, you see, that the time had come for me to clearly declare myself. I meant to propose the idea of marriage to Miss Stibbley. So it was a great relief that we would be at our leisure, that we would not be rushed. I could wait until the moment was exactly right before speaking.

Thanks to my aunt, I felt prepared; I knew exactly what I was going to say. I had confided in her a few days earlier – as soon as I had made the appointment with Miss Stibbley – what I intended to do.

"I suspected that something like this was in the wind, young man," she said, not at all discomposed by the news. "Yes, you will have my support. I think the two of you will suit very well. I only hope her parents will be as pleased with the match as I am. Now, I trust you have a fine speech prepared for the occasion."

I stared at her blankly. "A speech? What do you mean?"

"Heavens! Was there ever such a clueless young man? Very well, let me make myself clearer. You cannot expect the girl to know what you want without opening your mouth, so what had you planned to say to her?"

"I had not anything *planned*. I suppose I thought that when the moment was right, I would simply tell her what was in my heart: that I love her and would be honored if she would accept my hand. Something like that."

"Oh, dear me, no! That will not do at all. A girl likes to feel the gentleman cares enough to put some thought into the proposal. She likes to have something romantic to remember later on in life, too. Thank goodness you mentioned it to me first, while there is still time to get it right, or she might have turned you down in a fit of pique. *If he cannot take the trouble to do better than that at this most important moment, why should I marry him? It will surely be all downhill from here!*

No, no, my boy, you must not give her any such reason to reject you."

I thought it a bit silly, to be honest. Either the girl liked the idea of marrying me or she did not; the exact words used should make little difference. Still, I appreciated my aunt's imparting to me the female point of view. This was uncharted territory for me, and I had to get it right the first time, for I would likely never have a second chance. Besides, Miss Stibbley certainly deserved the finest proposal I could give her. So I set about working on it from that very hour. When I thought I had the words exactly right, I committed them to memory so that I would be ready.

Now the moment was approaching. I had collected Miss Stibbley at her home in Hanover Square as before, then travelled to and entered the Park by the same gate. The difference would be that this time I would be taking the long way round, skirting the northern perimeter and then Kensington Gardens on the west end. We talked of many things along the way, but always in my mind was the important business ahead. When we reached the path that led to the bridge over the Serpentine, I pulled the carriage off the road and helped my companion down.

"Let us see if your swans are about today," I suggested. "We can look a distance in both directions from the bridge."

"Oh, yes, let's do!" Miss Stibbley quickly agreed. She took my arm and we set a brisk pace up the path.

I looked down at her eager, smiling face, feeling satisfaction in the knowledge that I had played a part in raising that smile to her lips, which I hoped would only widen when I shortly told her what I had on my mind. She was looking remarkably pretty, I thought, not that that was at all unusual. It was probably only my heightened state of awareness that made me think there was a special glow about her. Or perhaps she knew exactly what I intended. I would not have put it past her, as quick and perceptive as she seemed to be.

I saw the pair of swans gliding over the water a moment before she did, and I took their presence as a good omen.

"There they are, Mr. Knightley!" Miss Stibbley cried as we approached the midpoint of the footbridge. "Are not they the most beautiful things you have ever seen?"

I resisted the temptation of saying at once what I was thinking. No, lovely as a swan might be, it was not the most beautiful creature I had ever beheld; Miss Stibbley was. Instead, I held my peace to allow her to bask in the moment for a little, creating a memory she would hopefully treasure in years to come. Secondarily, I wished to allow time for another couple to stroll on past and out of hearing. Then at last, I took both of Miss Stibbley's hands and gently turned her towards me.

"Miss Stibbley," I began, staring directly into her bright, expressive eyes. Perhaps that was a mistake, though, for I felt transfixed and my mind went blank. I forgot every single word of the speech I had so meticulously composed to tell her.

"Yes, Mr. Knightley?" she prompted when I said no more. "What did you wish to say to me?"

I had to answer her something, so I reverted to my original plan: speaking from my heart. "Miss Stibbley – Julia – you must know how I feel about you. I have adored you ever since the first moment I saw you. Could you…? I mean, would you consider…? Of course I must consult your father, but if he gives his consent, will you do me the great honor of marrying me?"

There. The words were out. Not eloquent or even entirely fluent, but she would understand me. I awaited her answer.

"I would be pleased to, Mr. Knightley," she said with a shy smile. I could hardly believe my good fortune!

I fervently pressed her hands and brought them to my lips, first one and then the other. I desired to kiss her perfectly formed mouth instead, of course, but I would not presume to do so in public, even on such a momentous occasion.

"That is excellent news!" I exclaimed, my excitement bubbling over along with a gush of words. "You have made me so happy, my dearest Julia. May I call you by your Christian name now, at least when we are alone? You may call me George, if you wish. And I am sorry that the proposal was not more eloquent. I did have something finer prepared, I assure you. But then, when I looked into your eyes, I forgot everything except how much I love you."

She was laughing at me, but I did not care. She had said yes, and that was all that mattered. Well, not quite. There was one other important question left to be answered.

"Do you think your father will look favorably on my suit?" I asked more soberly as we began walking back to the phaeton, arm in arm, the swans forgotten.

"I do not see why he should object," she said. "Mama has been keeping him informed by the post about my most serious suitors – the eligibles for whom I had any liking at all. So he is not unfamiliar with your name and reputation, at least."

"Really? That is encouraging. And how do you think your mother will feel about our news when she hears it? I can never tell if she likes me or not."

"Mama? Oh, I would venture to say that she does not *dis*like you, but…"

"Allow me to guess. She would like me much better if I had a title and a great deal more money."

I had spoken lightly and so Miss Stibbley knew it was safe to laugh. "What ambitious mama would not prefer to see her only daughter married to a rich lord? Of course, she would! But she would like me to be happy as well. Besides, I have no particular claims that would make a grand match eligible."

"I disagree, my dear. You could marry anybody you want."

"By marrying you, that is just what I will be doing," she said, smiling up at me.

Her words and the affection in her eyes made my heart sing. This lovely young woman, who could have any man she chose, wanted *me* for her husband! It seemed truly miraculous.

Who was I to deserve her? I was nothing special, just a simple, plain-spoken man. And yet she apparently saw something in me worthy of her love.

After returning to the carriage, we drove at a very leisurely pace along the Serpentine, on to Hyde Park Corner, and eventually completing the full circuit back to where we had entered the park.

"I want you to see Donwell Abbey as soon as may be," I told Miss Stibbley along the way.

"Oh, yes!" she agreed. "As soon as may be."

"I hope you will like it very well, for we will spend most of our time there in future."

"May we not come to town for the season each year? I do so love the shops and the dancing and the gaiety and the larger society one finds here."

"If it is that important to you, my dear – not for the entire season but for periodic visits. It's not far, after all. I expect that my brother John will reside here when he has finished his education in the law a few years hence, so that will be another enjoyable reason to come. My life and my work are at Donwell, though, so for the most part, that is where I must be. Besides, I adore the place uncommonly. I can hardly wait to introduce you to Donwell and to all my friends, Julia! I know you will love them as I do."

Now that the first flurry of excitement was over, we both fell a little quieter on the return drive to Hanover Square, each of us lost in our own pleasant reveries. Only one more hurdle to get over, and then the future looked very bright indeed.

I could see the years stretching pleasantly out in front of us – together at Donwell, spending quiet evenings in comfort before the fire. I pictured myself in my favorite chair with a book in my hand. Instead of reading it, however, my gaze rests on my beautiful wife. Julia is at the pianoforte, filling the house with exquisite song. When she finishes, she looks across at me and smiles a smile that bespeaks love and contentment. But there is an invitation in her eyes, too, I notice. It brings me out of my chair and to her side at once. She rises as well and is soon in my arms...

Yes, in due time, there would be children too. Then perhaps I would be able to keep my promise to Miles, naming our first son after him.

-21-
Joy and Reveling

Mrs. Stibbley was more animated in her receiving of our news than I had expected. Julia burst out with it as soon as she saw her mother and was immediately taken into her embrace.

"Well done, my darling!" said Mrs. Stibbley. "You have certainly found yourself a handsome and agreeable husband. In your first season too! And are you happy, my angel? Yes, of course you are! I can see that for myself. Wait until your father hears the news!"

I cleared my throat to remind my future mother-in-law of my presence. "I will of course be ready to ask for Mr. Stibbley's consent in form as soon as possible."

"Naturally, naturally. As soon as possible, although there can be no difficulty. I was not at first sure you would come up to scratch, Mr. Knightley, but now you have carried away quite a prize, if I do say so myself. There are many others half in love with my daughter too, some perhaps more… But no matter; she has made her choice and all will be well."

"I am a most fortunate man, Mrs. Stibbley."

"Mama, can we remove to Surrey at once? Mr. Knightley has invited us to Donwell."

"Well, now, let me think. I will need to write immediately to summon your father, of course. Nothing can go forward without his approval, as you know. But if he is to come as far as London anyway, a little farther will not be much of an inconvenience. No doubt he would like to approve the estate where his daughter will be mistress along with the gentleman who would be her husband. Mr. Knightley," she said, turning to me, "you had better be on your way, for there is much to be done. Will we see you tonight at the Rafferty's musicale? Julia is to sing, you know."

"I would not miss it for the world," I declared.

Then Mrs. Stibbley added, "I am sure you both understand that we can make no announcement of the engagement until Mr. Stibbley has officially sanctioned it, so for now it will be our little secret. Agreed?"

"Yes, Mama," said Julia.

"Yes, of course, Mrs. Stibbley," I agreed. I understood the reason, but I knew it would be nearly impossible to hide my prosperous love. It was no doubt written on my face, especially when I looked at Julia.

"Mama," Julia said, "would you leave us a moment so that I might tell Mr. Knightley good-bye?"

"Very well, you sly creature. I suppose lovers must have their privacy, and now that you are engaged, I think it will be all right. Just a few minutes, though." Then she left the room without closing the door.

"What a clever girl you are, my dear Julia," I said, moving closer to her.

She looked up at me through a thick fringe of lashes. "I thought perhaps you should like to kiss me good-bye. I would like that too."

"May we always find ourselves in such perfect accord, my darling," I said just before taking her into a gentle embrace and lowering my lips to hers.

That first kiss was everything I could have wished for. Julia's lips were soft and as velvety as rose petals. They were also warm and very receptive, making the kiss mutual instead of one-sided. We pressed and held, moved a little and pressed again, until a warning sounded in my brain and I knew it was time to break it off.

"Is that all?" she asked with a bit of a pout.

"For now, it had better be. But think of all the kisses in our future." I was thinking of that and more as I reluctantly released her and stepped back. "I must go. As your mama pointed out, there is much to be done. Until tonight," I said in parting.

"Until tonight," she repeated as I turned to go.

No doubt I was grinning like a fool on the short drive back to Berkley Square, for no announcement was necessary when I was met there by my aunt. She took one look at me and said, "I collect the lady accepted you. Well, congratulations, dear boy! I am sure you will be very happy together. When is the wedding to be and where?"

"I have not the least idea as to all that, Aunt. I imagine the bride's family will decide, and I expect to simply do what I am told. First, however, the ladies will travel with me to Donwell, that Miss Stibbley may see her future home. Mr. Stibbley is to join us there to give his blessing. Until then, no announcement will be made."

"So you will be leaving me presently. I must say that I am sorry to see your visit come to an end so soon, Nephew, although for a joyous reason."

"You have been exceedingly kind, Aunt Phoebe. I owe you a great deal."

"Stuff and nonsense. It was my pleasure, and you know it. Now, you must take my travelling coach when you go."

"I could not," I protested.

"You will allow me to do this one last thing for you. I insist. You cannot escort your bride and her mother in a hired coach or by the mail!"

"I thought I would send for Mr. Woodhouse's carriage."

"Fiddlesticks. Mine is already here and my coachman far too idle. They can be easily there and back within the same day. But I think it is high time, nephew, that you do something about getting a respectable carriage of your own!"

I agreed and thanked her. I had no pretentions to grandeur myself, but I must be prepared to keep Julia in some style. One does not acquire a rare gem only to house it in a broken-down box or display a Leonardo without a suitable frame.

Setting up a proper carriage would be a priority, but first… Suddenly, I knew there was something I must do without delay. "Excuse me, Aunt Phoebe," I said, already heading for the stairs, "but I have a letter to write."

Actually, I had two. The first was long and utilitarian. It went to William Larkins with some added instructions for the household staff enclosed.

I should have seen to some of these necessary items before ever leaving Donwell for London. I *would* have, had I any expectation that when I returned it would be with a beautiful bride in hand. However, I had been so sure at the time that nothing would come of my brief foray into the marriage market that it never occurred to me to make a few basic improvements first.

Not that I had any intention of deluding Miss Stibbley or her parents into believing me something I was not or that Donwell was excessively grand. I would tell only the truth. But neither did I wish them to think I was the sort of man to let his home go to wrack and ruin from neglect. Along with the necessary preparation of guest rooms and the laying in of extra food stores, I could immediately think of half a dozen items of general maintenance I wanted addressed before the Stibbleys arrived. And there was no time to lose.

My second letter was a brief but heartfelt note to Mr. and Mrs. Woodhouse:

Dearest Friends,

    How can I ever thank you enough for sending me into London? Forgive me for ever doubting you, Mrs. Woodhouse, when you said I was in need of a wife. Indeed, I did not know until I found her exactly how right you were. How could I have been so foolish as to think myself happy alone before?

I can imagine your surprise at this news, but it is quite true. I met Miss Julia Stibbley almost as soon as I arrived in town, and a whirlwind courtship ensued. She is an absolute angel with a face and a voice to match, and she has just this day done me the great honor of consenting to be my wife.

I am soon to entertain Miss Stibbley and her parents at Donwell and will take the first available opportunity to introduce them all to your acquaintance. Julia's mother is all accommodating to our wishes, and so we only await her father's arrival and blessing to make our happiness complete. I wanted you both to be among the first to know.

Remember me to the girls. With many thanks and best wishes,

George Knightley

Once the letters were on their way, I felt relieved, confident that all would be in order when we arrived at Donwell. Then it was time to dress for our evening engagement.

How different were my sensations at seeing Julia and hearing her sing this time, knowing she was now promised to be my wife. When she took her turn at the pianoforte, her eyes seemed to be trained in my direction as if she sang for me alone. If that did not give away our new status as a definite couple, the amount of time we spent together otherwise must have. Nobody who was paying any attention could have failed to observe it. Perhaps some commented, but I did not care. The whole world might know that we were in love, as far as I was concerned.

I was glad it was not a ball, where I would have been obliged to watch Julia dancing with other men most of the night. This was much better. We stood and talked or sat side by side as the other musicians performed. I could not concentrate on their songs, however, so aware was I of Julia's nearness. I hoped and trusted we would be married very soon.

Looking back, I would have to count that day – the drive in the park with Julia, the accepted proposal, the kiss, and reveling in each other's company at the musicale – as the happiest day of my life. I was to marry the girl of my dreams, and all was well. The future looked bright and uncomplicated. Such is the naivety of youth.

Returning Home

Three days later, after settling my affairs and bidding Aunt Phoebe a fond farewell, I collected Julia and her mother, along with the lady's maid they shared, and we set off for Surrey.

My spirits were flying high at the thought of being home again in just a matter of a few hours. Though my time in town had been much more enjoyable and successful than I could have imagined, I had been away from my beloved Donwell longer than I liked. So I could hardly wait to see the house, the grounds, and my dear friends again. Then there was the anticipated pleasure of acquainting Miss Stibbley with these treasures as well. I was sure my friends would all consider her a delightful addition to Highbury society. And no doubt they would think me a very lucky man, as I did myself.

Even the weather was fine, boding well for pleasant travel.

"This is a very comfortable carriage," said Mrs. Stibbley conversationally after we had been underway for fifteen or twenty minutes.

"Yes," I agreed. "My aunt was kind to give me the loan of it for our journey."

"Your aunt? Do you mean to say that this carriage belongs to Lady Anvert and not yourself?"

"That is correct, Mrs. Stibbley."

She looked surprised. "And the other? – that pretty little phaeton you took Julia driving in?"

"The same. My aunt has been very generous."

"Apparently."

"Of course, I have some conveyances of my own, Mrs. Stibbley – a spanking gig, plus an outmoded travelling coach I never use – but no carriage suitable for my trip into town. As a single man, I prefer to walk or ride most places. Now, of course, all that will change," I said, smiling across at Julia. "I mean to set up a proper carriage and horses before we are married."

"I should think so!" said her mother decidedly. "You cannot expect a gently bred young lady like Julia to be traipsing about dirty country lanes on foot or to go on horseback just because you are fond of it yourself."

"Quite so, Mrs. Stibbley," I agreed. "Although I hope Julia and I may enjoy many a country walk together when the weather is commodious. I do so enjoy the exercise, and fresh air is very beneficial for the health. Besides, there is no sense in troubling servants and horses when one only wants to go a distance of half a mile. Would not you agree, Miss Stibbley?"

Instead of answering, she looked down at the delicate slippers she wore, no doubt picturing them covered in dirt and worse.

I hurried on. "Country walks, of course, can only be safely undertaken with proper footwear. You said you spent much of your youth in the country, Julia, so you must have worn more serviceable shoes at one time."

"I did," she said, "as a child, but I cannot say that I possess anything suitable to a country walk any longer." She paused. "Perhaps I will need to acquire a pair of half boots?" she finished on a tentative note.

"Ford's in Highbury is the place for it. I daresay they will have just what you need."

"How reassuring," said Mrs. Stibbley, but I thought I detected a note of derision in her tone.

We drove along in silence for some minutes, and I could not help wondering what Julia was thinking. The conversation had not gone as well as I had hoped so far. Was she, like her mother seemed to be, put off by the fact that we were riding in a borrowed carriage? Julia's lack of enthusiasm for the country and its occupations did not overly concern me, for I fully trusted Donwell and Highbury to work their magic on her, as they apparently had on my own mother when she married. Julia would soon love them as I did. There was no denying that town had its necessary functions, but what person in his right mind would choose to live surrounded by noise, smoke, and London's crush of people all the year round, when they could be enjoying the charming verdure of the English countryside?

Looking across at Julia's serene countenance, my worries receded to the shadows. She was gazing back at me with a burning affection that mirrored my own sentiments. There could be nothing amiss as long as she loved me. Any little differences or adjustments would soon be smoothed over, and we would be happy together all of our days.

Still, judging from what had already passed, I began to think I should give the ladies some preparation for what they would find at our destination. "Perhaps I should tell you a little more about Donwell before you see the place," I suggested.

"Oh, yes!" Julia exclaimed. "Do. I am more curious than you can know."

"Very well, then. First, it is a fine estate, though I say it myself, and the size of the house is not in the least deficient. But I would caution you not to expect too much. Keep in mind that Donwell has been without a mistress for several years now, since my mother's decease. And even before that... What I mean is that it is at present, and has been for some time, a bachelor residence. I am the only one who lives there, except when my brother is home from school. And I have been used to living very quietly, you see. I have not been in the habit of entertaining except on a small scale."

Here I paused, waiting for some response.

The two ladies looked at each other, and then Mrs. Stibbley asked, "What is it that you are trying to tell us, Mr. Knightley?"

"Just this. You will no doubt notice that the servants are few and some of the rooms are shut up, unused. I do not expect it to remain so once Donwell has a mistress again. Julia, I realize that you will naturally wish to make some changes. We will undoubtedly entertain more. We will require more servants and the carriage I mentioned before. Be assured that I will not deny your wishes for anything reasonable, and I look forward to seeing the place returned to what it was years ago, when my mother and father were both living. So I hope you both will endeavor to see beyond Donwell's current state to what it can and will be in the future."

For a moment, neither of the ladies responded. In fact, they looked a little stunned.

"Dear me, Mr. Knightley," said Julia at last. "You do not paint a very pretty picture of my future home. I hope the place is not too dreary, for I doubt my imagination will be equal to the task of picturing something very different."

I leant forward and took her gloved hand. "No, not dreary, my dear. I assure you it is not that. I simply wanted you to understand, so that you would not set your expectations too high, which would only lead to disappointment."

Mrs. Stibbley then delivered herself of her considered opinion on the subject. "I cannot say that I am pleased to hear things may not yet be in proper order, Mr. Knightley. And I certainly do not intend to release my darling daughter to a home in disarray. Still, if the land and situation are good, the rest can be corrected – before the wedding if necessary, or at least after it – provided you are prepared to invest the necessary funds."

"Very true," I agreed. "Improvements can and will be made. I am not a miserly man. I believe in spending wisely, but there is no wiser expenditure than investing in one's own home and property."

Afterward, I was sure I had made the right decision by forewarning the ladies. Far better that their expectations should be somewhat lowered, so that they might be pleasantly surprised instead of disappointed when they saw Donwell.

The rest of the drive passed pleasantly enough, and as we neared Highbury, my excitement built. I pointed out sights of interest in the neighborhood and then in the village itself, with the knowledge that these would soon be Julia's nearer connections – the places she would frequent and the people who would make up her daily interactions.

"There is Ford's, which I mentioned to you before," I told her, pointing through the window on one side of the carriage. "Everybody must shop there every week of their lives. And The Crown Inn. The large room above is used for dances and other assemblies. The church and parsonage are just there," I said, when they came into view on the other side. "Mr. Bates is the rector, and he lives with his wife and an unmarried daughter. Although we will normally attend church in Donwell parish, the Bateses are my very good friends. They are the best sort of people you would ever care to meet, humble and kindhearted. I took lessons from old Mr. Bates when I was a boy."

Julia looked with interest, nodding or murmuring her understanding without adding much comment.

"Is that all there is to the place, Mr. Knightley?" Mrs. Stibbley asked when we had passed through Highbury and out the other end in the span of a few minutes. "I thought you said it was good sized town."

"I suppose not quite large enough to be called a proper town, Mrs. Stibbley. I believe I described it as a large and populous village. Highbury can provide for most needs. Whatever may not be found here must be got from London, which, as you have now seen for yourself, is a very easy distance away. Now, here," I said to direct their attention to the window again. "Here is the place to turn to reach Hartfield, the seat of the other principal family in the neighborhood and my dearest friends: the Woodhouses. Although in truth, I rarely come this way myself, for there is a very pleasant path that is much more direct. I walk to Hartfield and back nearly every day. The

Woodhouses are as close as family to me. I can hardly wait for them to meet you, Julia, for it was Mrs. Woodhouse's idea that I should go to town in search of a wife, for which I am now very grateful."

"As am I, and I hope I will meet with Mrs. Woodhouse's approval."

"You cannot fail to, my dear Julia! Now, what would you say to my collecting a small party of friends together at Donwell? It would be the easiest way for you to meet everybody and for them to meet you. Perhaps you would even consent to play and sing for us. Unless you should be overwhelmed by the numbers in some way. I know they would all be strangers to start, but they will soon be *your* friends as well."

"How many would there be of the party?"

"Let me see. We should have Mr. and Mrs. Woodhouse, of course, the three Bateses, Mr. Weston, Mr. and Mrs. Cole, Mrs. Goddard, and possibly the Fords and Miss Taylor. That would make an even dozen, should they all accept. Plus we ourselves, of course. Sixteen, if your father should arrive by then. What do you think, Mrs. Stibbley? Is it too many?"

"Julia often performs before larger crowds than that! She did the night you met her."

"Yes, but it would be a lot of new names and faces to try to remember all at once, Mama," said Julia.

"True," her mother agreed. "Are these all people of good family and breeding, Mr. Knightley?" her mother inquired. "It would surprise me if in such a rural area you could collect even a dozen gentlefolk. I know of no Coles in good society. And what about the Fords you mentioned? They must be the proprietors of the shop you pointed out to us and therefore in trade. Julia is unaccustomed to keeping such low company."

Here I had to exert myself to hold my temper… and my tongue. "All those I have named are perfectly respectable people for your daughter to associate with, I assure you, Mrs. Stibbley. In the country, one cannot afford to be overly fastidious or one would have few friends indeed."

"I am sure they are all delightful, Mr. Knightley," Julia said, "but perhaps we could invite fewer to start – just your very closest friends. That way I would have more time for each one and not so many names to learn."

I would not have excluded any of my friends on account of my future mother-in-law's prejudice. But it was quite another matter to limit the guest list in order to make my betrothed's introduction into Highbury society as comfortable as possible. So I said, "Of course, my dear, if you wish it. Then just the Bateses and Woodhouses, who will bring Miss Taylor. Only six plus ourselves. Would that be more to your liking?"

Julia's smile was radiant. "That sounds perfect. Thank you."

"Then it is settled. Now, look about yourselves. We have been driving on Donwell land for several minutes already, and the house comes into view momentarily, just on your right side. Wait for it. Wait for it. And... there it is."

I rapped on the roof to signal the coachman to stop.

"A fine prospect, I will grant you," said Mrs. Stibbley. "What do you think, Julia? How do you like your new house?"

"I like it. I like it very well indeed."

-23-

Taking the Tour

I was not surprised that Donwell made a good first impression. Especially when assisted by fine weather, it really was quite an impressive and beautiful bucolic scene from that elevated vantage point. Gently rolling hills, some dotted with sheep, gave the house and grounds a pleasant backdrop, with the stream meandering through the meadowland to one side. Timber here and there. I never grew tired of the prospect or took for granted my good fortune at living in such a place.

Everything was green and gleaming bright in the early summer sunshine that day. And from a distance, the little things did not show. The stables appeared well kept, and nobody could tell that they were mostly empty. The house looked impressive, sprawling over a large plot surrounded by gardens. Nobody could tell from a quarter mile away that the landscaping had become overgrown or that the house failed to live up to all its promise on the inside. That would become apparent soon enough, I knew.

This was a momentous occasion, I realized then, as we all admired the view. More so than I had apprehended before. Introducing Julia to Donwell was really like introducing my two best friends to each other. Since I could not imagine a life without both of them in it, it was essential that they liked each other – well, that Julia should like Donwell – even more so than that she liked Mr. and Mrs. Woodhouse. Julia would be living in the company of Donwell every day, just as she would be with me. The three of us must all get along well together.

But then I chided myself for my foolishness. Of course Julia would approve of Donwell! How could she not? Quite apart from its luxurious size and obvious charm, if she loved me, she must love this place that was so great a part of me. To do otherwise would make no more sense than saying she loved my right arm but could not abide my left.

I signaled to the coachman to drive on.

Mrs. Stibbley remained calmly upright in her seat, but it seemed Julia could not get enough of the views. Now that we were actually within sight of the house, everything was of more interest, I suppose.

Soon we had arrived at the front door, however, and the carriage came to a stop. I alit at once so that I could help the ladies out myself, Mrs. Stibbley first followed by Julia and then the maid. They paused a moment to take in the front façade from closer range, and then we proceeded up the steps.

Although I had no true butler, Harry, the indoor man, opened the door for us. I was pleased to see him looking so smart, wearing his seldom-used livery, just as I had requested in my instructions sent by the post. Most of the other servants were there to meet us as well, all looking clean and orderly. Each nodded or curtseyed as I named them to Julia.

"Harry, here, will manage all butler and footman duties. This is Mrs. Hodges, the cook, and Mrs. Pepperidge, the house-keeper. Annie is the head housemaid. Any one of them will be glad to assist you with whatever you need while you are here. Just ring the bell." Noticing that Julia was looking a little tired, I asked, "Would you like to be taken to your rooms now?"

"Yes, please," Julia said at once. "I am a little fatigued by the journey."

"Of course. Mrs. Pepperidge will show you the way, and Harry will bring up your things. When you are both rested and refreshed, I look forward to showing you more of the house. And then we will dine at seven."

When they had gone upstairs, I turned to Mrs. Hodges. "Is everything in a fair train for dinner tonight and so forth?"

"Yes, sir. I did think it strange that you wanted it so late, but I do as I'm told."

"Town hours, Mrs. Hodges, at least for now. And be aware that I mean to give a small dinner party as soon as you can be ready. Just ten of us at the most, and it needn't be anything grand. I will trust you with the menu as usual, and hire a girl from the village to help. Harry can wait table, with Annie to assist him. Now, where is William Larkins?"

"He's in your study, sir, as you requested."

"Very good," I said. "I will see him directly."

I was very glad that my guests had retired upstairs, leaving me at least a brief interval on my own to see to necessary business, which included a conference with my trusted estate manager. We had made an exchange of letters while I was gone, of course, but there was nothing like a face-to-face conversation on the premises to make me feel I was in control again. That is what I needed – to be on my land and up to date after all the distractions of town. What happened at Donwell was my responsibility, and I would not cede it to another, even William Larkins. His report reassured me that all was well and that the specific concerns, about which I had written him, had been addressed, at least so far as it was possible to do so.

As we were concluding our business, Harry knocked to tell me that the ladies were coming downstairs again. I rose at once and went out to meet them. I saw as they descended that both of them had changed, and Julia looked refreshed and blooming.

"I hope you both found your rooms comfortable," I said as they reached me. I had given them the best available, of course, so I did not doubt the answer.

"Very comfortable, yes," said Julia.

Mrs. Stibbley allowed her daughter's answer to stand uncontested.

"Good. Should you like a little tour now?" I continued. With the expected affirmative response, I took Julia's hand, drew it through to rest on my arm, and led the two ladies across the large entry hall to a pair of elegant double doors, which I opened. "The drawing room," I said, allowing the ladies to precede me in.

Mrs. Stibbley walked about, examining the space and furnishings with a practiced eye. "The size is very generous," she said. "One might even say it is a stately room. But Julia, you must have it completely new furnished before you even *think* of entertaining any of our London friends here. They will judge it very rustic as it is, and outmoded. This stodgy old sofa, for example. The rugs. Dreadful!" She shook her head and sighed. "Everything must go, I'm afraid."

"Some of the furnishings are not too bad, I think, Mama," Julia said in a conciliatory tone. "And consider, perhaps there may be family heirlooms among these things. Are there, Mr. Knightley?" she asked, turning to me.

"Well, if not true heirlooms, then certainly family favorites. This was my mother's chair," I said, going to a matched pair of wingbacks. I ran my left hand across the top of the first before repeating the gesture with the second. "And my father always sat in this other one. To this day, I can still picture them seated here, though they have both been gone a long time."

"See, Mama," said Julia. "Some updates are no doubt needed, but there can be no occasion for getting rid of everything."

"My dear child, have I taught you nothing? Having a mix of styles will spoil the whole effect! I did not let sentiment stand in the way when I new furnished your apartment at home, did I?"

"No, Mama," Julia answered with downcast eyes.

"There. You see? If Mr. Knightley must keep these musty old chairs, they can be moved to some out-of-the way corner or other, but they must not be allowed to remain where you will wish to impress and entertain your guests. It will be expensive, of course, but so very worth it."

We moved from room to room with similar results – Mrs. Stibbley always finding fault, always finding that a great deal of money must be spent to set things to right. Julia, however, seemed much less dissatisfied with what she saw, which was a great relief. And when at last we came to the music room, I had the pleasure of seeing her go to the instrument at once, exclaiming in delight, "A Broadwood grand!"

"Do you like it?" I asked, even though I could see that she did.

"Oh, yes! It is quite beautiful. May I try it?"

"Of course!" I said with a laugh. "I ordered it freshly tuned just for you." This was another of the preparations that I had made while still in London. I had sent an expert on ahead to be sure the pianoforte would be in excellent condition when Julia arrived. A musician of the first order, like her, deserved a first-class instrument to play.

She sat down, took a deep breath to compose herself, and then she began to play. Soon she was singing as well.

I leant back against the doorframe to watch and listen. She seemed to have travelled away somewhere, into a world of her own, immersed in the music and oblivious to everything else. I was likewise oblivious to everything but Julia. This was the realization of the scene I had pictured again and again, with some variation, ever since the first night I had met her: Julia at Donwell, filling my house – our house – with song.

"She is quite a talent as well as a great beauty."

I started when Mrs. Stibbley spoke, for I had quite forgot her existence.

"A diamond of the first water, as they say," she added.

"Yes, she is," I agreed, hoping that would be enough to satisfy the woman. I wanted to focus on my future wife, not spoil the song by making idle conversation with her mother. But I did not get my way.

"Mr. Stibbley and I shall miss hearing her so often as we have been used to doing," she said. "Still, this is not the end. After you are married, you may visit us in Herefordshire, and we will visit here very often. Mr. Stibbley fairly dotes on his only daughter, you know. Sons are all very well, he says, but he cannot be long apart from Julia. It has been very hard on him, you understand, having us away in London these many weeks. And the prospect of Julia marrying is not pleasant to either of us. But we must do what is best for our children. That is a parent's first duty. Do not you agree, Mr. Knightley?"

"What? Oh, yes, of course. A parent's duty. I had excellent parents as well, Mrs. Stibbley, who set me a fine example."

"I am glad to hear it. You must have keenly felt the loss of them dying so early."

"Yes, I did and still do, very keenly."

When she fell silent, I hoped the conversation would be allowed to rest there.

"But then, on the other hand," she continued a minute later, "you might not be in a position to marry at your young age, were it not for that misfortune. There is always a silver lining, you see, if one is willing to look for it. It is a fine thing to inherit early."

I was spared the necessity of commenting on Mrs. Stibbley's last piece of questionable philosophy by Julia finishing just then and rising.

"It is an excellent instrument," she said, giving the pianoforte a final, affectionate stroke before stepping away.

"I am so glad you approve, Miss Stibbley," I said. "Naturally, you can play it whenever you wish. It will always be a very great pleasure to me to listen to you."

–24–
Making Plans

The next morning, while the ladies were still abed, I rode to Highbury, to the parsonage, to invite the Bates family to Donwell the following day for dinner. I was not afraid of coming in on them too soon, for I knew they were early risers. And neither did I need to tell them the occasion for the gathering, for it was no secret that I had gone to town seeking a wife and not come home empty handed.

After my invitation had been civilly accepted by Mr. and Mrs. Bates, Miss Bates, who was even then on the wrong side of thirty and had taken to wearing a cap, addressed me in animated spirits.

"Then shall we meet your young lady, Mr. Knightley?" And before I could answer her first question, she continued on to the second. "Is she *very* pretty? I did not see her myself, but I spoke to Mrs. Partridge last night at evensong, and she said she had caught a glimpse of her, or so she supposed it was, in a carriage passing through yesterday. 'A very grand carriage,' she said, and that she saw you and two fine ladies in it. And so of course I told her that she must be mistaken, that it could not have been you, Mr. Knightley. 'Mr. Knightley does not own a grand carriage,' I reminded her. But I suppose it must have been you and your lady after all."

"Yes, it was, Miss Bates," I confirmed. "Myself, Miss Stibbley, and her mother. We were travelling in my aunt's carriage, you see. And you surely shall…"

"Oh! Well, of course," she interrupted cheerfully. "All is now made clear. We were both correct then, in our own ways – Mrs. Partridge and myself – for she said she had seen you, and I said it could not have been your carriage. I will be sure to explain it to her at my next opportunity, and we shall have such a laugh over it. Do not you think we shall, Mr. Knightley? But how exciting about meeting Miss Stibbley!"

Having accomplished what I had come for, I soon excused myself so that I could proceed to Hartfield with the same mission, plus an even more heartfelt reunion. I had only been away a few weeks, but it seemed much longer.

When I was received in the drawing room, I shook Mr. Woodhouse's hand and warmly pressed his wife's. That would not do for her, though. Her eyes bright, she laid hold of my shoulders and rose on her toes to kiss my cheek.

"What excellent news you sent us, George! I mean Mr. Knightley. I have not stopped smiling ever since we received your letter."

"My dear," said Mr. Woodhouse, "you must calm yourself. Mr. Perry said that too much excitement is not good for a lady in your... in your delicate condition."

"Oh, fiddlesticks, Mr. Woodhouse! I am perfectly well, and nothing could do me more good than to see this dear boy of ours so happy. Now, George, when shall we meet your lady love?"

"Tomorrow night. Will you come to dine? I have invited the Bateses as well."

"Of course! I have not yet taken to hiding myself away, and we would not miss it for the world, would we, my dear?"

"Yes, of course we will come, Mr. Knightley," said Mr. Woodhouse. "There should be plenty of light for safe travel, provided we do not stay too long. We must not stay over long in any case. Mrs. Woodhouse needs her rest. Perry says that adequate rest is vital."

"How you do fuss, Mr. Woodhouse!" scolded his wife. "I promise to rest before *and* afterward. Will that do? Now,

George, do tell us more about your lady. Who are her people and from where does she come? Oh, and I must know how you met and where the proposal took place. This is the most excitement our little community has seen in years!"

It would have been a pleasure to me to speak of Julia in any case, but to one who I knew held my concerns close to her heart, it was an utter joy. I could have happily gone on for an hour or more, I suppose, and no doubt Mrs. Woodhouse would have been ready to listen to it all. But after twenty minutes or so, I felt I really must return to Donwell before I was much missed. "Until tomorrow," I said while taking leave of my friends. "Do bring Miss Taylor too, if the girls can spare her."

I found the ladies at breakfast and joined them. After greetings had been exchanged, I told them, "I have good news. I have been about securing our guests for dinner tomorrow."

"So it is only Papa we do not know about," added Julia. "I do hope he will be here in time."

"He will no doubt come as soon as he is able, Julia," said Mrs. Stibbley. "Whether it will be tomorrow or the next day, I cannot guess."

"What do you say to a tour of the gardens after breakfast, ladies?" I asked. "Before it gets too hot? I think it is likely to be a very warm day."

Mrs. Stibbley declined, as I had hoped she would, for I naturally craved some time alone with Julia. Besides, certain things her mother had said the day before had rubbed me the wrong way, so to speak.

Julia and I covered some of the same ground again as we walked and talked together, and I was reassured that she did not share all her mother's views. She was not put off by Donwell's out-of-date furnishings or other supposed deficiencies. She was not particularly worried about the confined society of its rural situation. She said she thought she could learn to love living in the country again, so long as she had her music, and provided we could go into town now and again to visit friends, to attend the theatre, and an occasional ball.

"Yes, of course," I said. "I do so want you to be happy, Julia."

She looked up at me with love in her eyes and simply said, "I am sure I shall be, George."

We shared a chaste kiss and moved forward again. "I know it may not be as gay as town here, but you will not be bored. There will be much to occupy you. The house could use *some* improvements; I do not dispute that fact. You will need to organize the staff as you see fit. And then you can spend as much time as you like with your music."

"I will wish to revitalize the gardens as well," she suggested.

"By all means! You can have one or two of the field workers whenever there is less to do on the farm, or perhaps we will need to consider hiring a gardener, at least temporarily. What improvements do you have in mind?"

"Oh, I would not change very much, not at first. The general design seems pleasing enough, just a little overgrown. Once things have been cut back and tidied and I have studied the result for a while, then I will reevaluate. One thing could be started right away, however."

"You have only to name it."

"I would definitely like to make more of the river – restoring the view of it from the house to start, and then creating a gently curving gravel walk from here down to the bank," she said gesturing with her hand. "And perhaps we could build some kind of summerhouse or gazebo there as well. It would provide a destination and a reason to linger by the water, which would be so pleasant in the summer."

"An inspired idea, Julia," I enthused, and she looked pleased. "I can picture it now."

And I could. Not only the gravel path down to the stream, but walking it myself with this beautiful creature on my arm, whiling away an hour or two with her in that future gazebo, sitting side by side, watching the flowing water and listening to its splash and burble, going so far as to imagine Julia expecting our first child before bringing myself back to the present.

"With your touch, Julia, I know Donwell will soon be restored to its glory," I said, briefly turning my mind back to the days when my parents both lived, and when Miles was still with us – before my uncle Spencer came to spoil it all. Thoughts of those dark days I kept to myself, and I soon dismissed from my mind. They had no bearing on our current situation and should not be allowed to poison our happiness. Someday, after Julia and I had been married for a time, I would tell her the whole painful story. But not now.

It was much more pleasant to dream of the days ahead than dwell on what was behind me, and the coming years looked very rosy. With this bright angel by my side, anything seemed possible. We continued to stroll along the garden path with the birds singing and the sun at our backs, happily making plans for the future, blithely fashioning our castles in the air.

The trouble with castles in the air, however, is that there is no substance to them. They can so easily dissolve into mist and blow away with the first contrary breeze.

-25-
Dinner Party

Mr. Stibbley did not come the next day, which in hindsight I took as a great blessing, for it meant that Julia and I had one last day of felicity – one final day to enjoy each other with our dreams for the future still intact.

Had he come sooner, I am convinced the dinner with our friends would have been spoilt. As it was, however, it came off very well. Julia and I played the host and hostess, giving our first party as a couple, or so it seemed. What pride and delight I took in introducing her to the Bateses, who arrived first, and then to Mr. and Mrs. Woodhouse along with Miss Taylor.

Julia behaved very prettily, I thought, as we shared general conversation in the drawing room before dinner. To my eye at least, she was everything that was graceful, charming, and amiable. Likewise, everybody was vastly kind to her and to her mama. I had never doubted that it would be so, that they should all like each other exceedingly.

Mrs. Hodges outdid herself with the dinner. Even Mrs. Stibbley was forced to admit that she had rarely consumed a finer meal. It was perhaps a mistake to have seated my future mother-in-law so near to Miss Bates, however. Better that I should have given her the parents instead of the voluble daughter for a dinner companion. From my position, I could not hear much of their conversation, but I caught Mrs. Stibbley more than once looking askance at that lady as she ran on and on.

At my end, however, I had Mr. and Mrs. Woodhouse carrying on very well with Julia. Although Mr. Woodhouse had not at first been of the opinion that my marrying early would be a good thing, his natural tenderness towards the female sex, when met with Julia's sweetness, could not but leave him fully converted to the idea. And there was never any doubt of our having Mrs. Woodhouse's approbation. She was such an accomplished conversationalist, gently encouraging Julia, that it was a pleasure to be of that cozy enclave.

At the proper time, Mrs. Stibbley caught her daughter's eye and gave her a meaningful nod, whereupon Julia stood, saying, "Ladies?" to signal their traditional withdrawal. But that left only the three of us men – myself, Mr. Bates, and Mr. Woodhouse – staring at one another across the table. Since none of us smoked or were particularly interested in strong drink, we followed to the drawing room mere minutes later.

I arrived in time, to see Mrs. Stibbley vacate her seat. She beckoned to me in a stage whisper that everybody could hear perfectly well. "Mr. Knightley," she said, "do come and take my place beside Miss Bates. I believe I have enjoyed her company and copious conversation nearly as long as I can bear to. I very much fear one of my sick headaches coming on. You understand."

That was badly done, I thought. But my focus that moment could not be on Mrs. Stibbley's abysmal manners; I was all concern for our good Miss Bates, whom I had known all my life, that she should not feel the slight too much.

"With the greatest pleasure," I said, ignoring all but the first part of Mrs. Stibbley's ungenerous speech and directing my warmest smile at Hetty, who looked a little shaken. "What would you say to a little music?" I asked her.

"Oh, yes, do let us have some music," she answered me cheerfully. "I need not ask if Miss Stibbley is musical, for her reputation precedes her. I have heard… I forget now who told me first. Mrs. Parker perhaps, or maybe it was Miss Catkins, or you may have mentioned it yourself, Mr. Knightley, when you came to the parsonage to give invitation. But I suppose that is neither here nor there. In any case, the whole village seems to be talking about what a superior performer Miss Stibbley is. I myself never learnt to play, as you know, but I dearly love to listen to others. Do you suppose she would oblige us? Miss Stibbley, I mean? Or is it asking too much on so short an acquaintance. I would not discomfit her for the world, you know. I should be the last to demand anything of her so soon, since I have nothing to contribute myself."

"Never fear, Miss Bates," I said, patting her hand. "Miss Stibbley is very accustomed to performing. I cannot imagine a small assembly such as this can hold any terrors for her." I turned to Julia, who was a few feet away sitting beside Miss Taylor. "Would you mind, my dear?" I asked.

"Not at all," she answered, "but perhaps one of the other ladies would care to go first. Miss Taylor, would you?"

It was very considerate of Julia, for nobody would choose to follow a far superior musician if it could be helped.

Miss Taylor did consent to play and sing for us, and so she moved to the instrument, which sits in an alcove attached to the drawing room. She is not a great talent but nevertheless her two songs were very pleasing to hear. She had certainly mastered the musical arts well enough to teach the fundamentals to children, which I knew she had been doing for Isabella and Emma since coming to Hartfield. She had told me once that Isabella was accomplishing something worthwhile through steady application, but Emma could never be taught to sit still long enough, at least not yet. That I could well imagine.

With a little encouragement, Mrs. Woodhouse agreed to follow with a brief, humorous song, perfectly suited to her lilting voice. Everybody laughed and applauded her efforts as well, which gave great entertainment.

Then it was Julia's turn. She began with something very fast moving – Mozart, from The Marriage of Figaro – followed by a Bach largo and two other pieces unfamiliar to me, to which she added her voice.

Words fail me for how to describe her performance or my attendant feelings of pride and joy in hearing her, in watching what I believed then to be the first of many such occasions, when Julia, as my wife, would delight our friends with her musical talent. She appeared in all her glory, there at the center of everybody's adoring attention, in her best looks and sound, and I was very nearly in raptures throughout.

Finally, though, when she admitted to being a little tired, we had to be content to let her quit the instrument. Then after much praise of Julia's performance, we all subsided into general conversation for another hour before our guests began to be ready to depart.

Mrs. Woodhouse took me aside for a moment for some private parting words. "You have found yourself a true treasure, George!" she said, brimming with enthusiasm. "I cannot tell you how much I like her already and how I look forward to becoming better acquainted with her in the months and years to come. I am so very pleased for you both! When is the wedding to be?"

"Soon, I hope. We expect Mr. Stibbley at any moment, and then we shall see, for nothing can go forward until we have his blessing."

"That is a mere formality, I trust. Well, as I say, I could not be more pleased for you both. Good night, dear George."

When everybody had gone, I hoped Mrs. Stibbley might take herself off to bed, leaving Julia alone with me for a little while. I longed to discuss the evening with her, to praise and reassure her of the good impression she had made, and to hear her praise of my friends in return.

Unfortunately, Mrs. Stibbley showed no inclination to leave us on our own, and it was *her* opinion of the evening and of my friends that I heard instead.

"*Well*, Mr. Knightley," she began almost at once, uninvited, "I suppose that was not too bad for a start!"

"What do you mean?" I asked.

"It is much like this house. There is great potential, but some of the outmoded furniture must go!"

"I still have not the pleasure of understanding you, madam. Are you suggesting that my friends are outmoded and not good enough for your daughter?"

"Oh, the Woodhouses are very well, I suppose. A little too countrified for my taste, although I daresay one cannot expect anything much better of rural society. It sounds as if they spend very little time in London, if any, so they lack that town polish. One can always tell. And why they should have thought it fitting to bring their governess with them tonight, I have no idea."

"I specifically invited Miss Taylor to be of the party. She is a gentleman's daughter and perfectly respectable company for anybody."

Mrs. Stibbley carried on as if she had not heard.

"But I had hoped you could produce something better than the Bateses. *He* is not too bad, I suppose, and Mrs. Bates barely said a word. But the daughter!" Here she rolled her eyes in an exaggerated way. "She more than made up for it. I am not sure she ever drew breath, although she must have done. Nobody could talk for three hours straight otherwise."

"Mama," Julia began, "you exaggerate. I thought they were all..."

"I know you would be polite," her mother interrupted. "You are such a dear girl, and you would not wish to say a word against Mr. Knightley's friends. But in marriage, it is as well to be honest going in. You are used to the best society, and your husband should know it. Never mind, though. Just as with the house, a remedy is within reach. Your society can be easily augmented by often having friends from London visiting or going frequently to London yourselves. Surely Mr. Knightley would not begrudge you that. Would you, Mr. Knightley?"

I hardly knew what to say. I could not allow Mrs. Stibbley's statements to go unchallenged, as if I agreed with them. Neither did I wish to create an unpleasant scene. Using milder language and tone than I really felt, I said, "I expect Julia and I will be able to come to a reasonable arrangement between ourselves – some mutually acceptable compromise. I would not see her cut off from friends she values, just as I have no intention of giving up mine."

I looked to Julia for her concurrence.

She smiled at me, saying, "I agree. I think your friends are very pleasant people; I trust you will like mine as well."

There. That was all that needed to be said, all that I needed to know. In the end, I was marrying Julia, not her mother, and I was perfectly willing to compromise for the sake of harmony. I could learn to spend more time in town, if that was necessary to my wife's happiness. We could even host an occasional house party at Donwell, inviting some of her friends. So I foresaw no insurmountable problem in the issue Mrs. Stibbley had raised.

If only that had been the biggest trouble successfully got over, but worse was yet to come. Much worse.

-26-
End of a Dream

How shall I describe the significance of the following day's events? Other than the tragically premature deaths of my parents and my brother Miles, nothing in my life has been more devastating. So much so that I spent years trying to banish the recollections from my mind. I can look back on it calmly enough now, but at the time, the loss of Julia was much like another death in the family. Indeed, as it came to pass, she could not have been more irretrievably gone from me than if she had truly died. And as with the others, I mourned. But one eventually becomes reconciled, and the sting has finally gone.

Mr. Stibbley arrived in the middle of the afternoon, and at first I was glad to see him, for here was the opportunity to re-move the last obstacle to our marriage plans, Julia's and mine. I anticipated convincing him that I was sincerely devoted to and well able to care for his daughter, whom no doubt he cherished as much as I did. He would see that her future home was commodious and hear our plans for improvements. I hoped to find in him a sensible gentleman I could admire, perhaps someone I could even look up to as a father to help fill the place of the one I had lost too soon. I would have been satisfied, however, simply to gain his respect and receive his blessing.

Julia and her mother warmly welcomed Mr. Stibbley just inside the door, and then, smiling and blushing, Julia said, "Papa, this is Mr. George Knightley."

He gave me a stern look, bowed slightly, and said only, "Mr. Knightley."

"Welcome to Donwell, sir," I said in return. "I hope your journey was tolerably comfortable."

"Yes, well, that's as may be," he mumbled. "We have much to discuss, Mr. Knightley, but first I would like to wash and change."

"Of course. Of course!" I said quickly. "You must be fatigued from your travels. Julia, would you care to show your father to his rooms?"

"Certainly," she said. "Come with me, Papa." She led the way upstairs, chattering to him as they went. Harry, who had just brought in Mr. Stibbley's luggage from his carriage, followed them up.

I watched them go and then turned to Mrs. Stibbley. "Your husband, madam, he did not seem very happy to be here," I said with my first niggling of concern.

She fluttered and fussed. "Oh, well, it is just his way, I suppose. Mr. Stibbley is not given to outward shows of good humor, though he can be just as agreeable as any other man. And then one must make some allowance for how far he has travelled." She laughed nervously. "I daresay there is nothing more to it than that."

I was not entirely reassured, however, especially when Julia returned downstairs. She came to my side, her brow furrowed. "Papa seems sadly out of spirits," she reported. "He sent me away, saying he was tired. But perhaps he will be revived by some rest and then one of Mrs. Hodges fine dinners."

"Yes, let us hope so," I agreed.

It did seem to be the case. At dinner, Mr. Stibbley was more animated, talking mostly to his wife and daughter about commonplace things – their acquaintances and the news from home. It was difficult for me to have much share in such a conversation – of people and places I knew nothing about – but I asked an occasional question and received civil replies.

Toward the end of the meal, Mrs. Stibbley asked her husband, "Did you stop last night in London, my dear? From what you wrote in your last letter, we had expected you by yesterday. In fact, we had nearly counted on it, for Mr. Knightley gave a small dinner party in our honor and had hoped you would arrive in time."

Ignoring the rest, he answered the first. "Yes, I spent last night in town, and the two nights prior. I found I had more business there than I expected. Hence, the delay."

"Well, I suppose it does not much matter," she continued. "You will meet the Woodhouses some other time. They are, I gather, the only family in this area worth knowing."

"Yes, perhaps another time," he said, letting the matter drop.

When everybody had finished, Mr. Stibbley motioned to his wife, saying, "You and Julia run along now. I want a few words with Mr. Knightley."

The ladies were all knowing smiles as they withdrew, no doubt thinking, as I was, that this was the moment for the requisite ritual of asking the father's consent.

When they had gone and the door closed behind them, I began. "Mr. Stibbley, I know you are already aware of my desire to marry your daughter. You should understand that I love Julia most sincerely, sir, and if you grant us permission to wed, I swear to you that you will have no occasion to regret it. I intend to make her a very good husband, to spend the rest of my life making her happy."

"Hmmm," he rumbled deep in his throat and then only silently stared back at me.

I had hoped to receive and affirmative answer at once. "A mere formality." That is what Mrs. Stibbley had told me. And yet the longer the silence held, the more anxious I became. Finally, after what seemed an age, Mr. Stibbley spoke.

"A very fine speech, Mr. Knightley. I will give you that much. And no doubt you are sincere, for I know of no actual harm in you…"

I felt my blood turn to ice, for I knew at once what the next word out of his mouth would be.

"…But, despite all that, I must refuse my permission."

I sat in shocked confusion. "Refuse? But why, sir? I assure you that I am well able to provide a comfortable life for your daughter, and I will treasure her more than my own life."

"That may well be, Mr. Knightley, but there are other considerations. It is my responsibility, as her father, to procure the most advantageous match possible for my only daughter, and the truth is that you do not qualify as such. To put it plainly, sir, Julia deserves better."

I was growing desperate. "I beg to know in what way you find me lacking, Mr. Stibbley. Needless to say, I would do anything possible to improve your opinion of me."

"Save your breath, Mr. Knightley. There is no remedy for a family that is unacceptable. You see, I have had you investigated. *That* was the business which kept me in town. And so I know all about your thieving uncle."

There it was again. I could not believe that I had worked so hard to overcome all the damage Uncle Spencer had done, only to have his specter rise up again, all these years later, threatening to spoil the finest thing that had ever happened to me. Was it fair that something I had no control over should be held against me forever?

"But sir, that was long ago and nothing to do with me. There is not another blemish anywhere on my family history. I can promise you that."

He went on as if having heard nothing I had said. "Besides, I have received another offer for Julia's hand from a man of title and far superior wealth, who spent some time with her while she was still in town. He wrote to me, and I have just come from meeting with him. I am bound to say, Mr. Knightley, that his suit surpasses yours in every respect."

"Every respect, perhaps, except in affection! Does it not matter to you, sir, that your daughter loves *me* and not this other man?"

"She is young and does not yet know her own mind. Though she may protest now, she will obey me. Then one day she will thank me as well, for it has always been her ambition to be a *Lady*, not a mere Missus Somebody-or-other. She has only temporarily forgot." He rose, signaling that the conversation was coming to a close. "I must go to explain matters to my wife and daughter. I am sure you will understand that your presence is not wanted for that. You may make your good-byes in the morning before we depart."

So saying, Mr. Stibbley quit the room.

I remained where I was, held suspended in a state of utter shock. I simply could not believe what had just happened. *It must be a nightmare*, I reasoned, and yet I could not awaken myself from it.

How long I remained in that attitude, I know not. I only know that I was at last roused from my stupor by the sound of Julia wailing. I instantly arose and followed the sound to the drawing room doors, remaining there some minutes, undecided as to what I should do. Barging in where I was not wanted would only alienate Mr. Stibbley further, and in any case, I would never be allowed to hold Julia in my arms to comfort her, as I wished to do.

So I was still standing there when the doors opened and the three Stibbleys emerged.

"Oh, George!" cried Julia, reaching out when she saw me. Our hands touched briefly before her parents escorted her away, one on either side. They disappeared upstairs, not to be seen again that evening.

I was beside myself, wracked by grief and nearly frantic. My reason told me that there must be a solution, if I could only discover in time what it was. When I at last despaired of any chance of affecting a change that night, I went up to my own room. Sleep evaded me, however. I tossed and turned, my agitated mind determined that my body should be likewise restless. I puzzled and puzzled the problem, coming to no very brilliant solutions. Still, I resolved to try Mr. Stibbley again in the morning. Perhaps the ladies might have succeeded in swaying him, at least a little, where I had failed.

In the early morning, long before it was fully light, I must have finally lapsed into an exhausted sleep, waking in alarm a few hours later. Dressing quickly, I then made my way downstairs as soon as possible, only to find that the Stibbleys had been down before me. They had already breakfasted and called for their carriage.

"Mr. Stibbley, please," I began when I found him watching through the window for the approach of his equipage. "For Julia's sake, listen to me, I beg you."

"None of that, Mr. Knightley. A gentleman never begs."

"Then let me appeal to your reason. There must be some way we can resolve this disagreement."

"This is not a debate, young man," he said coldly. "This is my decision to make, and I have made it. I will not change my mind, no matter what you or anybody else may say."

Having heard my voice, Julia came running from the next room and threw herself into my arms, crying and calling my name. "George, oh, George, what a disaster! Cannot we do something? I love you, George, and I do not want to marry Lord Blankenship!"

So Mr. Stibbley's man was Lord Blankenship, whom I had met, but he was much too old for a lively girl like Julia! I could not dwell on that, though. For the moment, I simply held her tight for as long as I was allowed to, whispering assurances of my steadfast love into her ear, promising to continue the fight as long as necessary, and asking her to do the same.

Much too soon, Julia was torn from my arms and put into the carriage by her father. Mrs. Stibbley looked back at me with something like regret in her eyes. Then she shrugged and turned away as well.

I kept my promise to Julia, although I had no way of knowing if she was even aware of that fact. I did not give her up. I kept on fighting, by which I mean that I did the only thing I could, the only thing that I believed had any chance of succeeding with Mr. Stibbley. I wrote him bold but respectful letters dwelling on my financial solvency, the advantages for life and wellbeing of Donwell's situation, my willingness to accommodate Julia's every wish, and the necessity for true affection in marriage. I appealed to his unquestioned fondness for his child and his desire to see her happily settled. Finally, since I knew not what sources Mr. Stibbley had enlisted for his "investigations," I offered interviews with my own solicitor as well as with Mr. Woodhouse, to be sure the man was in possession of the true facts before his decision became final.

I sent some version of this correspondence every week without fail, and yet I never once received a reply, that is until about two months into my campaign, when this brief missive arrived to put an end to my already dwindling hopes:

> *Mr. Knightley –*
>
> *It is just as I told you that day at Donwell. You might have saved your breath then and your ink since, for Julia has obeyed her father, as I knew she would. She has done her duty and married Lord Blankenship. I trust that now you will finally see the pointlessness of further protestations and cease the deluge of letters. What God has joined together, no man dare seek to separate.*
>
> *Mr. Laurence Stibbley, esq.*

I was soon able to independently confirm that it was true; Julia had married Lord Blankenship.

Whether it had been God's will that had joined the two or Mr. Stibbley's, the fact was that Julia now belonged to another man, and I had no business thinking of her for my own wife any longer. Now, there was only one proper expression of my earnest love for her, and that was to pray she would not suffer as I did over the destruction of our plans – or at least that her suffering would be of short duration. I must pray that her husband would be kind to her, and that she would soon become content in her new situation. I suppose I should have also prayed that she could love the man and find a superior happiness with him than what she had enjoyed so briefly with me. But that I could not do, not for some time.

-27-
Parting Words

It seems that calamities often come in multiples, rather than one at a time. It had been true in that earlier period of my life, and it was true again at this juncture.

I shall not attempt to describe my devastation at losing Julia. Looking back, it hardly seems reasonable that I should have suffered so much over a person who had been known to me only a short time, for the loss of the future with her that I had in view for only a matter of weeks. But, as most everybody knows, first love is often a violent affair.

I was still reeling from its effects when a second blow fell. Although it was not primarily my own misfortune, still I felt it very keenly when Mrs. Woodhouse died. It was like losing my mother all over again, for Mrs. Woodhouse had all but adopted me after I had been left bereft of both my parents.

Her time came, and she was brought to bed with her fourth child, but things went horribly wrong somehow. I never was informed of the details. People hardly speak of such things. However, the result was that neither the child nor the mother survived the ordeal.

A great tragedy. I had never known a more gracious and lively woman. Such a treasure to her family! Such a friend to me and to the community. Such a loss to all who knew her.

The only blessing in the case was that Miss Taylor was already established as a much-loved member of the household, so I knew the girls would be well looked after. She would distract and console them. She would be their security and, going forward, fill the place of their mother as satisfactorily as anybody could do. She also effectively functioned as mistress of the house from that day, directing the servants and so forth.

Mr. Woodhouse, of course, was quite incapable himself. He would have had no idea how to go about it in any case, having always left domestic matters entirely to his wife. Moreover, for a long time his grief utterly overwhelmed and consumed him. Between Miss Taylor, myself, and the Bateses, Mr. Woodhouse was never left to suffer alone. But one feels so helpless, so useless at such a time. Good intentions and devotion can only go so far; they cannot fill the place of the missed loved one. I knew that all too well.

Mr. Woodhouse survived but never truly recovered. His grief over his wife's death left him a permanently altered man. Life had dealt him a very harsh blow – a second one, really – and he could never again trust it completely.

Thus began his own slow decline to the dear but sadly diminished man he is today. Year by year, he became more fretful – for himself, his daughters, and others he cared about – worrying more and more over every detail of safety and health. He began to regard any ache or pain as a harbinger of disaster. Rich food was bound to curdle the stomach. A chill draft was sure to bring on an infection of the lungs. A carriage ride beyond the friendly confines of Highbury could not help but meet with accident or highwaymen or both.

Before, he had been the strong one, always there for me when I needed him. Now the roles were reversing. It was my turn to watch over him, to be strong for his sake. That has been my duty and privilege ever since.

I will never forget the final conversation I had with Mrs. Woodhouse – although neither of us had any idea at the time that it was to be our last. It was about a fortnight before her sad demise, and I had only recently learnt of Julia's marriage. Heavy with child by this time, Mrs. Woodhouse nonetheless came to call late one morning, bringing me a gift of some of her special cherry preserves, which she knew I favored. Her presence was the true gift, however. It always made me feel better, if only temporarily.

"I have been thinking, George," she said a few minutes into our quiet conversation in the sunny little parlor, where she liked to sit when she came to Donwell. "Although I was enchanted by Miss Stibbley, there must be some reason you were not supposed to marry her."

"Her father certainly had his reasons. He said I wasn't good enough for her."

"That is not what I mean at all, and you know it. I am speaking of a much higher authority. God must have had a reason for not allowing your marriage to go forward. He does not always give us what we want, of course, but there is always a reason behind it. At least, I believe so. Although it is easy to thank Him for the blessings we receive, we are also to thank Him for the blessings denied for our own good. Perhaps He knew it would not be a happy match in the end. Perhaps He has something else in mind for you, something even better – some*one* even better, at least better for *you*."

"I cannot imagine there could be anybody better than Julia."

"I know you cannot, not now while the wound is still so fresh. In time, though, it may turn out to be so. You may look back and see how the hand of Providence worked for your own good. You must allow it is possible."

While I knew, intellectually, that she was right, emotionally I could not agree. I gave her a weak smile and said nothing.

After a bit, she continued. "I know that I was the one who encouraged you to seek out a wife, but I begin to believe I was very wrong in doing so. You yourself were not so inclined, and you would have been spared a great deal of pain if I had not pressed you to go to London for the season."

"I do not blame you, Mrs. Woodhouse. I could never blame you."

"Thank you, George. You are very good to say so. Still, considering how it has turned out, I wish we had both listened to my husband instead. Remember? It was his opinion that you should not be in a hurry, that you might do better to wait until you were older before marrying, as he did. After all, if Mr. Woodhouse had married at your age, it would have been to somebody else, for I was still in the schoolroom at the time. Perhaps the same is true for you. Perhaps your perfect mate is still too young."

She stopped at this, but I had the distinct impression from the look on her face that she had something more on her mind – something in particular. "What are you trying to say, Mrs. Woodhouse?"

"Very well. I will tell you, although I hardly know if I should. An idea has started in my brain somehow, and I simply cannot get rid of it. It occurs to me that perhaps you were not to marry Miss Stibbley because you are supposed to wait for somebody else." She paused, looking uncomfortable. Then she finished in a rush. "And perhaps that somebody is Isabella. There, I have said it, come what may."

I don't know what I had expected her to say, but not this. Isabella? She was not yet fourteen! It was impossible to consider her in such a light.

"Mrs. Woodhouse, Isabella is little more than a child!"

"She is *now*, but five years hence she will be eighteen – a perfectly respectable age at which a girl might be married. That is exactly my point, you see. She is too young now, but she will not be if you wait a little while. Of course, I freely admit it is only *my* idea, not a prophetic word from God. Still, I cannot help thinking it makes perfect sense, and nothing would please me more than having you for a son-in-law, George. Mr. Woodhouse and I count you as part of our family already, but this would make it official." Her eyes sparkled, telling me that she really was delighted with this inspiration of hers. Also delighted, I suspected, in having successfully shocked me out of my gloomy mindset for a bit.

Before I could formulate a response, she went on. "Though the gap in your ages may seem wide now, it will not always seem so. While a man of four-and-twenty can have nothing to do with a girl of thirteen or fourteen, men of twenty-nine and thirty often marry young ladies a decade or more younger than themselves. You must allow it is true. Why, Mr. Woodhouse is a full sixteen years my senior, and look how well that has turned out!"

I often thought of that conversation over the years, not only because it was the last time I spoke to Mrs. Woodhouse but because of the topic. Once something like that has been said aloud, it is impossible to forget, and it was a good while before I could be in company with Isabella without feeling an awkward flush of consciousness.

After Julia, I had no interest in trying again for a bride. I focused once more on Donwell, time passed, and my heart eventually mended. But no other suitable young lady ever happened to come in my way, and I never made any effort to seek one out.

I hardly know how the rumors got started. Perhaps Mrs. Woodhouse had mentioned her matchmaking scheme to a friend or two before she died, or perhaps the same idea sprang up independently in other minds. Somehow, though, all Highbury began to talk of a future match between Isabella and myself. Granted, it was a natural enough pairing, especially once Isabella had developed into a comely young lady. The eldest son of one principal family being set to marry the eldest daughter of the other would hardly have come as a surprise to anybody.

Soon, it was spoken of as a settled thing, and I began to believe it myself! It was not that I had at some point made a conscious decision to wait for Isabella; I had not. But somehow the years had passed and there we were, in the very situation Mrs. Woodhouse had described; I was still single and her daughter now of a marriageable age.

Doubtless Isabella had heard the gossip too. How she felt about it, though, I had no idea, since I never was so bold as to broach the subject with her. To do so would be tantamount to a proposal, and I judged that neither of us was ready for that. She was still young. If it was meant to be, I reasoned, love would blossom between us at the proper time.

Meanwhile, we would go on as we were: good friends, seeing each other very frequently. Mrs. Woodhouse's death had changed much but not my habit of walking to Hartfield nearly every day. If anything, I felt my friendship and support were needed more than ever, especially by the poor widowed gentleman.

– 28 –

Caring for Donwell

Through the years, through all the highs and lows, the comings and goings of people, the one constant in my life has been Donwell. Land is solid and dependable. It will not die or disappear. Donwell is there every morning when I wake up and still there at night when I close my eyes. It has embraced me when I was lonely, given me purpose when I sorely needed something to do, and responded generously to my efforts. I give to Donwell, and it always gives in return. I am very blessed to be its caretaker. I am also gratified to be in a position to open Donwell's sustaining lands to others.

I have been very fortunate in my tenants, who are and have been, nearly without exception, honest and hardworking. I had some trouble with Mr. Walsh at first. Although the estate records showed he had paid my father his rent in a timely manner, I suppose he decided to put me to the test. No doubt he thought he could bully and browbeat a mere boy – for I was little more when I became master – into taking less. And so his payments were either late or fell short of the amount, occasionally both. This went on for some time as I was over tolerant in the beginning, wanting to keep everybody's goodwill. But when Mr. Walsh failed to pay the whole amount yet again, I knew I had to confront him.

"Mr. Walsh, I need a word with you," I said when I rode over to his farm and found him crossing from the house towards the barn.

"Can't stop now, boy. I have a full day of man's work to do."

I rode ahead a few paces to block his way, and tried again in my most commanding tone. "It is 'Mr. Knightley' to you, Mr. Walsh, and you *will* stop for five minutes and hear what I have to say."

He answered nothing but remained in place, which I hoped meant he was prepared to comply. I dismounted.

Once we were both standing on the same level, I was reminded of what a large man he was – no taller than I, but burley and in his prime. If we had somehow come to blows, no doubt I would have got the worst of it. He put his meaty fists on his hips and sneered at me in defiance. "Hurry up, then," he said. "Get on with it!" he added when I hesitated.

I felt my confidence and resolve ebbing away, that is until I suddenly remembered Mr. Woodhouse and how he had faced down Uncle Spencer. His example gave me the boldness I needed.

"Very well, Mr. Walsh, I will state my business concisely so you may get back to your work, as you are so anxious to do. The problem, as you must know, is that you have become negligent in paying your rents."

Here, he opened his mouth to protest, but I forestalled him, saying quickly, "There is no use arguing with me; the record speaks for itself. The truth is that, like the other tenants, *all* of whom have managed to pay what they owe on time, your harvest was good. I know this for a fact." Here I noticed something else to help make my case. "You must be doing very well for yourself, indeed, for if I am not mistaken, that fine bull I see in the pen across the way is newly purchased."

I paused for his response, but he only hemmed and hawed, shuffling his feet from side to side.

"Now see here, Mr. Walsh," I continued. "I have been exceedingly lenient with you until now, but no more. I shall expect the full amount promptly at the quarter day, including everything you owe from the previous shortfalls. Otherwise, I shall have no choice but to begin looking for new tenants for this farm. I had much rather not, but I will on no account allow you to continue treating me with such disrespect. Do I make myself clear?"

His defiant stare held a few moments longer before he finally dropped his eyes and gave me a begrudging, "Yes, sir, Mr. Knightly."

"Very well, then. I am glad we understand one another. Good day to you." Not waiting for anything in answer, I threw myself up into the saddle and rode away.

Like Mr. Woodhouse had admitted to, I had been quaking on the inside as I delivered my ultimatum. It must not have shown, however, for I had no more trouble with Mr. Walsh.

The other tenants were more pleasant and straightforward. A few even became friends. I tried to copy my father's example: being firm but fair, treating tenants well, expecting the same in return, and making it known that my door was always open to hear their concerns. If a tenant was late with the rent for good reason, I was not a tyrant. I had experienced enough of financial hardships that were not of my own making to sympathize with others caught up by circumstances beyond their control.

That is how I came to my friendship with Mr. Robert Martin – the father first and then the son. The Martins were a fine family of five when I first knew them. They had the large farm between Donwell Abbey proper and the mill on the river. Abby-Mill Farm it is called. So it is an easy walk between us. The Martins had been tenants there as long as I could remember: a middle-aged man, his wife, their son, named after his father, and two daughters. My father had always spoken well of them. The family remains there still, though somewhat changed in its makeup.

Nine or ten years ago, the senior Robert Martin became violently ill and died, by default leaving the farm for his son to manage. The younger Robert Martin, being then only fifteen years of age (a like age to when similar events had overtaken me years earlier), naturally engaged my deepest sympathy. Notwithstanding the disparity of our stations, our situations bore a striking resemblance: early loss of a father, financial woes, and heavy responsibility come too soon. It was well behind me by then, but it still loomed large in my memory.

Grief is no respecter of rank, of course; is a universal experience that crosses over dividing lines into every level of society. So I do not think it would be stating it too strong to say that I understood much of what the young Mr. Martin was suffering. Despite grieving himself, as I had, he could not allow that grief to immobilize him, for he now had the work of two men to do – his own and that even larger portion which he had inherited from his father. In addition, there was his widowed mother and younger siblings depending on him. Yes, these were circumstances I understood very well.

They were all hard-working, from what I observed, but inevitably they fell behind. That is when Robert came to me. I had been half expecting to hear from him, and had been on the point of stopping by Abby-Mill Farm myself on more than one occasion. Farmers are a proud and resourceful sort of people, though, so I hesitated to interfere where I might not be wanted.

I had attended the funeral but had not spoken to any of the family since. So when young Mr. Martin presented himself at my door, I was not very much surprised. I happened to see him coming and was the only one immediately to hand, so I did the expedient thing and let him in myself.

Had he known of it, Mr. Woodhouse would probably have censured me for this break with normal protocol, but I could not see the sense in standing on artificial ceremony, especially when it flew in the face of convenience and common sense. I still cannot. Besides, Donwell was hardly flush with a full complement of servants even then. We had learnt to do with less when times were lean, and we had gone on afterward in much the same manner.

"Good morning, Mr. Martin," I said when I opened the door. "Do come in."

He was clean and tidy, and wearing what was probably his Sunday best. When he saw me, he looked surprised and quickly snatched the cap from his head. "Mr. Knightley, sir," he said with a little hesitation. "I need to speak with you, if it would not trouble you over much."

"No trouble at all. Let us go into my study and you can tell me what is on your mind." We went in, and I sat in what I had finally become accustomed to thinking of *my* chair behind *my* desk. "Please, be seated, Robert," I invited.

"If it's all the same to you, Mr. Knightley, I'll stand."

"As you wish." I waited for him to begin.

He shifted his weight from side to side and back again, apparently gathering his thoughts, and then he plunged in. "You see, Mr. Knightley, it's like this. I was reading my Bible last night – Luke, chapter 14 – and it decided me that I needed to speak to you."

Hardly the opening I had expected, but I nodded, encouraging him to continue.

"There's this part about a king plannin' to go to war against another. But it says a wise king will first consider if he has enough men to prevail in battle, and if not, he will try to negotiate terms of peace instead. That's where I saw myself, Mr. Knightley. It's like I'm in a war, battling with too few men. So I come to ask for terms of peace."

"Very well, Robert, but I'm not sure I quite follow you. We are hardly at war with each other, are we?"

"Oh, no, sir! That story just put me in mind that I needed to explain my situation to you now and ask your advice instead of blundering ahead when I know it's likely I'll fail. You see, without my father, it's been a tough go."

"Yes, I can certainly understand that."

"Ma manages the house right enough, and the girls do the milking and the dairy works and the chickens, but the field-work is all left to me now. You know the farm, Mr. Knightley. It's too much for one man…"

And that man little more than a boy, I was thinking.

"…So as I see it, I must decide whether to leave off farming part of it or hire me some help. Now to my mind, it don't make much sense to have good land I'm paying rent on laying there doing nothing. So my idea is to hire a boy from the village. I was thinking of young Billy Figgins. Do you know him? He is twelve next month. Big for his age, too. And from what I hear, the family could use some extra blunt. If he comes to work for me, it helps me and his family both."

"Sound reasoning, Robert. I like the idea."

"Thank you, sir. The thing is, though – and this is the part I wanted to talk to you about – I will need to start paying him now, but I won't see the results until harvest. That means I might not be able to make up my full rent until then."

"Oh, I see. That is why you have come to negotiate *terms of peace*."

"Yes, sir. I will pay you everything, but I'm asking if you can see your way clear to wait a little."

I remained silent for a minute, not because I was undecided but because I wanted to put as much thought into my answer as his well-considered question deserved.

"First, Robert, I want to compliment you on your business acumen. You are quite right that it makes no sense to leave valuable land lying fallow. It is also forward thinking to understand that often one must invest something now to reap greater rewards later. You have obviously put much thought into the problem and your proposed solution. But what I appreciate most is your honest, forthright dealings – coming to me straightaway. And so yes, Mr. Martin, your plan has my full support. With a young man of sense and integrity at the helm, I know you will make a success of Abbey-Mill and that you will pay me when you can." I stood and shook his hand.

He returned the gesture with enthusiasm and a smile. "Thank you, sir. You can depend on me."

Before he left, I invited him to keep me abreast of how things went on at Abbey-Mill Farm, and I told him I would be glad to talk over any problems or questions that might arise.

Here was somebody worth encouraging. Here was somebody I wanted to see happy and successful.

Robert availed himself of my invitation from time to time. Farm business always began these visits but rarely ended them. It was a pleasure to me to converse on any topic with a young man of such good sense, and over the years I came to count Robert Martin a valued friend.

– 29 –

A Bachelor Still

As I have said before, everybody expected me to marry Isabella, especially when my brief London season ended with me still a bachelor. I had come to expect it too. Since the first seed was planted by Mrs. Woodhouse just before she died, the idea had gradually grown on me until I thought it would be the most natural thing in the world. At twenty, Isabella was fresh and lovely and everything I could reasonably have asked for in a wife.

These general expectations came to nothing, however, for Isabella had other plans.

Perhaps I should have foreseen the outcome as inevitable. John and Isabella were closer in age and had always spent a great deal of time together whenever he was home from school, and then from Oxford. Still, when John came to tell me he intended to apply for Isabella's hand... Well, I must say that I was taken completely off my guard.

John and I were close in some ways and not in others. With the loss of the rest of our family, we had naturally clung to each other from early on. Although because of circumstances, I had been forced to take more of a parental role with him than would normally have been the case between brothers only a handful of years apart in age. The dissimilarity of our temperaments also limited our camaraderie to some degree, I think, and then there was the fact that John was away most of the time. Still, there was nobody else whose welfare was more important to me.

"You cannot be serious, John!" I said when I was enough recovered from the shock of his announcement to speak.

He had set up his practice of law in London after completing his education but had come home for the Easter holidays. "And why not, I should like to know?" he asked, defiantly, jutting his chin out in the way he had always done when attempting to stand up to his older brothers.

"Because Isabella is intended for *me*. You know that."

"Very well, then. Are you planning to propose marriage to her?"

The question drew me up short, and I could not answer at first. "Not this minute," I hedged.

"Then, when?" he demanded. "Next week, next month, next year?"

"I cannot say exactly! When the time is right, I suppose. That should be nothing to you, my dear boy. It is between myself and Isabella."

"Have you spoken to her about it?"

"No, of course not! Not in so many words."

"Then how do you know what her wishes might be? How do you know she would not rather marry me? After all, I am not a 'boy' any longer, no matter what you may say."

"It is understood; that is all. Her mother made the match before she died, and her father... See here, John, I do not need to explain these things to you. You know the facts equally well."

"I know certain plans were made. I know some wished it so. But there has never been anything legally or morally binding. Therefore, the way I see it, there exists no definite impediment to Isabella marrying me instead, if she is agreeable."

"And I suppose you think she will be agreeable, that she is even now pining away in eager hope of your addressing her."

Here he smiled slyly. "I must say that I have good reason to believe she may be."

Yes, he looked very sure of himself. I could no longer doubt that he had received the positive encouragement from the lady required to support such an air of certainty. I felt oddly deflated by this. I think it was that while the probability existed of my marrying Isabella at some point in time, the future had held the prospect of... I can hardly say what, just something more than my current existence.

"Mr. Woodhouse will not like it," I said. "He will not encourage your suit." That was my only solid argument with which to temper John's confidence, and it sounded weak even to me. When did such an impediment ever stand in the way of the boldness engendered by prosperous young love? Mr. Woodhouse was no Mr. Stibbley, after all. Not anymore.

"Mr. Woodhouse? Bah! Mr. Woodhouse would keep Isabella a virtual prisoner at Hartfield all her life, if he could. You know that as well as I do. I would not see her suffer that fate, would you? – to grow old left sitting on the shelf?"

"No, I suppose not," I admitted resignedly. "But it will be a heavy loss to him, poor old gentleman. And we owe him so much. Perhaps you were too young to remember."

"Oh, I remember. You would never let me forget it. But are you proposing that Isabella should be sacrificed to that debt? Are she and I to repay Mr. Woodhouse with our lives, to forfeit our future happiness for something with which we had nothing to do?"

I had no answer to this, and so John, no doubt smelling victory in the air, hurried on.

"And before you feel too sorry for the old gentleman, consider, he will still have Emma. And Miss Taylor too! It is not as if he would be totally abandoned if Isabella goes."

"I suppose you mean to carry her off to London."

"Of course. We must be where I find my source of income. You know that. As the younger son, I am obliged to make my own way in the world."

"You will always have a home at Donwell."

"I thank you, Brother, but I would prefer to provide for my wife and any children myself. And it is only sixteen miles off. Depend on it, we will be visiting Donwell and Hartfield very often."

"You speak as a man with his plans already accomplished."

"To tell you the truth," he said cheerfully, "I see my future very clearly: excellent employment, a charming house in the best part of town, the most amiable wife imaginable, two children – a boy and a girl – three at most, I think."

"A picture of perfect contentment."

"Yes." He looked warily at me. "Now George, old friend, you do not really mean to oppose us, do you? I cannot believe you are in love with Isabella yourself."

I paused, sighed, and then laid my hand on his shoulder. "No, John. If Mr. Woodhouse consents to the match, I will not oppose it."

What else could I do? It was so obviously a *fait accompli*. My pride might suffer from the knowledge that Isabella preferred my brother to myself, but I soon concluded that my heart would not much feel the blow. My attachment to Isabella had never been deep, and it had by this time subsided to a calmness that could not justify violent agonies of any kind. She was my dear friend, and as my sister-in-law, she was sure of remaining ever so.

No, I would be happy for them to have found love and contentment together. I would be happy to have John raise up another generation of Knightleys – something I now doubted I would ever accomplish myself.

My only real reservation was for my old friend Mr. Woodhouse. Although he would not be left without people remaining at home to love and console him, John's argument was faulty. You cannot say to a man who is losing a beloved child, "Oh, you mustn't mind. After all, you still have another to spare." You may as well tell him the same about his two arms or his two legs! I could only hope John would be true to his word and bring his family to visit his father-in-law very often.

And so John got his way. Isabella accepted his proposal, as he had known she would. And Mr. Woodhouse was soon applied to as well. We spoke on the subject on one of my regular visits to Hartfield – the first following his learning of the young couple's intentions – where I found myself in the awkward position of switching sides, obliged to argue the opposite opinion to what I had so recently taken a stand for in my conversation with John.

"What do you think of this sad business with John and Isabella?" Mr. Woodhouse asked immediately. "I think it a very bad notion, and I am sorry they ever thought of it. Poor Isabella! Is she to be carried away from the only home she has ever known? And all the way to London too?"

"She seems perfectly willing."

"We shall never see her again!"

"'Tis only sixteen miles, my dear sir – sixteen miles of very good roads, I might add. The distance will be no impediment at all. They will be visiting here very often. You will see."

"Travel is no trifling matter! Such an undertaking as going sixteen miles and then back again is not to be considered lightly, especially when the weather is inclement. Why, anything may happen! – accident, illness, highwaymen. The possibilities send my mind spinning."

"But consider, sir, these types of misfortunes are very rare. People range safely to and fro every day. It is only because you so infrequently stir from home yourself that it seems such a fearsome undertaking. John is quite used to travelling, though, and you can depend on his knowing how it may be safely managed. As he recently reminded me, he is not a green boy anymore."

A new and surely winning argument occurred to me. "John and Isabella *will* come to visit, I promise you, and with their children, too, in years to come. Think of it, Mr. Woodhouse:

grandchildren. That must be ample compensation for the loss of Isabella's daily company. Should not you like to see little ones about Hartfield again?"

"Oh, dear. I suppose I might, but at what cost? Small children seem to be always carrying with them one kind of sickness or another, and Emma's constitution is not robust."

"Nonsense. Fear for your own safety if you like, Mr. Woodhouse, but not for Emma's. She is strong as an ox and never ill."

"You may scoff, Mr. Knightley, and think me nonsensical. I know that children are to be counted as a blessing from God, but the risk to the mother is something dreadful. That is the worst of it. Mothers so often... Well, you know what I mean, George, and why I cannot help but think of such a calamity. Poor Isabella! I shudder to consider what could happen... happen again. No, I would not see her put at risk of that kind of peril for all the world! I think she should not do it!"

"True, there are risks. Life is full of risks we cannot avoid."

"But that is my point. Do not you see? These are risks that *can* be avoided if Isabella would only stay home and not be married."

"Now, Mr. Woodhouse, you know your Bible; you know that the philosophy you suggest is not God's design. A man is to *leave his father and mother and be joined to his wife*."

"Aha! A *man* is. It does not say that a *woman* is to leave her father and her comfortable home."

I had to laugh. "Mr. Woodhouse, you are too clever for me." Then I leant forward and looked him steadily in the eye. "But what we are really talking about here is Isabella's happiness. She and John love each other and wish to be married, sir. Can you deny them that chance for happiness? Consider your own example. Even knowing that it would not last forever, would you have given up those happy years you had with Mrs. Woodhouse?"

And so Mr. Woodhouse was ultimately persuaded to relent. The wedding took place, and Isabella left Hartfield. Now, years later, Miss Taylor has gone as well, becoming Mrs. Weston. There is only Emma left. Emma, now a grown woman of twenty, is Mr. Woodhouse's whole world. I doubt he would survive her leaving too.

I could not do it to him, not that there is any reason to suppose she would wish to remove to Donwell as my wife. To Emma, I am just an old friend, almost a brother. She thinks only of Frank Churchill.

Part Three

~~~

The Present Day

–30 –
A Friend Ever Dearer

I have put off thinking about Emma for as long as I can. But since I have now transcribed all the significant events of my past, I can delay confronting the current dilemma no longer.

While she was only a child in my recollections, it was easy enough to sidestep the conflict Emma now poses in my mind, for she was just a minor character at the periphery of my consciousness, the young offspring of my friends and nothing more. The girl I knew then seems like a different person altogether from the woman she is now become.

She no longer represents a minor presence in my life. She will not be kept to the periphery of my consciousness anymore. In truth, it has been some time since that was the case. Ever since Isabella married and removed with John to London, Emma has been advancing to the forefront – both in my notice and at Hartfield. It was she who then claimed the position of mistress of the house. It was she to whom I spoke more and more when I visited Hartfield.

Although there had never been a romantic thought about her cross my mind until recently, I could not have denied that I looked forward to seeing her at Hartfield nearly every day. Unlike most people of my acquaintance, she challenged me, and I never knew what to expect. She was impertinent and funny and difficult and charming all at once. She was a friend who grew ever dearer to me, a person who had at some point without my knowing it become absolutely essential to my happiness. A day without a word and a smile from Emma seemed sadly lackluster.

Although my musings have now brought me nearly to the present, I cannot help relating one more incident from days gone by – one of my strong, earlier recollections of Emma – because it served to establish the manner in which Emma and I related to each other ever after, how we got into the habit of saying whatever we like to each other.

Emma must have been twelve at the time – on the very cusp of adolescence – and I had been trying to correct some bad behavior on her part. What she had done on that particular occasion, I do not even recall, for she seemed always to be straying into error of one kind or another. No, "straying" implies accident, whereas Emma's youthful transgressions were usually of a more willful nature. Boundaries had to be tested. Her strength must be proved.

I just remember saying, "As your friend, Emma – and one older and more experienced – it is my duty to correct you when I see you doing wrong."

"Oh, so we are friends now, are we? The way you preach at me sometimes, I might have mistaken you for a rector."

"I have one thing in common with Mr. Bates, Emma – and with your father and Miss Taylor as well. We all care for the development of your character. We all care that you should learn to govern your temper and your fancies in order to do what is right. But believe me, I had much rather you gave me no cause to correct you. Then indeed, I could simply be your friend."

"I see. Well, although I cannot at present guarantee the first, I will help you with the second. If we are to be friends, and as you already call me by my given name, I will return the favor by calling you George."

"George?"

"That is your name, I believe."

"Well… yes, of course it is, but you know you should address me as Mr. Knightley," I said mildly. "Even your father does."

"Then why do not you address me as Miss Woodhouse? Or Miss Emma, when my sister is by?"

"That is entirely different, and you know it. You are a still a girl, Emma. A mere child."

"I am nearly thirteen! I shall soon be old enough to dance at balls. And so please do address me as Miss Woodhouse, George."

"Emma!" cried Miss Taylor, coming into the room. "Apologize to Mr. Knightley at once."

"So sorry," she said in an affected way and with a roll of the eyes. "Please do forgive me, George."

"Now you are simply being impertinent," I returned, trying to hide my amusement. "I cannot speak to you when you are like this."

"As you wish. Since we obviously cannot yet be friends, I may as well leave you. Good day, George!" And she gaily skipped from the room.

When I was sure she had gone, I laughed aloud and I turned to Miss Taylor, who stood with her arms crossed. "Cannot you do anything with the girl?" I asked.

"I try, but you know her disposition, Mr. Knightley."

"Yes, I do. She is entirely too full of herself. Always has been."

"One can hardly blame her. With all her faults, she is an excellent creature – so very bright and lively."

"The trouble is, she knows it," I grumbled.

"Soon she will be pretty too, I'm afraid."

"That may be, for she indeed has the look of it, so much like her mother. We must sincerely hope she does not add vanity of person to her list of conceits."

Miss Taylor shook her head and gave a little laugh of chagrin. "I used to think what a good governess I was, when I had only dear, tractable Isabella in my charge, for she always did everything I said. She has the gentle spirit of her father. But Emma…"

"Yes, 'But Emma!' That is the beginning of every sentence. '*But Emma*, you should not say such things.' '*But Emma*, please do as you were told.' '*But Emma*, why cannot you be more like your sister?'"

"For all of that, I do love her so, and I must admit to admiring her indomitable spirit too, much as it vexes me at times."

I sighed. "There is a great deal of truth in what you say, Miss Taylor, though I hate to admit it. I suppose we would not like Emma so well as we do if she were nothing more than a mere copy of her sister. She has the wit and vivacity of her mother, but she has not yet learnt to rein in her self-will. I fear what will become of her if she never does. And her father is no help, of course, for he can never find any fault in her."

"Do not worry, Mr. Knightley," Miss Taylor said with a more cheerful tone. "Between the two of us, we will see her right, and her own good sense, you know, will ultimately assist us. I believe Emma will turn out very well."

Miss Taylor and I enacted many versions of this same conversation over the coming years, often failing to see eye to eye. Though I held Miss Taylor in terms of warm friendship, even esteem, I could not help feeling her judgement sometimes faulty where Emma was concerned, her unqualified affection for the girl interfering with her otherwise good sense.

~~*~~

Not many months ago, in fact, we two again exchanged words on that same favorite subject – Emma – specifically Emma's new and questionable friendship with Harriet Smith. Whilst I considered it a bad thing, not likely to do either of them any good, the new Mrs. Weston argued the opposite point of view.

"Mr. Weston would undoubtedly support me," she said. "We were speaking of it only yesterday, and agreeing how fortunate it was for Emma, that there should be such a girl in Highbury for her to associate with. Mr. Knightley, I shall not allow you to be a fair judge in this case. You are so much used to live alone, that you do not know the value of a companion…"

Here, she was wrong. I was *accustomed* to living alone, yes, but that did not mean I liked it. A week never went by – a day, really – when I did not miss my brother Miles and wish him back again. But this I could not say.

"…and perhaps no man can be a good judge of the comfort a woman feels in the society of one of her own sex, after being used to it all her life. I can imagine your objection to Harriet Smith. She is not the superior young woman which Emma's friend ought to be."

On this much we could agree, although I stated it more decidedly. "I think her the very worst sort of companion that Emma could possibly have! She knows nothing herself, and looks upon Emma as knowing everything. Her ignorance is hourly flattery. How can Emma imagine she has anything to learn herself, while Harriet is presenting such a delightful example of inferiority?"

"I either depend more upon Emma's good sense than you do, or I am more anxious for her present comfort, for I cannot lament the acquaintance. How well she looked last night!"

I recognized a favorite diversionary tactic. "Oh, you would rather talk of her person than her mind, would you? Very well; I shall not attempt to deny Emma's being pretty. I confess that I have seldom seen a face or figure more pleasing to me than hers. But I am a partial old friend."

Even this would not satisfy Mrs. Weston. She must go on to extol the superiority of every feature: eye, countenance, complexion, height, bloom, and air. "She is loveliness itself, Mr. Knightley. Is she not?"

"I have not a fault to find with her person," I conceded. "I think her all you describe. I love to look at her; and I will add this praise, that I do not think her personally vain. Considering how very handsome she is, she appears to be little occupied with it. Her vanity lies another way. Mrs. Weston, I am not to be talked out of my dislike of her intimacy with Harriet Smith, or my dread of its doing them both harm."

"And I, Mr. Knightley, am equally stout in my confidence of its not doing either of them any injury. With all dear Emma's little faults and mischiefs, she is an excellent creature. Where shall we see a better daughter, a kinder sister, or a truer friend? No, no; she has qualities which may be trusted. I am convinced she will never lead anyone really wrong. She will make no lasting blunder. Where Emma errs once, she is in the right a hundred times."

I could only hope Mrs. Weston was correct. "Very well," I said resignedly. "I will not plague you anymore. Emma shall be an angel, and I will keep my spleen to myself."

I did truly judge Emma's mismatched friendship a bad thing, and I would argue that the evidence since has been on my side of the question, at least as to doing Miss Smith a disservice. She might have been happily married to my good friend Robert Martin by now, had it not been for Emma's well-intentioned but misguided interference.

Then it seemed that Mr. Elton, the handsome young rector of the parish, who had taken the place vacated by old Mr. Bates upon his death, was soon admitted as a third to Emma's and Miss Smith's intimacy. He was very often to be found with them, I noticed, especially once the scheme of Emma's painting Harriet's portrait was proposed. Emma told me of it herself when I called at Hartfield one evening.

"Can you guess what I have been working at today, Mr. Knightley?" she teasingly asked, coming into the room after I had been speaking to her father for several minutes.

"Have you truly been working at something, Emma?" I asked. "I cannot guess, for I have not the least notion what it might be. I daresay you would not call it 'work' to be reading or walking or talking with your friend Miss Smith, or engaging in any of your other usual occupations. Was Miss Smith indeed with you again today?"

"She was, and without her I could not have achieved anything at all." Again, there was that spark of mischief in her eye.

"Now I *am* intrigued, but I still cannot guess. Work that required Miss Smith's help? You see, there I am entirely at a loss."

"Not her help exactly, but at least her presence. Does not that give you a clue?" She paused only a moment before going on. "Very well, Mr. Knightley, if you will not guess, I suppose I shall have to tell you. I have been working at painting a portrait of Miss Smith. Now, what do you say to that?"

"I admit that I am surprised. Dear Emma, I thought you had quite given up portraiture."

"Yes, I did forswear ever drawing anybody again, but then I could not help thinking how charming a subject Harriet would make. And Mr. Elton so particularly encouraged us both that we relented. It will be a whole-length in watercolors and is already well underway. We three worked at it very happily together for the better part of the day, Harriet posing, I painting, and Mr. Elton reading to us. You cannot imagine how well we got on."

"Mr. Elton? I am amazed he could spare you so much time from his duties. He has been coming to Hartfield very often, I think."

"Perhaps he has," Emma agreed with a sly smile. "I think he must be very devoted to his parish visits... and especially to visiting Papa, of course."

Here, Mr. Woodhouse joined in. "Oh, yes! It is just as Emma says. I miss my old friend Mr. Bates, but Mr. Elton is a very pleasant young man, and so solicitous of my health and wellbeing – mine and Emma's both. Whenever he comes, he is sure to ask us each more than once how we do. And then, you know, he always has something very pretty to say in response. A very pleasant young man indeed. One can find no fault in him."

That was debatable. According to my observations, Mr. Elton was a rather vain, ambitious young man, who would no doubt be glad to connect himself well if he could. So it struck me that it was more likely Emma, and not her father, who was the real object of Mr. Elton's frequent visits. I trusted there was no danger in it, however, for I could not imagine Emma falling for his tactics; they were too obvious.

What surprised me, though, was that Emma would even allow his attentions. I suppose she felt an obligation to be particularly civil to him, as rector, and then perhaps her own vanity could not help but be flattered. I even considered that her penchant for matchmaking might be involved. Did she have in view a union between the cleric and her friend Miss Smith? No, she must see that would never do either.

But I simply said, "How kind of him. May one see the picture?"

"Oh, no, Mr. Knightley!" answered the fair artist. "It is not yet finished. Perhaps if you come again tomorrow it will be, for we three have a definite appointment to continue the work in the morning."

I was indeed admitted to the privilege of viewing the finished painting the next afternoon, along with Mr. Woodhouse, Mrs. Weston, Mr. Elton, and the subject herself: Harriet Smith. I thought it was very well done, especially for Emma's first effort in a long while. Everybody else was pleased with the picture too. In its praise, however, Mr. Elton outdid us all. He was in continual raptures, defending it through every minor criticism offered. He would not allow that Emma had made the subject too tall or enhanced her features in any way.

"I never saw such a resemblance in my life!" he raved. "Oh, it is most admirable! I cannot keep my eyes from it. I never saw such a likeness." And then he insisted on claiming for himself the commission of taking the picture to London to have it framed.

I must say that I was embarrassed by the whole thing – embarrassed for Mr. Elton at making such an unbecoming display, and for Emma at having no choice but to be the object of his fawning attentions. She hardly seemed aware of any excesses, however. She just exchanged smiling looks with Harriet.

I had no notion of it then, but in hindsight, I suppose I should suspect my own motives and prejudices as potentially distorting my judgement in these affairs. Were Mr. Elton's attentions really as excessive as they seemed at the time? Was Harriet Smith really as unworthy a friend as I thought her to be? Or was I unconsciously jealous of the time and attention Emma gave to these others? Jealous of her partiality for her new friends and her dependence upon their flattering opinions? I honestly cannot say.

If it was not true of Mr. Elton or Harriet Smith, however, it would soon be true of somebody else. Two months after this event, Mr. Frank Churchill arrived in Highbury to further upset the status quo. His presence would teach me to know my own mind, for he represented a much greater threat to my place in Emma's heart and life than Harriet Smith ever could.

−31−
Visitor Delayed

I am not always finding fault with Emma. Even when she was young, I hope I was as quick to praise as to correct. As Mrs. Weston argued, Emma has some very excellent qualities. She has a quick mind, ready wit, and general good sense, although in the inexperience of youth, sometimes misapplied. She is very compassionate too. The distresses of the poor are as sure of relief from her personal kindness, counsel, and patience, as from her purse.

And never has there been a more loving and dutiful daughter; of that I am perfectly convinced. Although I have a great fondness for Mr. Woodhouse myself, my attentions to him must pale by comparison to Emma's. As he has grown more withdrawn and infirmed, Emma's gentle forbearances seem to only multiply in compensation. I find this particularly admirable since, in my observation, young people are rarely sympathetic to the foibles of the old. But Mr. Woodhouse's habits and inclinations are always her first consideration, and often have I seen her forego some pleasure of her own for the sake of her father.

I say this not with the blind admiration of a would-be lover but as an impartial observer. And nobody, I think, can dispute its truth.

Me, she does not treat with the same style of respect. Nor indeed should she. I am not so much older as to demand her deference, and as I have related before, we are close friends in the habit of saying what we like to each other, which often leads us into debate, either because of earnest disagreement or as a form of enjoyable entertainment.

One topic upon which we genuinely disagreed from the start, however, was Frank Churchill.

Mr. Frank Churchill is Mr. Weston's son by his first wife, who was raised after her early death by her sister. In honor of his aunt and uncle, and as their heir, Frank took their name. The young gentleman sees his father from time to time in London, but has been promising a visit to Highbury for as long as anybody can remember. That visit was particularly due in consideration of his father's recent marriage – a bride visit to the new Mrs. Weston, formerly Miss Taylor. And still he did not come. One date after another was set for it, only to be cancelled under some pretext or other, most often by the excuse of Mrs. Churchill's poor health.

Much had been made of a letter Mr. Frank Churchill sent from Weymouth to the new Mrs. Weston on the occasion of her marriage. Although not the attention due her, she professed at the time to being very pleased with it herself, and she hesitated not to share it with all those who could be made interested to read it afterward. Again there was the promise of a visit in the offing, and again he did not come.

Emma herself told me of the most recent delay in January, when I walked to Hartfield the evening of the day this latest disappointment was known. "He is not coming," she said flatly without preamble.

"Who? Not Mr. Churchill, I hope. Not again!"

"Yes, I'm afraid so, Mr. Knightley. Mrs. Weston is so *very* disappointed."

"I shouldn't wonder. She has every right to be – disappointed and more."

"And indeed, so am I. So shall all Highbury be, for we are denied the pleasure of looking on a handsome new face, of meeting with somebody who is bound to be agreeable and entertaining in every way. What an addition to our confined society he would be, were he ever allowed to come! Oh, those Churchills! They are to blame, of course, being so disobliging as to not let him go anywhere at all."

"The Churchills *are* very likely in fault," I agreed coolly, not wanting an argument. Then I could not seem to stop myself from adding, "But I daresay he might have come if he truly wished to, for we know he somehow managed to go to Weymouth when he chose."

Emma's eyes flashed. "I do not know why you should say so. He wishes exceedingly to come, as his letters always say, but his uncle and aunt will not spare him."

No doubt my disdain for the young man was perfectly apparent. "I cannot believe he has no power in coming – a man of three- or four-and-twenty with no want of money? He only lacks resolution, for there is one thing, Emma, which a man can always do if he chooses, and that is his duty. It is Frank Churchill's clear duty to pay this attention to his father, and he knows it."

"That is easily said, and easily felt by you, who have always been your own master. You are the worst judge in the world, Mr. Knightley, of the difficulties of dependence. You do not know what it is to have tempers to manage."

I was very happy to tell her exactly how it might be managed and she to tell me why I was completely mistaken. Back and forth we went – me assailing Frank Churchill's character and actions (or inaction, in this case), and she defending him as an amiable young man at every turn.

"You seem determined to think ill of him," she said at last.

"Me!" I retorted. "Not at all. I should be as ready to acknowledge Frank Churchill's merits as any other man's, but I hear of none except that he is well grown, good looking, and has fine manners."

"Well, even if he has nothing else but these things to recommend him, he would be a treasure at Highbury. We do not often look upon fine young men, well-bred and agreeable. Cannot you imagine, Mr. Knightley, what a sensation his coming will produce? There will be but one subject throughout the parishes of Donwell and Highbury, but one interest, one object of curiosity. It will be all Mr. Frank Churchill. We shall think and speak of nobody else."

"I trust you will excuse *me* from being so much overpowered by Mr. Churchill," I said with a healthy dose of sarcasm.

"Very well, I will say no more about him! We are both prejudiced – I for him and you against – and so we have no chance of agreeing till he is really here."

"Prejudiced? I am not prejudiced in the least. Being prejudiced requires some level of deliberation, and Frank Churchill is a person I never think of from one month's end to another!"

She looked a little taken aback at my vehemence and thankfully changed the subject.

I admit I was vexed with Emma for her blind defense of Mr. Churchill – a man she had never met – taking his part over mine, and refusing to even consider the arguments I and common sense put forward. She was not a flighty miss with no brains in her head, who must be excused for not knowing any better, and it distressed me to see her so determined to act as if she were. But perhaps it was pure stubbornness. Once she had taken a stand, no matter how insupportable, she was determined to fight for it to the end.

Was I any better, though? Again in hindsight, I see the situation more clearly. I must admit my own closed-mindedness. I was not the least bit willing to consider that Frank Churchill might turn out the highly admirable young man she represented him. I was not happy to think of everybody, especially Emma, being so overawed by his good looks and charm as to make it impossible to think or speak of anything else. That people should suddenly behave as if there were nobody else in the neighborhood worth looking at or listening to appalled me.

I liked to think my friends and neighbors had more sense than that; I liked to think Emma did as well. Also, I had the prescience to suspect that if and when Mr. Frank Churchill actually made his appearance in Highbury, nothing would ever be the same again. I could not have articulated then why I was certain that would be a bad thing. Some changes are for the better, after all.

Looking back, I am sure I should not have much minded if the whole world were in love with Mr. Churchill, if only there had been one exception. If only Emma had not been caught up in his spell. It was Emma's fascination with him, her seemingly boundless enthusiasm for this man of her imagination, her insistence that the addition of his society was absolutely indispensable to her... This is what truly rankled me, I think.

"We do not often look upon fine young men, well-bred and agreeable."

Only later did it register that she had said this while looking directly at me. Which could mean only one thing, that she did not class me in this category. I was somehow lacking. Was it that she did not consider me fine, well-bred and agreeable? Since I occasionally dared to differ with her, perhaps I could not be considered agreeable. And then there was that the other descriptor I no doubt failed to meet; in her eyes at least, I was far from "young." Either that or I had become invisible altogether because of overfamiliarity. She did not consider me a man, not really, only a friend or an older brother, almost a household fixture that had always been there – comfortable, but easily disregarded when something more interesting came along.

Six months before, I would hardly have minded, but now... Now, of course, I was mortified.

A Suitable Companion

Instead of Frank Churchill arriving in January as promised, another person loosely belonging to Highbury came instead: Miss Jane Fairfax. The orphaned granddaughter of Mrs. Bates (and the niece of Miss Bates), Miss Fairfax is a very genteel young lady who comes to stay with her relations from time to time. And so, unlike with Mr. Churchill, all Highbury has had the good fortune to become acquainted with her over the years since she first went away as a very young child.

Because of the similarity in their ages and stations, I had always expected Emma and Miss Fairfax to form a strong bond of friendship. However, it has never developed. They cannot help civilly meeting, of course, whenever Jane comes to Highbury. Emma knows and does her duty by Jane but never goes much beyond it. Now, especially in light of the issue of Harriet Smith, I could not help hinting to Emma once again at this more appropriate companion. I was determined to be entirely politic in how I did so, though, not implying fault to Emma or belittling Miss Smith – only the benefit to furthering a potentially valuable friendship.

"You are always so gracious, Emma, especially to those less fortunate than yourself. Won't you try again with Miss Fairfax?" I asked when it was known that she had arrived at the Bateses.' "Like your mother, Mrs. Fairfax was a fine woman, and like you, Jane has had the misfortune to grow up without her. That gives you much in common for a start. And soon she is to go out as a governess, you know. That must arouse your compassion."

Rather than addressing my main question, Emma seized on one part of it. "It has always seemed so unfair to me, Mr. Knightley, that you remember my mother much better than *I* do. Tell me again what she was like. You know Papa cannot bear to speak of her."

I was not blind to the fact that this was undoubtedly Emma's way of avoiding the subject of Jane Fairfax, at least for a time. And yet I could not find it in my heart to object, for Emma was right; it was not fair that she should have no more than a few indistinct remembrances of her own mother. Or was that actually a kindness, in that she could not violently miss a treasure she did not remember having once possessed?

In any case, the topic often incited a reoccurring conversation between us, one pleasurable for us both. Emma would ask about her mother, and I would spend the next ten or fifteen minutes talking about old times and trying to conjure up some new anecdote to relate to her. It was not an onerous task, for Mrs. Woodhouse had been one of my favorite people, and I wanted Emma to know what kind of woman had given her life. I saw so much of her mother in her, so much potential, some of it not yet fully realized.

"Very well, Emma," I said. "We shall take a little detour, if you like. Hmm." I thought for a moment. "Did I ever tell you about the time your mother gave me a birthday surprise?"

"No, I am sure you did not. How delightful! Of what age were you then?"

"Much too old for birthday parties, I assure you. However, your mother did not look at it that way. It was my twenty-first birthday, which is an important milestone, of course, and I believe she was concerned that I had nobody to acknowledge it. By then, you see, only John remained of my family, and he was away at school. So without giving a hint as to any particular reason why, your dear mama insisted I come to dinner again, as she so often did. I have told you before that Hartfield has always been a second home to me, especially after my parents and Miles died."

"Yes. No wonder, then, that you are so comfortable here. It was good of Mama not to let you dine alone on your birthday."

"Very good of her, yes, and I was definitely not alone! I arrived to find the three Bateses here as well as your whole family and Miss Taylor. And there wasn't only dinner, but cake and punch and silly songs sung and laughter and games played late into the night. I will never forget it. Nothing could make up for what I had lost, but I certainly could not feel sorry for myself that day, not with such friends at hand. Your mother intuitively knew what I must otherwise feel, and she took compassion on me. But that was always her way – putting herself in the place of the other person and doing what was needed to help."

Emma was silent for a minute, enjoying the picture I had painted for her, I supposed. Then she took me by surprise by saying, "You make me feel quite ashamed of myself, Mr. Knightley."

"What?" I leant forward to touch her hand. "Dearest Emma, I meant to do no such thing!"

"I know you did not. Still, I feel it. I feel that my mother would be thinking now of Miss Fairfax, newly arrived in Highbury after two years away, and wondering what she could do to make sure Jane felt welcomed and appreciated. Do not you think so?"

"Perhaps, but…" I trailed off, not knowing what more to say.

"I will visit Jane at once, Mr. Knightley," she said decisively, rising to her feet, "just as I intended to do tomorrow anyway. But I will also promise to try again to like her better. Perhaps if I am warm, she will drop her reserve a little and we can become friends at last."

"That is very good of you, Emma," I said, proud of her and hoping for the best.

I was gratified to learn, by her own report the following day, that Emma had indeed visited the Bateses. "Jane is certainly more handsome than I remembered her," she said. "Elegant too. In fact, I would say that is the reigning quality of her style of beauty: elegance."

I could not get her to say much beyond at the time, but I soon had the satisfaction of witnessing some of Emma's efforts at an evening party at Hartfield, where I saw only proper behavior and pleasing attentions on each side.

I was again at Hartfield the morning after on business, talking Mr. Woodhouse into what was necessary and getting him to say that he understood what to do. As we put our papers away, Emma joined us.

Wishing to express my approbation to her circumspectly, I began, "A very pleasant evening, last night, Emma. You and Miss Fairfax gave us some excellent music. What a luxury it is to sit at one's ease and be entertained a whole evening by two such accomplished young women."

"One much more accomplished than the other," she added.

"I was equally pleased with you both," I said, determined to keep in a positive vein. "I am sure Miss Fairfax must have found the evening pleasant too. You left nothing undone in your attentions to her, Emma."

"I am happy you approve," she said, smiling gently, "but I hope I am not often deficient in what is due to guests at Hartfield."

"No, never, my dear!" cried her father instantly.

"No," I said nearly at the same time. "You are not often deficient, not in either manner or comprehension. I think you understand me, therefore."

By her arch look, I knew that she did.

"Miss Fairfax is so very reserved," was all she said, however, and we could not then agree if that was to be counted a fault or a virtue.

"I hope everybody had a pleasant evening," Mr. Woodhouse presently said in his quiet way. "I had. Once, I felt the fire rather too much, but then I moved back my chair a little – only a very little – and it did not disturb me again. Miss Bates was very chatty and good-humored, as she always is, though she speaks rather too quick, I think. However, she is very agreeable. And Mrs. Bates too, in a different way. I like old friends best, but Miss Jane Fairfax is a very pretty sort of young lady, a very pretty and well-behaved young lady indeed. She must have found the evening agreeable, Mr. Knightley, because she had Emma with her."

"True, sir," I said, adding with some anxiety and a look in Emma's direction, "and Emma, because she had Miss Fairfax."

Seeming to want to reassure me, Emma said very sincerely, "She is a sort of elegant creature that one cannot keep one's eyes from. I am always watching her to admire. And I do pity her from my heart for her fate."

I was satisfied, and I had just thought of moving on to share a piece of news with my friends when Miss Bates and Miss Fairfax walked into the room.

Miss Bates bubbled over at once with gratitude – to Emma and Mr. Woodhouse for the evening party, and to me for a hind-quarter of pork I had sent over – and then she erupted with the very same news I had intended to give: Mr. Elton was going to marry.

Mr. Elton had gone away for a few weeks at Bath just after Christmas. There, he had apparently procured the favor of a Miss Augusta Hawkins, publishing the news by letter to Mr. Cole, a mutual friend of us all. That is where I had acquired the information an hour and a half before.

This should be great compensation to Emma, I thought. Having been deprived of the anticipated amusement of seeing and talking of Mr. Frank Churchill, what could be better to fill that void than another piece of sensational news? The young rector marrying must be a story that engaged everybody's interest. But somehow, Emma did not seem to enjoy it.

Though Emma did not delight in the news of Mr. Elton's engagement, others did. Certainly the man himself returned to

Highbury very happy, self-satisfied, and eager for everybody's congratulations. And his well-wishers were many. Suddenly, because of his interesting situation, he was more kindly spoken of than ever before, universally proclaimed a very fine young man, as if he had proven himself amiable by convincing this one other person to be his companion for life. He and his prospective bride were the talk of the whole village, as Emma had expected Mr. Churchill to be, and when Mr. Elton again set off for Bath, there was a general expectation that he would not enter Highbury again without bringing his bride.

-33-

A Fine Young Man

Barely had the excitement over Mr. Elton's engagement died away a little when the talk began again about Frank Churchill's coming. Mr. Weston now spoke of it as a certainty. For his and his wife's sake, I hoped it might be true this time.

Then, in February, the young man so long talked of, so high in Emma's interest, was actually among us at last, his stay intended to be a full fortnight. This much I had from Mrs. Hodges when she returned from the shops in the village, where the news was already widely known and spoken of.

When Mr. Weston brought his son by Donwell on purpose to meet me, I happened to be out. I met with no more success when I returned the call at Randalls. And so the next report I had of the young man was the following day, when I went to Hartfield. There I found Emma very ready to speak on that subject and that subject only.

"Papa is taking his exercise," Emma explained with a nod through the window by which she stood in the back drawing room.

I came to stand beside her, my own gaze following hers to find my old friend dutifully pacing the perimeter of the large walled garden. "Ah," I said, then allowed a companionable silence to settle between us for a minute.

"Oh, Mr. Knightley!" she then said, "You must tell me your opinion of Frank Churchill, now that he has come. I have not seen you since then."

"You have the advantage of me, Emma, for I have yet to lay eyes on him. It seems we keep missing each other. So for now you are safe; you may tell me what you think of him without my being able to challenge a word you say."

"Well, then, this *is* a singular opportunity, and yet I think that even *you* will have to admit him to be a fine young man when you meet him."

"Is he handsome and charming enough to satisfy all your ideas, Emma?"

"He certainly is *very* good looking. His height is just what I can like too, and such a well-bred air and ease of address, like one rarely meets with, and a general readiness to talk. He has a great deal of his father's spirit and liveliness in his counten-ance as well; of that, at least, you must approve, Mr. Knightley. I felt at once that I should like him extremely."

"Is that so?" I said noncommittally, turning my attention back to Mr. Woodhouse's progress in the garden. For some reason that I could not at the time quite put my finger on, it pained me to see the eager animation in her face when she spoke of Frank Churchill, the sparkling brightness in her eye. Her enthusiasm for the man before she had seen him could be at least somewhat discounted; now her approbation must be taken more seriously.

I told myself that it was simply a very natural concern – concern that she should not be taken in by this stranger who had come into our midst. Yes, he was Mr. Weston's son, but he had been raised by people about whom we knew almost nothing. On so short an acquaintance, to let one's guard down could be dangerous. Emma was young and relatively naïve, I was afraid. Having been sheltered so thoroughly from the outside world, she did not know what men could be like.

"So where is the young man today?" I presently inquired. "Having got on so splendidly together, I should have expected to find him here at Hartfield again."

Her enthusiasm seemed to fade a bit. "He has gone to town on business," she answered defensively.

"To town? But he has only just arrived. It must have been something quite urgent, I suppose."

"Oh, yes, very urgent, I understand."

I waited, expecting her to tell me more. Her face, at first impassive, soon contorted in a series of mild agonies before she finally broke into an uncontrollable splutter of laughter. "He has gone to get his hair cut," she then confessed.

I was speechless at this. It was so absurd a behavior as I could not deprecate enough, and I knew I should find great difficulty remaining civil if once I got started. So it was better that I should exert myself to say nothing at all except, "Indeed." I then turned from the window and took my usual chair to wait for Mr. Woodhouse's return. Picking up a newspaper that was at hand, I attempted to read, finally relieving my feelings a bit by muttering to myself, "Just the trifling, silly fellow I took him for."

~~*~~

The next time I saw Emma was at the Cole's party. Her carriage followed mine to the door, so I was in the happy position of being available to hand her out.

She smiled warmly at me and said, "I am quite glad to see you, Mr. Knightley."

I was pleased to see her too, of course, especially since I was not sure she would accept the invitation. Doing right must have won out in the internal debate that had no doubt been fought in her mind, for the Coles, although perfectly respectable people, where not on the same social plane.

"This is coming as you should do, like a gentleman," she continued.

"What?" I said, feigning incomprehension, although I knew perfectly well she meant the carriage and horses, which I rarely employed for so short a journey. Indeed, I had only done so on this occasion so that I might send them next to convey the ladies of the Bates household.

"Oh, the carriage, do you mean?" I said. "How lucky that we should arrive at the same moment, for if we had met in the drawing room instead, I doubt whether you would have discerned me to be more of a gentleman than usual tonight. You might not have distinguished how I came by my look or manner alone."

"Oh, yes I should. I am sure that I should," she said playfully, taking my proffered arm. "There is always a look of consciousness about them when people behave in a way they know to be beneath them. I daresay you think you carry it off well, Mr. Knightley, all bravado and an affected air of unconcern, and yet I always know. But now, you see, I shall really be very happy to walk into the house with you."

"Nonsensical girl!" I declared, shaking my head and smiling down at her as we went on in to join our hosts and those guest who had arrived before us.

Emma must have been pleased she had come, that whatever little hesitation of pride she might have felt at first had been surmounted. For she was received with a cordial respect which could not but gratify and given all the consequence she might have wished for. Then when the Westons arrived, all their kindest looks and strongest admiration were for her – all three of them. But I did receive a small share as well.

"Mr. Knightley! At last," said Mr. Weston. "May I present to you my son, Mr. Frank Churchill?"

We bowed to each other and exchanged only the minimum of customary civilities before Mr. Churchill turned his attention to Emma, who was still at my side.

He gave her an appreciative perusal before telling her, "Miss Woodhouse, may I say that you are looking particularly well this evening?"

She was, of course, and I suddenly wished I had thought to mention something along those lines – her hair, her dress, her radiant countenance – before we had come in, before Mr. Churchill could.

"You may, Mr. Churchill," Emma said, giving him an especially dazzling smile. She released herself from my arm and the two strolled off together as of one accord.

"Do not they look well together," said Mr. Weston, glowing with cheerful satisfaction. Instead of waiting for an answer, however, he posed another question. "Well, Mr. Knightley, what do you think of my son, now you have finally met him?"

"My dear," Mrs. Weston cut in. "I know you are proud of Frank, but you should not go about begging everybody's compliments, especially after only a two minute acquaintance."

"That is quite all right, Mrs. Weston," I said. "Mr. Weston and I are old friends. I do not mind telling him that his son seems to be just as I have been told: a very fine young man."

"There, you see, my dear," said the proud father to his wife. "I knew I should hear a sensible opinion from my good friend Mr. Knightley. Frank *is* a very fine young man. Indeed, how could anybody think otherwise?"

I was glad he was satisfied, and I hoped I would not be called upon for anything further. Yes, he was a handsome young man – there was no denying it – but that did not hold much sway with me. And there was something about him that I inherently did not like or trust. I especially did not trust him near Emma.

And yet at Emma's side he remained for most of the evening, maneuvering so well as to arrange to be seated by her in the dining room. Or perhaps that was due to Mr. and Mrs. Weston's good offices, for they seemed always delighted to see the two paired together, I noticed.

It was a rather large party at dinner that night, even without the lesser ladies (Miss Bates, Miss Fairfax, and Miss Smith), who were to come later in the evening. And so it was impossible to hear everything from one end of the table to the other. That is until a tale of particular interest drew everybody in.

Mrs. Cole was telling that she had called earlier on Mrs. and Miss Bates, and as soon as she entered the room had been struck by the sight of a large, very elegant pianoforte. Miss Bates had then explained to her that the instrument had arrived the day before from Broadwood's, entirely unexpected and with no note as to the sender. It was clearly meant as a present for Miss Fairfax, but even she was bewildered by the gift.

Although the story was told with an air of intrigue, everybody soon agreed that the instrument could have come from only one source – from Colonel Campbell, in whose family Jane had been raised as a companion to his daughter. The only wonder was that it should have been given without notice or explanation.

The conversation soon moved on to other topics, except perhaps between Emma and Mr. Churchill. From where I sat, I could hear nothing of what was said between them in low voices, but those two had their heads together in a conspiratorial way for several minutes more afterward.

My surmise – that Mr. Churchill might be more caught up in the mystery of the pianoforte than most – was borne out by what he said immediately after dinner was over and the ladies withdrew. "Well, my dear sirs," he began, "now that it is just between ourselves, what is your true opinion of this pianoforte and of the mysterious donor? Was not it a generous gift?"

As the youngest and the newest to the neighborhood, I was amazed that he should presume to direct the opening of the conversation. That honor should by rights have gone to our host Mr. Cole. Everybody was, of course, too polite to give Mr. Churchill the set down he probably deserved.

Mr. Cole simply said, "Undoubtedly."

"Generous but ill-advised," I added. I would have been content to leave it at that, but Mr. Churchill was not.

"How do you mean, sir?" he challenged at once.

"Just this. I wonder if Colonel Campbell stopped to think of the difficulty it would be to the Bateses to have to make room for such a large article in their very small apartment. And arriving unannounced, as it did, the ladies had no time to even prepare for it. He would have done much better to consult with them first and abide by their wishes, instead of foisting upon them something that must be inconvenient if not downright unwelcome."

"But prior consultation would have removed the element of surprise," objected Mr. Churchill.

"Exactly."

"Have you no romance in your soul, Mr. Knightley? Come now, you must at some point have known the pleasure of being given a surprise."

I thought of Mrs. Woodhouse's birthday surprise for me. Then I thought of Uncle Spencer, and I said gravely, "Unfortunately, Mr. Churchill, most of the surprises in my life have been remarkably *un*pleasant."

"Now, gentlemen," said Mr. Cole in a placating voice..."

Only then did I realize that I had allowed myself to become over warm in my tone.

"...if I may be so bold, I would like to suggest a change of subject. Perhaps we might take this opportunity to discuss parish business for just a few minutes. You will recall that there are one or two items requiring our prompt attention."

Mr. Weston was quick to follow Mr. Cole's lead, and the rest of us just as readily acquiesced, the previous line having proven unproductive. But Mr. Churchill apparently could not interest himself in such a mundane conversation as what followed, for he soon excused himself to rejoin the ladies.

When the after-dinner guests arrived, Miss Smith was admitted to the privilege of meeting Mr. Churchill. The others – Miss Bates and Miss Fairfax – had done so already, I found. As for Mr. Churchill himself, he continued to single Emma out for his particular attentions, although I noticed Miss Fairfax also gained a share.

After tea, these same two ladies were again petitioned to give us some music, this time at the Cole's grand pianoforte. Emma played and sang first, and I was enjoying her performance, at least until Frank Churchill joined her unexpectedly in her song. She stumbled a little from the surprise of it but then happily carried on to the end.

Frank then laughed at his own insolence. "You must forgive me, Miss Woodhouse, for barging in on your performance. But when music moves me, I cannot remain in my seat."

"You are forgiven, sir," she said, smiling at him. "I enjoyed singing with you exceedingly. You have a fine voice, which could only improve my poor song."

"Not at all, Miss Woodhouse! I am the lucky one, that you so graciously allowed my intrusion."

"You will find that Frank's knowledge of music is quite comprehensive," eagerly volunteered Mr. Weston, "as is his taste and appreciation for it."

"This is too much praise, my dear sir," his son disclaimed. "I own to loving music, but as to the rest... Well, though I know little of the matter, I believe I am an indifferent musician myself. If Miss Woodhouse does not think me a disagreeable partner, however," he said turning back to her, "perhaps we could sing another?"

"Gladly," she said, evincing genuine pleasure at the prospect. They decided something between themselves and began.

Emma relinquished the instrument afterward, but there was no getting rid of Frank Churchill. He stayed to sing with Miss Fairfax as well, having apparently done so before at Weymouth. During their second song, I glanced back and noticed Emma sitting off by herself. So I went to join her.

"How well she plays," I said, with a nod in Miss Fairfax's direction. I restrained myself from any comment upon Mr. Churchill's interference. "Do not you think so?"

"Of course. There's no denying she is a superior musician. That is why I was happy to go first. Nobody can follow her."

"As you say."

We were silent for a minute, listening again.

Then she said, "It was kind of you to send your carriage for her and for Miss Bates. I should have thought of it myself, of course. No doubt my mother would have. Is not that just the sort of humane attention she was known for? But you can imagine how impossible my father would deem it, that James should put-to for such a purpose."

"Quite out of the question, yes, but I am sure you must often wish for the power to do such kindnesses." I smiled at this pleasing conviction. I was gratified that Emma could benefit by her mother's example, even though it came to her secondhand.

She then asked my opinion of the surprise gift of the pianoforte, and I answered her much the same way I had Frank Churchill, only calmer – the inconvenience overpowering any pleasure.

I was soon distracted, however, by what was going forward at the instrument. Miss Fairfax's voice began to falter towards the end of her second song with Mr. Churchill, and yet he insisted they should sing a third together. Others called for more as well.

I had heard enough and could restrain my opinion no longer. "That fellow thinks of nothing but showing off his own voice," I muttered and then arrested Miss Bates, who was at that moment passing by me, touching her arm. "Miss Bates," I said, "you must interfere at once or your niece will sing herself hoarse. You see how they have no mercy on her, begging for more than she is able to give." Good woman that she is, Miss Bates stepped forward without delay to rescue her niece.

Before the party broke up, there was a bit of dancing, in which Emma took part and I did not. Then, being late, the carriages were called for and everybody took leave.

Good food, good company, good music: all in all, it was a very rewarding evening... or at least it should have been. Instead of contentment, however, I felt dissatisfied and irritable when I got home to Donwell. Rather than accepting help,

I testily insisted on struggling off with my clothes myself, leaving them in disarray about the dressing room. Then, though I felt bone tired, sleep would not come.

Scenes from the party kept reenacting themselves before my mind's eye – Frank Churchill speaking and laughing conspiratorially with Emma, singing with her, dancing with her... The more I dwelt on these things, the more agitated I became.

Frank was a showoff, a coxcomb, a vain parading peacock. What of it? Had I not suffered fools of his type and worse calmly enough before? Why, then, did this particular fool have the power to discompose me so, when others had not? The answer finally came to me early the following morning.

– 34 –

Admitting the Truth

I must have finally slept, because I woke to find the sun up
and the birds singing. I did not feel rested, however, and
soon remembered why. I had been most unsettled by the
doings at the Coles' party the night before, in particular, Mr.
Frank Churchill's.

Upon closer scrutiny, however, it was not Frank Churchill
himself that disturbed me so much as it was the braggart's very
obvious attentions to Emma. No, that still did not quite go to
the heart of the matter, for his attentions to her could do no
harm if she ignored them. But she did not. She enjoyed and
encouraged them. She had so obviously reveled in them.

Yes, now we had come a bit closer to the truth. I was
worried for Emma; of course I was! I naturally desired to
preserve her from Mr. Churchill's unwholesome influence, for
her own sake and for her father's. Had I not deliberately and
voluntarily taken on some responsibility for doing so when
Mrs. Woodhouse died?

For a moment, I convinced myself that was all this nagging
apprehension was due to. I need look no further. But then I did,
and I heard an accusation – from my conscience or another
teller of deep truth. *You would be just as upset, or nearly so,
no matter who the man was. You know you would. The truth is,
you want to be first in Emma's eyes yourself.*

Initially, I denied it. Had I not told Mrs. Weston only a few
months before that I should like to see Emma in love and in

some doubt of a return? Yes, I had, but now, upon repeat, the very idea seemed like a calamity of epic proportions. Emma in love with some other man? Emma perhaps to marry him? No.

I could deceive myself no longer. Though I had never seen it before, the truth was that I unconsciously thought of keeping Emma to myself. I wanted to be first in her eyes as she had somehow, without my realizing it, become first in mine. The truth was, I was in love with her. I was in love with Emma Woodhouse.

There. I had admitted it. I had not needed to do anything about that unconscious truth before, because nothing threatened it. Nothing threatened my position in Emma's life until Frank Churchill arrived.

Now, however, the danger was real. Emma, who had always said she would never marry... Emma, who seemed permanently affixed at Hartfield and willingly so, was suddenly looking vulnerable. For the first time, she had fallen under the influence of somebody who fascinated her enough to perhaps make her forget all her former convictions, who perhaps had the power to convince her to marry and go away from us all – away from me – into a life of... I could not even envision the rest, and I did not want to, for it was impossible to imagine Emma Woodhouse living anywhere other than Highbury. Emma so far north as Enscombe in Yorkshire? Impossible!

And yet my thinking or saying so did nothing to prevent its actually happening. After all, I had been perfectly ready, years ago, to remove Miss Stibbley from her home in Herefordshire without a qualm. And she had been perfectly willing to come away. (How long since I had thought of that unfortunate episode!) Youthful, passionate love had overruled every other consideration – everything except her formidable father, that is.

There was a father in this case also, of course, although he could hardly be called formidable. Not anymore. And yet, if he could be properly motivated... Nothing, I was sure, would be more likely to rouse Mr. Woodhouse to action than a risk of

Emma's leaving him. It might be worth a try. Mrs. Weston – my usual potential ally where Emma was concerned – would be of no help here, I collected. And so I quickly resolved to go to Hartfield at once, to have a little talk with my old friend.

As to such an action possibly being premature, I soon settled that question. Although I had seen them together only once, over the course of one interminable evening, Emma and Mr. Churchill had been acquainted longer. They had met several times, and their degree of intimacy seemed already well advanced. Here again, I thought of the example of Miss Stibbley and myself. I had been smitten the first time I saw her and thinking of marriage soon afterward. No, it was not too soon to take what prudent measures were available.

Rather than walking to Hartfield, as I usually did, I went on horseback, since I planned to continue on an errand to Kingston afterward. All along my way, I considered what I should say to Mr. Woodhouse. After all, I had only my personal observations and intuition as evidence. Hopefully that would be enough to at least put him on his guard.

It seemed auspicious that I found Mr. Woodhouse alone when I arrived.

"I am sorry that Emma should not be here," he told me. "Not five minutes ago, she left to walk into the village with Miss Smith, who had business at Ford's or some such thing. Did not you see them on your way?"

"No, we must have just missed each other, but no matter. It is really you, sir, I have come to see."

"Ah. Then you may as well come in and be seated," he said. "I have a cozy little fire in the library."

As soon as we were settled, I proceeded in a calm and sober manner to relate to my dear friend my observations from the previous night, since he had not been there to witness these things for himself, and what I feared it would lead to. "I can prove nothing sinister against Mr. Churchill," I said in conclusion. "Not yet, at least. I only mean to put you on your guard by telling you that he exerts an unhealthy degree of influence over your daughter, as well as charming everybody else, it seems. For Emma's sake as well as your own, my dear sir, I urge you to do what you can to keep her out of harm's way. You know what it would mean to your comfort and peace should Mr. Churchill convince Emma to marry him."

Mr. Woodhouse smiled benignly. "Mr. Knightley," he said patiently, "you are a true friend. Indeed, nobody could have been more solicitous for our welfare – Emma's and mine – these many years than you yourself. But I really believe you have taken your solicitude too far in this case. Emma to marry and leave Hartfield? Impossible! She would never do such a thing to me, and I will not accuse her of it. You have let your imagination get the better of you, I think, which is so unlike yourself in general. And as for Mr. Frank Churchill, he seems a perfectly amiable young man to me, although perhaps a little careless of draughts. But he is Mr. Weston's son, you must remember, so I cannot imagine there is any real harm in him. I am sure you must be mistaken."

Further urging did no good. My appeal fell on deaf ears.

I had expected to carry my point on the strength of Mr. Woodhouse's ever-present fears – including his fear of the disruption of his personal comforts – but instead I had run up against another side of his character: his unwillingness to think badly of anybody he knew. Although always objecting to every marriage that was arranged, it seemed Mr. Woodhouse never suffered beforehand from the apprehension of it. And now, he could not be made to think so ill of any person's understanding – much less his own daughter's – as to suppose she meant to marry till it were proved against her. Unfortunately, by then it would be too late.

I left Hartfield discouraged but not entirely downcast. For the moment at least, I had done all I could; I took consolation in that. And as my mother had been fond of saying, "You must leave something for God to do." So I prayed that God would do what was necessary to keep Emma and Mr. Woodhouse safe from harm. That is what I wanted, even over and above the granting of my personal wishes in the case. God's ideas and mine as to what was best did not always align, I had noticed, but I had to continue trusting that His ways were best.

~~*~~

My road from Hartfield to Kingston took me through the village, where Miss Bates espied me from one of the windows of her upstairs apartment. She called out to me. As usual, she had more to say than her words could succinctly communicate. She would thank me again for the carriage the night before, and ask me to come up. In return, I asked after their health and welfare, especially that of Miss Fairfax, and I asked if I might do anything for them in Kingston.

"No, I thank you," she answered. "But do come in. Who do you think is here? Miss Woodhouse and Miss Smith; so kind as to call to hear the new pianoforte. Do leave up your horse at the Crown and come in."

I drew up short at the idea of seeing Emma so soon after admitting to myself the feelings I had for her. I certainly could not avoid seeing her for long, though, not in so confined a society and especially not when my longstanding habits had been exactly contrariwise. Besides, I was just as much in desire as dread to be in her company again, if only I could conceal my inconvenient sentiments. I would not have anybody catch me out gazing at Emma like a moonstruck calf! I would not have *her* suspect me either. There, I believed I was safe, since it would be very far from her mind to envision in me a lover.

I was on the point of agreeing to go in when Miss Bates's added intelligence that Mr. Frank Churchill was present as well changed my mind. Frank Churchill was the last person I wanted to see at that moment, especially in company with Emma. "No, not now, thank you," I said. "I must get on to Kingston as fast as I can. Besides, your room is full. I will call another day and hear the pianoforte."

Although I held fast to my decision, many more words were forthcoming – complimenting the delightful dancing the night before, extending a hearty thanks for the apples I had sent, etc. – before I was finally on my way. With Miss Bates's heart of gratitude, she might have kept me there all afternoon, extolling my "goodness" to the entire neighborhood, but I would not stay to hear it. When I gave gifts out of my abundance, it was in concern for my neighbor, not with the hope of receiving public praise. Shame on me if I did *not* share what I had with those less fortunate.

~~*~~

The fortnight granted by his aunt and uncle was nearly at an end, and so I expected to presently hear of Frank Churchill's imminent departure (and hopefully that he was unlikely to come to Highbury again anytime soon). If he left and did not return, perhaps the harm done to us all would be minimal. Instead, Emma informed me that the young man had requested leave to extend his stay, expressly for the purpose of attending a ball to be given in his honor at the Crown by the Westons.

Evidently, Emma expected to provoke some kind of violent response from me with this news. I could not oblige her. I had little opinion about a ball one way or the other; it was only the prospect of Frank Churchill's staying longer that chafed. "A ball?" I said, unperturbed. "Oh, yes, that will be pleasant for you, Emma."

"Pleasant? I thought you would have more to say on the subject than that!"

"I could tell you more, but I doubt you will like it any better than the answer I have already given you."

"Oh, I see how it is. You have taken offence. Poor Mr. Knightley. Since you were not consulted before about the arrangements, you are now determined to show no interest."

"Believe me, I do not have to pretend indifference when it comes to a ball."

"Though you do not like dancing yourself, you must have something good to say about this famous scheme!"

"Very well, Emma. Since you insist, here is a more comprehensive answer for you. If the Westons think it worthwhile, I have nothing to say against a ball, but that they shall not choose my pleasures for me. Oh, yes! I must be there, of course; I could not refuse. And I will keep as much awake as I can, but truly, I would rather be at home, looking over William Larkins's accounts. It is no pleasure to me to watch other people dancing. Fine dancing, I believe, like virtue, must be its own reward. Those who are standing by are usually thinking of something else entirely."

I was right in supposing this answer would not please her either. Still, I could almost be sorry when I later heard that the ball had been cancelled – sorry indeed for Emma, but not for myself. It seemed Frank Churchill had been summoned back to Enscombe; Mrs. Churchill was unwell again.

"...So you may spend the evening with William Larkins now and be happy," Emma concluded morosely upon delivering this news to me.

Poor thing. She looked so deflated that I could not triumph even a little at her expense. "My dear Emma," I said, leaning forward, "you know I cannot regret it for myself, but do not imagine me so heartless as to rejoice in the disappointment of so many others. I think of you. You have few opportunities of dancing and must feel the loss of this ball exceedingly. You are very sadly out of luck, I am afraid, and I am sorry for that. Truly I am."

The good news was that Frank Churchill had gone... forever, I hoped.

-35-

The Parson Takes a Wife

Everybody was agog to see Mrs. Elton when she arrived with her new husband in Highbury. She was declared, as all brides are allowed to be, charming, handsome, accomplished, and very smartly dressed. Upon making her acquaintance myself, I could detect nothing remarkable in the former Miss Hawkins, and I heard of nothing superior to a fortune of ten thousand pounds that could have recommended her to any man of sense. Therefore, my opinion of Mr. Elton did not improve by his choice, but I sincerely wished them both very happy.

Emma, when I had occasion to hear her opinion, was more outspoken in her disapprobation.

"An insufferable woman!" she pronounced Mrs. Elton to be. "I could not have believed it. A little upstart, vulgar creature, with her 'Mr. E' and her *'caro sposo',* and all her airs of pert pretension and underbred finery. You will be pleased and flattered, I'm sure, Mr. Knightley, to learn that she discovered you to be a gentleman. I am certain that relieves your mind. And Mrs. Weston! Mrs. Elton was astonished that the person who had brought me up should be such a lady! I could hardly keep my countenance. To think, we shall be forced to meet with her everywhere we go from now on!"

"Perhaps not. After she has been here a while, she will naturally form friends at her own level, and then you will not see her over much."

"Oh! If that is what you think, Mr. Knightley, you completely mistake the matter. Mrs. Elton imagines I *am* of her level – and you too, I daresay – or she is of ours! You should have heard her talk on and on about how much Hartfield resembles Maple Grove, her brother's seat, putting us on an equal footing in her mind. And she is already speaking in terms of 'we,' as if she and I were bosom friends! – how *we* should unite to form a musical club, how *we* must set the example for others to follow, how we should unite our efforts to bring *poor Jane Fairfax* forward.

"Oh, I know you might agree with that idea, Mr. Knightley, but really, even Miss Fairfax does not deserve to be pitied and patronized by such a person as Mrs. Elton! '*We* have carriages to convey her, and *we* live in a style which could not make the addition of Jane Fairfax the least inconvenient.' You see how she has already insinuated herself into our lives? We shall never be rid of her now."

I allowed Emma to carry on in this way as long as she wanted (or needed). Better that she should say these things to me, where they could do no harm, than to have them burst forth somewhere less appropriate. Though I secretly agreed with her about nearly everything, I did not wish to add fuel to the fire. Instead, I only nodded occasionally to show I was listening and murmured my understanding of her feelings. I knew she would soon have done and feel better for having got all her ill temper out of her system.

However, some of the same refrain came forward again from Emma when Mrs. Weston happened to be also with us a different day – in particular, the wonder that Miss Fairfax seemed to willingly accept the Eltons' attentions – walking, sitting, and spending time with them apparently of her own volition.

"We cannot suppose that she has any great enjoyment at the vicarage, my dear Emma," said Mrs. Weston, "but it must be better than being always at home. Her aunt is a good creature, but, as a constant companion, must be very tiresome. We must consider what Miss Fairfax quits before we condemn her taste for what she goes to."

To this sentiment, I felt compelled to add something myself for Emma to consider. "You are right, Mrs. Weston," I said warmly. "Miss Fairfax is as capable as any of us of forming a just opinion of Mrs. Elton. Could she have had her choice of companions, she would not have chosen her. But she receives attentions from Mrs. Elton, which nobody else pays her."

Emma understood my thinly veiled reproach. She colored and presently replied, "Such attentions as Mrs. Elton's, I should have imagined, would rather disgust than gratify Miss Fairfax."

Mrs. Weston quickly moved the conversation on from this sore point, saying, "I shouldn't wonder if Miss Fairfax were to have been drawn on beyond her own inclination by her aunt's eagerness. Poor Miss Bates may very likely have committed her niece and hurried her into a greater appearance of intimacy with the Eltons than Jane's own good sense would have dictated, in spite of the very natural wish of a little change of society."

Both ladies looked to me for my opinion, so I added one more thought. "We must also take into consideration that Mrs. Elton likely does not talk *to* Miss Fairfax in the same way she talks *of* her to others. One may suppose that Miss Fairfax awes Mrs. Elton by her superiority of mind and manner, and that, face to face, Mrs. Elton treats her with all the respect which she has a claim to."

"I know how highly *you* think of Jane Fairfax," said Emma in such a way as to give me the idea she meant more by it than was at first apparent.

"It is no secret," I said, warily, suspecting what lay ahead and hoping I was wrong. "Anybody may know how highly I think of her." I immediately busied myself with the buttons of my leather gaiters, affecting to appear nonchalant.

Emma hesitated a moment and then plunged ahead. "And yet, perhaps you may hardly be aware yourself how high it is.

The extent of your admiration may take you by surprise some day or other."

Although agitated within, I answered her calmly enough, "Oh, you are arrived there, are you? But you are miserably behindhand, Emma. Mr. Cole told me of the same suspicion weeks ago. That will never be, however, I can assure you. I daresay Miss Fairfax would not have me if I asked her, and I am very sure I shall never ask her."

It pained me that Emma should be so ready to see me married to somebody else. Clearly she suffered no worries over losing my time and attention as I did hers.

"Is that what you want, Emma?" I asked for clarity's sake. "You have been settling that I should marry Jane Fairfax?"

"No indeed!" she said at once. "You have scolded me too much for match-making for me to presume to take such a liberty with *you*. Upon my word, I have not the smallest wish for your marrying Jane Fairfax or anybody. You could not sit with us in this comfortable way if you were married."

I rolled this statement over in my mind a little. Perhaps my company held some value to Emma after all. "Jane Fairfax is a very charming young woman," I said presently, "but even she has a fault. She has not the open temper which a man would wish for in a wife. I told Mr. Cole he was mistaken; he begged my pardon and said no more. I will tell you the same, Emma. I admire Miss Fairfax, but I have no thought beyond. And now, I hope, there is an end to it."

Regardless of their true opinions of Mrs. Elton, the inmates of Highbury all seemed very ready to pay her and her husband the marked attentions due upon their marriage. Invitations flowed in so rapidly that Mrs. Elton soon had the pleasure of apprehending they were never to have a disengaged day.

"I see how it is," she said to those collected outside the church after divine services one Sunday. "I see what a life I am to lead among you. Upon my word, we shall be absolutely dissipated. We really seem quite the fashion. If this is living in the country, it is not very formidable. A woman with fewer resources than I have need not be at a loss."

Emma knew she could do no less than others, and so a dinner for the Eltons at Hartfield there must be. I was pleased to hear that Jane Fairfax was to be included on the guest list, along with the Westons, the Eltons and myself. A little variation took place when the day arrived, however. Mr. Weston was unexpectedly called to London on business, and my brother John just as unexpectedly arrived from there, bringing his two young sons with him.

Poor Miss Fairfax. After what occurred at the dinner, being invited may have seemed no treat for her in the end. Mrs. Elton's proprietary attitude towards her, her officious interference, was nearly beyond bearing. The woman seemed to feel she had a right to tell her supposed protégé if she might go to the post office for her own letters or not, and to whom she should contract herself out as a governess. There was quite a to-do on the former over dinner and the latter among the ladies afterward, according to Emma's information.

Just as the whole party was reassembled in the drawing room, Mr. Weston was finally able to join us, his mood more cheerful than one might expect after travelling so far. It seems he had in his possession news to share of a nature he believed would be as universally pleasing to others as it was to himself. His son Frank Churchill was returning to Highbury.

At his announcement, I could not help turning to regard Emma's reception of the news. But if it excited a flutter of joyful agitation within her breast, she hid it well. She seemed rather more contemplative than openly celebratory. Needless to say, I did not feel like celebrating the news either.

The topic did give a fresh subject for conversation, however, especially since Mrs. Elton had never met the young man. The whole history of his life and his current situation must be canvassed for her benefit, with opinions given on his looks, manners, and character. Yet her ignorance of the subject was no bar to Mrs. Elton; she must have her share of the conversation regardless.

"Enscombe one hundred and ninety miles north of London? That is sixty-five miles farther than Maple Grove. But what is distance to people of large fortune? You would be amazed to hear how my brother, Mr. Suckling, flies about! Twice in one week he and Mr. Bragge went to London and back again with four horses."

"The evil of the distance," explained Mr. Weston, "is Mrs. Churchill's delicate health. As we understand it, she sometimes has not been able to leave the sofa for a week together, much less travel."

"Oh! But if she is really ill, why not go to Bath?"

And then she was off on another of her favorite topics, dispensing advice according to her vast experience and expertise.

Later, when the Westons sat down to cards with Mr. Woodhouse and Mr. Elton, the remaining five of us were left to our own powers – powers insufficient for the occasion it appeared.

I was little disposed for conversation by then, feeling ridiculously sulky over the news of Frank Churchill's imminent return. Mrs. Elton looked to be wanting more continual attention than anybody was prepared to pay her. Jane Fairfax was always reserved, of course, and even Emma seemed a little subdued. Thank heaven my brother was in a talkative mood.

"Well, Emma, it is good of you to agree to entertain my boys for a few days."

"It will be my pleasure, I'm sure," she said.

"You have your sister's letter, which no doubt gives instructions from A to Z of what is to be done with them. I will only add my more concise request that you not spoil them too much."

"I rather hope to satisfy you both," said Emma, "for I shall do all in my power to make them happy, which will be enough for Isabella, I daresay. And happiness does not come from false indulgence."

"Very well, but if you find them troublesome, you must send them home again," continued John.

"You think that likely, do you?"

"I hope I am aware that Henry and John may be too noisy for your father, and perhaps they may be an encumbrance to you at a time when your engagements must be increasing. If they begin to weary you, I only beg you to send them home, as I said before."

"No," I protested, "there can be no need for that. When Emma is too busy, let the boys be sent to me at Donwell. They are my nephews too, and I shall certainly be at my leisure."

"Upon my word," exclaimed Emma, "you do amuse me, the pair of you! I should like to know how many of all my numerous engagements take place without your being of the party, Mr. Knightley; and why I am to be supposed in danger of wanting leisure to attend to my dear little boys. These amazing engagements of mine – what have they been? Dining once with the Coles and having a ball talked of, which never took place. If Aunt Emma has not time for her nephews, I do not think they would fare much better with Uncle George, who is absent about five hours to my one, and who when home is either reading to himself or settling his accounts."

I tried not to smile at this – first, at Emma's very rare use of my Christian name and second, at her bundling our names together as aunt and uncle to John and Isabella's children. For so we were already, and it would be doubly true if we ever were to marry.

-36-

Seen in a New Light

That night, I had an inspiration built upon some of the conversation at the dinner party at Hartfield. I would set aside my other plans to accomplish two things at once: to claim a little more time with Emma before Mr. Churchill's return, and to simultaneously do my share for contributing to the care and entertainment of our visiting nephews. I would rise early, and if the weather were even reasonably fine, I would propose a little outing.

April could be so changeable, but the sky was blue when I awakened. That was all the encouragement I needed. I asked Mrs. Hodges to assemble a cold collation into a basket while I saw to the horses and carriage. Normally I would have taken the gig and driven myself, if I had wanted a carriage of any kind, but I had something different in mind for the day. So in the stables I pressed into service Webster, who was one of Donwell's former workers that I had been able to hire again after Uncle Spencer's leaving. He would drive and tend the horses, leaving me free to give my full attention to my guests. I only hoped Emma had not made other plans.

When the carriage pulled up at Hartfield's front door, I sprang out and rang the bell.

The butler's eyes popped wide when he opened to find me standing there. "Mr. Knightley!" he said in amazement.

"Yes, yes, I know, Pinkerton," I said in answer to his unspoken question. "When is the last time I ever came to the front door rather than letting myself in from the garden? I shouldn't wonder at your surprise, but would you tell Miss Woodhouse that I am here nonetheless?"

"Certainly, sir," he said, still looking perplexed. "Would you care to... Would you care to wait in the drawing room, sir?"

"Of course," I said, feeling a bit awkward also, to be so formal in a house I knew as well as my own. It was part of the point I was trying to make, though. This was a different kind of occasion, and I wanted Emma to notice it. I wanted her to see me more in the light of a gentleman caller than a member of the family to be taken for granted.

She did notice at once that something was unusual.

"Mr. Knightley?" she said in puzzlement when she came in a few minutes later. "What can you mean by coming in all this state this morning?"

"I have come to propose an outing for you and the boys. My carriage is here and Webster to drive it."

"A carriage and horses?"

"Yes, and I have a picnic in a basket and fishing gear for Henry and John. Won't you take a drive with me, Emma? No Harriet Smith today?"

"No, not with the boys here."

"Ah, so then you are at liberty, if you would care to come."

"Yes, I suppose I am, and it sounds delightful, although I am still a bit overwhelmed. What a surprise you have given me, Mr. Knightley."

I could not help being pleased to hear it. "So you will come?"

"Yes, certainly. Only give me a few minutes to collect my wits and get the boys organized."

"Excellent. The carriage is open. Still, there will be room for your maid, if you believe it more proper."

"In an open carriage with your man and our nephews to chaperone? I hardly think it necessary, Mr. Knightley! We are practically brother and sister, after all." With that cheerful sally, she turned to leave the room, adding over her shoulder, "I won't be twenty minutes!"

I was delighted by her approbation. Everything was going as I had hoped – well, except for that "brother and sister" remark – and I was too excited to sit idle and wait. So I wandered to the back of the house to find my old friend for a short chat.

"Fishing?" Mr. Woodhouse exclaimed when I had related my plan. "But Henry and John do not have any idea how to catch a fish. They have been raised in town, you know."

"Then it is high time they learnt! Do not you agree, Mr. Woodhouse? No boy should grow up without the chance to cast a line and feel the thrill of landing a fine trout to be cooked for his supper."

"I daresay they do not know how to swim, Mr. Knightley, and neither does Emma. Oh, dear."

"Now, sir, before you allow your fears to run away with you, consider. You know that Emma will not go near the water herself. And do you think I will permit either of those dear boys out of my sight for one second?"

"No, I suppose not."

"Quite right. I am an excellent swimmer myself, if it should come to that. Plus the piece of water I have in mind is shallow and quiet. I believe either of the boys might walk with his head and shoulders above the surface all the way to the other side."

"Oh, dear, I think that had better not be attempted, Mr. Knightley."

"Certainly not. Rest assured, Mr. Woodhouse. I do not expect anybody to get so much as a boot wet."

At this point, Henry came running into the room followed closely by his brother. They whooped and hollered with delight, throwing themselves at me and attacking me with questions. "Are we really going to learn how to catch fish, Uncle George?" That was the gist of it, over and over again.

"I am sorry, Mr. Knightley," said Emma, coming in as well. "Once they learnt of your plan, I could not hold them back for anything."

She had changed into a pink walking dress, which looked very becoming I noticed amid the confusion and noise. "'Tis no trouble to me, Emma," I said, laughing and fending my nephews off as well as I might. "I am delighted by their enthusiasm. But let us be on our way, children, so that we do not disturb your grandpapa with our noise, shall we?"

I did not have to ask them twice. They raced for the door and were energetically exploring the carriage interior, Webster in nervous attendance, by the time Emma and I could catch them up. "Now do sit down like gentlemen. There," I told them firmly, pointing to the backward-facing seat. I waited until they had settled before helping Emma in and following myself.

We set off at once, Emma and I sitting side by side facing forward. As for Henry and John, they spent very little time sitting properly at all. They were bouncing to test the springs, or turning to look ahead and pester Webster with questions. *Where are we going? How long till we get there? Will there be very many fish to catch, do you suppose? Who do you think will catch most, me or John? Me, of course, for I am older. Do not you think so?*

"This is quite unlike you, Mr. Knightley," said Emma, while the boys were thus occupied. "Being so spontaneous, I mean."

"I disagree."

She looked her skepticism.

"Well, I suppose I do generally think and plan ahead; I will not apologize for that. My experience in life has required me to do so. But sometimes, like today, Emma, I am struck by an inspiration that must be put into action at once. And if I have taken you by surprise, so much the better. After all, it would be a shame if we knew each other so well that there were no surprises left between us. Do not you think so?"

"That is true enough. I enjoy surprises – pleasant ones, at least. I simply have not yet learnt to expect them from you."

I smiled. "If you expected them, then they wouldn't be surprises, would they?"

We both laughed.

"I suppose not," she admitted.

"Now, I will promise you this. If you enjoy today, I will contrive to produce other pleasant surprises for you in future. How will that be?"

This is as much as we had time for before the boys claimed our attention again. But Emma was smiling at me, and that was enough.

~~*~~

When we arrived, I made the boys sit still until I had given them careful instruction about how we would proceed. I told them there would be no mad dash for the water. There would be reasonable calm and following instructions, or it would be back in the carriage to head for home again.

"Yes, Uncle George," they said when I asked if they understood and agreed to this.

I helped Emma to alight, and only then were Henry and John allowed to get down.

"The ground is quite uneven, Emma," I said. "Do take my arm." And she did so.

"What a pretty spot!" she said as we approached the gentle bank of the river. "Oh, but I see we are not the first to find it today."

She was right. A well-dressed man seemed to be preparing to leave as we arrived. He tipped his cap to me, saying, "Good morning."

I returned the salutation and asked, "Had you any luck, sir?"

"Good luck indeed, but I believe I left some fish for you and your family too."

I smiled and said, "I thank you kindly."

"That man took us for your wife and children," said Emma after he was out of hearing.

"I daresay he did," I answered, and I left it at that. However, the thought went a long way towards creating a very pleasant picture in my mind, towards feeding my unfounded dreams for Emma and myself.

"Now, if you have everything you need for your comfort, Emma," I said presently, "I will get the boys started before their short supply of patience is quite run though."

Webster had brought the things from the carriage to a flat spot under a tree, which I had indicated to him. From there, Emma could have a close view of our aspiring little fishermen.

"Perhaps I should like to try my hand as well," Emma said.

This time, it was she who had surprised *me*. "Should you?" I asked. "Truly?"

"Why not?"

"No reason that I can think of, only never tell your father or he shall eat me alive!"

So I had three eager students to instruct in the art of persuading a fish to take the bait. As it happened, Emma was the first to land one – a fine brown trout. She was practically giddy with excitement as she held high the wriggling fish on her line, that is until I told her what was to come next.

"Well done, Emma! If you are to be a true fisherman, though – fisherwoman, rather – you have more work to do."

She looked at me questioningly.

"Catching the thing is only the first step," I explained. "You must naturally kill it and clean out the entrails, so that you can later eat it."

She looked at me askance. "But I do not even like trout! Please, cannot we put it back instead?"

I laughed. "As you wish." Taking the fish in hand to remove the hook, I said, "You, sir, are a very lucky trout. Miss Woodhouse refuses to eat you, and so back into the water you go. Take care, though, that you do not fall victim to one of these other anglers. They may not be so compassionate." I let the trout swim from my hands, and in a moment he had disappeared.

"Care to try for another?" I asked Emma, ready to bait her line again. "If you succeed, I promise to let that one go as well."

"No!" she said quickly. "No, thank you, Mr. Knightley. Now that I have discovered that I can do it, I am satisfied. I will leave it to you and the boys from here. I shall just sit and read my book, if it is all the same to you."

"By all means. I do applaud you for being so game in the first place, though. Not one girl in a dozen would have even attempted it."

Despite being bested by their aunt, the boys continued at it, undaunted, with only periodic help from me. This left me free to keep watch from beside Emma much of the time.

"You have made yourself more of a hero than ever to our nephews this day," said Emma during one of these pleasant intervals. "Their talk will be nothing but Uncle George and fishing for days, I declare. I only hope your brother will not mind your being such a favorite with them."

"An uncle – or an aunt – may spoil a child from time to time, but it is their parents whom they truly love. Nobody can usurp their place in the child's affections." It was a serious reflection, since I was wondering if I should ever know the other side of this equation, if I should ever find myself in the role of the parent instead of the doting uncle. From how she answered, I had the idea that Emma understood.

"No doubt you are correct, Mr. Knightley. You must remember, though, that there are some advantages to being only the aunt or uncle. One only takes on the work and weight of responsibility for a short time. Then one may give it all back to its rightful owner. I cannot imagine myself in my sister's place. Five children! Still…"

At that moment, little John began to holler, "I've got one, Uncle George! I think I've got one! What shall I do?"

I sprang to my feet to assist him.

When Henry and John had caught two trout apiece, we stopped to consume our picnic. Then, while discussing the question of if there was to be any more fishing that day or not, the changeable weather intervened to answer. I heard a distant rumbling and checked the sky, which I then saw had turned ominously dark.

"Pardon me, Mr. Knightley," said Webster, hurrying towards us. "Storms 'a coming. I've put the top up on the carriage, but you might want to start for home as soon as may be."

"Of course," I said, instantly acceding to the wisdom of his advice. "Emma, take the boys and go to the carriage at once. Webster and I will collect these things and be with you presently."

We worked quickly, but not quickly enough to altogether avoid the rain that soon began to fall. Fortunately, Emma and the boys were dry when I joined them. Little John, afraid of thunder, was huddled tight against his aunt's side, and so I sat down my damp self next to Henry.

"A shame about the rain," Emma said as we started off for home. "It was such a lovely day when we set out, and we were all having such a fine time. Thank you, Mr. Knightley."

"My pleasure, Emma," said I.

I felt a surge of warmth between us that tempted me to go on – to tell her that this could be just the beginning of many, many other days of a similar nature. I wished this day to prefigure for her our possible future together, our future family, what it could be. But it was likely that only *I* had that kind of thought in mind, only *I* indulged dreams of that sort. Though, by all appearances, she enjoyed the day with me as well, Emma's mind would probably soon move on to the superior felicity of anticipating Frank Churchill's return.

-37-
Shall We Dance?

The first issue of Frank Churchill's return – his now being fixed as near as Richmond with his adoptive parents – was that the scheme for Mr. Weston's ball was immediately revived. And with it were revived all Emma's joy and anticipation for it. How much was due to the thought of dancing with Mr. Churchill and how much to the pleasure of the ball itself, I could not judge.

"You *will* be there?" Emma questioned me.

"I said I would before, and nothing has changed except the date. So, yes, I will be there, but I will not dance."

"Oh, sometimes you make me so angry, Mr. Knightley! I shall hate to see you among the standers-by, classed with the husbands and fathers and whist players. You do not belong there, as if you were a tired, old man. You belong among the dancers, for you have a grace and energy that would perfectly suit the activity. If you would but try, I am sure you would enjoy it."

I could not tell her the truth – that I *had* once enjoyed dancing, very much, in fact. I had danced and danced with Julia Stibbley during our whirlwind courtship. But the joy of it had expired along with our ill-fated engagement, and I'd not danced in the many years since. Not once. I had made no vow or conscious decision against it, as if in judgement or compliment to Julia. I suppose that, afterwards, dancing was inherently bound up in my mind with courtship and being in love, hazards which I instinctively guarded against for my own protection.

It was gratifying, however, to hear that Emma did not think the exercise beyond my capabilities, that she ranked me more with the active young men than with the stodgy old fellows standing by. Nevertheless, when the night arrived, I stationed myself off to the side, where I could observe without being in the way. There was only one lady with whom I could have had any interest in dancing, and she obviously preferred another.

Everybody was there, of course, except Mr. Woodhouse, who almost never strayed from his own home and hearth in the evening. I noticed at once that Mr. Churchill was already at Emma's side, even before the music began. Then they were joined by Mr. and Mrs. Weston for a brief but busy little conference, their four heads together over something of mutual interest. Although I could hear no more than a word or two, I could guess by what happened next that it was about the realization that Mrs. Elton must be asked to begin the ball, and perhaps the question of who should be her partner.

For Emma to stand second, especially to a Mrs. Elton, must have been a blow indeed. At least she retained her preferred partner for the first two dances, however, since the young man's father undertook the task of escorting Mrs. Elton to the floor.

The dancing began and everybody was happy. Thanks to the careful attentions of Mrs. Weston, not a detail had been overlooked, and the ball was a great success from the start. There even seemed enough willing partners so that no young lady who wished to dance was forced to sit down instead. This was lucky for me; I could stand by with a clear conscience knowing I was not needed.

So, whilst everybody else was enjoying the evening, I tortured myself by following Emma and Mr. Churchill's progress down the room and back with my eyes. To spend half an hour or more together watching Emma gracefully move to the music – for she was undeniably an elegant dancer – should have been in every way a delight to me. That she must have a partner, and that her partner must be Frank Churchill… There was the rub.

They moved well together, I had to admit, and their great pleasure in each other's company was clear for all to see. They laughed and smiled nearly through the whole of their time together. I could find nothing to censure, however – certainly not in the lady, but not in the gentleman either. I discerned no leering looks or improper touches, no hands holding too long or heads bent too near each other. If I had hoped to find fault with Emma's partner, I failed.

"Do not they look well together, Mr. Knightley?" asked a lady at my elbow. "Miss Woodhouse and Mr. Churchill, I mean?"

Roused from my silent glowering, I looked to find it was Mrs. Crabtree. "Oh, yes," I answered as civilly as I could. "They might have been made for each other," I added with a sarcasm that I hoped she hadn't heard. That seemed to satisfy my companion, and we both returned our attention to the dancers.

Passing near me, Emma twice caught my eye, easily drawing a smile from me, despite everything. I could not be put out with her. After all, she was only behaving as any young lady of her age must be expected to behave at the first ball she has attended in many months. I had no wish to spoil it for her by my own sullen mood.

The ball proceeded pleasantly enough, and I relaxed a little when Emma was at last forced to move on to dance with somebody besides Frank Churchill. Then, shortly before the supper break, I noticed a change in Emma's countenance, which was now no longer wreathed in smiles. Following the direction of her eye, I soon discovered the trouble: her very particular friend, Harriet Smith, was sitting down in want of a partner, the only lady disengaged. Something had taken place to upset the perfect balance that had so happily existed before.

Mr. Elton, who had been dancing enthusiastically until this time, had for some reason withdrawn. One gentleman standing out naturally resulted in one lady with no partner.

Granted, it is no crime for one who is tired to take some time to rest from his exertions. However, Mr. Elton did not look the least bit fatigued. He was using his liberty to speak cheerfully and strut himself about the room. He had my full attention now, and I saw him more than once glance at Miss Smith with a smug expression, clearly enjoying her discomfort and knowing he had the credit of it himself. The snub was deliberate, then, although at the time I could not think why he should have done it.

When he came by Mrs. Weston, I was near enough to hear what passed between them. She suggested he might be so good as to dance with Miss Smith, but he flatly refused.

"You must excuse me, Mrs. Weston," he said. "I am an old married man, and my dancing days are over." This from the man whom we had all seen carrying on most enthusiastically only ten minutes before.

Not the actions of a gentleman.

Mr. Elton's pointed snub had not escaped Miss Smith's notice either. She looked mortified and miserable. Immediately, I knew I had to do something – to redeem my sex, to rescue Emma's friend, to make up for her ill treatment at the hands of one who had decided to be cruel. A clergyman, of all people, should have behaved better.

Mr. Elton tried to waylay me, but I had no time for him; I cut him as short as I decently could and made a path to Miss Smith's side without delay. She took my offered hand, and I led her into the set.

Then and only then did I question acting so hastily. I had followed good principles but with little forethought, and now I would see if it had been a great mistake. Would I remember the dance steps after the intervening years of inactivity? Or would I make a hash of it, exposing Miss Smith to more embarrassment than if I had left her where she was.

I believe I moved a little wrong once or twice, but the steps came back to me with surprising ease. And looking across at Miss Smith, I knew I had done the right thing. She could not have appeared happier. Emma confirmed it for me. When I passed her in the set, her eyes conveyed her gratitude, warming my heart and making my slight sacrifice entirely worthwhile.

Following our two dances together, I took Miss Smith through to the supper, where we had an enjoyable conversation. Harriet was certainly no prodigy, but she surprised me by having more common sense and proper feeling than I had credited her with heretofore. I began to understand what Robert Martin had seen in her and to sympathize more sincerely with his loss.

In the pauses, I turned my mind to the question of why Mr. Elton had snubbed Miss Smith, remembering a fleeting suspicion I'd had months before, when he and Emma and Miss Smith had been so inseparable. Could tonight's unpleasantness be the latterly consequences of Emma's matchmaking efforts at the time? That was my passing thought.

I had no opportunity to speak to Emma until after the supper was over. Then I saw her off to one side by herself, watching me – waiting for me, it seemed. Her eyes invited me to come and be thanked.

"Mr. Knightley, how good you are!" she said at once when we had taken each other's hands in greeting. "You continue to surprise me. Not wanting to dance at all and yet doing so for poor Harriet's sake!"

"It was no great sacrifice, and I did it as much for you as for Miss Smith. I saw how distressed you were."

"I thank you again and again."

"Say no more about it, Emma. Mr. Elton's unpardonable rudeness was reason enough for me to act, and my guess is that Mrs. Elton is not innocent in this matter either. It seems to me they aimed at wounding more than Harriet. But what I do not understand is why. What has made them your enemies when so recently Mrs. Elton courted your friendship?" I waited but received no answer. "*She* ought not to be angry with you, whatever cause *he* may have. Now confess, Emma. You did want him to marry Harriet."

She sighed. "I did, and they cannot forgive me. I was fully convinced of Mr. Elton's being in love with Harriet, but it was... It was something else altogether. I have made one blunder after another, it seems. He must have only recently told his wife about the affair, and now they both despise me."

A thought occurred to me, which might serve to lighten the atmosphere. "Perhaps you may not need to worry, after all, about how to fend off Mrs. Elton's overfamiliarity. She may no longer want you as her bosom friend."

She gave a wry smile. "That is some comfort, I suppose, but otherwise I must own myself to have been completely mistaken in Mr. Elton. There is a littleness about him, which you discovered and I did not."

"And in return for your acknowledging so much, I will do you the justice to say that you would have chosen for him better than he has chosen for himself. Harriet Smith has some first-rate qualities. An unpretending, artless girl is infinitely to be preferred by any man of sense and taste to such a woman as Mrs. Elton. Your friend surprised me, Emma. I found Harriet far more conversable than I expected."

Emma smiled her gratitude.

The chance of any further conversation was then interrupted by Mr. Weston calling on everybody to begin dancing again. "Come, Miss Woodhouse. Come, Miss Otway, Miss Fairfax. What are you all doing? Everybody is lazy! Everybody is asleep! Emma, do set your companions the example."

"I am ready whenever I am wanted," said Emma.

"Whom are you going to dance with?" I said before I could stop myself. I held my breath while she looked at me steadily a moment. Then she replied as I had dared to hope she would.

"With you, if you will ask me."

"Will you, Emma?" I said, offering her my hand.

"Indeed I will. You have shown that you can dance, as I always suspected. And you know we are not really so much brother and sister as to make it at all improper."

"Brother and sister! No, indeed!"

What I felt when I led her to the floor may be imagined. To have Emma so near, her hands in mine, to have her moving in and out of my arms through the dance, to have her concentrated attention focused on myself and myself alone for those many minutes together... My thoughts and impressions were too rich and complex for words. It was joy, longing, love, pride... and nothing brotherly about it.

For what she felt, I could only use my powers of observation. This is what I know: she looked at me very steadily throughout – with affection, certainly, and with something else in her eye I could not decipher. It seemed like an unspoken question or possibly confusion. Only in my most wildly optimistic musings did I afterwards consider that it might signify a dawning realization that there had been a fundamental shift in our relationship. Brother and sister? No, indeed.

–38 –

Jealousy and Duplicity

W hatever optimistic visions had been conjured up by my dancing with Emma that night were quickly overthrown. It had no doubt been only the stirring music. Or perhaps it had been the quixotic setting. More likely it had been my own wishful thinking that had produced the stars I had imagined seeing in Emma's eyes.

Things soon reverted to normal, or at least what passed for normal since Mr. Weston's son had come to Highbury. Frank Churchill was still talked of everywhere. He was still constantly seen in Emma's company. Her mind was still full of *him*. When I would visit Hartfield, I would see Emma but I would hear nothing except Frank Churchill.

"Did I tell you what Frank Churchill did the other day?" she would say to me, or, "Frank Churchill said the most amusing thing when he was here this morning."

Then I had to hear, over and over again from everybody of my acquaintance, how the man had rescued Harriet Smith from the gypsies. Frank Churchill, the coxcomb, had been bad enough; Frank Churchill, the celebrated hero, was more than I could bear.

I freely admit that it was a raging case of jealousy at work, exaggerating my honest dislike for the man into something ugly and unreasonable. Had Emma not been in the case, surely I could have ignored or tolerated him a good deal better. But I do not think it was jealousy, prejudice, or my imagination either when I recently began to suspect Frank Churchill of playing some kind of double game.

My suspicions were first aroused when I was dining at Randalls one evening earlier this month. The Eltons and Jane Fairfax were there as well, but not Emma. And I saw a look – more than a single look – at Miss Fairfax, which from the ardent admirer of Miss Woodhouse seemed out of place.

Everything had declared that Emma was Frank Churchill's object – his own attentions, his father's hints, his mother-in-law's guarded silence. It was all in unison. Words, conduct, discretion, and indiscretion all told the same story. So what business had he to be making sheep's eyes at another woman?

Once observed, such things cannot go unobserved. The more I watched, the more signs and signals I saw between the pair. Miss Fairfax was more circumspect, but I caught her sometimes looking back at Mr. Churchill. I could not persuade myself to think the looks void of meaning, however I might wish it for Emma sake.

Then there was the day we had all met walking and ended up back at Hartfield – the business about Mr. Churchill's supposed dream that Mr. Perry had intentions of setting up a carriage. Frank Churchill seemed determined to catch Jane's eye after that, but she refused. He would not be ignored, however; he forced a response from her with the game of alphabets – the words "blunder" and "Dixon." Jane's deep blushes must have given great satisfaction; he had won the contest between them.

It was all a rollicking game, a joke, to Mr. Churchill – passing meaningful looks to one lady in secret whilst making a show of flirting with another publicly. I did not understand such behavior.

Frank and Jane had met each other before, in Weymouth; that much was openly acknowledged. But it was described as only a slight acquaintance. I began to wonder if it had been more. Had there been some private liking, or even a decided involvement between them at one time? If so, their understanding must have run onto the rocks, for he had come to Highbury and pursued Emma. And yet, for some reason, he must keep Jane on a string as well.

Something was not right.

I was indignant at such unfeeling double dealings. Jane could not help but be aware of it, and I was sorry for her. But it was for Emma that I most feared, for she seemed blind to anything but Mr. Churchill's preference for herself.

I remained at Hartfield that evening after the others had gone, my thoughts full of what I had seen. I must, I decided, as a concerned friend, give Emma some hint. I must give her some warning. It was my clear duty as well as my desire. I could not see her in considerable danger without trying to preserve her. A gently leading question seemed the best way to begin, in the hopes she would quickly be able to explain away all my fears.

"Pray, Emma, may I ask in what lay the great amusement, the poignant sting, of the last word given to you and Miss Fairfax? – how it could be so very entertaining to the one and so very distressing to the other."

"Oh!" she cried in evident embarrassment, "It all meant exactly nothing, Mr. Knightley – a mere joke among ourselves."

I waited, hoping she would elaborate, but she did not. Should I say more, I wondered, or would it be only fruitless interference? Nevertheless, I would risk anything rather than her welfare. I would encounter whatever censure might come rather than deal with my conscience over the remembrance of some neglect of duty that might have spared her pain.

"My dear Emma," I said at last, very earnestly, "do you think you perfectly understand the degree of acquaintance between the gentleman and lady we have been speaking of?"

"Between Mr. Frank Churchill and Miss Fairfax? Oh, yes, perfectly! Why do you ask?"

"It is just that I have lately imagined that I saw symptoms of attachment between them – certain expressive looks not meant to be public. Have you never had any reason to think he admired her, or perhaps had in the past, or that she admired him?"

"Oh, Mr. Knightley, you amuse me excessively!" she said, actually laughing. "I am delighted to find that you can vouch-safe to let your imagination wander after all, but it will not do. Your imaginings go too far. There is no admiration between them, I do assure you. And the business with the alphabets... Well, other very different feelings are to blame there – a great deal of nonsense but not admiration. That is, I presume there is none on her side, and I will answer for that being true on his. Believe me, I can swear to the gentleman's indifference."

The confidence and satisfaction with which she spoke these things staggered me. Every word of her answer unasham-edly acknowledged her intimacy with Mr. Churchill and all but declared that her own affections were thoroughly engaged by him.

What more was there to ask or say? Here was the truth I had been unprepared to hear but now must somehow learn to accept. I believe I could have come to abide it, had I thought my dearest Emma safe in Mr. Churchill's care, had he been a different sort of character, had he been a kind and principled man worthy of her devotion. But how could I ever entrust her into the hands of such a careless fellow, such a disingenuous and double-dealing example of man, who had already proved inclined to sport with the delicate feelings of respectable ladies?

"Now, Mr. Knightley," Emma continued in lively good humor, "you must tell me what you meant before. Let me hear the particulars of these 'expressive looks' and 'symptoms of attachment' between Frank and Jane. I am sure to find them diverting, and we will both laugh when I have explained how you went wrong!"

This was almost the worst, that Emma had been taught to make sport of such things herself. *Oh, that Frank Churchill had never come to Highbury!,* I thought once again. We should all have been a lot better off without his influence, especially my dear Emma.

"You must excuse me," I said stiffly, getting to my feet, "but I can find no humor in such things. And since I cannot be useful to you, I may as well take my leave."

"No, do stay, please, and do not be cross," she said in a soothing way. "We can talk of something else, if you like, only do sit down again, Mr. Knightley."

I was not cross with her, only very sad. "Forgive me, Emma. I am not fit company tonight, and the fire is too warm. I need the coolness of the night air to make me reasonable again." I hastily bowed, said goodnight, and left her to walk home to Donwell by myself.

~~*~~

I deliberately stayed away from Highbury, and especially Hartfield, for the next few days, to spare myself anything further on these unhappy themes. I did not wish to hear Frank Churchill's name mentioned. I did not wish to see him with Emma or hear her talk of him. I did not even want to think about my suspicions of his double dealings or the danger to my friends. Neither Mr. Woodhouse nor Emma herself would listen to my warnings in any case.

As at other times of personal distress, I took my solace in Donwell. I caught up on my accounts with William Larkins, and then I went out on horseback to tour the land, visiting my tenants along the way. I saved Abbey-Mill Farm for last. Robert Martin was my closest friend among the tenants, and I always looked forward to our conversations.

Lately, however, my feelings at meeting him were more mixed on account of his lingering disappointment over Harriet Smith, for which I held myself partly responsible. There must have been something I could have done to spare him, I reasoned. Had I encouraged him to wait before making his declaration or warned him off the match entirely, he might have fared better. From the other approach, might I have intervened more strongly with Emma herself, curtailing her influence over Harriet before any harm was done? And so, when I came to Abbey Mill Farm, I hoped to avoid the subject of Harriet Smith altogether.

Robert Martin received me as warmly as ever, and he took me to his barn to show me a litter of ten fine piglets that had just been born. "I plan to keep two or three for our own needs and sell the rest," he said.

"They should bring a good price," I told him. "They look healthy and strong."

"That they are, Mr. Knightley, in fine fettle. Mable is me best sow, and she always gives me two big litters a year."

We stood there a while longer, admiring the wriggling little creatures, energetically suckling their mother. New life never ceases to amaze and fascinate me. Finally, I asked, "Is everything else well on the farm, Robert? Are you keeping up all right?"

"Oh, yes," he said. "All is well. Billie is a steady man, and he works as hard as I do. I have never been sorry for hiring him those years ago."

"Good," I said. However, I was not completely reassured. Robert's words were nothing but positive, but his demeanor did not fully match them. As a friend, I felt compelled to try again. "Is anything the matter, Robert? Is there anything I can do for you?"

"No, sir," he said. "I thank you kindly, Mr. Knightley, but there is nothing the matter with me that time and hard work will not cure."

I did not press him. He was a proud and independent young man, I knew, and there was little to be gained by attempting to force from him a confession he clearly did not wish to make. Still, I believed I understood what ailed him. Once again, I saw a similarity in our plights. We were both suffering the woes of unrequited love. There seemed no help for me with Emma, since her affections were thoroughly engaged by another man.

But I knew of nobody else in Harriet's case, especially since Mr. Elton had married. So perhaps there was still hope for Robert.

I decided I would keep an eye out for something I might do for him. I could at least get to know Miss Smith a little better. Perhaps then I could determine if there were any point to suggesting Robert try her again.

Exploring to Donwell

I could not avoid my friends forever, and the fine weather of mid-June made them eager for schemes of visits and excursions that the fates seemed determined to overthrow. First Mrs. Elton's great relations, the Sucklings, were definitely coming to Highbury. Then they definitely were not, at least not until the autumn. Next, an exploration to Box Hill was proposed and universally applauded. But it was of necessity postponed as well on account of a lame carriage horse.

"Is not this most vexatious, Knightley?" Mrs. Elton cried in dismay. "And such weather for exploring! These delays and disappointments are quite odious. What are we to do? The year will wear away at this rate, and nothing done."

"Then you had better explore to Donwell," I said without thinking it through. "That may be done without horses. Come and eat my strawberries. They are ripening fast."

I regretted making the spontaneous gesture almost at once, for Mrs. Elton immediately seized on the idea and proceeded to make all her own what she so obviously took as a compliment to herself.

"Oh! I should like it above all things!" she enthused. "You may depend on me; I certainly will come. You may leave everything to me. Only give me carte-blanche. I am Lady Patroness, you know. It is my party. I will bring friends with me."

"I hope you will bring Elton," I said, trying to rein her in, "but I will not trouble you to give any other invitations."

"Now you are looking very sly. But consider; you need not be afraid of delegating power to me. Married women, you know, may be safely authorized. Leave it to me. I will invite your guests."

With measured calmness, I tried again. "There is but one married woman in the world whom I can ever allow to invite what guests she pleases to Donwell."

"Mrs. Weston, I suppose," said Mrs. Elton, looking cha-grinned.

"No. Mrs. Knightley; and till she is in being, I will manage such matters myself."

In this manner, I wrested control of the affair back from her into my own hands again, though not without many further attempts on her part to help and advise me – as to guests, time of day, attire, style, baskets, riding on donkeys, and eating on the ground. I think I just managed to spare Mrs. Hodges having Mrs. Elton to interfere in her realm.

I remained adamant about the meal being spread on the dining room table and not on the ground – for the convenience of the servants and for the comfort of the guests too. I was thinking particularly of Mr. Woodhouse, whom I knew would be made ill by the prospect of any of his friends sitting down out of doors to eat. He must not, under pretense of a morning drive and an hour or two spent at Donwell, be tempted away to his misery. No, every effort would be made for his comfort and entertainment. I would bring out my collections that he was so fond of looking at – my books of engravings and my cabinets of curiosities. And he was sure to find companions in his daughter, Mrs. Weston, Miss Bates, and myself.

I was also considering Emma. I knew she had been every bit as dismayed with the delay of the Box Hill scheme as had Mrs. Elton. It was in no small measure with the thought of giving pleasure to her that I had first proposed the idea. Of course, in this I expected to please myself as well. To have

Emma at Donwell again after a long absence; to have her view my home with a more mature eye; to properly appreciate its style, size, and grounds; to perhaps think that being mistress of the place might be something indeed...

No, this was going too far. Such speculations were not only pointless but unsafe as well.

In any case, the invitations were so well received as to not admit a single failure; everybody readily accepted. Mr. Weston was so enthusiastic that, unasked, he promised to get his son Frank over to join us. Naturally, I could not but say he would be very welcome.

The day was warm, and everybody came prepared to enjoy themselves, all except Frank Churchill. He had written that he would surely come and then failed to appear.

After Emma and I got Mr. Woodhouse comfortably settled with Mrs. Weston to keep him company, Emma began to look about herself.

As we slowly strolled through the great hall, I said, "It is so very long since you have been here, Emma, that I think you shall need to take some little time to reacquaint yourself with the house and grounds again."

"It *has* been a long time, Mr. Knightley."

"Above a year, I believe."

"Indeed. I must refresh and correct my memory on some points. I had forgot... well, the size of the place, for one thing. Considerably larger than Hartfield – house and grounds – and totally unlike it with its rambling style. This room is especially handsome," she said gazing at the exceptionally high ceiling and hanging tapestries.

"I am glad you approve."

"One must be insensible not to approve, I think. Altogether, Donwell is just what it ought to be, Mr. Knightley – a proper home for a true gentleman and his family."

"Or a gentleman with no family?"

"You have family, Mr. Knightley, and how proud you must be to think of passing your legacy on to our dear little nephew Henry!"

My pleasure at Emma's looking on Donwell with such open admiration could not survive this blow, the blow of knowing she thought of its all going to Henry. Although I am as fond of the boy as any uncle can be, I would have preferred Emma should think of me as a man still young enough to marry and have sons of his own. It was one more evidence that any hopes I harbored for her were in vain.

"Of course," I said, blandly. "Come, we must join the others picking strawberries. We will have been missed by now."

Since my own case seemed hopeless, I had in mind trying to advance Robert Martin's cause by speaking with Harriet Smith, if possible. Yet she was nearly always with Emma, which would not do, for Emma must never be given any reason to suspect the object I had in view.

Later in the day, however, I saw my chance. Emma had gone into the house to check on her father, and Harriet was on her own a little apart from the others. I went to her and said, "Miss Smith, would you care to see the lime walk? We will have shade there and a view as well."

She looked up at me with that child-like wonder I had observed in her before. "Oh, Mr. Knightley," she said tremulously, "I can think of nothing I would like better."

I indicated the direction, and we walked off together, talking of nothing in particular at first – the warm weather, the gardens, the strawberries. But then I introduced a subject that I hoped might eventually elicit from her some more valuable information. I asked how she liked living at Mrs. Goddard's school.

"Oh, ever so much, Mr. Knightley. Mrs. Goddard is vastly kind to me… and to all the other girls too, of course. But I think she shows me particular kindness, almost like a mother, for she has been nearly that to me since I came. In fact, she once said that I was the daughter she never had. Is not that a sure sign of true affection?"

"Indeed it is, Miss Smith. And I daresay you have many friends among the girls as well."

"Oh, yes. There are one or two that I like ever so much – Peggy Mallkus and Jenny Carter. Oh, and Susan Henderson too! I must not forget Susan. Still, they are all younger than I am, you know, and so it is difficult to be on real terms of intimacy and equality. When one is grown, one wants a friend of one's own age."

"Like Elizabeth Martin," I suggested. "She is just your age, I think, and I understand you spent last summer with her at Abbey-Mill Farm."

"That's right. It was the happiest summer of my life. Oh, but I must not think of that, for now I have Miss Woodhouse, and nobody could be a better friend to me than she! She is always so good."

I nodded, and we walked on.

"As kind as Mrs. Goddard is to you," I resumed presently, "you cannot mean to always stay with her, I think. You must eventually wish for a home of your own, Miss Smith."

She blushed, looked conscious, and dropped her eyes, no doubt thinking of the opportunity she had already rejected, which she had no way of knowing that I was aware of. "Of course," she answered, "but I hardly know when that may be, Mr. Knightley. I have no name or portion to attract anybody."

"Perhaps your father may make himself known and arrange something for you."

"Oh! I do not think I should like that at all! That is, I should very much like to meet my father, but I should not like an arranged marriage."

"Such things happen every day, Miss Smith, and they often turn out well."

"But it would take me away from..." She stumbled, stopped, and began again. "It would no doubt take me away from Highbury. And all the people one cares about are in

Highbury, after all – Mrs. Goddard, Miss Woodhouse, and... and... others."

"Very true. Ah, here we are. I wanted you to see the view from this spot. I think it extremely pretty. What say you?"

Miss Smith withdrew her eyes from me and dutifully cast them out over the downward slope beyond the low stone wall we had been walking beside. A half mile distant was a bank of considerable abruptness and grandeur, well clothed with wood. At the bottom of the bank, favorably placed and sheltered, lay a neat little farm, with meadows in front and the river making a handsome curve about it.

"Why, that is Abbey-Mill Farm!" Harriet exclaimed.

"So it is. Where you spent the summer with your friends. It makes a pretty prospect, does it not, Miss Smith?"

She did not answer, just stood there gazing at the bucolic splendor with something I could almost believe to be longing. Was she imagining herself mistress of that tidy house below, the co-beneficiary of its prosperous crops, herds, flocks, and orchards? The wife of its honorable and hard-working pro-prietor? How could she help it? At that moment, watching her, I began to think not so badly of Robert Martin's chances. But then I saw Emma approaching and immediately changed the subject.

"I often consult with my tenants about farming matters," I said in a business-like tone, drawing Harriet's attention away from Abbey-Mill Farm to myself once again. "Do you know anything about crop rotation, Miss Smith, or animal hus-bandry?"

"Oh, no, I am sure I do not. Mrs. Goddard teaches nothing about farming at her school."

I smiled at Emma as she came up to us, knowing she had heard some of the last but none of what had gone before. "Emma, won't you walk with us? How does your father go on?"

We took a few more turns together along the short avenue of limes, the three of us together. The shade and the breeze there were most refreshing, and I found it easily the pleasantest part of the day.

We did not end particularly well, however. Miss Fairfax insisted on walking home early by herself – most inadvisable, especially in the heat of the day. This Emma related to me after the lady had already gone, so there was nothing I could do for her. Then Frank Churchill finally did arrive, although why he bothered to come so late in the day, I cannot imagine. It served to set Mrs. Weston's mind at rest, however, for she had been fretting that some mischance had overtaken her son-in-law.

-40-
Box Hill

Now I have arrived at my last day in Highbury, the day that convinced me I had no choice but to come away to London. It was the day of the wretched excursion to Box Hill, which was the next after everybody had been to Donwell. The carriage horse had quickly mended and the weather continued fine, so there was nothing at all to prevent the scheme from going forward without further delay.

It began well. Mr. Weston directed the whole, officiating safely between Hartfield and the vicarage, and everybody was in good time. Emma and Harriet Smith went together in one carriage; Miss Bates and Miss Fairfax with the Eltons; and the remaining gentlemen on horseback. Mrs. Weston, in her delicate condition, chose to remain behind to keep Mr. Woodhouse company.

Seven miles we travelled in expectancy of great enjoyment, and indeed, everybody had a burst of admiration on first arriving, especially those who had not seen the impressive vistas of Box Hill before. But once the initial flush of pleasure was over, a sort of languor set in, a want of spirits. Or at least a want of unity, for we soon separated into parties to explore – the Eltons on their own, Emma and Harriet with Frank Churchill, and I with Miss Bates and her niece.

When we did collect later to sit down together, the situation only grew worse. Two hours had been allowed for our stay, but one quarter of that would have been sufficient. And more advisable, as it turned out. We had seen what there was to see, and now there was only left the task of trying to think of something new to say to the same collection of people we had spent hours with the day before. Not all of us were on the best of terms either, which did not help. The Eltons were known to be at odds with Emma and Harriet, and I had not yet learnt to get along with Mr. Churchill. What followed would not change my opinion of him either, except to convince me I had been right before in disliking him.

He began to make a great display of flirting with Emma and then demanding attention from everybody else as well, as if he were some kind of showman. Outside of his father, Emma was the only one who seemed entertained by his ridiculous antics. No doubt pleased at being so flattered and singled out for his particular attentions, Emma grew gay and easy. She laughed at all his jests and witticisms, and she smiled at him excessively.

"Ladies and gentlemen," he addressed us at one point, with a bold voice and a sweeping gesture of his arm. "I am ordered by Miss Woodhouse – who, wherever she is, presides – to say that she desires to know what you are all thinking of."

This was met with half-hearted laughter from some and a good deal of comment to the purpose by Miss Bates. In my turn, I responded by saying, "Is Miss Woodhouse sure that she would like to hear what we are all thinking of?" My thoughts, I knew, certainly were nothing she would wish to hear.

I believe she understood me, but she only laughed again, crying, "Oh! No, no. Upon no account in the world. It is the very last thing I would stand the brunt of just now."

Mrs. Elton ventured a scathing remark against the idea of young ladies ordering married women to do anything at all, her husband then advising her that it was best passed off as a joke.

Soon Mr. Churchill tried again. "I am ordered by Miss Woodhouse to say that she waves her right of knowing exactly what you may all be thinking of and only requires something very entertaining from each of you – either one thing very clever, be it prose or verse, two things moderately clever, or three things very dull indeed. For her part, she engages to laugh heartily at them all!"

"Oh, very well!" exclaimed Miss Bates, laughing too. "Then I need not be uneasy. 'Three things very dull' will just do for me. I shall be sure to say three dull things as soon as ever I open my mouth, shan't I? Do not you think I shall?" She looked round at her friends with the most good-humored dependence on everybody's benevolent assent.

Oh, that we had all just laughed with her and moved on. But Emma could not resist adding something more. She could not resist doing as Mr. Churchill had suggested a minute before – telling us all exactly what she was thinking.

"Ah, ma'am, but there may be a difficulty," she said. "Pardon me, but you will be limited as to number – only three at once."

I winced to hear it. Yes, we all understood and could not disagree. Others had probably been thinking something similar, but it should never have been uttered aloud.

Miss Bates also understood and was pained. "Ah, well, to be sure," she murmured to herself and then turned to me. "Yes, I see what she means, Mr. Knightley, and I will try to hold my tongue. I must make myself very disagreeable, or she would not have said such a thing to an old friend."

I squeezed her hand, and Mr. Weston tried to rescue us by telling an indifferent conundrum, which was entirely too flattering to Emma, especially under the circumstances. But any chance of resurrecting our lost good spirits had gone. People broke away from the group again under various excuses, and everybody was heartily relieved when at last the servants announced that the carriages were ready to take us home again.

One thing more had to be done, however. Whether it would do any good or not, I knew I must speak to Emma. No doubt any influence I once had with her was fading, but still I must try, and so I came alongside her before she reached her carriage.

"Emma," I said in a low voice, though there was nobody nearby. "I must once more speak to you as I have been used to do – a privilege rather endured than allowed, perhaps, but still I must use it. I cannot see you acting so wrong without some remonstrance. How could you be so unfeeling to Miss Bates? How could you be so insolent in your wit to a woman of her character, age, and situation? I would not have thought it possible."

Emma blushed in consciousness but then attempted to laugh it away. "How could I help saying what I did? Nobody could have helped it."

"And yet everybody *did* help it, everybody but you."

"It was not so very bad. I daresay Miss Bates did not even understand me."

"I assure you she did! She felt your full meaning. I wish you could have heard how she has talked of it since – with what candor and generosity, honoring your forbearance and kindness to her, when her society must be so irksome to you."

"Oh!" she cried, now showing some distress. "I know there is not a better creature in the world. But you must allow that what is good and what is ridiculous are most unfortunately blended in her."

"Granted, and were she prosperous, were she your equal in situation, I would not quarrel with you for some liberties of manner. But, Emma, consider how far this is from being the case! Miss Bates is poor. She has sunk from the comforts she was born to, and if she live to old age, must sink further still. Her sadly reduced situation should secure your compassion, not your ridicule. It was badly done, Emma! You, whom she has known from an infant, when her notice of you was an honor. To have you now – in thoughtless spirits and the pride of the moment – laugh at her, humble her before her niece and others, some of whom would be guided by your treatment of her."

She made no answer, and so I continued "This is not pleasant for me to say or for you to hear, Emma, but I must... I *will* tell you the truth while I can, proving myself your friend by very faithful counsel, and trusting that you will sometime or other do my confidence in you greater justice than you do now."

There was so much more I could have said, that I wished to say. I wanted to tell her that I believed in her implicitly, that I loved her no matter what, but that I could not bear to see her acting unkindly, demeaning herself by wounding a tender heart like Miss Bates. It was unworthy of her. I wanted to ask, "Can you not now see what Frank Churchill's influence has done to you?" For I placed the blame squarely on his shoulders, at least I wished to. It was not so much that Emma had no selfishness or malice in her – we all do – just that Churchill's flattery and bad example seemed to bring out the worst in her.

All of these things I could have said, but I did not. Neither did Emma say anything at all. She only looked angry and sullen, averting her face from me as I handed her into her carriage. Then I turned to walk off and the horses were in motion, taking her away.

Afterwards, of course, I was filled with remorse. I had been too harsh and perhaps left her with the impression that I despised her now, which could not have been further from the truth. I loved her more than ever, having added to my longstanding friendship and concern the passion of a deeper kind of affection. If I did not love her so fiercely, it would not cut me so deep to see her behaving badly, to see her devoted to another man and guided by him. I feared that my words to Emma just then had burnt my last bridge to her heart, that she would never again be my darling friend on such terms as I had come to depend, even before I had become her unacknowledged lover.

This is why I could not go away the next day without seeing her. How could I let the last words between us on the old footing be ones of such acrimony? No, I wanted – I needed

– the assurance that she did not hate me. That might be all the consolation left to me if she married Mr. Churchill.

And so I waited half an hour at Hartfield that next morning, my nerves on edge, sitting with Miss Smith and Mr. Woodhouse, until Emma returned. According to Mr. Woodhouse's information, she was calling on Mrs. and Miss Bates. I was encouraged to hear it, thinking perhaps my words the day before had not been thrown away after all. Perhaps she had found some truth and value in them?

I rose the moment she finally entered. And when our eyes met, I immediately saw that she did not hate me. Such a relief! Instead, her eyes begged my approval and that we should be friends again. I wanted to go to her at once. Indeed, were it not for the safeguard of others present, I might have done so, for I longed to take her into my arms and feel that all was forgiven between us. I longed to tell her the truth about everything – that I loved her and could not bear the thought of her marrying Frank Churchill. I wanted everything restored as it was before… only better. Instead, I was obliged to hold myself in check, to appear calm and indifferent when I was anything but.

"I would not go away without seeing you," I told her in as neutral a tone as I could affect, "but I have no time to spare, and therefore must now be gone directly. I am off to London, to spend a few days with John and Isabella. Have you anything to send or say, besides the 'love,' which nobody can carry?"

She looked confused, perhaps even distressed. "No, nothing at all. But wait, is not this a sudden scheme?"

"It is, rather," I said, "although I have been thinking of it for some little time."

I told myself to go without further delay, to stop staring at Emma, admiring how well she looked with that becoming blush upon her cheek. Somehow, though, I could not bring myself to submit to my own good advice. And then Mr. Woodhouse was talking, praising his daughter's kindness to the Bateses, which served to heighten Emma's color even more. But her wan smile and a slight shake of her head clearly told me she knew this praise was unjust and undeserved.

I was very proud of her at that moment – for apparently acknowledging her mistake, repenting of it, and humbling herself in order to attempt some reparation to Miss Bates. What an excellent creature she is – flawed, like the rest of us, but excellent nonetheless! Head and shoulders above most other women at her worst, and at her best, showing signs of fulfilling all the potential inherited from her mother.

No further words were spoken between us, but just as I had understood her silent communication moments before, I am certain she could not have failed to read the warm glow of regard I felt burning in my heart for her then. She knew I did not despise her, not even a little bit.

Did I reach for her hand then, or did she offer it? However it came about, I took and pressed it, holding it for a moment and even going so far as to lift it partway to my lips before stopping myself. It was impossible now, in light of my in-tensified feelings for Emma, that I could have kissed her hand without conveying more significance than I ought. So I released it instead and tore myself away from her, leaving the room and the house at once.

-41-

A Change of Scene

I travelled on horseback to London, surprising my brother and his wife by arriving unheralded on their doorstep in Brunswick Square late that same day. Having no reasonable explanation to offer for my unexpected presence there, I mumbled something about a sudden inclination for a change – a variation of scene. It was true enough as far as it went, for I was very much inclined to exchange Highbury society, pervaded as it was by Mr. Churchill, for anything else.

John and Isabella looked each to the other, and then John said, "Of course, George. You are welcome to stay with us... as long as you choose. Uh, the children will be delighted to see you... as are we."

"Certainly," said Isabella. "Is there anything else you would wish to do while you are here? Shall we form some kind of evening party for you? Gather your London friends and make merry?"

"No!" I nearly shouted. Then I tried again. "No, thank you, Isabella. It is exceedingly kind of you to offer, but I should like to remain very unobtrusive whilst I am here, if you don't mind. I will be happy to play with the children and spend evenings with you both, but that is all. I have some thinking – and perhaps some writing – to do, for which quiet and solitude will be most desirable."

"Quiet and solitude? Hah!" John retorted. "My dear brother, have you lost your mind? You might have had quiet and solitude aplenty at home, alone in that big house of yours, but not here! May I remind you that I have five small children?"

He was right; it made no sense to have come, not in any way that I was prepared to explain. But my friends indulged my whims just the same, only occasionally shaking their heads at me or shrugging when I did not behave in a reasonable way – keeping to my room for hours at a time or, when the walls began closing in on me, going out for long walks on the city streets without purpose or destination.

It was on one of these walks – I was minding my own business and thinking myself just one more anonymous face amongst the metropolitan throng – when I heard my name called out. I turned, and there, at the open window of a very fine carriage, I saw the last face I had expected. I recognized her at once, though. It is Julia Stibbley – Lady Blankenship, that is. She beckoned me with her hand, but I hesitated. My first inclination was to walk away, pretending I have not seen her. It was too late for that, however, and I had no justification for cutting her. So I went.

Making a neat bow in front of her, I said with a neutral air, "Lady Blankenship."

"Oh, George, it is so good to see you," she told me with warmth. "Could we... I mean, do you have a minute or two?"

I gave a non-committal shrug.

"Could we walk a little, then, or do I ask too much?"

In answer, I opened the carriage door and offered her my hand, which she took to alight. After she instructed the coachman to wait for her, we strolled slowly on, saying nothing at first.

After a sideways glance at my companion, I had to admit to myself that she was just as lovely as ever – face just as handsome and figure still trim – only a slightly more mature style of beauty. Her attire was obviously stylish and expensive – more expensive than I could have afforded to give her. It suited her, though, and no doubt the London life she always preferred. How strange it was to see her again after fourteen years, to be walking side-by-side with her again, as I once thought to do for the rest of my life.

"I hope you do not mind that I called you by your Christian name," she began. "I know I should say 'Mr. Knightley,' especially now, but that is not how I think of you. You became 'George' to me before we parted, and so you remain to me still. On the same grounds, you may call me 'Julia' if you like. There is nobody here to notice or object."

"Thank you, my lady. You may call me what you wish, but I have had to learn to think of you as a married woman. You are not the girl I knew as 'Julia' so long ago, not anymore."

Her expression dimmed a little. "I suppose that means you have not forgiven me."

"On the contrary. I harbor no resentment, and I sincerely wished you well in my heart long ago."

"That is good of you." After a minute, she went on with more intense feeling. "I *did* protest against marrying Blankenship, you know, as long and as violently as I could. I cried and pleaded and would not eat. It did no good, though. My father had all the power, and I had none. Then, when I heard nothing from you…" She trailed off.

"I wrote dozens of letters," I objected, "to your father, of course, but I hoped you would hear of it. He never told you?"

She shook her head.

"I shouldn't be surprised. I sent a letter every week – to prove my constancy and to continue begging your father to reconsider. He never answered, though, not until he finally wrote to say you were married and I must give up my campaign. Then there was nothing left for me to do."

"I wish I had known," she said.

"Would it have made a difference?"

"Not in the outcome, I suppose. I would have been constrained by my father to marry Blankenship in any case. But I should have liked knowing you cared enough to try."

"Of course I did."

We walked on in silence for a bit. Then, to offer her an olive branch, I said, "You are certainly looking well, Julia."

She gave me a half smile. "Thank you, as are you, George."

"I hope you have been happy as well," I added tentatively, more question than statement.

She paused before answering. Looking off into the distance, she said in a measured way, "I have learnt to be content… most of the time, at least. That is the best I can say for myself. I must be satisfied in the knowledge that I have done my duty – to my father by marrying according to his will and to my husband ever after. I have been mistress of his houses, played hostess to his parties, sung for his friends, and most importantly, I have given him an heir."

"You have a son?"

She gave me a brighter smile at this. "Yes. Harry is eleven and the light of my existence. It seems we, none of us, gets everything we desire, but life always gives us *some* compensations."

I thought of Donwell. I thought of my nieces and nephews. "Yes, so it does."

"Have you never married, George?"

"No, and now I probably never shall," I said, thinking of my hopeless passion for Emma. "My brother John has children, though, so a Knightley will inherit Donwell when the time comes."

"Oh, how is dear Donwell? And what of the improvements we discussed? The gravel path down to that lovely little river? You see; I still remember. And the gazebo I envisioned by the water?"

I shook my head. "Donwell prospers, and the grounds are kept tidy enough. But I had no heart for those other things after…"

"Of course. Forgive me. I know I have no right even to ask." We walked on a bit further until presently, she slowed, sighed, and said, "I should be getting back. I am expected at home shortly. There is this dinner party at the Livingstons' tonight, you see," she finished weakly, almost apologetically.

I nodded without comment and we reversed course. Neither of us spoke. What was there left to say? And yet I was somehow reluctant to see this unexpected interlude come to an end.

When we were still a little distance from her carriage, Julia stopped and laid a hand on my sleeve. Speaking in a hushed voice, she said, "Mr. Knightley, George, I cannot help thinking, seeing you again and all... Since you have never married and my husband is... Well, what I mean to say is, who knows what might happen in the future?"

I had to put a stop to this unhealthy line. "The future is in God's hands, Julia. It is our job to do the best we can in the present, not spoil it by longing for... By hoping for something else that can never be." I needed to remember this as well.

"But if you feel the same as I do..."

I answered nothing at first, only stared at her hand on my sleeve until she at last withdrew it. Then I said, "Lady Blankenship, I will always think of you fondly, in honor of what we once were to each other, but I have no aspirations concerning you for the future. You must believe me when I tell you that I am fully reconciled to leaving the past where it belongs: in the past. My mind and my heart have moved on."

"Oh! Well, it appears that I have been supplanted. There is somebody else who holds a higher place in your affections now."

"You were not supplanted; you surrendered that place long ago. But yes, there is somebody else now, though it may also come to nothing."

"I see," she said, after which she paused so long that I wondered if she would say anything more. "Then I suppose I must hope she will be wiser – or luckier – than I was, that she will stop at nothing to marry you and make you happy. Good bye, George."

I bowed and remained standing where I was as she continued on her way. When she glanced back, I had one last look at her pretty face before she disappeared into her carriage.

I was not sorry for the encounter. No, in some ways it helped to exorcise a ghost from my past. It was good to know Julia was well and had not been ill used by the man she married instead of me. It was good to have seen her, but I did not wish her back again. If there had been any doubt in my mind about that before, it was gone.

Other than this ancillary benefit, however, coming away to town has not made my mind any easier. If I had meant to stop worrying that Emma would throw herself away on Frank Churchill, I utterly failed. If I meant to learn indifference towards her and my perpetual bachelor state, I came to the wrong place. For there is far too much domestic happiness in my brother's house, and the name of woman wears too amiable a form. Isabella is too much like her sister, only differing enough to remind me of all the ways Emma is superior.

Nevertheless, I stay, vigorously battling on day after day, trying to get the better of this deplorable situation.

-42-
News from Highbury

For ten days now, I have hidden myself away here in Brunswick Square, living in the past and trying not to think of what my future will be without Emma. We are friends again; that is something. But what does it avail when she will soon be gone from us and another man's wife? Everything is at an end, not just for myself but for poor, unsuspecting Mr. Woodhouse. I pity Emma, too, for she deserves a better fate than to be the wife of a Frank Churchill.

Ten days have been insufficient to reconcile me to this inevitable outcome. My escapes into the past have not done me as much good as I had hoped either. These extensive reveries in which I have indulged myself, have at least served one useful purpose, however; they have reminded me, over and over again, of my primal and abiding attachment to my land. That has been the one truly unshakable constant in my life. We lost my father, but we still had Donwell. I then lost Mother and Miles, but Donwell lived on, despite my uncle's plundering. Julia was taken from me as well, but Donwell remained.

Whatever my griefs and losses, I could always turn to Donwell for solace. I could pour my love and devotion, my sweat and tears, into her and know that it would not go for nothing. Donwell has always been faithful. She has always yielded to my hand, giving back more than she received. Donwell will never die or desert me. So perhaps, I now try telling myself, I can survive this coming blow like all the others. Losing Donwell is the one thing I could *never* survive.

When Emma has gone, I will continue on. There is no question about that. If not happiness or even contentment, I will at least find occupation enough in caring for Donwell. When the time comes, I wish to leave the estate to little Henry in better condition than *I* found it, that Donwell might itself carry on long after I too have gone.

My other job will be to console and support Mr. Woodhouse as well as I can. He has many friends to share in that labor of love. However, the truth is that none of us can ever take the place of his youngest daughter. Isabella and the children will probably visit even more frequently than before. But Emma will be so far away in Yorkshire and caught up in her new life... I cannot imagine she will be able to come into Surrey more than twice a year. She will write, of course, but letters are not the same as being here, not to a father who needs to gaze upon her face and touch her hand to feel secure each day. Not to a father who looks forward to nothing so much as hearing his beloved daughter's voice. And not to me.

I may survive Emma's departure, but I am not so certain Mr. Woodhouse will, not at his age and with his weakened disposition. After the early loss of his little son and his wife, he took Isabella's leaving very hard. Then he mourned the loss of Miss Taylor nearly as much, though she only went as far as Randalls to be Mrs. Weston. Now Emma?

How could I have ever thought, in my most optimistic moments, of taking Emma away myself? Though nothing like the distance to Yorkshire, even a removal to Donwell would have seemed a tragedy to Mr. Woodhouse. And yet, given the choice between the two, I know having Emma at Donwell must seem to him the lesser of the two evils. The choice is not his, however... or mine. It is Emma's, and she can think only of Frank Churchill.

~~*~~

There is nothing more to say or write; my fruitless musings are at an end. And so I put down my pen at last and sit, staring at the wall without seeing it. For how long, I know not.

But then somebody begins knocking outside the door to my room. "George," I hear John saying, "do stop moping; there's a good fellow. Come out and join the living. The children are asking for you, and a letter has arrived in the morning post, from Highbury I expect. If you are not curious to see what it says, my wife is."

"Very well," I answer through the door. It is indeed time that I got out of this room, after all.

The children attack me the moment I appear, and I surrender to them, meaning to take the time to tickle and tease and toss them in the air quite as much as they could desire. I have neglected them far too long as it is. As for the letter, I am in no hurry. I cannot consider it with anything other than dread for what it might tell me. Will it be the announcement of Emma's engagement, which I have been every day half expecting? And so I carry on playing with the children.

"When will you take us fishing again, Uncle George?" asks Henry.

"Next time you come to Hartfield," I say. Grabbing hold of him, I add villainously, "For now, though, you shall be tickled instead. Aha!"

He shrieks and laughs as he half-heartedly struggles to free himself, and we both tumble to the floor. The little ones pile on top of us, adding their own noise to the growing commotion.

"My turn!" demands little John. "It is my turn to be tickled now, Uncle George."

I happily oblige him, and the others too, until at last their mother comes in.

"That will be enough for now, children!" she cries loudly, clapping her hands for their attention. "Uncle George has an important letter to read."

Gradually, I am released. Then I have no choice but to rise and face the ominous missive. "What makes you think it is important, Isabella?" I ask, tidying myself as we move to a pair of chairs by the window.

"Nothing in particular, but news from Highbury is always of interest to me." We sit, and she hands me the slim packet, obviously eager for me to open it.

"It is from Mr. Weston," I say, recognizing his scrawling hand in the direction. "Parish business, no doubt. Nothing of much consequence to you in that, I daresay."

She sighs and takes up her knitting.

I break the seal and beginning to read what is indeed, to my relief, a page and a half of parish business. But then, towards the end, a change of subject demands my full attention:

By the by, although I am loathe to speak of it, you may as well know the unpleasant news now, lest you come home only to have it take you by surprise. Brace yourself for something unexpected. It concerns Frank and a romantic attachment. Well in truth, it is an engagement...

I must make some involuntary sound at reading this, for Isabella is instantly at attention. "What is it?" she cries. "Is anything the matter?"

"One moment, please." I say, focusing again on the page in my hand.

...Frank is engaged, and has been secretly for some time, to Miss Fairfax.

Miss Fairfax. Oh, Miss Fairfax! I close my eyes and slowly release the breath I had been holding. My instant sense of relief is incredible. It is as if the dread of certain death has suddenly lifted, replaced by the promise of new life! I try not to let all this show in my features, however, lest Isabella should guess how much this news has affected me. "So that was the scoundrel's double game," I mutter.

"George, for heaven's sake, what is it?" Isabella demands all the louder.

"All is well," I tell her, "surprising but well. Mr. Frank Churchill is engaged to marry Jane Fairfax. That is the news in a nutshell. Allow me to finish and I will tell you more.

I ignore Isabella's exclamations and return to the letter.

> *They met at Weymouth, as you no doubt remember, and there they fell madly in love. But the understanding between them had to be kept a great secret, lest Mrs. Churchill should hear of it. She never would have approved, of course, and Frank feared being disinherited. So he felt he had to come among us playing a part, behaving very unengaged. We were all convinced.*
>
> *Everything is changed now, however. Mrs. Churchill has died, and her husband means to make no difficulties for Frank. He has made it up to Miss Fairfax and there is harmony between them again. Mrs. Weston and I have forgiven Frank his little deception. We hope everybody else will as well. Young lovers are inherently selfish, and so there is no use anybody holding a grudge against them...*

After this, there is only the closing salutation, and so I turn to Isabella to explain the rest. Then I add in sudden resolve, "I must go at once."

"What? Why so suddenly? I thought you said all is well."

"It is... at least I hope it is. In truth, I am concerned for Emma's feelings. Mr. Churchill, the rogue, flirted with her outrageously, and I am afraid she liked it."

"You think her heart had become entangled?"

"Exactly, and this announcement will have hit her as a very cruel blow."

"Oh, dear. Poor Emma! Yes, go to her at once, George! I only wish I could myself."

I call for my horse to be readied, take leave of my brother and his family as quickly as possible, and I am on the road for Highbury within forty minutes.

The weather is very wet, but that is no deterrent to me. Emma is paramount; she is nearly all I think of as I ride, and my questions on her account abound. How long has she known, and how did she hear the news? Mr. Weston's brief account did not say. Is she heartbroken by Mr. Churchill's desertion? My own heart aches in compassion for what she must be feeling. What can I possibly say that will be of service to her, when no mere words can heal or even soften such a crushing disappointment?

I know these are the same sixteen miles between London and Highbury that I have travelled countless times before. To-day, however, they seem both interminably long and yet still not long enough for me to think how I shall behave when I arrive – what I shall say to her.

All that matters is Emma's safety. And yet I cannot seem to stop my mind from wandering a bit as I ride. I think of poor Jane Fairfax. I am truly sorry for her. Such a sweet young wo-man deserves a superior fate, and I wish she may make a better man out of her husband than he is now. I hope he will realize his good fortune and endeavor to eventually deserve her. I believe such things sometimes happen. At least she will be mistress of her own fine house instead of having to go out as a governess. There is some consolation for her friends in that.

I think of Mr. and Mrs. Weston, considering what must be their embarrassment that their much-touted 'fine young man' should turn out to be a fraud. Although Mr. Weston made somewhat light of his son's "little deception" in his letter, I know him well enough to read between his few lines on the subject and hear his deep disappointment. Emma aside, I would like to do Frank Churchill an injury just for the pain and mortification his actions have exposed his parents to.

It is easier than ever for me to criticize Mr. Frank Churchill, for I now have not just suspicions but solid evidence of his perfidy. And I am feeling quite sanctimonious until my own self-interest comes forward.

I tell myself to stay focused on helping Emma weather this storm, but there are still a few miles to cover, and I cannot seem to keep my mind from galloping ahead too. I cannot ignore the fact that, whether she may like it or not, Emma is free. She will *not* marry Mr. Churchill, as I have so long feared. She is safe from that fate. And the next thought that follows is that there still may be a chance for me – however small and far off, a chance.

-43-

Reunion and Accord

I stop at Donwell only long enough to stable my horse, change my clothes, and take a little nourishment before hurriedly walking on to Hartfield. I would not have stayed even that long, except I had rather not arrive until after dinner, for I would see Emma alone. Luck is with me. I find Mr. Woodhouse settled in a cozy conclave with Mr. Perry, so I am not needed there.

"Perhaps I will just speak to Emma for a few minutes," I casually suggest after general civilities have passed between us, "if she is at liberty."

"Yes, do, Mr. Knightley," Mr. Woodhouse encourages. "She has gone out of doors. I told her she had much better not, what with all the damp. But as soon as the weather cleared, she could not be detained inside any longer. No doubt you will find her poking about amongst the shrubbery."

I thank him, bow myself out, and go in search of Emma.

I find her taking a turn in the garden. When she looks up, I see I have caught her by surprise. A few long strides bring me to her. "Emma," I simply say in a tone of sympathy, taking both her hands in mine. For a moment that is enough for me, for she is alive, apparently well, and I am with her again.

"Mr. Knightley, this is most unexpected! I did not know you were back."

"Only just."

"And how did you leave our mutual friends in Brunswick Square? All well, I hope."

"Yes, they were perfectly well when I left them this morning."

"You chose a very wet day for your ride."

"Indeed, but it could not be helped. Shall we walk?" We step off together in the direction she had been going when I came upon her. Silence reigns. For the life of me I cannot think what to say next. All the easy part has been got through already, and the difficult remains. I try and fail to get a better view of her face to judge her feelings by. She seems determined to avoid my scrutiny and to maintain the unnatural silence between us. Finally, though, she breaks it.

With what seems like a forced brightness, she says, "You have some surprising news to hear, now you are come back."

"Have I?" I say quietly, watching her. "What sort of news?"

"Oh, the best sort: a wedding."

She volunteered no more, and so I said, "If you mean Miss Fairfax and Mr. Churchill, I have heard it already. A letter from Mr. Weston informed me this morning."

"You probably have been less surprised than any of us, for you had your suspicions. I wish I had attended to them, but I seem to have been doomed to blindness."

She gives me far too much credit. Yes, I had suspected some past attachment between the pair and some double dealings on his part, but I had lately been more convinced than ever that his real intentions were all for Emma. And so I tell her the simple truth. "I did not expect it either." Then I can delay no longer; I must face the thing head on. I stop, draw her arm through mine, and press it to my heart.

"Time, my dearest Emma. Time will heal the wound," I say as steadily as can, although a myriad of emotions threaten to overcome me. Then I blunder on, still pressing her arm tightly to myself. "Abominable scoundrel! Never mind; he will soon be gone. They will be away in Yorkshire and not visit often, so you shall be spared seeing them. I am sorry for *her*, though. She deserves a better fate."

Emma smiles composedly up at me. "You are very kind," she says, "but you are mistaken. I must set you right. I am not in need of that sort of compassion. My blindness to what was going on led me to act in a way that I must always be ashamed of, but I have no other reason to regret that I was not in the secret earlier."

I cannot believe what she seems to be telling me. "Emma!" I cry, "Can this be true? No, I understand you. Your exertions are commendable, and he is certainly no object of regret. I confess that from your manners I could never be sure to what degree your affections were entangled, but I hope it will not be long before he is indeed nothing to you again. He is a disgrace to the name of man. And is he to be rewarded with that sweet young woman? – Jane, Jane, I fear you will be a miserable creature."

"Mr. Knightley," Emma says, "no doubt my manners are entirely to blame, but I cannot allow you to continue in your error. You must believe me when I tell you that I have never truly been attached to the person we are speaking of."

Her words are music to my ears, and yet I must hear more before I am thoroughly convinced. After a little hesitation, she goes on.

"I have very little to say for my own conduct, I'm afraid. I could attempt many excuses, but it all comes down to this; my vanity was flattered, and I allowed myself to be pleased. For some time, however, I have had no idea of his attentions meaning anything serious. And now I tolerably comprehend his behavior. He never wished to attach me. It was merely a blind to conceal his real situation. No one, I am sure, could have been more effectually blinded than myself, except somehow I have been kept safe. He has imposed on me, yes, but he has not injured me."

I take a minute to think this through before accepting it and relaxing a bit. "You cannot imagine how relieved I am to hear it, Emma. I had thought that… Well, never mind. It is enough to know that you are safe. I suppose I must now wish Mr. Churchill well for Jane's sake. With such a woman for a wife, he has a chance of improvement."

"I have no doubt of their being happy together," Emma says. "I believe them to be very mutually and sincerely attached."

Considering the difference in our situations, I am suddenly angry with Mr. Churchill all over again. I cannot tell Emma why, and so I only declare, "He is a most fortunate man! Everything turns out for his good. So early in life to have drawn such a prize, too. He meets with a young woman of beauty and character by chance in a watering place, gains her affection at once, and cannot even weary her by negligent treatment. His aunt is in the way; his aunt dies. His friends are eager to promote his happiness. He has used everybody ill, and they are all delighted to forgive him. Yes, he is a fortunate man indeed!"

Emma looks puzzled at my outburst. "You speak as if you envied him."

"I do envy him, Emma. In one respect he is the object of my envy." I stop abruptly. I am on the brink of revealing something to her that I never intended. I only want her invitation to do so, but she remains silent. I must be mad, for I boldly push ahead anyway. "You will not ask me the point of my envy? You are determined, I see, to have no curiosity." Still she says nothing. "Well, perhaps you are wise, but I cannot be. Emma, I must tell you what you will not ask, though I may wish it unsaid the next moment."

Now she does speak, almost pleading, "Oh, then don't speak it! Don't speak it! Take a little time to consider. Do not commit yourself."

She might just as well have slapped me hard across the face. I am mortified, although it is a kindness she has done me. Emma has plainly seen the truth and had the good sense to stop me before I could say something too foolish to be forgiven or forgotten, something we should both have regretted. She would at least preserve our friendship if she can. I should thank her for that, I suppose. Perhaps someday I will be able to do so, but not now.

We have almost completed our circuit and reached the house again. I have no intention of going in, though. I cannot see Mr. Woodhouse now, or Mr. Perry. I cannot linger in Emma's presence either, speaking lightly of commonplace things. It would be too much for me. I need to be gone as soon as possible. I am looking left and right for my best way of escape when Emma places a hand on my sleeve.

"Please don't go, Mr. Knightley," she says in an apologetic way, her face a puzzle of various emotions. "Not yet. Let me make amends. I stopped you ungraciously just now and gave you pain. This is no way to treat a friend." She took a deep breath and continued with resolve. "As my friend, you may speak openly to me on any subject or ask my opinion about anything you have in contemplation. Indeed, as my old friend, you may command me. I will hear whatever you like and tell you exactly what I think."

"As a *friend*," I repeat, feeling lower than ever, for that word, spoken thrice for emphasis, only makes Emma's sentiments about me all the clearer. We are friends, and that is how we are to remain. Very well, then, I will put that friendship to the test. I have already gone too far for concealment in any case.

Impulsively, I say, "Emma, I accept your offer, and as your friend I refer myself to you for your opinion. Tell me then, have I no chance of succeeding?" Looking earnestly into her eyes, I go on. "My dearest Emma, for dearest you will always be to me, whatever the outcome of this conversation. My dearest, most beloved Emma, tell me at once. Say 'no' if it must be said." I pause a moment. "And yet you say nothing. I cannot make speeches, Emma. If I loved you less, I might be able to talk about it more, but you know what I am. You hear nothing but truth from me. I have blamed you and lectured you, and you have borne it as no other woman in England would have borne it. Bear with the truth I would tell you now, dearest Emma. God knows, I have been a very indifferent lover. But you understand me; I see that you do. You understand my feelings, and you will return them if you can."

"Do you mean..." she says uncertainly. "Can you really mean to tell me that you are in love? With *me*?"

I nod cautiously, balancing on the knife's edge between hope and despair, for I still cannot read her feelings.

"But I thought... I thought you wished to tell me..." She stops herself.

"Tell you what, my dear?"

"Oh, forget what *I* thought!" she says, growing animated. "It is of no account. This news of yours is *so* much better! Mr. Knightley – my own, dearest Mr. Knightley – I *do* return your feelings. Although I had not realized it until... until very recently, I think I have loved you for quite some time."

"You love me too?" I ask in disbelief, and then take the next step. "Will you marry me, then, Emma? Please say you will."

She leans a little closer and looks up at me with a wide smile. "Yes," she says, "I will be very happy to."

Joy explodes through my brain and I feel like dancing! I am the most fortunate of men! I begin to take her into my arms, desperate to kiss her.

"Wait," she says, with a glance at the house. Then Emma clasps my hand and, laughing, tows me across to the side of the garden, where the denser shrubbery furnishes privacy from the windows. Now there is no holding us back. We are in each other's arms, with our lips meeting a moment later – tentatively at first but soon deep and sure of ourselves. Alongside the restrained passion, there is a sense of oneness and belonging as never before, of trust and coming home. Of, at last, completeness. With my arms round my sweet, darling friend, I never wish to let go.

For a long time, I do not. And then I am torn between the need to simply hold Emma tight and the need to share what is in my heart. I know we soon must go inside and act as if nothing has changed, to behave with the usual constraint. But not just yet. I want more time with Emma first, and she says the same. So we find a private place to sit, where we can talk, continue holding hands, and steal a kiss now and again. There is so much to tell – so much I want Emma to know and so much I want to learn from her.

I confess my jealousy of Frank Churchill to her at once. Then I add, "I still do not like the man, but I must thank him on one account. He has been infinitely useful with respect to enlightening me to my own feelings for you, dearest Emma. When I thought he would marry you and take you away from me, I nearly went mad. That is when I knew I did not just care for you as a friend, as I had so long told myself; I was in love with you. Yet there was nothing to be done, for you were by then thoroughly attached to Mr. Churchill, or so I supposed. I could not bear to see it, and so I went away – to forget you or at least to become indifferent to you. Going to London was of no use, however; I was miserable still. Then Mr. Weston's letter arrived this morning, and I had to come home at once to see how you bore the scoundrel's desertion. I came to be near you, to give you comfort, if I could. I had no idea of anything beyond that being possible!"

"Nor I," she said.

"And you?" I asked. "You said you were not acquainted with your true feelings either until recently. Do tell me how you knew at last, if you will."

"What? Oh! Certainly. Well, let me think how to put it into words." After a moment she began again. "I suppose I had the first inkling at the ball at the Crown last month, though I did not recognize it for what it was: a sign of romantic attachment. I honored you for your gallantry to Harriet and thought, not for the first time, what a superior man you were."

"No need for flattery, Emma."

"You asked the question, Mr. Knightley, and so you shall have to bear with the truth I tell you now, as you required of me before."

"Fair enough."

"Then, I suppose *I* must give Frank Churchill some credit also. He was everything my girlish fancy could have imagined, and I expected to fall in love with him, even wished to. But I did not. As much as he entertained me, as much as I enjoyed his company, there was still something wanting. I could not help sometimes comparing his behavior to what it should have been. I compared it with yours, and I would think, 'Mr. Knightley would never carry on so. He would not do or say such-and-such.'"

"But a woman will rarely fall in love with a man simply because his behavior is correct."

"Perhaps not, Mr. Knightley, but when I asked myself why I held you up as the example of manly excellence, the ideal in all things… When I asked myself why I could not fall in love with Frank… It occurred to me that my heart might already be engaged, that I might already be in love with somebody else. And when I looked a little closer, it was you I saw. I think it has always been you."

It is a good answer, and I savor each word. Yet I can sense there is more to the story, which Emma hesitates to give. "You only *might* be in love?" I say, hoping she will tell me the rest.

She blushes and looks away before speaking. "Yes, well, I am not at liberty to go into details, but like you, Mr. Knightley, I had occasion to consider how I would feel if you were ever to marry somebody else." She looks at me again. "*That* is when I knew for certain I was in love with you, and that if you should marry anybody, it must be me."

I gently take her beautiful face in my hands and kiss her – softly, then more deeply. She is not a passive recipient but an active participant, sometimes leading the way and sometimes allowing me to. We take our time to explore and sample, delighting in the pleasure of these new sensations. Her lips taste so sweet, as I somehow knew they would, and she is both firm and yielding at the same time.

Oh, the joy of this hour! – our mutual love and passion finally discovered and shared! I can hardly believe it; Emma loves me, and she has agreed to be my wife! We will be married as soon as possible, and I will take her home with me to Donwell…

Here my happy reverie runs aground. My conscience pulls me up short. I have been thinking only of myself – myself and Emma. What of poor Mr. Woodhouse?

-44-

The Cost of Keeping Promises

Poor Mr. Woodhouse. Little does he suspect what is being plotted against him in the breast of the man who he considers his most trusted friend in the world, the man who has always sworn to put Woodhouse interests above his own.

And so, entirely unsuspicious, he cordially receives me when Emma and I at last come back into the house. He anxiously hopes I have not caught cold on my wet ride from town. In childlike innocence, no premonition of impending evil enters his imagination. I am astonished that neither does he seem to detect anything extraordinary in the looks or manners of either of his companions at the tea table.

How can he not know that something incredible has happened? How can he not notice Emma's high color and distraction? How can he not see the way we look at each other now? How can he not sense my heightened and conflicting spirits – on one side jubilant and on the other wracked with guilt?

Instead, still his good self, he comfortably repeats to us all the little articles of local news he had received through Mr. Perry's visit: Mrs. Perry's having fully recovered from her cold, Mr. Evans having lamed his horse, and the new shipment of gloves that has arrived at Ford's. In comparison to the trifles he speaks of, Emma and I have news of monumental importance. This we will not share, however. Not yet.

Emma seems all aflutter with happiness, and so I am sure she has yet to consider what our plans will mean to her father. When she does, however, I know very well what she will tell me. She will say that we cannot marry, for her father would never consider removing to Donwell with her, and she will never leave him behind. I hope to have worked out a better solution for us all before then.

I cannot resist walking to Hartfield the next morning, just to see Emma's face and to confirm again by look and word all we said and felt the evening before. But again, we say nothing about the matter of Mr. Woodhouse, not over breakfast with him, of course, and not even when we take a quick turn in the garden on our own before I go. We must be allowed to enjoy our happiness while we can.

When I come again in the evening, after thinking on the subject all the day long, I am prepared. Yet I must wait for an opportunity. Mr. Woodhouse himself is still by, and then I find that Mrs. Weston has sent over for Emma's perusal a very long letter from Mr. Churchill, full of explanations and apologies. Emma has read it and is fully satisfied, and now, at her insistence, I must read it as well. Although what he writes fails to entirely exonerate him in my opinion, it brings me a little more in charity with him. I am at least now convinced that he is truly attached to Miss Fairfax. He must, therefore, benefit from her steadiness and delicacy of principle in the gradual improvement of his own character.

At last, however, Mr. Woodhouse takes himself off to bed and the odious letter can be set aside. For the moment, we remain in our traditional places – I in what has come to be considered *my* chair, and Emma across from me on the settee she likes so much.

"Now I must speak to you about something else," I begin. "I have another person's interest at present so much at heart that I cannot think any longer about Frank Churchill. Ever since I left you this morning, Emma, my mind has been hard at work on one subject only: how to ask you to marry me without attacking the happiness of your father."

Her response is immediate and as predicted. "Oh, Mr. Knightley, I have been making myself miserable over the same question, and it is no good. While my dear father lives, any change in my situation is impossible. I cannot marry you because I can never quit him. I will not do it!" she cries, eyes quickly welling with tears.

Reaching across to give her my handkerchief, I say, "You are quite right in the main, dearest Emma. There can be no thought of your leaving your father, or of trying to induce him to remove to Donwell with you either. I am convinced it ought not to be attempted, and so I would never ask it. But there is an alternative. So long as your father's happiness requires that Hartfield continue to be your home..." I pause, and Emma looks up in hopeful expectation. "...then let it be my home as well."

This is not an easy solution for me to propose. My leaving Donwell, even to go only so far away as Hartfield, seemed nearly impossible, ridiculous, absurd, when the thought first occurred to me. Donwell has been my home all my life, my heritage, the lifeline on which I depend in good times and in bad. Yes, it seems nearly impossible to live elsewhere, but not as impossible as living without Emma, now that we have found each other at last.

Emma is surprised. "You would do that? Leave Donwell? How can you even think it? It would be sacrificing a great deal – your comfortable home and some portion of your independence – just for me."

"And for your father."

"But could you bear it?"

"I wonder why nobody asks a bride if she can bear giving up *her* lifelong home and independence just to be married. In any case, I know this idea is a little unconventional, Emma, but it is the only way. And I shall bear the change gladly, if it means having you for my wife. Promise you will consider the scheme. After reflection, I trust you will find that our mutual good outweighs every drawback."

"I will! Oh, thank you, Mr. Knightley. You are so good to us!" She leaps up and comes across to kiss me. "Thank you, again and again."

A pleasant way to be thanked, I discover. The posture is awkward, though – me sitting, her standing – and so once more a better scheme is needed. Again, I have the solution. A quick tug in the right place and Emma tumbles neatly into my lap – a perfect position from which to thank me as much as she likes.

~~*~~

The next time I speak to her in private, Emma readily gives her full concurrence to the idea of my living at Hartfield after we are married. So that is happily settled between us.

"You must allow me to be the one to inform my father, though," she tells me. "It is my duty and I will do it."

"Very well, if you really think it best. Otherwise, I would gladly stand by your side and do what I can to ease the way when you impart the news to him. I know it will be difficult."

"I daresay that the way I explain it to him, he will barely mind. He is so sincerely fond of you, Mr. Knightley, that it must seem like gaining a son, not losing a daughter, to have you staying at Hartfield."

"I am here so much as it is – usually until after he has gone to bed every evening and often back before breakfast – that I sometimes wonder if he will notice any difference. When will you tell him? I hardly need say that I am ready for church any-time."

"As am I, but I think it must wait until after Mrs. Weston is safely delivered. Do not you agree? One matter of worry and agitation at a time is enough for Papa."

"Agreed. And so, another fortnight, is it?"

"Yes, a fortnight at least. I am almost glad of it. We shall have the secret joy, leisure, and peace of our engagement all to ourselves for a time."

"I have waited this long to be married, Emma. I don't suppose another fortnight will overly tax me."

I hear the shuffling footfalls coming, easily identified as Mr. Woodhouse's, and the subject is therefore at an end.

"Ah, Mr. Knightley, how good of you to give up your evening to us again," he says, taking his usual seat."

"My pleasure, as always," I say, thinking it has never been truer.

"What have you been speaking of, the two of you together?"

"We were speaking of Mrs. Weston, Papa," Emma says seamlessly. "Of how glad we shall all be when she is safely delivered."

"Yes, it is a very bad business," he returns. "Poor Miss Taylor. How unfortunate that Mr. Weston should have ever thought of her. And now, she must undergo this terrifying ordeal."

"I am sure all will be well, Papa. Remember Mr. Perry's opinion. He said she is very healthy, and there is no reason to expect the least bit of trouble. Now, here is some news that will surprise you both, I think. Miss Smith is going to London!"

"Miss Smith?" questions Mr. Woodhouse. "She had much better stay at home! You must tell her so, Emma. What can she want in town that she cannot find here in Highbury?"

"A dentist, Papa. Harriet has a bad tooth and is in want of a dentist. I have written to Isabella, and it is all arranged. Harriet is to stay at least a fortnight in Brunswick Square so that she can have her tooth attended to. But I hope she may also have some amusement while she is there."

Emma's mention of Miss Smith brings that young lady back to my mind for the first time in a good while, and it suddenly strikes me that I have never once seen her at Hartfield since my return from town. Perhaps it is her indisposition that has kept her away.

In any case, hearing her name reminds me of my resolution to do something in that line for Robert Martin if I could. And so my brain involuntarily begins to formulate a plan. Not that I intend to take up matchmaking myself, after scolding Emma for it so often in the past. I only mean to give encouragement to the poor young man... and possibly opportunity. If Harriet Smith is to be staying with John and Isabella, it would not be so terribly unlikely that Robert Martin could have some legitimate reason to be in the neighborhood too. If he could see her again – in a fresh setting and away from his detractors – and more to the purpose, if she should see him and be reminded of all his many good qualities... Well, I would not go beyond. Something must be left for God and chance to do.

As soon as I know Miss Smith to be in town, I drop by Abbey-Mill Farm to have a good, long visit with my old friend. During the course of our conversation on general topics, I ask Robert, "Have you by chance any business taking you into London soon? The reason I ask is that I have some papers that I am wanting to get to my brother John. I had rather not trust them to the post if there should be a way of having them hand delivered instead. I would go myself, but it is impossible for me to leave Donwell again so soon."

"Well," he says, scratching his head in thought, "although I had made no definite plan as yet, I do have a few things I must tend to in town before long. I can go now as well as any other time, especially if it will be of service to you, Mr. Knightley."

"Good man," I said, reaching to shake his hand. "I am much obliged to you. Oh, I suppose I should mention, in case you have not heard, that Miss Smith is currently staying with John and Isabella in Brunswick Square. I don't know if that information is of any interest to you or not. Just make of it what you will." The seeds are now sown. I must wait to see if any harvest will result.

-45-
Important Revelations

It is soon known that Mrs. Weston has been safely delivered of a baby girl, which exactly suits all Emma's ideas.

"It would have been quite a pity that anyone who so well knows how to teach girls should not have their powers in exercise again," she tells me. "She practiced on Isabella and me, and now you will see her own daughter educated on the perfected plan."

"That is to say that she will indulge this child even more than she did you, all the while believing she does not indulge her at all. This will be the only difference."

"Poor child!" Emma cries in mock horror. "What will become of her?"

"Nothing so very bad," I answer mildly. "The fate of thousands. She will be disagreeable in infancy and learn to correct herself as she grows older. In fact, I am losing all my bitterness against spoilt children, my dearest Emma. I, who am owing all my present happiness to you, would not it be the worst kind of ingratitude in me to be severe on them?"

Emma laughs, as I hoped she would, and then says, "But I had the assistance of all your earnest endeavors to counteract the indulgence of other people. I doubt whether my own sense would have corrected me without it."

"Do you? I have no such doubts. Nature gave you good understanding through your mother and a tender heart through your father. Miss Taylor gave you principles. You must have done very well without my interference. The good was all to myself, by making you an object of tenderest affection to me."

"I am sure you were of use to me!" Emma objects. "I was very often influenced rightly by you – oftener than I would own at the time, Mr. Knightley."

"*Mr. Knightley.* You always call me 'Mr. Knightley,' while I call you 'Emma.' It does not seem right, not anymore. It is too formal. I want you to call me something else now, but what?"

"I once called you 'George' in one of my amiable fits, seven or eight years ago."

"Yes, I remember. Cannot you call me 'George' now?"

"Impossible! I never can call you anything but 'Mr. Knightley.' I will not even attempt to copy Mrs. Elton's style by calling you Mr. K.," she added laughing.

~~*~~

John and Isabella were the first to be let in on our secret, the necessary communication being sent by Emma in the same letter that announced the good news from Randalls. We have since received their return communication assuring us that they fully enter into our happiness.

Now the time has come that the news of our engagement must spread further. Emma is still resolved to break it to her father alone, but she agrees that I will come in behind to follow the beginning she makes.

Emma, no doubt employing all the gentle reasonings we have discussed in advance, does indeed make the important disclosure to Mr. Woodhouse. When I come in, however, she shakes her head slightly to tell me he has not taken it as well as we had hoped.

Mr. Woodhouse does indeed look distressed, poor man, but he is kind anyway, holding out his hand to me when I approach. "Oh, Mr. Knightley, dear Mr. Knightley, what is this that Emma tells me? – that it is all decided that you two are to be married? How can this be?"

I take and press his hand firmly before releasing it and sitting down nearby. "My dear sir, I know this must come as a shock to you, and for that I am truly sorry. But it is quite true; Emma and I are to be married, and then I am to come to live here, with your permission. Everything possible is to be done to preserve your comfort, which is why Emma will remain at Hartfield. The only change is that I will be here even a little more than I usually am. I hope you will not dislike that too much."

"As to that, I am always glad to see you here, Mr. Knightley. You have been like a son to me since you were a boy."

"And you like a father to me, my old friend. Now it will be so indeed." I am suddenly reminded of a conversation I had with Mrs. Woodhouse years ago. "Did you know, Mr. Woodhouse, that it was your blessed late wife who first had the idea that I would one day marry your daughter?"

"Mrs. Woodhouse had the idea you would marry Emma?"

"Not exactly. I believe she had Isabella in mind for me at the time. This was after my engagement to Miss Stibbley fell through. You will remember that."

"Yes, of course. She was a very pretty kind of young lady, but then she went away to be married to somebody else. It was a sad time for you."

"Very much so, and in her kindness, Mrs. Woodhouse called to give me what wisdom and consolation she could. She said that perhaps I was prevented from marrying Miss Stibbley because I was to wait until I was older to wed, as you did. Perhaps I must wait until the wife God intended for me should be grown up, and that perhaps it would turn out that that lady would be her daughter. How surprised – and pleased, I should hope – Mrs. Woodhouse would be to know her idea will soon come to pass. Do not you think so? She said that nothing should make her happier than to have me as her son-in-law one day. Was not that kind of her to say?"

"Yes, very kind, but then she was always so very kind."

We sit together in silence for a few minutes, no doubt both thinking of that dear lady long lost to us.

Finally, Mr. Woodhouse says in a far-off way, "Mrs. Woodhouse was wise as well as kind, and we were happy together, though I was so much older than she."

"It was a good match, sir. I can only hope to be as fortunate."

He looks at me and nods, and I have the feeling that he is well on his way to accepting what is to happen.

Emma has been sitting across the room from us, listening unobtrusively. When our eyes meet, she gives me a look so full of love that I nearly melt on the spot.

"Thank you," she silently mouths.

~~*~~

The news of our engagement gives universal surprise wherever it spreads, nowhere more so than at Randalls. But Mr. and Mrs. Weston quickly accustom themselves to it and celebrate with us.

"It is a secret, I conclude," says Mr. Weston after we tell them. "These matters are always secret till it is found out that everybody knows them."

Which is pretty much the case.

Now that our secret is out, we look forward to setting a date for the wedding itself. "I have been thinking," Emma says, "we should be married in October, while the John Knightleys are still here. That way we might be gone for a bit of a wedding tour – to the seaside, perhaps? – without leaving my poor father alone."

I agree at once, and we begin making happy plans. But there is something less pleasant niggling at my brain, something prompted by Emma's mention of John and Isabella's upcoming visit. I know that Harriet Smith, who has been in Brunswick Square all this time, will be travelling back with them, and I must speak to Emma before she arrives. I must prepare her for what I have just learnt myself.

After a silent minute to gather my thoughts and my courage, I begin. "I have something to tell you, Emma, some news."

She looks up quickly. "Good or bad?"

"I do not know which it ought to be called."

"Oh, good, I am sure, for I see it in your countenance. You are trying not to smile."

"I am afraid, dear Emma, that *you* will not smile when you hear it."

"Indeed? But why so? What pleases you is sure to please me."

"There is at least one subject upon which we do not think alike. Can you not guess? No? Then I shall tell you straight out. The subject is Harriet Smith, and the news is that she is to marry Robert Martin."

Emma gives a great start and exclaims, "Impossible!"

"I know this is difficult for you to hear, Emma, but it is indeed true. I have had it from Robert Martin himself. He came to tell me the news this morning, and a happier man I have never seen. I wish you could feel like I do, that this is a good thing for your friend. In time, however, I trust you may."

"You mistake me, Mr. Knightley. You quite mistake me. It is not that such a circumstance would now make me unhappy, but that I cannot believe it. You cannot mean that Robert Martin has actually proposed again and Harriet has in fact accepted him. Good God! Tell me how this could have happened."

"It is a very simple story, really. Robert had some business in town, and so I asked him to take charge of some papers which I was wanting to get to my brother. When he delivered them to John at his chambers, John asked him to join a planned family party to Astley's that evening and then to dinner the following day. At some point – I am not aware of the details – Robert found an opportunity of speaking to Harriet, and he did not speak in vain."

Emma has covered her mouth, so it is difficult for me to read her expression.

"Emma, my love," I continue, "I am afraid this gives you more uneasiness than you will admit, but let me assure you that you could not wish your friend in safer hands. I will also answer for your thinking better and better of Robert Martin as you know him more."

I want her to look up and smile, to speak, to let me know that all is well, that she can learn to be as happy about this news as I am. And then she does.

"You need not be at any further pains to reconcile me to the match, Mr. Knightley," she says evenly. "I think Harriet is doing extremely well. I do not at all doubt your estimation of your friend's character and respectability. I have been silent from surprise, merely excessive surprise. You cannot imagine how suddenly it has come upon me, how peculiarly unprepared I was, for I had reason to believe her very lately more determined against Mr. Martin than she was before!" Then she laughs and gives me a bright smile. "I must have been misinformed. I am perfectly satisfied and most sincerely wish them happy."

"My dearest Emma, you are materially changed since we talked on this subject before," I say, still a bit incredulous at her reaction.

"I hope so! – for at that time I was a fool," she says, laughing merrily again.

So I suppose I must believe that, however it may have come about, Emma is truly pleased for her friend. And no doubt the intimacy that has existed between the two will gradually subside – if it has not, indeed, already begun to do so – since they both now have new objects for their affection as well as new occupations for their time and interest. I can henceforth enjoy thinking how Emma and I shall meet with the Martins on the most cordial terms – at Donwell, Hartfield, or Abbey-Mill Farm.

I am determined that the same shall be true for when we in future meet with Mr. and Mrs. Frank Churchill. Had he harmed Emma in any way, it would be a different story. But as it is, and with my future wife's encouragement, I find I can forget his former folly – or at least choose to overlook it – and wish him well. I hear they will marry in November, after his deep mourning for his aunt has been lifted.

It seems that the priceless love of Emma Woodhouse has put me in charity with all the rest of the world, even Mr. Churchill.

-46-
Epilogue

These things I now look back upon from the perspective of a twelve-month of wedded bliss.

There was a last-minute crisis Emma and I had to get past before all could be accomplished. Mr. Woodhouse, who had apparently only ever accepted the idea of our marrying as theoretical, as something consigned to the distant future, grew miserable when he realized it was a fact after all, one soon to overtake him. Emma could not bear to see him so unhappy, and her courage nearly failed. I was not unsympathetic – to Emma or to Mr. Woodhouse either – but I was quite sure that when once the event were over, her father's distress would be soon over too. Still she hesitated; she could not proceed.

I never wavered in my conviction that this marriage would be for the benefit of all concerned, including Mr. Woodhouse. My only qualms came when I remembered my ancient promise to always put his *wishes*, as well as his needs, ahead of my own. Was I betraying my old mentor and benefactor, to whom I owed so much, by forcing this unwanted change upon him, even for his own good?

In this awful state of suspense, we were befriended, not by any sudden alteration of Mr. Woodhouse's nervous system, but by the same system of fears operating in another way. Mrs. Weston's poultry house was robbed one night of all her turkeys, and other poultry yards in the neighborhood suffered similar thefts. Pilfering was housebreaking to Mr. Wood-house's mind, and suddenly the thought of having one of the Knightley brothers, upon whom he had long depended, always at Hartfield to protect him and his, seemed a very good idea after all. Thus, with his voluntary and cheerful consent, we were able to fix an immediate date and be married, our consciences clear.

The wedding was a simple affair with only a small band of our true friends and well-wishers to witness the ceremony. No pomp or parade, no ostentatious display of finery. Emma did not desire any of that, and neither did I. It would have been wasted on me, in any case, for I only had eyes for my darling bride. When she walked up the aisle, when she stood before me as we exchanged our vows, I thought I had never seen anything quite so beautiful. Knowing Emma as thoroughly as I did – that her beauty ran through and through, not just skin deep – I could not believe my good fortune. In truth, I still cannot all these months later.

Our wedding trip to the seaside was an unadulterated pleasure. I shall never forget the look of wonder on Emma's face when she beheld the vast ocean and its waves for the first time. At that moment, I did not look at the sea myself; I preferred to watch her enjoying the view of it instead. That was worth far more.

One cannot expect the weather to be constantly fair in October, and indeed it was not. But we had enough sunshine for exploring the local environs, walking on the beach, and collecting shells – shells which Emma now keeps in a jar on her table in the morning room, where she does her correspondence. When the weather was poor – and even sometimes when it was fine, truth be told – well, then there were other wonders to explore and indoor entertainments enough to happily occupy ourselves for many hours. We were newlyweds, after all.

We only stayed away a fortnight, for we had promised to be back at Hartfield before John and Isabella would be forced to return to London. But that did not mean the honeymoon was over. Hartfield is a big house, so Emma and I have privacy enough.

We three get along quite well with the new arrangements. Despite all his little quirks and foibles, his fears and fancies – or maybe partly because of them – Mr. Woodhouse has always been dear to me. Now, as a nearer relation, he is even dearer. I am glad to be able to keep my promise where he is concerned, to repay some of what I owe him. I will now be even closer at hand to look out for his comfort in his waning years. And his mind may be set at ease knowing that his daughter will continue safe in my care after he is gone.

Much as I assured him, little has changed from his perspective. I spend much of each day about my business at Donwell, as before, and then I am at Hartfield every evening (instead of only *almost* every evening). We have long chats and play at backgammon or some other game. Sometimes Emma will favor us with a little music. Then Mr. Woodhouse toddles off to bed, leaving Emma and me alone.

At first, once the scare over the poultry thieves had passed, I think Mr. Woodhouse liked to pretend that I went home to Donwell every night like I had used to do, for in the morning he would often say something like, "Oh, Mr. Knightley, how good of you to join us so early in the day. Emma, my dear, is not it good of him?" But then it must have become impossible for him to persist in his little self-deception any longer, for there was proof, growing more obvious by the day, that his daughter was indeed a married woman.

Our first child, Emma's and mine, was born at the end of July – a strong, healthy boy. Thankfully, all Mr. Woodhouse's extreme but understandable fears came to nothing, only serving to excite my own alarm for Emma's safety more than otherwise would be. Anybody inclined to lament for poor little Henry, being thus deprived of the hope of inheriting Donwell, should be comforted to know that Mr. Woodhouse has decided to leave Hartfield to his oldest grandson and namesake.

I have spent much time over the years thinking about my promises on Mr. Woodhouse's account, but I never forgot another promise made just as long ago. I had nearly given up hope that it would ever be in my power to fulfill it, however. Now, though, thanks to Emma, that is happily changed…

Emma comes over to where I am writing these things down at the escritoire in our shared bedchamber. I look up and smile at her, and she bends to kiss me.

"How is the baby?" I ask, standing to join her.

"He is sleeping peacefully, just as I daresay he was half an hour ago, when you checked on him last." Drawing her brows together, she studies my face, tracing her finger down the slope of my nose and along my jawline. "I cannot decide who he looks like most. He has a small nose, like mine, but otherwise it is a mystery to me."

"Too early to tell, I believe." I kiss her again and then take my turn gazing at *her* face. "When we have a daughter some-day, Emma, I hope she will look just like you – so beautiful."

"Then it is only fair that our son should look exactly like his handsome father."

"Maybe our *second* son," I say. "Nothing would make me happier than that this one should look like his namesake: Miles."

"Your dear brother, yes. I wish I had known him."

"I wish you had too. He was a lot like me, only with a nobler heart, I think. I have tried to live out as best I could the life that should have been his, and now our son will someday carry on his name and his legacy: Mr. Miles Knightley, master of Donwell Abbey."

"Not *too* soon, if you please. I am perfectly satisfied with Mr. George Knightley being master for now."

"Master of what, though? That is the question. Donwell sits nearly deserted, and this house belongs to your father."

"I will give you the title *Master of My Heart*, if you prom-ise not to grow too conceited."

"Very well, Mrs. Knightley, I accept."

When I kiss her again, this time lingering much longer, I consider how far we have come and to what a glorious pass. This happiness has been a long time in the making for me, and the road I have travelled sometimes very hard. Now, however, all the years of waiting and striving have been rewarded, my patience and suffering along the way fully compensated. Any journey that ends with Emma in my arms is one I shall always count worth taking.

Someday I will live at Donwell again, not alone this time but with my own growing family about me. For now, though, I am content. Wherever Emma and I are together, that is home.

The End

About the Author

Shannon Winslow has been writing for the fans of Jane Austen for well over a decade now, but she takes a little different approach from most other authors in the genre. She explains. "Since I'm just sappy enough to believe there's only one true story for the characters I've grown to love (and Jane Austen wrote it), I amuse myself with adding onto rather than varying from canon. I delight in expanding on what Jane Austen gave us and filling in blanks in the record with prequel, sequel, and supplemental views."

Her body of work so far:

- *The Darcys of Pemberley*
- *Return to Longbourn*
- *Miss Georgiana of Pemberley*
- *The Ladies of Rosings Park*
- *For Myself Alone*
- *The Persuasion of Miss Jane Austen*
- *Murder at Northanger Abbey*
- *Fitzwilliam Darcy in His Own Words*
- *Colonel Brandon in His Own Words*
- *Mr. Knightley in His Own Words*
- *Leap of Hope: Chance at an Austen Kind of Life*
- *Leap of Faith: Second Chance at the Dream*
- *Prayer & Praise: a Jane Austen Devotional*

Her two sons grown, Ms. Winslow lives wither husband in the log home they built in the countryside south of Seattle, where she writes and paints in her studio facing Mt. Rainier.

Learn more about the author and her work at her website/blog:
www.shannonwinslow.com

.

www.ingramcontent.com/pod-product-compliance
Lightning Source LLC
Chambersburg PA
CBHW020405260626
47156CB00007B/2244